QUEERING TRIBAL FOLKTALES
FROM EAST AND NORTHEAST INDIA

This book explores queer potentialities in the tribal folktales of India. It elucidates the queer elements in the oral narratives of four Indigenous communities from East India and Northeast India, which are found to be significant repositories of gender fluidity and nonnormative desires. Departing from the popular understanding that 'Otherness' results largely from undue exposure to Western permissiveness, the author reveals how minority sexualities actually have their roots in Indigenous cultures and do not necessarily constitute a mimicry of the West. The volume endeavours to demystify the politics behind such vindictive propagation to sensitise the queerphobic 'mainstream' about the essential endogenous presence of the queer in the spaces that are aboriginal.

On the basis of extensive interdisciplinary research, this book is a first of its kind in the study of Indigenous queer narratives. It will be useful to scholars and researchers of queer studies, gender studies, tribal and Indigenous studies, literature, cultural studies, postcolonialism, sociology, political studies and South Asian studies.

Kaustav Chakraborty is an assistant professor in the Department of English, Southfield (formerly Loreto) College, Darjeeling, India. He was a fellow at the Indian Institute of Advanced Study, Shimla, India. His recent publications include *Tales and Alternatives: Revisiting Select Tribal Folktales* (2017), *The Politics of Belonging in Contemporary India: Anxiety and Intimacy* (2019), *Indian Drama in English* (2014) and *Tagore and Nationalism* (coedited, 2017). His research interests include Indigenous literature and culture, queer theory and cultural studies.

QUEERING TRIBAL FOLKTALES FROM EAST AND NORTHEAST INDIA

Kaustav Chakraborty

LONDON AND NEW YORK

First published 2021
by Routledge
2 Park Square, Milton Park, Abingdon, Oxon OX14 4RN

and by Routledge
52 Vanderbilt Avenue, New York, NY 10017

Routledge is an imprint of the Taylor & Francis Group, an informa business

British Library Cataloguing-in-Publication Data
A catalogue record for this book is available from the British Library

Library of Congress Cataloging-in-Publication Data
Names: Chakraborty, Kaustav, author.
Title: Queering tribal folktales from east and northeast India / Kaustav Chakraborty.
Description: Abingdon, Oxon ; New York, NY : Taylor & Francis Group, 2021. | Includes bibliographical references and index.
Identifiers: LCCN 2020031487 (print) | LCCN 2020031488 (ebook) | ISBN 9780367541835 (hardback) | ISBN 9781003093497 (ebook)
Subjects: LCSH: Folklore—India. | Folk literature—India—History and criticism. | Sexual minorities—India—Folklore. | Sexual minorities in literature.
Classification: LCC GR305 .C4328 2021 (print) | LCC GR305 (ebook) | DDC 398.20954—dc23
LC record available at https://lccn.loc.gov/2020031487
LC ebook record available at https://lccn.loc.gov/2020031488

ISBN: 978-0-367-54183-5 (hbk)
ISBN: 978-1-003-09349-7 (ebk)

Typeset in Sabon
by Apex CoVantage, LLC

To

Supriyo, for teaching me how to explore. . .

&

Sahan, for reminding me what I should never look for!

CONTENTS

PREFACE

My grandmother's narratives about a toad man or a pumpkin prince seem to have inculcated in me a keen interest for folktales. Later on, having discovered my own sexual nonnormativity, I found myself more attracted to all that are seen as the Other of the 'mainstream': the 'belittled' traditions of the tribal people and the folktales as the nonelite Other of the 'classical'/'popular' literatures. This study has tried to bring together the categories that are equally, but differently, perceived as nonnormative—queer identity, Indigeneity and tribal folktales.

The Indian Supreme Court judgement, on September 6, 2018, while reading down Section 377 of the Indian Penal Code, has affirmed that constitutional rights should be defended and guaranteed over the majoritarian ethos. The majoritarian resistance after the de-criminalising of queer desire in India has proven how intolerant the 'mainstream' is towards all that are differently normal. A nonconformist, who is located in the 'mainstream' only to be otherised by the sociocultural taboos of the 'mainstream', finds oneself under the surveillance of the censoring mobocracy. Even the tribal communities are the victims of state-sponsored neocolonial impositions. The tribal folktales reveal how the ethnic communities are not phobic towards the dissident erotic. I hope that this endeavour of mine allows me to imagine an increasing intimacy between the wretched of the 'mainstream' and the Indigenous communities of India, where the 'mainstream' Indian queer people as the 'outsiders within' would choose to tribalise with Indigenous wisdom and ethnic alternatives.

The importance of sexual autonomy for asserting one's individual liberty was not unacknowledged in the civilisational domain that we call India. Scholars like Saleem Kidwai, Ruth Vanita, Vinay Lal, Giti Thadani, Mrinalini Sinha, Devdutt Pattanaik and many others have already revealed how with the domination of European hypermasculinity, queernormativity has gradually been otherised—a tenacity that has been ultimately internalised and reproduced by the 'mainstream' in postcolonial India. Hence, despite the historical judgement of decriminalising same-sex intimacy that can be perceived as a decolonising effort of the Indian judiciary, one can hardly deny that queer phobia continues to prevail as a major inhibition in contemporary India. The fact remains that even now 'mainstream' India considers queer as an aberration by perceiving it as a mere mimicry of the West. To establish a counterdiscourse of an Indigenous queer, I have engaged myself in making the Indian nonnormative tribal visible through a queer reading of tribal folktales. On the one hand, this book seeks to draw back the curtain on the continual process of (neo)colonisation on Indigenous persons and cultures through an examination of changing nature of folktales deriving from Toto, Rabha, Lepcha and Limbu cultures, and on the other hand – pertaining to the field of LGBTQ+ studies – it attempts not merely to focus on same-sex relations but also to understand/deconstruct larger social norms that are labelled 'nonnormative' by the 'mainstream' and thereby pursues to extend the scope and merit of queer studies. Apart from rediscovering/decolonising the queernormative heritage of the Indian Indigenous past, despite the ravages of the colonisers and the neocolonial 'mainstream' and the state, through the strategic folktales of the rebel tribal storytellers, I hope that this book also helps to underscore the significance of the tribal 'modernity' of alternatives; the ethnic accommodation of alternatives, as opposed to the stereotyped 'mainstream' perspectives, is the basis on which the tribalscapes appear to be more progressive than the shrinking liberal spaces in the contemporary Indian 'mainstream'.

The tribal folktales are highly metaphorical. Hence, one may question whether the assertions I make about the meanings of the folktales are at all valid or whether the folktales are used to prove a predetermined result. I authenticate my argument by positioning myself as a cultural insider-outsider. As a person born in Jalpaiguri, I have grown up with an intimate sense of belonging with the neighbouring ethnic communities. Thereafter, while living for more than 13 years in Darjeeling, I have closely studied the ethnic cultures of the hills. Moreover, as a part of my UGC project, I have interpreted the tribal tales with the help of the representatives of each of the Indigenous communities, who as the cultural insiders have affirmed that my take on the tales are not arbitrary or misrepresented. In this regard, I am thankful to all the storytellers, research associates and cotranslators, without whom it would not have been possible to complete this project. I am also extremely indebted to Manprasad Subba, Dhaniram Toto, Daychand Rava, Norbu Tshering Lepcha, Ananta Rava, Jenisha Singh, Binod Pradhan, Mandika Sinha, Mouna Lama, Gazala Fareedi, Vagesh Pawaiya, Sidharth Syangden, Dipti Tamang, Brianson Lepcha, Benoy Pradhan, Dinesh Chandra Ray, Srikanta Roy Chowdhury, Mahesh Pradhan and Pathik Roy for their support, encouragement and input. To further authenticate my argument, I would have loved to cite multiple readings of a folktale by other scholars who have asserted the same meaning. Unfortunately, I have failed to come across any scholarly work on the queer reading of the tribal tales from India.

I am thankful to the University Grants Commission, New Delhi, for sanctioning a major research project, due to which I managed to identify and translate the folktales of the Toto, Rabha, Lepcha and Limbu communities. I am indebted to all my friends from the Indian Institute of Advanced Study, Shimla, for their suggestions and engagement with my work. I also wish to acknowledge the contribution of Professor M.T. Ansari, University of Hyderabad, who allayed many of my doubts, referred to various important books and took an active interest in my work. I also thank the entire Routledge team, especially Antara Ray Chaudhary and Anvitaa Bajaj, for their interest, involvement and assistance.

Darjeeling and Jalpaiguri   **Kaustav Chakraborty**

1

INTRODUCTION

Folktales, nonnormativity and queer Indigeneity

Few foreigners are so foreign as I.

(Le Guin, 1996: 23)

Every culture is first and foremost a particular experience of
time, and no new culture is possible without an alteration of
this experience. The original task of a genuine revolution,
therefore, is never merely 'to change the world', but also—and
above all—to 'change time'.

(Agamben, 1993: 91)

Censored desires, contested categories

July 2, 2009, was a day of deliverance for Indian nonheterosexuals when
they felt that after the Delhi High Court judgement, decriminalisation of
sexual dissidents would pave way for a gradual social inclusion of those
who refuse to act straight. The reinstalling of the ban on sexual minorities
by the Supreme Court of India on December 11, 2013, has been a major
setback for those who had thought that sexual heterogeneity was, after all,
an attribute which had ceased to be an offence. The Supreme Court reo-
pened the debate on Section 377 by referring it to a five-judge bench, and
the queer citizens of India witnessed a historic moment on September 6,
2018, when the Supreme Court of India declared that criminalising queers
for any consensual relationship was unreasonable, illogical and hard to
defend. The Supreme Court judgement while reading down Section 377 of
the Indian Penal Code asserted that constitutional rights need to be safe-
guarded and assured over majoritarian prejudices, which by its implication
makes clear that the majoritarian notion of gender and sexuality in India
even now excludes queers.[1] The major resistance in contemporary India
comes largely from those who popularise that queer[2] as an identity is an
'imported disease' and therefore antitraditional.[3] This endeavour of queering the select tribal folktales of four Indigenous communities of East India
(from the region known as North Bengal)[4] and Sikkim[5] is a counter-attempt

1

to show how endogenous[6] queers existed even before the arrival of colonisers in our societies.[7] Julian C.H. Lee has rightly observed that in countries like 'India, laws that restrict and attitudes that stigmatize homosexuality have been adopted as Indigenous by politicians who portray the "West" as their country's Other, and sexual minority cultures within their countries as being the result of undue exposure to Western permissiveness' (Lee, 2011: 140). *Queering Tribal Folktales from East and Northeast India* is an endeavour to demystify the politics behind such vindictive propagation by revealing how the sexual cultures that have been minoritised through surveillance and penalty actually have their roots in the Indigenous cultures of the tribal communities in India. The political integrant of the 'belated'[8] task of 'reading *behind*' these originally oral tribal folktales might be useful as 'the catalyst that mediates the political struggle of the contingent' (Afzal-Khan and Seshadri-Crooks, 2000: 72) ostracised populations of queers and tribals, through the proposed 'tribalisation'[9] as a means of stepping into the domains of alter-modernities that, unlike 'mainstream'[10] India, are not prejudiced against people who have different sexual orientations.

By 'nonnormative sex/gender practices', I mostly refer to those who are seen as the Other of the 'mainstream' 'type or form of sexual activity that *is marked by a coincidence between socially privileged sexual acts and privileged gender constructs*' (Schutte, 1997: 42; emphasis in original). Foucault has motivated us to acknowledge that the 'normalising' of a particular norm as 'natural'/'prevalent'/'dominant' through propaganda and repetition has resulted in the expansion of the power of a particular group of a population in a society while excluding a huge section of other dissimilar norms as nonnormative. When a particular norm is made to function as 'the universal prescription for all' (Foucault, 2006: 55) in comparison to which 'a certain exercise of power is founded and legitimized' (Foucault, 2003: 50), the prescriptive character that gets associated with the selected norm facilitates a disciplinary command by introducing 'with it a principle of both qualification and correction . . . [that] is always linked to a positive technique of intervention and transformation, to a sort of normative project' (ibid.). Thus, as the determinant of what ought to be regarded as the normal, the norm gets projected like an 'optimal model' (Foucault, 2007: 57)—'something that can be applied to both a body one wishes to discipline and a population one wishes to regularise' (ibid.: 252–253).

According to Foucault, although the norm determines the normal in the disciplinary context, in terms of biopower, 'the normal comes first, and the norm is deduced from it' (ibid.: 63). Uniting his notions of the disciplinary power and biopower, Foucault then formulates the concept of normalising societies, where the normalising norms get officially 'normatised' by the governmentality as 'natural'/'normal' and, thereby, function as the tool of differentiating all that does not match the normalising norms, as the nonnormative 'abnormal'. Rejecting 'as self-evident the things that are proposed to us' (Foucault, 1980b), with an effort 'to seek out in our reflection those things that have never been thought or imagined' (ibid.), this study of tribal imagination as manifested in the folktales is critical in that it tries to read the possibilities of a queernormative antiquity—now perceived as nonnormative by the neocolonial state and the 'mainstream'—in these tribal folktales in an effort 'to think differently, instead of legitimating what is already known' (Foucault, 1990: 9). Upholding queer as quintessentially antinormative, queernormativity often has been regarded as antithetical to queer leftism because of its expected alignment with right-wing politics (Lamont, 2017: 634). However, influenced by the usage of 'queernormativity' in an article published recently by Dan Michael Fielding (2020), I have used 'queernormative' (and the allied terms like 'homonormative') to represent an empowered queer who can redefine the normative by a strategic transforming of heteronormative activities into celebrations of queer love, sex, coupling, family and so on and who can repurpose supposedly heteronormative narratives to serve queer interests (Fielding, 2020: 5–6). Hence, moving beyond the existing apprehension regarding the term 'queernormative', which has been generally seen as an attempt to fit into the state-recognised frameworks or substitute one set of norms for another, the term has been used in this book to refer to a movement towards an 'adaptive construction and deconstruction of "the normal"' through which it can be asserted that 'queer is as normal as straight and straight is just as problematic as queer' (ibid.: 18).

I have consciously used 'tribal' instead of Hindi words like *adivasi* or *janajati* because of the linguistic hegemony that these vernacular terms carry with them and, therefore, are not much well received by many of the North East Indian ethnic communities who fail to connect with Sanskrit genealogy. If *tribal* is colonial, then both *adivasi* or *janajati* (finally paving way for the Hindi-Hindutva term *vanavasi*) become the markers of neocolonial linguistic politics of the state in its nation-building mode, so far as the North East Indian Indigeneity is concerned. Even the proponents of the term *adivasi* have recognised the limitation in the acceptability of the term among the pan-Indian tribal communities and the connotative vantage of the term 'tribal' to signify *adivasi* or *janajati*.[11] Moreover, from the '1980s the main contender of the term "tribe" has been that of "indigenous people"' (Rycroft and Dasgupta, 2011: 25).

The extremely contested categories like 'tribes of India' and 'Indigenous' communities have been propagated through the means of knowledge manufactured by British colonisers: 'Knowledge of subject races or Orientals is what makes their management easy and profitable; knowledge gives power, more power requires more knowledge' (Said, 1978: 36). Gyan Prakash while hinting at the connection 'between classification and colonialism' (Prakash,

1992: 156) has exposed that the colonisers have ensured that people with certain distinctions ought to be

> classified according to races and tribes, [who] should sit each in his own stall, should receive and converse with the Public, and submit to being photographed, printed, and taken off in casts, and otherwise reasonably dealt with, in the interests of science.
>
> (ibid.: 158)

Colonial anthropology, in order to camouflage the colonial hegemony as a civilising mission, has resulted in delineating people, who have been framed as tribes, in terms of primitivism, racial lowliness and barbarism. The Indian anthropologists in the first half of the twentieth century, while arguing to tag all the so-called Indigenous people as 'all Hindus' on the basis of an ardent Hindu nationalism, have ultimately designated them as 'backward Hindus' (Ghurye, 1959: 20). Arjun Appadurai's critique of all the 'officially enforced labeling activities' (Appadurai, 1993: 326) has elucidated how only by reinscribing primitivism, aloofness, overall backwardness and so on to the tribal communities, the scheduled tribe status as an administrative category has been conferred by the Indian state. The postcolonial Indian ethnography has failed to bring the history of the people classified as 'tribal'/'Indigenous' out of the stereotypes of labelling them as isolated, backward and completely different from the ones who are treated as 'civilised' ones. This has ended in the 'provincialising' of the 'Western' modernity, mediated by a cultural nationalism of the Hindu nationalists' 'mission civilisation' that has fulfilled its aim by erasing the unique 'alternative modernities' of these people, by stigmatising them as uncivilised, and, thereafter, overruled by a homogeneity that is imagined as Indianness. The nationalists have tried to resolve major challenge of 'mainstreaming' the tribal/Indigenous communities, who according to Beteille have mostly remained in India as distantly related with the state (Beteille, 1986: 316), by altering the disposition of the tribes in relation to their 'direct, unalloyed satisfaction in the pleasures of the senses—in such areas as food, drink, sex, dance and song—whereas caste people maintain a certain ambivalence about such pleasures' (Xaxa, 1999: 1520). Hence, the ambivalence regarding the portrayal of queer desire as depicted in contemporary rendition of the tribal tales can be interpreted as the outcome of the Hindu nationalists' imposition of a taboo regarding non-'mainstream' desires in the process of linking tribal people with a structured 'civilisational identity'. The classification of 'folk' as the nonelite Other of the cultured nationals justifies the intention of the national elites to mould the 'other modernities' into the nationalised version of modernity. The folklore of the tribal communities, perceived by the nation makers as the hub of a traditional backwardness has become the major target of the statist agents. Internalising the disciplinary agenda of 'governmentality', the elite Indian nation builders have become the spokespeople of the state-sanctioned modernity and have thereby started interfering with the folk-lores of Indigeneity so that a state-sanctioned ethos can be 'written' into the bodies, minds and habitus of tribal folk (Gupta, 2001). It is in these constructions of the debatable categories of tribe and folk where the layers of erasures and marginalisations of 'nonnormative' desires and sexualities by the mainstream lie. My multidirectional analysis of tribal folktales can assist in revealing how moving beyond certain well-entrenched and 'obvious' renditions of sex and gender in a given community can break novel ground in queer studies and—relatedly—open the possibility for queer analysis in the remnants of the 'pretextual' and the oral in that community's collective sense of the (historical and present-day) self. There cannot be a chronological sequence of the folktales. Rather, the mythistory approach, specifically an a-chronological approach, has been adopted as the sequence of the folktales, and this approach does not involve development but rather the arranging of ideas along a continuum to highlight the stages of colonisation/neocolonisation and the consequential erasure of dissident desires. My approach might seem to be loaded with 'imagination' to some ethno-anthropological critics, but that is not a hindrance, given what Toni Morrison (1993) has said about 'imagination': conventionally seen as a tool just to perceive the world with the outcome of constructing/getting constructed, imagination can also be seen as a means of sharing through the interpretation of shared imagination.

Teaching us how to bypass certain aspects of our identity by favouring certain other aspects, the 'intersectionality theory directs us to researching the standpoint of those identities located at the site of intersection' (Rahman, 2010: 951). In the same way, this work aims at an intersectional understanding of oppression faced by the queer people and the tribal community, with an emancipatory effort towards social justice. 'Recognition struggles', according to Carol Mueller, gain legitimate momentum through 'the contingent definitions of means, ends, and fields of action that exist in a state of tension arising from a system of social relationships as well as systems of meaning' (Mueller, 2003: 276). Driven by a conscious politics of belonging, to bridge the experiences of the queer marginality with that of marginalised Indigeneity, my positioning is grounded on an intersectionality of gender(queer) Indigeneity—having much resemblances with the 'Indigenist' epistemology of class Indigeneity intersectionality (Kjosavik, 2003). Queerness and Indigeneity are the identities that suffer the common internal colonialism of the state,[12] where either they are pushed out to the periphery as the nonnormative Other of the 'mainstream' or are compelled to give up their intrinsic nonconformity and get nationalised after being converted into useful citizens of the state. Hence, a queer, even if coincidentally located in the 'mainstream', can possibly get a more generous space for a dialogic relationship in a mode of 'pluriculturality' with the 'First Nations'[13] than with the normatised citizens of the nation-state.

Fredric Jameson's definition of narrative as a 'socially symbolic act' under-stands literature as a dramatic manifestation of the complex intertwining of the historical, the political and the psychological.[14] I have attempted a psy-chological reading of the tribal tales under the motif of 'measuring silences' and measuring both 'what the text cannot say' and 'what it refuses to say' about the mythistory of antinormative time and space (Macherey, 1978: 87). My search for the 'origins' of tribal imagination is not merely out of nostalgia but also out of a search for combating the strategic majoritarian Othering of the marginal people with differences. Despite Judith Halber-stam's warning against the method of 'perverse presentism',[15] this retrospec-tive politics—of a curable return to the resourceful past with the hope of finding a remedy for the politically restrained present, according to Nishant Shahani, who has attempted to 'insist [on] the value of preserving retro-spection as a mode of doing the history of homosexuality' (Shahani, 2012: 70)—is important as a mode of treating the present as 'the "fulcrum point" through which the past is reframed' so that the 'queer retrosexualities axi-omatically lapse into a reification of the "now"' (ibid.).

The chapters of the book

Folklore studies have two major aspects: collection/identification and inter-pretation. Some of the folktales that I have collected and translated with the help of cotranslators who belong to Indigenous communities have been previously documented by other scholars as well; however, none of them has tried to interpret these folktales through a queer lens. There has always been a deficit in interpretative studies of folktales, compared to the ample studies available on the models of methods of collection.[16] Hence, this book is more about interpretation than about the identification/collection of the folktales of the four Indian tribal communities. The interpretative method, combining mythistory, psychoanalysis, theories of sexuality, gender and so on, can be best expressed through the term 'eclecticism'.[17] An elaboration on the mode of selection and interpretation of the tribal tales is provided in the next chapter. To separate folktales from 'faketales', I have selected only those folktales that appear in almost similar versions in the previously published materials. I have chosen the four tribal communities in the North Bengal region, rather than a single one, to study how, on the basis of a com-monality of their culturally diverse nonnormative attributes, different ethnic groups and queers, signifying a resistance to the 'normalising' categories of subordination, can strive for 'self-formation' as an antimajoritarian identity. This identity, which is not labelled from above by statist regimes, can assist in fortifying a collective agency—established by the collective recollection of the queer/antinormative aspects of the past in order to 'resignify' them for an unfettered future—in the attempt to 'self-formulate' the assembled 'minoritised'. The nonnormative collective of queer people and Indigenous peoples, while refusing to 'conform to the individualist norm where the "autonomy" or sovereignty of the self is an ultimate and untouchable value' (Bennett and Bhabha, 1998: 44), can also expedite the counterhegemonic potency 'to trigger uncontrollable movements and deterritorializations of the mean or majority' (Deleuze and Guattari, 1988: 106).

In the chapter 'In the company of an-other: methodology, debates and concerns', having cited extensively from a wide range of theoretical works, I have tried to justify my choice of subject and establish my position as an interlocutor from the 'outside' who is adopting, in order to empower himself, the strategy of engaging with the nonnormative transgressions of the tribal communities.[18] In doing so, drawing from various theoretical positions, I have striven to interweave a network of diverse perspectives in a rhizomatic interconnection, since 'Network, not hierarchy, will free the richness of the aesthetic, oral or literary' (Thiong'o, 2012: 85). Inspired by a 'polyversal inclusivity' that asserts how '[w]e are more similar to each other than we are different' (Eisenstein, 2004: 176), I have aspired for a 'Globalectical reading' that tolerates the mode of 'declassifying theory' into a more interconnected mechanism for understanding the links between the otherised self and an-other.[19] The dialogic approach that has been chosen as the mode of communication between the Fourth World and the Third World can give rise to the question about the validity of using such categories. Despite having been conscious of the ever-changing dynamics of the world where old barriers are being broken down and new ones are being created, categories like that of the Third World, nevertheless, seems to be important. Recognising the differences in the world order serves initially as an invocation to resist the nonlocal ways of understanding that have been constantly dumped by the overbearing First World upon the local understanding of the world[20] and, thereafter, as a possible means of solidarity that can be formulated as 'the critique of dominance within [one's] own societies' (Niranjana, 2007: 104). Even Homi K. Bhabha in his new foreword to Fanon's *The Wretched of the Earth* has treated these categories as forces of opposition against the shadow of globalisation—the another form of the colonial extraction that often darkens the postcolonial world (Bhabha, 2004: xii). Bringing together all the major theoretical perspectives related to agency, translation, memory, story as history, queer transgression, folktale as a literary genre, the methodology of selecting and interpreting folktales and community formation, this chapter underscores the interdisciplinarity of the book.

The next chapter, '"Wandering between two worlds": "mainstream" ethos, transgression and narratives of the anarcho-dissidence in Toto', engages in a psychoanalytical study of the folktales of the Toto community. The Toto, as one of the Indigenous tribal groups, can be traced only to Totopara, an enclave located at the foothills of the Himalayas in the Alipurduar district (it was a part of Jalpaiguri district until June 25, 2014, when Alipurduar as the 20th district of West Bengal was carved out from Jalpaiguri) that shares its border with Bhutan. The total Toto population consists of 1387 individuals, as per the census report of 2011, out of which 737 are men and 650 are women. Examining the select folktales under the three broad themes— 'From Leading Grandmother to Misleading Witch', 'Dissident Intimacies' and 'Evil as Emancipation'—it has been assuredly confirmed that the emphatic desire of the Toto community to transgress the norms of the 'mainstream' subverts all the attempts that have been programmed to impose majoritarian values and nationally normatised standards on them, which subsequently provides transgressive, nontribal queers with a space for dialogic collaboration. The 'mainstream' in relation to the Indigenous communities needs to be understood as a machinery of settler colonialism.[21] The Toto folklore, with transgressive agencies, illustrates the process of the subtle suppression of undocumented time and then-prevalent, uncensored desire as nonhistorical, since the criterion of being included as a historical society is usually fulfilled at the cost of the suppression of the unwritten/oral histories as obsolete. The vigilant regimes of the state have been proactive in interleaving the tribality with the complex network of market, desire and well-being/welfare that constitutes the 'mainstream'. Toto society, therefore, is under the compulsion of narrowing down the traditional consideration of sexuality, as an unrestricted potential of human possibility in terms of intimacy and longing, towards the prescriptive model of the implementation of normatised eroticity and desire. Even then, a psychological appraisal of projection and fantasy in the select Toto oral literature through a queer lens would divulge the tension resulting from the distinctive survival of 'objects-in-thought' and 'objects-in-reality', which becomes the crucial ground for alluding to the queer counternormative impulse.

The chapter 'Discord as defilement: consensual incest in Limbu folktales and "mainstreaming" the feminine' deals with the tribal oral tales of the Limbu community, also recognised as Subba. Limbus consider themselves the descendants of the eight *Kirati/Kirata* (Indo-Mongoloid) chiefs of Nepal who had migrated from Mongolia and can be found in various parts of the present-day Sikkim and Darjeeling. As a member of the Tibeto-Burmese family of languages, Limbus have their own Kirat-Sirijonga script. Beginning with Yumanism, the traditional faith of the Limbus, which offers the feminine principle with the foremost agency, it has been argued that with the invasion of the patriarchal 'mainstream' various taboos got imposed on the Limbu liberal codes of feminine conduct, one of which is the adult female's right to opt for a consensual incestuous relationship. Addressing the issue of adult incest from the woman's perspective of empowerment, the Limbu folktales evidently bring out the essential androcentrism of the taboo, imposed on consensual incest at the cost of denying women agency. This further exposes the 'mainstream' politics of turning any alternative

Indigenous culture of difference into something abject, similar to the 'mainstream' agenda of proscribing nonconformist queers.

In the chapter 'Stages in the proscription of homoeroticity: Lepcha folktales and mythistory', the discussion on homonormativity[22] is based on the folktales of the Lepcha community. 'Lepcha' as a misnomer for the Rong community has been popularised by the nonnatives' entry into their land and confusing the identity of the Indigenous people of Darjeeling and Sikkim with 'Lapchao'—the name of the place of their residence. The poem 'Ode to the Origin of Rongs' elucidates the Lepcha genealogy: according to it, Achyuk, Menlong and many others are the ancestors of the Rong community, whose land is 'a *leemayel lyang* [land of wealth]' (qtd. in Chattopadhyay, 2013: 84).

A queer reading of the four Lepcha folktales exposes the gradual eradication of the queer tribalscape by the intruding colonial and the postcolonial/neocolonial, heteropatriarchal[23] state. The chapter in its four major segments reveals how an Indigenous gay space has been narrowed down by the structuring of closets by the trespassing colonisers, only to force tribal people, strategically, to internalise the colonial model of a compulsory heteronormativity, which thereby paved way for the expurgation of homoerotic Indigeneity by strategic association with the notion of an alien. The popular misconception of queer being an import into India, thereby, seems to be an outcome of propaganda meant to wipe out Indigenous sexual dissidents, led by foreigners and copied by the successive coloniality of the Indian state. The recurrent discriminating of queers in India is the extension of the European classification of a 'normative' sexuality that as a means of regulating diverse Indigenous sexuality becomes one of the major pillars of the production and maintenance of governmentality.

'Manly women, womanly men: genderqueer in select Rabha tales' involves a revisiting of seven folktales of the Rabha community. Rabha, generally believed to be one of the sections of the Bodo group, are actually known as Koch or Koch-Rabha in the Cooch Behar, Alipurduar and Jalpaiguri districts of North Bengal. 'The Koch is Rabha, Rabha is Koch' is a popular slogan, and although they acknowledge themselves as Koch, in the census reports, they have been designated as Rabhas (Saha, 2015: 21). Rabhas also live in various parts of Assam and Meghalaya. The search for an Indigenous ideal that would also assist in moving beyond the binaries of the sex/gender categories has persuaded me to come across the genderqueer figures of the Rabha folktales. These genderqueer men and women, as the debris of a demolished ethnic time, are important Indigenous, decolonising models to be emulated by all who find themselves victimised in their present struggle against the tabooed, neocolonial time. It has been argued that these Rabha folktale characters should make us aware of the genderqueer *absence* in the present epoch of gender fixities that has to be revived in the long run to overcome 'boundary situations'.[24]

Guided by the deep conviction that the disruptions created by the powerful agencies of authority can be combated only by borrowing the virtues of tribal imagination, the title of the concluding chapter, 'Queer India as neo-Bahujan: towards a possible assembling', hints at my possible response to the beats of the tribal customs by queers located in, and censored by, the 'mainstream'—a positive response that can actually offer the radical rhythm of becoming liberated[25] and thus civilised. Nontribal queers need to come together with the Indigenous communities to cocreate a 'third' space of anti-assimilative resistance against statist homogenising practices.

The conclusion, despite the risk of seeming utopian, comes from my firmly held belief that 'we should be interested in the commonalities that go beyond the ideological justifications for sectarianism' (Fox, 2011: 109) and come to the realisation that the state has made us outstandingly terrified of ourselves.[26] The tribal people who do not have any significant share in framing the policies which affect them most, apart from becoming the worst victims of 'inclusive exclusion' imposed by the state, are the most dependable companions for queers to fight against the discrimination sanctioned by society. Experiencing the five stages of grief—denial, anger, bargaining, depression and acceptance—as formulated by Elizabeth Kübler-Ross (1969), queer Indians, in an intimate bond with the tribal Dalit Bahujan, can gradually start admitting that there cannot be a worse threat, since present-day authoritarianism is already excessive enough to instigate an emancipatory defiance.

Towards a queer activism

This 'belated reading' of the folktales has also made me aware—more so while listening to the oral performance of storytelling based on repetitive recollections for unearthing buried 'ideas' via memory's 'power to revive again, in our minds those ideas, which after imprinting have disappeared, or have been as it were laid aside out of sight' (Locke, 2007: 75)—of the process of how socially constructed 'abject' people can easily be made invisible 'if they be not sometimes renewed by repeated exercise of the senses, or reflection' (ibid.: 76). Folklore as a 'contemporary prehistory' (Corso, 2018) provides extant evidence, despite its being mutilated and adulterated, that offers an outlook that is completely opposed to that of the official version of normativity.[27] The conviction that politics is intrinsically sexual has become stronger because of contemporary Indian 'juridico-political' discourses, which have further motivated readings into the tribal folktales of oral traditions from a queer perspective. Adding a queer perspective to tribal folktales is important to illustrating the (neo)colonial politics so that by 'sexualising the political', with the revelation of the taboos being imposed by the interloping 'mainstream', 'it becomes possible to wrest sexuality discourse from its various minoritarianisms, opening it up to a genuinely universal emancipatory struggle beyond the reach of capitalism's complicity with the continuing proliferation and deconstruction of sexual and gender identities' (Penney, 2014: 1–2).

Sexual politics in order to be effective has to critically consider the immediate present and become, in Judith Butler's term, 'sexual politics *now*' (Oleksy, 2009: 18). Conjoining sexual politics of freedom with the time that is 'now' permits a space for critiquing against the majoritarian violence, together with the prospect of getting support from those who are differently yet equally minoritised.[28] The bleak Indian sexual scenario emerging out of the decriminalising and recriminalising of queers has become gloomy, despite the historic judgement by the Supreme Court, due to right-wing political rhetoric.[29] The antiqueer odium was popularised immediately after the Supreme Court's partially striking down of the colonial-era provisions of Section 377 of the Indian Penal Code, and the right-wing regime is endeavouring at what Rosi Braidotti calls a 'politically conservative return of God' in an attempt to naturalise differences with the target of using them as 'natural' categories,[30] to sustain structural discriminations (ibid.: 41). In the name of morality,[31] the agencies of governmentality have been implementing all the hard-edged sets of proprieties and rules at the cost of an ethical good that could have been functional in legitimising diverse modes of 'becoming'. Having understood the dangers of been turned into just another category of hegemonised 'sexual citizens', the demands that queers have made through their agitation against Article 377 is for an 'intimate citizenship'. Such a claim is pivotal in asserting the rights relating to 'those matters which relate to [their] most intimate desires, pleasures, and ways of being in the world' (Weeks, 1996: 83), out of an earnest realisation that remaining as non-citizens would 'maintain systems of exclusion and discrimination that brings real material harm to many people' (Bell and Binnie, 2000: 146). The most acute challenge before decriminalised queer Indian people is that of gaining widespread acceptability, because many Indians have internalised colonial homophobia. Queering the tribal folktales by illustrating instances of the inclusion of the non-'mainstream' desires in the queernormative[32] Indigenous sociocultural traditions in India is an endeavour to lay the groundwork for sensitising people to a queer 'natural'-cum-autochthonous identity.

Notes

1 See for instance, "Homophobic India? Survey Finds 56 Percent Respondents Would Refuse Organ from LGBTQ Donor", *News18*, November 12, 2019. www.news18.com/news/buzz/survey-finds-over-half-of-indians-would-refuse-organ-from-an-lgbtq-donor-2384117.html; "Not My Fault I Was Born Gay: 19-year-old Commits Suicide Over Homophobia", *India Today*, New Delhi, July 9, 2019. www.indiatoday.in/india/story/gay-man-suicide-homophobia-lgbt-helplines-1565041-2019-07-09 Accessed on June 6, 2020.

2 'Queer' as a term has been generally used to denote those otherwise unalike subjects who can collectively engage in a togetherness, as 'the oxymoronic community of differences' (Jagose, 1996: 112), mainly on the basis of their nonnormative identities and practices. 'Queer' is often an umbrella term used for the lesbian, gay, bisexual, transgender, transsexual, intersex, asexual and pansexual people along with their allies.

3 Swami Chakrapani, president of All India Hindu Mahasabha, in response to decriminalisation of same-sex intimacy, has said, 'It's shameful. We are giving credibility and legitimacy to mentally sick people' ("Religious and Political Silence on India's LGBTQ Decision Speaks Volumes", *Rewire.News*, September 7, 2018. https://rewire.news/religion-dispatches/2018/09/07/religious-and-political-silence-on-indias-lgbtq-decision-speaks-volumes/). Also see 'Homosexuality an 'Imported Disease', Says VHP', *Deccan Chronicle*, December 17, 2013. www.deccanchronicle.com/131216/news-current-affairs/article/homosexuality-imported-disease-says-vhp Accessed on August 22, 2019.

4 After the partition of 1947, North Bengal has referred to the following districts of West Bengal (a provincial state in India): Darjeeling, Kalimpong, Jalpaiguri, Alipurduar, Cooch Behar, North Dinajpur, South Dinajpur and Malda. Recently, Gour Banga has been popularly used to denote Malda and its adjacent places. In this work, I have focused mainly on the Himalayan belt (Darjeeling and Kalimpong districts of North Bengal and Sikkim) and the Dooars region (the Jalpaiguri, Cooch Behar and Alipurduar districts) of North Bengal. My hometown is Jalpaiguri, and for the past 13 years, I have been working in Darjeeling. The four Indigenous communities—Lepcha, Limbu, Toto and Rabha—are geographically interrelated. Any random picking of the other Indigenous communities in India, which can never be all inclusive, has been consciously avoided. My methodology is based on a definite locale where these four communities often come across one another and derives from my having coexisted with them in a shared domain for quite a long time. Since the politics of this work is aimed at showing how endogenous Indian queer identity is—by underscoring how one can come across the queernormative identity even in the cultures and tales of the Indian tribal community who are the Indigenous people of the soil—I have also restrained myself from including some comparative analysis of queer folktales from other parts of the world.

5 Sikkim is one of the provincial states of the region of Northeast India. The other states of Northeast India are Assam, Nagaland, Manipur, Mizoram, Meghalaya, Tripura and Arunachal Pradesh.

6 Hountondji has used the phrasing "to dwell on the origin of a cultural product or value that comes from, or at least is perceived by people as coming from inside their own society, as opposed to imported or "exogenous" products or values" (Hountondji, 1995: 6–7).

7 It is indeed unfortunate that queer is still regarded as non-Indian by the majority of the 'mainstream' India, despite the trailblazing works of Ruth Vanita and Saleem Kidwai (2000) and Devdutt Pattanaik (2008), to name just two. However, they have focused on the history of queer ideas and desires available in the written traditions of India. Hence, it appears to be easy for the rebuffing 'mainstream' to mar those representations as interpolations by the people who had arrived from outside or who are singled out as outsider. On the contrary, the oral tradition of an Indigenous community, which is regarded as the storehouse of 'the community's social norms, values and thoughts' and drawn from the realities of traditional society, cannot be discarded as a mere distortion (Sone, 2018: 142). Hence, I hope that this book, by associating queer identity with

Indigeneity, can provide a tougher challenge for those who are still reluctant to accept Indigenous queer people. It is interesting to come across 'The Eunuch Priesthood and Deity Daria' in Sen (1985) where, on the basis of a case study of Cachar district of Assam, Daria, the female deity riding on a tortoise, is worshipped by Gurma, the eunuch priest. I have, however, not come across any full-length work on Indigenous queer people in India. I have dealt with some of the issues before, and this book, in bits and pieces, draws on three of my published works: Chakraborty (2020a, 2020b, 2017).

8 Ali Behadad has defined 'belated reading' as 'not an orthodox reiteration or a reapplication of a previous theory; rather, it is an interventionary articulation of a new problematic through the detour—or, perhaps more accurately, retour—of an earlier practice' (Behadad, 1994: 3).

9 'Tribalisation', as conceptualised by S.L. Kalia, suggests the practice of adopting aspects of tribal living by the people of non-tribal origin (Kalia, 1959).

10 My conscious recurrent use of 'mainstream' is mainly influenced by Akeel Bilgrami, who has also considered the 'mainstream' to be an important route to majoritarian nationalism:

> a modern state of mind in which the very ideal of 'nation' has built into it as a form of necessity the ideal of nation-state, with its commitment to such things as development, national security, rigidly codified forms of an increasingly centralized policy, and above all the habit of exclusion of some other people
>
> (Bilgrami, 1998: 383)

As the 'culture' of the majorities who enjoy power and privileges in a society gets projected as the 'dominant culture', so too does the 'mainstream' constitute the national paradigm sanctioned by the ruling majorities and normatised by the state, where everything beyond the standardised framework gets marginalised. 'Mainstreaming' often becomes the governmental homogenising tool of erasing the multicultural praxes of differences. The power structure of the 'majoritarianised' is maintained by valorising the value system of the privileged as 'mainstream' 'normal'/'national', at the cost of minoritising a plethora of multicultural counternorms, through vigilance and repressive laws that effectively result in dehumanisation, polarisation, and a stereotype demonisation of the 'other' (Wolfensberger, 2002). It is the dominant 'mainstream' culture that, under the plea for 'culturalism', appropriates *tribalism* by fitting through distortions nonconformist Indigeneity within the frame of national discourses and institutions. Reinventing the norms that are suppressed is essential in order to uncloak the oppression of the 'mainstream' and to pave a way towards demarginalisation by establishing the legitimacy of counternorms that have been strategically bracketed off as 'marginal', 'antinational' or 'malevolent' by the 'mainstream' (Viollet, 1988).

11 'The Adivasi concept has gained widespread resonance and currency in contemporary India, but it has yet to supersede the concept of the 'tribe' in national arenas' (Rycroft and Dasgupta, 2011: 7).

12 'Silence around Native sexuality benefits the colonisers and erases queer Native people from their communities. Putting Native studies and queer studies in dialogue creates further possibilities to decolonize Native communities' (Finley, 2011: 40–41).

13 'Fourth World' is used more in this book than is 'First Nations', because 'First Nations' is more specifically used with the Indigenous people of the Americas; moreover, the word 'nation' itself has become immensely problematic for social scientists.

13

14 '[T]he aesthetic act is itself ideological, and the production of aesthetic or narrative form is to be seen as an ideological act in its own right, with the function of inventing imaginary or formal "solutions" to unresolvable social contradictions' (Jameson, 1981: 79).

15 For a detailed study, see Halberstam (1998: 50–59).

16 'There are certainly more citations to models of methods than there are to findings from tale studies' (Goldberg, 1986: 173)

17 Eclecticism, as suggested by Christine Goldberg, characterises the suitable trends of studying folktales: 'Folktales deserve to be approached from many directions. Each approach is self-limiting. . . . Approaches that may seem irrelevant to each other are all parts of a single question: why do tales take the forms they do?' (1986: 173).

18 The tribal societies are not static. There are internal dynamics of the tribal societies at the threshold of social transformation, and the folktales too are a part of ongoing revisions through variable oral performances. This endeavour of mine, however, is not about historicising of the folktales. Hence, an explanation of the historical and cultural reasons which sanction certain behaviours/ideologies as alternatives to that of the 'mainstream' in one type of tribal society and forbid it in another has not been undertaken in this study. It is a known fact that the tribal communities have their customary laws, and transgressing customary laws of a tribal society is a serious offence, for which severe punishment is often meted out by the traditional courts to transgressors of social customs and taboos. However, the diverse alternatives related to gender and sexuality that are available in these Indigenous alter modernities are beneficial for the transgressor of the 'mainstream' to initiate a dialogic communication and establish a sense of belonging through 'tribalisation' in their perusal of finding approval in order to overcome the anguish of otherisation on the basis of sexual marginalisation.

19 According to Ngũgĩ wa Thiong'o, reading 'globalectically'

> involves declassifying theory in the sense of making it accessible—a tool for clarifying interactive connections and interconnections of social phenomena and their mutual impact in the local and global space, a means of illuminating the internal and the external, the local and the global dynamics of social being. This may also mean the act of reading becoming also a process of self-examination.
>
> (Thiong'o, 2012: 61)

20 Clifford Geertz has deployed 'Third' World as 'an attempt to come to terms with the diversity of the ways human beings construct their lives in the act of leading them' (Geertz, 2000: 16).

21 Settler colonialism refers to the persistent sociopolitical endeavours by the colonisers/newcomers/nontribal settlers who enter into the tribal lands and gradually start to make claims of owning the lands through the strategic expunction of the traditional praxes of Indigenous people.

22 'Homonormativity' is often criticised as a posture of 'assimilation' with the 'mainstream' by trying to imitate the conventional values and fit into traditional institutions, like marriage, parenting and so on. There are possibilities that while struggling for approbation from the 'mainstream', the gay movement towards a homonornative India, seduced by neoliberal capitalism, may be ill-shaped as 'homocapitalist' (Rao, 2015: 38) or, by falling into the trap of hypernationalism, may also be easily aberrated to 'homonationalism' (Puar, 2007). Following the sectarian rhetoric of right-wing populism and targeting the progressive critics

of the populist governments as 'antinational foreign ideologues', an aggravated 'homopopulism' (Lotter and Fourie, 2020) seems to have accelerated queer-on-queer violence initiated by a section of the queer community's engaging with the politics of fear and intolerance, thereby colliding with those who seek to abuse non-jingoistic queer people. However, in this book, by 'homonormativity', I refer to the desired paradigm shift in the normalisation of homosexuality that entails accepting the basic demands of treating Indian homosexual people as endogenous (and not an import or a non-Indigenous identity) and of recognising the gay identity as differently normal by the Indian 'mainstream'. There lies, nevertheless, a risk that the 'regime of normalcy' attained through homonormativity (contrary to the 'radical individualism' of locating the gay selves—aimed at achieving an 'alternative respectability' (Orne, 2017: 220)—outside the societal strictures) may hamper the politics of making 'life choices distinct from those considered more socially expected, celebrated, and sanctioned' (Pfeffer, 2012: 578). Yet even if the homonormative plea seems to be premised on pleading the state for providing legal provisions with 'expectations for living a "good life"' (Schippers, 2016: 7), it can be argued that heterosexuals have questioned and refashioned traditional norms and conventional social institutions associated with heteronormativity (e.g., the advocacy of anti-childbirth by 'antinatalist' heterosexual couples). Similarly, once the recognitions of Indigenousness, equality and normalcy are achieved by the homosexuals of India, they too will try to readjust the interpersonal and reshape the institutionalised homonormative experiences and will learn not to remain confined only within the domain of sexuality but rather to join with other struggles against various kinds of depravities (Croce, 2015: 5). 'Homonornative', as deployed in this book in the context of pointing out the prevalent normalisation of homosexuality in the domains described in the tribal folktales, needs to be placed before the 'mainstream' so that the homophobic 'mainstream' can learn how to accept and cope up with non-heteronormativity. This might ultimately also challenge the notion of impossibility put forward by Rao regarding 'the intersectionality of queer and Adivasi' (2015: 41).

23 Heteropatriarchy is the social order that treats heterosexuality and patriarchy as 'normal' characteristics and all other configurations as 'abnormal'.

24 Elaborating on Arendt's use of this expression in *The Life of the Mind* (1981: 192), Roberto Esposito writes, 'It concerns an absence that is made a presence or a presence that resounds, silently, in an absence' (Esposito, 2015: 78).

25 An insinuation of a radical tribalism can be found in *Living in the End Times*, where Zizek claims that although the 'people's justice is harsh', 'no matter how unpalatable to our liberal tastes this may be, *we have no right to condemn it*', since the radical rebels 'in India are a starving tribal people to whom the minimum of a dignified life has been denied and who are fighting for their lives' (Zizek, 2010: 395).

26 'The people must be put in *terror* of themselves in order to give them *courage*' (Marx, 1975: 247).

27 Gramsci has argued that

> Folklore should instead be studied as 'conception of the world and life' implicit to a large extent in determinate (in time and space) strata of society and in opposition (also for the most part implicit, mechanical and objective) to 'official' conceptions of the world (or in a broader sense, the conceptions of the cultured parts of historically determinate societies) that have succeeded one another in the historical process.
>
> (Gramsci, 2015: 189)

For a discussion on the various alternatives related to ecological care, artistic calibres, social and gender stratifications as manifested in select tribal folktales, see Chakraborty (2017).

28 For a detailed discussion on a possible intimacy among the people who are differently but equally marginalised, see Chakraborty (2020a: 1–17).

29 Subramanian Swamy has expressed his annoyance by reaffirming homosexuality as a 'genetic disorder, like someone having six fingers'. "BJP mum on SC Verdict on Section 377", *Deccan Herald*, September 7, 2018. www.deccanherald.com/national/bjp-mum-sc-verdict-section-377-691575.html.

30 The latest instance of right-wing sexism is the stand taken by the central government of India before the Supreme Court, where it has been argued that women, because of their physical differences, are not suitable enough to be given command posts in the Indian army. For details, see "Justifying Sexism, Centre Says Women Can't Be Given Command Posts as Army Men Won't Accept It", *The Wire*, February 5, 2020. https://thewire.in/law/women-officers-indian-army-command-posts.

31 'I invite the gay community', said Baba Ramdev, 'to my yoga ashram and I guarantee to cure them of homosexuality'. Zakir Naik has remarked, 'Generally, naturally, no human being loves the same sex'. "'Disease', 'dangerous', 'curable': What key public figures in India think of homosexuality" by Kuwar Singh. September 6, 2018. *Quartz India*. https://qz.com/india/1380027/section-377-what-ramdev-adityanath-zakir-naik-think-of-gays/Accessed on August 22, 2019.

32 'Queernormative' refers to the perspective that promotes queer orientation as the normal/preferred sexuality. The queernormative depictions in the tribal folktales get interdicted as nonnormative by the queerphobic 'mainstream'.

2

IN THE COMPANY OF
AN-OTHER
Methodology, debates and concerns

[O]ne of the most basic of all human questions: who are you?
This is not a question that can be answered with a name nor
can it be answered satisfactorily in words. Rather, the question requires qualitative demonstrations. Answers emerge in
the lived experience of relationships developed in shared time
and place. Ultimately, answers are a sharing of perceptions,
attitudes, experiences, and, I think, compassion.

(Rose, 2009: 26)

The 'Third' in a dialogic intimacy with the 'Fourth'

The motivation for intimacy with my neighbouring Indigeneity comes
from the inner consciousness of what Patricia Hill Collins (1991) suggested as 'the outsider within'. This has resulted into a dialogic attempt to
communicate with the Fourth World so that its incommensurability would
enable self-actualisation for a censored citizen from the Third World. The
Fourth World is almost synonymous with the Indigenous.[1] As per Roxanne Dunbar Ortiz's adaptation of George Manuel's primary definition,
the term 'Fourth World' is

the name given to the Indigenous peoples descended from a country's aboriginal population and, who today are completely or partly
deprived of the right to their own territories and its riches. The
peoples of the 4th world have only limited influence or none at all
in the national states to which they belong.

(Ortiz, 1984: 82)

For someone like me, who represents the nonconformist from the Third
World, the Fourth World's Indigenous face has initially been that of a 'stranger' who, however, does not oppose me as 'obstacle or enemy' (Levinas,
1969: 215). Rather than a distanced reflective stance, a dialogic reflexivity
enables the self 'to be in the presence of others precisely inasmuch as the

17

Other has become content of our experience. This brings us to the conditions of possibility of intersubjective knowledge' (Fabian, 1983: 91–92). The dialogic framework also helps in perceiving the Indigenous existence as a paradigm not of premodernity but rather of alter-modernity and thereby not committing the error of the 'denial of coevalness' (ibid.: 31). This is one of the reasons why the term 'tribal' is preferred over *adivasi*, which can often be linked with remoteness. The dialogic nearness helps me to be in proximity with the face that communicates with me with an invitation for a relationship (Levinas, 1969: 198). The tribal face, that 'comes from a dimension of height', starts disclosing the Fourth World in front of me (ibid.: 215), and in the presence of the face of the 'other', I feel liberated to claim more of myself (Levinas, 1990: 294). Being situated in the 'mainstream' is not always a privilege. Many times, transgressing the societal norms in the 'mainstream' results in getting quickly labelled 'a nonnormative deviant'. Becker has rightly observed that

> deviance is created by society. . . . Social groups create deviance by making the rules whose infraction constitutes deviance and by applying those rules to particular persons and labelling them as outsiders. . . . The deviant is one to whom the label has successfully been applied; deviant behaviour is behaviour that people so label.
>
> (Becker, 1966: 9)

The homophobic comments that flooded social media immediately after consensual gay sex was decriminalised in India, along with the setbacks— such as the Supreme Court's dismissing of a review petition[2] seeking different civil rights related to same-sex marriage, surrogacy and adoption for the LGBTQ+ community and India's abstaining at the United Nations Human Rights Council from voting in favour of LGBTQ+ rights[3]—have given birth to renewed questions about the connection between the periphery and the core of social life, the margins and the centre, difference and identity, the normatised and the deviant and the possible mechanism that could plausibly bind the subalterns in a collectivity. In today's world it is difficult to be rebellious in a culture where seldom a common belief gets sustained in any form of collective action or shared identity. The contemporary nonconformist is left not with utopianism or nihilism but with isolation. It is only by having a strong sense of being 'together' if not collective (and thereby not sharing anything exactly identical per se) that we can start to comprehend and give an explanation for that which is outside, at the peripheries, or that which disregards the consensus. With the rising problem of generating and legitimatising a national culture that 'represents a special battlefield' (Fanon, 1990: 193), counter-endeavours are crucial to this battle in various ways. Denounced by the moral policing of the non-queer-friendly 'mainstream' and attempting to be mutually connected with the Indigenous societies whose take on sexuality and intimacy appears to be more cosmo-politan, I try to locate myself as a non-Indigenous ally, with a 'response-ability' (Venkateswar and Hughes, 2011: 246) to correlate the experience of the queer minorities with those of Indigenous communities. The Indigenous tribal world by its alter-modernity seems not to hesitate to be intimately together with the one dispossessed off the 'mainstream', thereby inviting for a dialogic interconnection. According to Bakhtin, 'a person's conscious-ness awakens wrapped in another's consciousness' (1984: 138). Bakhtinians argue that life itself is meant to be dialogic, to ask and respond, from the creative posture of 'outsideness': 'An event cannot be wholly known, cannot be seen, from inside its own unfolding as an event' (Holquist, 2002: 29).

The notion of 'outsideness' that enables the self to assimilate the subjec-tive perspective with that of the others results in self-actualisation, which further results in the manifestation of the consciousness of 'I-for-myself' against the background of 'I-for-the-other'. For Bakhtin, 'being' is a shared 'event' of cohabiting as a co-being, simultaneously sharing and cooperating with others, with implication/understanding arising on the frontier between two consciousness. This comes from the perception of the self as non-self-sufficient: 'A person has no internal sovereign territory, he is wholly and always on the boundary; looking inside himself, he looks into the eyes of another or with the eyes of another' (Bakhtin, 1984: 287).

Communication with an-other, however, may turn an individual sceptical when they are reminded that 'To undergo an experience with something—be it a thing, a person, or a god—means that this something befalls us, strikes us, comes over us, overwhelms and transforms us' (Heidegger, 1971: 57). Bataille answers back: 'there cannot be knowledge without a community of seekers, nor inner experience without a community of those who live it. . . . [C]ommunication is a phenomenon which is no way added to Dasein, but constitutes it' (Bataille, 1988: 24). Bataille also proclaims that truth can be traced only by tracking its progress from a single one to the other (Bataille, 1989: 62). Dialogic communion, apart from an engaging involvement with the other, is not a drive towards merging the self fully with another:

> The way in which I create myself is by means of a quest: I go out to the other in order to come back with a self. I live into another's consciousness. . . . But I must never completely meld with that ver-sion of things.
>
> (Clark and Holquist, 1984: 78)

The question of asserting self-identity of the nonnormative self through intersubjectivity, rather than altering it, or even without aiming for any sort of hybridised identity, provides a kind of compulsion for a person like me, to strive for togetherness with unprejudiced Indigeneity. Fabian aptly wrote that 'if it is true that recognizing others also means remembering them, then we should see relationships between self and other as a struggle for recognition, inter-personal as well as political' (Fabian, 2006: 145). Gayatri Spivak's speculation has pointed out the problem faced by a transgressive Third World individual of not being listened to by the censorious Third World 'mainstream': 'For me, the question "Who should speak?" is less crucial than "Who will listen?" . . . I should be listened to seriously; not with that kind of benevolent imperialism' (Spivak, 1990: 49).

Representing the socially disapproved 'queer India', I find myself denied a space, in the neocolonial state, not only to speak but also to be heard. The tribal subculture as an interlocutor 'other' with its huge gamut of cohabiting differences facilitates the nonnormative individual from the 'mainstream' to emerge as a non-subaltern, who is allowed to speak and who is listened to in a dialogic continuum. Engaging intimately with this inside-out/outside-in study may be the only potential strategy to empower the self and those who represent nonnormative transgressions.

Can the otherised speak for an-other?
The politics of belonging

In reference to the process of understanding a different tradition, Edward Said has raised some pertinent questions: 'Who writes? For whom is the writing being done? In what circumstances? These it seems to me are the questions whose answers provide us with the ingredients making a politics of interpretation' (Said, 1983: 7).

This is a study of the select tribal culture and its nonnormative transgressive elements of queernormativity as reflected in the tribal oral literature, carried out by a nontribal. For whom am I writing? Before addressing this vital question, I need to communicate the rationale on the basis of which a non-Indigenous individual, if at all, may be approved of carrying out research on Indigenous people. As reflected through Habermas's conceptualisation of the public sphere, a theory is legitimated by its distance from experience. According to Habermas, the precondition of theorising is to sustain a distance between theory and experience. Authorship cannot be dictated by experience; rather outsiders can formulate theorisation by virtue of their distance from experience (Strong and Sposito, 1995: 263–288). There are, however, multiple speculations on this highly debated issue. Given the fact that researchers of ethnography are 'positioned subjects' (Okely, 1992: 14), what is the advantage of neutrality that is often ascribed to the research done by the individual who might be representing the ethnic group under study? The expectation of objectivity is almost an illusion in ethnographic research; rather, what can be expected is intersubjectivity:

Exoticism certainly offers data which are immediately and easily descriptive because they are new, whereas familiarity blurs the object to be described. Both can prove to be deceptive. If one rejects the complicity of the strange and the illusion of the known, then ethnographic 'fields', distant or near, are revealed as on an equal footing

(Segalen and Zonabend, 1987: 111)

It is faulty to presume that the ethnographers carrying out fieldworks in their own societies can provide the insider's vision with strict neutrality. Inversely, being an individual representing the group is hardly 'a neutral, uninvolved position' (Nakleh, 1979: 344). Being an insider, the researcher gets often controlled by the researched group: 'indigenous anthropologists find themselves in a great variety of positions vis-à-vis the local groups that affect their self-perceived roles and the expectations of the local community' (Fahim and Helmer et al, 1980: 647). The taken-for-granted outlook that often seems to blur the vision of an endogenous researcher representing the Indigenous group of the researched results in a failure to go beyond the self-evident.[4] This issue can be handled with more precaution by someone representing other cultures:

Cross-cultural perspectives still have an important role to play in carrying out projects of repatriated ethnography, in defining novel approaches to taken-for-granted domestic phenomena, in framing questions, and in suggesting alternatives or possibilities among domestic subjects.

(Marcus and Fischer, 1986: 135–136)

Hence, my non-Indigeneity cannot be the basis of reproving my attempt for dialogic communication with tribal communities. The question of a fair, neutral stance is not only a problem with non-Indigenous researchers' studying the tribal world but a universal problem for even endogenous researchers: 'The tension between the need for both empathy and detachment is a problem facing all anthropologists' (Sarsby, 1984: 129). This tension regarding an impossible objectivity seems to be an intrinsic component of Indigenous ethnographic research, irrespective of whether it is done by a tribal researcher or by a nontribal researcher. Kirin Narayan seems to express a similar view: 'Writing texts that mix lively narrative and rigorous analysis involves enacting hybridity, regardless of our origins' (Narayan, 1993: 682).

All the foregoing arguments on this subject can yet again be challenged with the single question: how can the lived experience of the tribals be perceived/theorised by a nontribal? Subjective experiences are unique and marked by an absence of freedom: one can never have the freedom to choose, to leave or to modify experiences, but rather, one is compelled to continue to live in the provided inimitable situation of 'lack'. 'Mainstream' queer people,

21

however, can easily link the dearth of queer experiences with that of tribal experiences: they are marked by deficits. Yet again, one is not merely eligible to respond to and theorise about the situation of experience alone, acquired through one's being but can also theorise/speculate about the situations where one consciously places oneself. A contested queer person of Third World India will indubitably be drawn to consciously place themselves in a similar position to that of a tribal person, primarily on account of their sharing a lack of freedom in their experiences. Further, if experience of the affair becomes, from the perspective of the ethics of theorising, the sole marker of authenticity, then it would have been impossible to think of any reliable writing of history from any historians, because they did not actually experience antiquity (Sarukkai, 2007: 4043–4044).

The supposed polarity of the self and the 'other' that anticipates the subject/object divide needs further consideration in order to answer whom the writing is being done for. In the classical framework of an austerely objective ethno-anthropological study, the subjective self of the researcher is denied establishing any ethical relationship with the studied 'other', fortifying the binary of self and not-self. Bronislaw Malinowski (1922), while reaffirming the need of studying alien cultures, strategised the mode of participant-observer. Through the researcher's understanding of the target culture as 'not-other', the distance between the alien researcher gets reduced by their becoming of one among the natives. However, this methodology at times provokes theorising by the tourist researcher, whose sense of belonging is often dicey, and it eventually ends up as unmerited research.

The subject/object dichotomy has been given a different turn by M.N. Srinivas, who differentiates between a foreign anthropologist's studying Indigeneity in India and an Indian individual's studying Indigeneity in India. Srinivas has argued that since the Indian researcher and the Indian tribals reside in 'same cultural universe', not like the foreign researcher, it is 'self-in-the-other' that is operational unlike the non-self or non-other position (Srinivas, 1996: 656–657). This notion of self-in-the-other, which is a distinct feature of a nontribal Indian person's studying tribal people, can be further understood when one takes into account the way 'other' is understood in Indian vernacular. The 'other' in Indian vernacular has the common connotation of 'one more' or 'second', which bears the implication of considering 'other' as an extension of the self—that is, self-in-the-other. As Sarukkai has observed, 'For a person steeped in this tradition, this does make a qualitative difference in constructing the other' (Sarukkai, 1997: 1408).

This endeavour is not aimed at imitating that of the West or the (neo) colonising majority. Rather, it is a venture of a contested belonging, otherised by the 'mainstream', seeking inclusion in an-other marginalised culture through the intimate sharing of the burden of exclusion as well as a sharing of differences, unsanctioned by 'mainstream' societal norms. But can the otherised write for an-other? I try to address this question in this book by replacing the dichotomy between the self and the other with a politics of belonging through the realisation of the self-in-the-other. This book thus represents a writing about the otherised that includes both the (neocolonised) self and the (Indigenous) 'other'. Discovering the self-in-the-other through dialogism leads to the discovery that the culture of the 'other' is more cosmopolitan and thus humanist/neotraditional/alter-modernist in its inclusion of differences of perspectives/desires/orientations than the neocolonial 'mainstream'. The 'mainstream', to a large extent, provides the contrast of creating docile bodies and rendering the nonconformist as a disowned subhuman/nonhuman. Hence the non-Indigenous self of mine acknowledges itself being powerless due to the situatedness in the 'mainstream', compared to the world of tribals. Thereafter, it seeks to 'Indigenise', through intimacy with the Indigenous way of knowing/imagining, in order to gain the power of self-assertion. This, as a corollary, would argue that the Fourth World is more cosmopolitan/humanitarian and thereby a power provider as opposed to the myth of what Said has called the powerful 'positional-superiority' of the (neo)coloniser.

Memories turned into the tales and history

There can be no formation of identity sans memories, because the self and society are essentially 'steeped in memory' (Casey, 1987: ix). While trying to historically construe a particular ethnic group, it is crucial to discern their ethnic memory, in this case manifested through tribal folktales. Memory is the foundation based on which the folktales have been formulated. 'Contrary to Leroi-Gourhan who uses the term "ethnic memory" for all human societies', writes Jacques Le Goff, 'I will use it only to refer to the collective memory of people without writing' (Le Goff, 1992: 55). Ethnic/collective memory has multiple synonymous usages: local memory, cultural memory, traditional memory, popular memory, shared memory, social memory and so forth. How social groups create the image of the past, which are based on the agreed-on versions that get formulated through their communications about antiquity, is appositely reflected in their collective memory. Therefore, history can be regarded as social memory: 'a convenient piece of shorthand that sums up the rather complex process of selection and interpretation' (Olick and Robbins, 1998: 110). Recollecting the past through the retellings of folktales illustrates how some facets of times of yore resist attempts of restyling by the outsider-oppressors (Schudson, 1992). The subordinated tribal groups avow their identity and offer resistance against the diminutions of customary ethos by the dominant hegemonic culture, interfering frequently under the guise of a nation-building agenda, through their retention and mobilising of the different aspects of traditional/cultural history by habitually summoning ethnic memory. The tribal folktales transmitted through descriptions of remembered cultures have been termed by Roger

Sanjek (1993) as 'memory cultures': '[We] can speak of a real community as a "community of memory", one that does not forget its past . . . [and that] is involved in retelling its story' (Robert Bellah et al., 1985: 153).

To consider folkloristic as a serious engagement, first one needs to validate memory as a serious tool of understanding history or rather recognise 'history as an art of memory'. 'Historicism' is commonly understood as the objective knowing how the past really used to be (Gilbert, 1987). In a critical disagreement with the intention of 'historicism', Karl Popper has asserted his discomfort with historicism, with its notion of predicating a historical destiny, which for him is 'sheer superstition . . . [and] there can be no prediction of the course of human history by scientific or any other rational methods' (Popper, 1957: vii). Walter Benjamin argues that the responsibility of history, often assumed as the promise of history, which is to divulge the memory of suffering, is betrayed in the accounts of historiography/historicity, which is actually the history of the vanquisher. As a critique of historicism, Benjamin argues that the method of guarantying objectivity turns out to be an interpretation founded on 'absolutism of method' and missing out on the 'richness of layers' in history (Benjamin, 1972: VI, 95). The agenda of historicism in faithfully depicting what really happened ends up illustrating the most visible traces of the powerful over those who were oppressed, thus producing an 'eternal' image of the powerful and the universal history of legal impositions (Benjamin, 1968). Benjamin, who acknowledges the need of an interpretative or even a constructive history 'dedicated' to the nameless ones, critiques scientific historiography thus: the 'scientific' character of history

> is purchased at the expense of the total extirpation of all that which reminds it of its original meaning of remembrance [*Eingedenken*]. The false vitality of representation [*Vergegenwärtigung*], the removal of every echo of 'lament' [*Klage*] from history, signifies its final subjection to the modern concept of science.
>
> (Benjamin, 1972: I, 1231)

Only the history that is linked with a memory of the 'oppressed past' can create a historiographical method of responsibility towards the 'drudgery of the nameless' and provide resistance to those who benefit from 'scientific' fetishism (Benjamin, 1968). Benjamin has recommended an alternative: teasing history out of the established place in the stream of historicity. This 'ripping out of its context', what Benjamin calls 'destruction' or 'a citation without citation marks' (Benjamin, 1972: V, 572), is an effort of blasting the historical object out of 'the continuum of historical process' so that the object is rescued from the 'brutal grasp' (ibid.: 592) of context and unfolds itself as a 'force-field' for the prehistory and posthistory to polarise itself (ibid.: 587). Then, it will be easier to show how the object, apart from owing to sociohistorical processes, also gets constructed by its reception as a part of a progressive process. The constructive portion of historians' task lies in a constellative rearrangement of the components or works, which Benjamin equates with the montage method of the surrealists (ibid.: 575), broken out of the stream of tradition of received interpretation, what Gadamer terms 'effective history'.

Memory needs to be considered as a text that has to be interpreted, not as a lost fact that has to be rediscovered (King, 1996: 62). Relating history's recollection with the folktales' tradition of repetitions, Patrick H. Hutton argues that

> history is an art of memory because it mediates the encounter between two moments of memory: repetition and recollection. Repetition concerns the presence of the past. . . . Recollection concerns our present efforts to evoke the past. It is the moment of memory with which we consciously reconstruct images of the past in the selective way that suits the needs of our present situation.
>
> (Hutton, 1993: xx–xxi)

The tribal tales are narrated in a particular moment of time by an individual tribal storyteller, but even then while revealing the part of individual memory, the rendered tales also share the extended memory across generations and embody the time beyond the individual lifespan (d'Azevedo, 1962). How can memory that is characterised by change and reinterpretation in the course of recollecting the past, passing through remembering and forgetting, be considered as representative of history? There are multiple ways of answering this. Memory is history in the sense that it is the history of mentality. Even if the details are transcreated by revisions and distortions, the 'core truth' of memory regarding 'a discourse on original experience' remains more or less consistent over time (Pillemer, 1998). Moreover, as De Boeck observed, an individual's memory is always 'vivid with existential immediacy' (De Boeck, 1998: 39). The personal memory of an individual is always collectively structured and socially mediated: 'Nearly all personal memories are learned, inherited, or, at the very least, informed by a common stock of social memories' (Brundage, 2000: 4).

'Oral evidence by transforming the "objects" of study into "subjects" makes for a history which is not just richer, more vivid and heart-rending, but *truer*' (Thompson, 1988: 99). Oral history, according to Iggers, urges us to move from macro-history to micro-history, where the historical study gets centred more on the individual stories of the subject concerned than on any grand narrative (Iggers, 1997: 101–117). Our suspicion as to whether orality renders true or false information proves irrelevant the moment we look to oral history as the evidence derived from the social perception of a subject, in whatsoever personal, metaphorical or objective mode. These oral tales, like private letters, have social meaning from a historic event, narrated from the subjective micro-standpoint. Here another question arises: whether to treat the oral stories as history of the present narrator or history of the past. For Thompson, despite the subjective intervention by the present narrator, oral history in the form of oral stories that has been transmitted from one generation to another through oral/aural practices becomes a part of a greater oral tradition that forbids us from treating the stories as mere history of the present; rather, they must be treated also as history of the social past. Making use of Jan Vansina, Thompson has argued that because the older deviations and archaisms are left unharmed, despite the course of social change (with the obvious traces of the matters concealed), the story—apart from mirroring the history of the present of the narrative or providing a window into the history of author's/narrator's time and condition—also carries evidence of that history of what had happened before the history was transformed into a story (Thompson, 1988: 147). The people of the particular tribe live in a time continuum, where their understanding of the past, which is directed towards the future, cannot be understood without understanding the 'cultural heritage' of each society, which provides a trajectory of change from what was given as normal to the normalised vis-à-vis nonnormative, as reflected in their folk literature.

Oral history, while relating the past with the present of the informant, is implicated not just in memory but also in mimesis—the continuity of past by the recalling–cum–re-enactment of past through verbal and behavioural practices. Hearing and seeing are the two important modes of transmission of the folk material that relate the present with the past, both aurally and visually. This mimesis enabled Vansina to regard oral tradition as history. Because the oral literature provides a historical intentionality of an oral rendition, Vansina argues that an oral tradition needs to be considered a 'historiology' of the past—that is, an impression of how a section of people have analysed the history through the oral legacy (Vansina, 1985: 196). Thus, if not always a factual truth, the 'historiology' of the past that can be obtained from the oral tradition of the tribal tales indeed provides a present-day audience with a version of interpreted truth of the historical truths.

Even if it appears that the commemorative storytelling of an individual narrator is faulty, the individual narrative nevertheless exposes the revisions and continuities in the personal memory as the result of the alterations and continuities in attitudes/identities taking place in the collective lifestyle and customary praxes over a period of time and, as a corollary, makes known the subjective-cum-collective reactions/mentalities in response to such historical moments of rupture.

Pierre Nora has already shown that the historian's task is not to revisit the past with an ambition of resurrecting it as a living memory but to describe the images to reveal how collective memory once survived (Nora, 1984–92). Even an imprecise memory, revealing not what had happened but rather

26

what was expected becomes a history of the plausible—what Philippe Aries calls 'collective mentalities' (Ariès, 1882: 117, 185). Even if the real is different from the narrative, the transitory tribal communities through the shared collective memory increasingly invent themselves—'[we] modify the story of ourselves to maintain consistency'—and the myths that cannot be tested as authentic against the documented facts become 'the sources of [their] consciousness and [their] identity, the stuff of [them]' (Climo and Cattell, 2002: 35).

Remembering is selective, and the selection depends on the need of the past for the present. When a historian on discourse tries to understand the reality of the past through the countermemories in oral narratives, beneath the officially sanctioned ones, that mould the past (and thereby consign the images of past to commemorative represented forms) as it suits the present, the historian can get an index of the configurations of power in a society (Foucault, 1977: 151, 160). Finally if memory seems to be elusive from the perspective of history, then one can argue that all academic/scientific study of history that is based on the documents—written, recorded, documented, archived—are equally elusive, because both the makers and users of the documents have applied interpretative frameworks that bias the selection of data and ultimately the documents. Exposing history as an understanding founded on an imaginative reconstruction of the past, Gadamer asserts that the historians by their own experience of memory, through participation in their own tradition, have acquired the skill of interpreting the past: 'It is time to rescue the phenomenon of memory from being regarded merely as a psychological faculty and to see it as an essential element of the finite historical being' of humankind (Gadamer, 1989: 16). Based on this proposition, as William McNeill said, all history is actually 'mythohistory' (Ross, 1991: 166). Such a stance on history is also made by Archibald, for whom history is not an irretrievable fact but 'an inclusive conversation of multiple perspectives on enduring concerns' (Archibald, 1999: 166).

This study of the sociocultural history of Indigeneity through tribal folktales is an endeavour to add force to the underrated relationship between memory and history. History based on the memory of suffering can bring only the promise of resisting the suffering of the peripherals and the oppressed of the society. It also becomes a critique of archival works aimed at adding to the havoc of the historicised memory that comes not from within: 'The indiscriminate filling of archives is a troublesome-by-product of the new consciousness, the clearest expression yet of the "terroristic" effect of historicised memory' (Nora, 1996: 10). If the dominant culture, in its politics of inclusion, ends in excision of the collective memory celebrated in these folktales, then it would not only damage the tribal culture but also invite further antagonism towards the 'mainstream'. For a 'mainstream' deviant, it is important for the sake of an-other ally to advocate for the need for recognising the de-stereotyped 'culture of memory' of the neotraditional tribal 'community of memory', such as by revisiting the historical folktales in order to promote camaraderie through the acknowledgement of shared marginalisations.

Story as cultural history

Often, culture has been perceived as 'the story its members tell so as to make sense of all the different pieces of their social life' (Hinchman and Hinchman, 1997: 235). Roland Barthes observes that 'there does not exist, and never has existed, a people without narratives' (Polkinghorne, 1991: 135). Narratives, therefore, in a manner, create the community (Keeshing-Tobias, 1994: 120). The set of symbols, plots and characters offered by the stories of a particular community provide the members of that culture with the tools for understanding, negotiating and even creating their world (Bruner, 1986: 66) against the backdrop of the fudging internal colonisers. The culture 'speaks to itself' as the community members repeat and reproduce these canonical forms in their lives (Gergen and Gergen, 1988: 40). Culture emerges out of this sense of agreement that gets revealed through the sharing of a preserved memory, along with passing on the patterned manners/ideals through the regular retelling of the narratives (Berger and Kellner, 1964: 3).

Ethnography as a discourse can be treated as 'a genre of storytelling' (Hinchman and Hinchman, 1997: 264). Just as a story has a beginning, middle and an end, so too does a culture have a past, present and a future in its course of transformation. Anthropologists, in their ethnographical studies, do not simply describe the present but also try to connect the present in a lineal sequence of systematic relations with its reconstructed past and a constructed future, just like the format of a story. Bruner suggests that

> Stories give meaning to the present and enable us to see that present as part of a set of relationships involving a constituted past and a future. But narratives change, all stories are partial, all meanings incomplete. . . . With each new telling, the context varies. . . . The story is modified. . . . 'retellings become foretellings'. . . . Then anthropologists . . . must accept responsibility for understanding society as told and retold.
>
> (ibid.: 277)

Narrating stories is vital in the sense that the storytelling not only provides a plurality of viewpoints but also provides a narrative resistance to the version of reality sanctioned by the 'mainstream'. The storytelling that involves selectivity, the rearranging of incidents, redescription and simplification provides the present audience with an 'interpretive device' and 'a capsule view' of the 'world views' of the alternative reality of the tribal world. Even where the tales appear to be partially formed, one can find 'spots of time' in them. Retelling the particular 'past' stories one revisits the 'spots of time', making the narrating 'self' almost appear as a 'work in progress', which can be 'revised' as per the demand of present circumstances. The Gergens rightly pointed out that 'one's view of self in a given moment is fundamentally non-sensical unless it can be linked in some fashion with his or her past' (Gergen and Gergen, 1988: 255).

Storytelling enables us to 'translate our impressions of a distant event into a form that will allow a listener in an immediate situation to grasp its significance' (Bennett, 1978: 3). The reoralised stories provide a range of stock from which the self can choose to fit into available social roles and construct its own narratives of life. In this sense, stories, by acting as a stockroom of common memories revivified through storytelling, also narrate the common identity of communities. These tribal oral narrations must be treated as a narrative history rather than flights of fantasy, because 'stories are lived before being told' (MacIntyre, 1981: 197). Stories are indeed 'habitations', to use Miller Mair's words, that dominate the tribal thinking in such a manner that one needs to get involved with these tales seriously in order to understand the tribal world (Mair, 1988: 125).

This understanding is political, both for the teller and for the audience. These people retell stories to themselves and to the audience, to understand and address the complex dichotomy of 'is' and 'ought'. As argued by Gene Outka, 'our moral lives require narration' (Outka, 1980: 114). Stories of these tribal tales enchant us with their plurality in depicting the social (alter)realities as a collage of outlooks and values. Drawing on the fact that all human action is essentially teleological—that is, we can only find ourselves in the middle of a process of action by starting with some sort of derivation aimed at our anticipating of a projected end—David Carr relates storytelling to the narrating of experienced reality. Moreover, by integrating the past, present and future, storytelling also adds up to make identities stronger and more well-founded on both the personal level and the communitarian level (Hinchman and Hinchman, 1997: 21–23).

There are various reasons for the undying appeal of folk literature: as observed by Raphael Samuel (1994), these literatures represent popularised historical imagination; according to Jameson (1991), these oral traditions put into words the commodity fetishism and the atrophy of some authentic history; and as per critics like Shaw and Chase, the merit of these folk literatures lies in their capacity to provide the present listeners with a retro-fashion retreat into the individual and familial domain of nostalgia and, thereby, to facilitate an escape from the unpredictability of the future (Shaw and Chase, 1989: 3). The folktales epitomise the mnemonic rendition of the oral cultural legacy. Two approaches have been often undertaken while estimating the merit of these oral mnemocultural praxes—one that argues to maintain the foundational memory (remembrance for transmission) needed for (re)narrating the tales as passive and, therefore, almost the 'mirror' of the history of the community's previous traditions and another that, instead of asking for reflection and authenticity, strives to focus on the existing representations and fabrications of folktales, relating them to subjectivity, innovation and fantasy, and that finally treats memory as something actively produced. There is immense tension in both approaches: either in the form of anxiety pertaining to the loss and upsurge of memories embodied in objects of narration and the narrating subject (from the historic perspective) or in the possibility of the fabrication and transfer of the evoked experiences of unlived-through events (Landsberg, 1995) that impels the teller of the tales to embellish the inherited tales with rhetoric—metaphoric, metonymic—in addition to literary devices like transbiology, magic real, morphology and so on, all related to fantasy.

This book aims at looking deep into the folktales of the four endogenous tribes of North Bengal and Sikkim. The entire folk literature is essentially oral and anthologised by researchers as recently as 1991.[5] These folk accounts cannot be equated with the modern genre of short stories. They are tales because they are more about multiple possible signifiers without a focus on any particular engagement towards a signified goal that forms an important hallmark of modern short stories. Yet these tales, often resembling modern short stories, seem to revolve round a protagonist, charting their ultimate end in either failure or success. Hence, due to the characteristic hybridity, the word 'story' in the context of the tribal folktale can be regarded as an indicator of both folktale (to refer to a genre) and story (to refer to an account or a saga). The folktales, along with narrativising the world of imagination, also, in a sense, describe the extratextual[6] real world. The inherent dynamics of the inner texture of these tale texts are the 'mirrors' (Byrskog, 2002: 1) of the narrator, reflecting the self-contained world of the subject, while the intertexture of the series of tales in an extratextual mode become the 'windows' (ibid.), opening up to the extrafictional terrain of diachronic levels of sociocultural history.

One of the main reasons why one may be apprehensive about the validity of the folktales as realistic narratives, and whether these are relevant to history, is the extensive use of literary devices like the magic real, transbiology and so on. Although these tales are stories, they are inimitably connected to the past, with rudiments of reminiscences that get transmitted as remembrances of the past from time immemorial, without which these tales can be acknowledged as good stories, but not folktales. Moreover, a deconstructive reading of the usage of rhetorical devices would assist in making use of them both as signifiers of the sociocultural texture of the bygone era and as a 'focalization around the reception of extrafictional material from the past' (Abramowski, 1983: 343) that forms a component external to the story-tales. Like the dissimilar pearls collected at diverse times but strung all together into a single wreath, these folktales are historical objects: there is history, but the history in the course of turning up to us in our present times has become stories.

Ulrich Luz (1993), while dealing with the alleged distinction between history and story, has stated that the 'otherness' of the 'pastness' of the orally transmitted stories gets absorbed by the present-day time of the community through the collective oral synthesis of the present—hence, in all likelihood, story is history. Ulrich Luz, by using the theories of narratology, has asserted that the oral narratives that are rendered by some real author/narrator before some real listeners/audience are indeed history in their extrafictional dimensions. Moreover, while referring to story and history one needs to differentiate between the composer's/narrator's historical present that gets built into the stories (this history can be revealed by probing deep into the complex use of the literary devices and narrative techniques) and the role of history that has acted as an inducement in the process of devising the stories—that is, the differences between the intratextual and extratextual functions of history. Every time the oral folk stories get narrated, the 'pastness' gets absorbed by the present orality, with the promise that with its transmission in the future, this present will get stitched as a past along with the series of the patches of 'pastness', tailored to the tales. On the basis of these stitches of time, where the present gets tied up with the past and the past with the future present, Luz's study of the oral transmission charts out the possibility of a context where the intratextual and extratextual aspects of the stories somehow coincide, making these oral narratives, in Frei's words, 'realistic or history like' accounts (Frei, 1974: 14).

Robbins's interdisciplinary interpretative approach, called sociorhetorical criticism, attempting at establishing a logical methodological framework for an integrated interchange between studies with focus on story or on history, is focused mainly on bringing 'practices of interpretation together that are often separated from one another' and on integrating 'skills people use in ordinary life with exploration of the intricacies of language in a text', to provide 'a socially and culturally oriented approach to texts, forming a bridge between the disciplines of social-scientific and literary criticism' (Robbins, 1995: 277). Neither the listener/reader nor the author/renderer but rather the text with its rhetoric is central in this approach, and a dialogic understanding is needed for the narratorial and sociocultural dimensions of the language of the text. According to Robbins, a text has textures that include all the inner dynamics of language/rhetorical strategies that are used to negotiate meaning deep into the plot of the stories, along with the awareness of how sociohistorical locations as well as personal interests affect the interpretation. Accordingly, a text exhibits 'webs' of multiple textures like inner texture, intertexture, social and cultural texture, ideological texture and sacred texture, which in a complex way convey signification or meaning and effects of that meaning that can be communicated differently according to the different angles from which one approaches the text. Robbins critically upholds that the text is the 'place' where both implied author and implied hearer/reader are present and thereby meet, along with the modern critics of various paradigms.

This book follows the framework provided by Robbins and is an attempt to incorporate the inner texture and the intertexture in the course of the development of the oral folktale traditions of the four Indigenous communities, assuming that each oral folktale narrative has an inner texture which stands in some kind of relation to a diachronic dimension of its intertexture and thus relates primarily to that which Robbins calls historical intertexture. Robbins—unlike Luz, for whom orality forms the matrix to conceptualise the interaction between story and history, present and past—speaks of an oral-scribal intertexture (in other words, how an oral or a written tradition of past history affects the present story) that is manifested through the recitation, recontextualisation, reconfiguration, narrative amplification and thematic elaboration of specific traditions that are passed down by spoken or written texts. There are possible links between the oral-scribal intertexture and the historical intertexture, paving the way for a possible interaction between the story and history, because history is seen and accounted for different ways, depending on its medium.

To overcome the dichotomy between story and history (in the specific context of the 'gospel'), Francis Watson, approaching writing as a communicative speech act, maintains that there lies dynamics of the oral in the act of writing: the act of writing is just a mere overlaying of a secondary code upon the primary one of that of speech. He relies on Jürgen Habermas and Alistair McFadyen to portray human beings as communicators, not just captives of a language system (Watson, 1997: 107–123). The old tales have their essential foundation in the past; 'they are . . . about their own present and future, which are the present and future of this past' (ibid.: 53). Watson maintains that since the speech act theory of communication demonstrates that every text contains a determinate intention implanted into it, each text must therefore have a 'literal sense' that depends on 'authorial intention'. The oral performing of the past transmits the past into the present through the narrating of the past, and they, codified as written texts, do not imply an end of orality out of a schematic stabilising imprint of the past, but rather, the texts get persistently reoralised to serve as unassailable texts.[7] The multiple oral renditions provide a context for the past, present, history and story to interact even within the dynamics of a written discourse.

Folklorists often have to grapple with whether they can rely on the accuracy of the sources of oral history. Alessandro Portelli's article (Portelli, 1998: 63–74), which Thompson quotes, tries to resolve the problem: it argues that the apparent 'errors' of 'false', 'untrue' statements are also important as a part and parcel of oral history narrated through stories, because those imaginative/metaphorical renditions move beyond the factual accounts and, in the process, let us understand not only what happened in the past but also what people wanted and imagined to happen, which is equally important for our historical understanding. Thus, the oral story and oral history behind the formation/narration of the story are interlinked (Thompson, 1988: 139.).

My interpretative work is centred on searching for traces of encoded queernormative voices so as to study how these voices, which are nowadays labelled 'nonnormative', continue to remain as significant expressions of oral histories behind the textualised work of the tales. Some of the realistic elements in a text serve as windows through which one might get a holistic view of a tradition, while some other items in a text may be fictional ones, mirroring only the world of story itself. Yet the self-contained world of the story has evolved as the textualised narrativisation by a person from the real world, where the story, in spite of being conjured, shares the language of the narrating individual and thereafter got implanted in a common social system and reassures listeners that the story can also serve as an index of the sociocultural state of affairs of the teller of the tales.

The rhetoricians have provided a definition of 'narratio' which is similar to the accepted mode of writing history. In *Rhetorica ad Herennium*, Cicero defined narration as 'the exposition of events that have occurred or might have occurred' (Cicero, 1954: I 3:4); Cicero offered a similar definition in *De Inventione* (1949: I 19:27); and Quintilian, an expert on narrative, defined it as 'the persuasive exposition of that which has been done or is supposed to have been done' (cited in Byrskog, 2002: 203). These takes on narrative are almost identical to Lucian's concern regarding the vividness of a historical account (ibid.) and somewhat echo Aulus Gellius's notion of history writing: 'They thus assert history indeed to be either the exposition or the description of events that have occurred' (ibid.). Writing history, therefore, must have been almost an act of extensive narrative, for the ancient world.

Working on the connection between history and rhetoric, A.J. Woodman has shown (1988: 140–146) that history writing was almost regarded as a kind of rhetoric by classical historians. During Cicero and Quintilian's time, historians had to get rhetorical training to inscribe the past. The issue that follows from here is the concern over whether the impact of rhetoric gave birth to 'lying historians'. Addressing the issue, Robert G. Hall, in his first article, asserted that 'writers of narration ruled sovereignly over the historical data at their disposal', while in the second article, he observed that 'to dismiss rhetoric as antithetical to history is too hasty' (Hall, 1991: 313, 1997: 118). Historians, in their attempts at no longer producing mere facts but aiming for the target group to believe their findings, have been engaged in a narrativising process where the rhetorical devices they used came to be seen as supplementary, and not contradictory, to the factual credibility. The writing of history has therefore often been equated with oratory. History, with its use of rhetorical/oratory devices, has been viewed as the encoded traces of present-day people communicating with the past.

In these folktales, we find a similar circular structuring of history where one finds a constant reoralising of the texts: the living people interact with the past through memory, whereby the recalled past is investigated from the conceptual frames of their contemporary world and vice versa. The process of the reoralisation of the tribal folk literature makes the tales, as Margaret A. Mills stated, 'words to live by in the profoundest sense' (Mills, 1990: 232)—that is, construed by people, in quest of ascertaining and preserving shared meaning and cohesion. Hence, one's opting for (re)producing a particular tale reveals not the narrativised/interpreted history alone but instead one's own retelling of a crucial facet of the present. When history becomes the telling of tales, the story is revealed as the interpretation not only of the individual self but also of their larger tendencies/instincts. Bruce J. Malina has shown that the tribes of oral community exist as 'dyadic selves', thereby constantly requiring another to know themselves (1996: 73–82). Maurice Halbwachs in his influential work (1992) made us conscious of the working of the 'collective memory'. Elizabeth Tonkin has informed us of how the social construction of oral history and the stories of others, symbolising the 'collective past', shape an individual's take on the present. The selection of a particular folktale for re(production)/retelling shows how awareness of the 'I' in a particular time/context survives amid collective representations of the past: 'That one's self is both variable and vulnerable may be disconcerting to consider, but it does not follow that selves are non-existent' (Tonkin, 1992: 136). In the rendition of the tale by an individual, the story becomes their story, where in the endeavour of communicating something of the present through the reoralising of the past, the individual encodes their own interpretation of the presence of past in the present, just like the historian who was employing rhetoric and elaboration in writing history.

The crucial question, then, that might arise is the issue of subjectivity of selection, which remains unproblematic in the context of the oraliser but becomes problematic in relation to the teller of the story, like that of the researcher. Objectivity, conventionally, seems to be the guiding principle behind the researcher's selectivity and interpretation. However, in practice, even the historians seemed to have enjoyed a similar kind of interpretative selectivity.[8] Herodotus, in his endeavour of writing a history of Alyattes, has spoken only of those notable incidents according to his subjective standpoint, and Polybius, who outspokenly propagated his notion that a historian needs to be selective while highlighting the issues, according to subjectivity, remained understated by other historians (Polybius, 1922–1927: I 56:11; 179:7; XXIX 12:6). Even in the case of Xenophon,[9] the selection was never done on any objective criteria. Rather, he has been quite subjective: his method was to write whatever according to him was worth remembering and omit the rest which, he believed, did not deserve to be mentioned.

A historian makes sense of their reality by choosing subjective elements of elucidation. The investigative meets the interpretative through the historian's applying of their conceptual framework to narrativise a coherent story. Thus, history becomes their story, with extratextual-cum-extrafictional reality that results from the historian's explanatory urge, stopping them from acting as an objective fact bearer. Just as an historian's observation and questioning of the past from the conceptual framework/ viewpoint of the present, aimed at a communicative narrativisation of the past, is conveyed through almost that of a coherent story that connects the past with the present, revealing both the intratextual notions of the history of a 'realistic narrative' and the author/teller's effort to grasp their own state of affairs in view of the past, the oral folk stories, as Kelber (1987) indeed admits, at once serves as a 'window' to the past history and as a 'mirror' of the contemporary history. From this interrelation, one might finally move towards a synthesised view of history as story and story(-tales) as history.

From the telling into the written: translation of the oral tradition

Shared memory in the form of folktales finds meaning through the enactment of orality and, thereby, supports the tales' becoming real in the bodies of the tribal storytellers. To feel the power of the folktales is 'to sense the past in the present, to participate through sound in a . . . continuity story of struggle and survival that is generation old' (Climo and Cattell, 2002: 20) against the backdrop of encroachment from global and/or national/'mainstream' control. It is important to connect the metaphorically 'buried' tradition of orality with contemporary times and community activism. The oral tradition becomes an important oral/aural medium of fashioning the present self in continuation with the sociocultural norms and customs of the past (Frisch, 1990: 188). The politics of rendering oral tradition can be illustrated as something deeply relevant as a mode of connecting the aspiration that has its roots in times immemorial and yet is present continuous, despite the surveillance of neocolonial normative regimes. The stories of oral tradition are not altogether unknown but are mostly made invisible 'from the state of fear to the fear of the state' (Esposito, 2010: 29).

Oral literature did not need to be written down to be literature, and it continued long after writing was invented. Walter J. Ong has given us a useful term, 'oral residue', referring to the characteristics of orality which remain in the world of literacy even after the introduction of writing down oral tales (Ong, 1982: 36–57). Researchers have also not done enough to revisit the 'oral residue' of the tribal literature in an effort for social justice and the reinstitution of alternative visions reflected in the literature that has oral origins. Strangled between a personal/neotraditional subjectivity and the changed material facts, the contemporary tribal can find even in the residue of oral performances an important tool for the self 'to perceive the multiple, mutable ways of elaborating on'(Portelli, 2003: 16). Recreating identity and community through the recollection of the oral practices, which in a way becomes 'ethnography of practice' (Hamilton and Shopes, 2008: xiii), inculcates a demand for 'sharing authority' of the alternative ideologies, often framed as nonnormative by the homogenising agencies of the state and the non-Indigenous 'mainstream'.

The oral tradition—with its aural dimension of listening and remembering, performance and transmission, recollection, improvisation and articulation—involves representation and mediation, which makes orality a liminal process of making meaning social, collective and public. The distinction made by Kendall Philips between the 'publicness of memory' and the 'memory of publics' is relevant in this context (Phillips, 2004: 3–7). The 'memory of publics' denotes the shared public memories within which a group interacts and thereby both affects and is affected by the shared memory. The 'publicness of memory' scrutinises the politics of how certain memories are made public while others are made to be forgotten or at least revised and rephrased to fix their meaning, which otherwise can be problematic as nonnormative. Hence the study of the tribal tales, transmitted extensively through oral renditions, is useful in understanding the politics of public meaning making. While some safer tales, with ambitious but detailed description of reality are popularised, others are kept aside for revisions by substituting the 'affordable'—which nevertheless challenges the normative gaze of the 'mainstream'—with the oblique instruments of transbiology and magic realism. The tribal oral literature brings out the tribal power struggle with the agencies of the state/mainstream as the most vital component of oral history. In the words of Walter Ong,

> Oral tradition in that case covers what one hears of what has happened in the past, distant or recent. . . . Literacy has little or no effect on oral history, except that eventually, when literacy becomes widespread and begins to be used for recording, and finally for writing, literature, the *writing* of history is an important part of that larger development.
>
> (1982: 22)

The long absence of a script[10] among the stateless tribal peoples can be understood as a resistance towards literacy, viewed by them as a technology of dominance through administration and statecraft (Scott, 2009: 228). Their apathy towards literacy has led them to rely on endogenous 'knowledges that resist bureaucratic codification' (Richards, 1993: 20). As Claude Lévi-Strauss notes, 'Writing appears to be necessary for the centralised, stratified state to reproduce itself. Writing is a strange thing. . . . It seems rather to favor the exploitation than the enlightenment' of humankind (Lévi-Strauss, 1968: 291).

However, soon the tribal communities, with their increasing contact with the nontribal world, resulting in their adoption of agricultural works that require keeping records, must have realised that writing can be seen as a mode of 'relationism' rather than reductionism for the evolution of consciousness: '[writing] intensifies the sense of self and fosters more conscious interaction between persons. Writing is consciousness-raising' (Ong, 1982: 174). Moreover, the oral tradition that was originally viewed as a democratic medium of voicing the self through subjective renditions has slowly become rigidified with rules and thus a dominated realm of the privileged; writing slowly became the means of voicing those who were excluded from democratic politics[11] (Steiner, 1994: 227). Thus, the choice of welcoming literacy and the culture of writing by the tribal world, with its rising conflict with the intruding state/mainstream, can be justified on the basis of Tarn Steiner's statement: 'if speech is the hallmark of the democratic city, then writing is associated with those out of sympathy with its radical politics' (ibid.: 7). By then, they might have also realised that 'there is nothing about writing, in and of itself, that requires a text to be fixed for all times and places. Writing, like speaking, is a performance' (Tedlock, 2000: 257).

These days, scholars have more often tended to recognise 'oral' and 'written' as interconnected cultural realms, rather than rigidly differentiating between orality and literacy (Stock, 1987). Written cultures and oral cultures are not, however, mutually exclusive. Both oral practices and literary practices are in fact textual practices. The 'texts' in the forms of colours, dresses, fetishes and so on, as a part of oral performances, have 'texts' in the form of books and documents as their written counterparts[12] (Scott, 2009: 227).

Translations of the tribal folklore of the Toto, Rabha, Limbu and Lepcha communities into English are indeed a difficult task. The folklore tradition, which is always accompanied by terms like 'orality'/'performative' and 'transmission', makes it quite obvious that the texture of a folklore— the language pattern and the specific phonemes and morphemes used—is untranslatable; the text alone can be translated. Hence, for the purpose of translation, the text of a specific item of folklore can be considered a single version rendered by an individual: 'For purposes of analysis, the text may be considered independent of its texture' (Dundes, 1980: 23). Haroldo de Campos (1981) has provided a host of connotations that factor into the diverse approaches of translators: transluciferation, transcreation, transtextualisation, translumination, reimagination and poetic reorchestration, among others.

Hence, some elaboration has to be made regarding my stance on translation. The translated text is a distinct and separate entity that works in conjunction with the source text; the translated text, following the source text to represent its 'afterlife', in a sense provides a 'continued life' to the source texts (Benjamin, 1969: 77). The question that arises is about the nature of the translated text, the mode through which the source text is made to be reborn as a hybrid text, revealing faithfulness as well as 'translational' shifts (thus making it 'transnational'). 'Anuvad', the Sanskrit term for translation, means 'saying after or again, repeating by way of explanation, explanatory repetition or reiteration with corroboration or illustration, explanatory reference to anything already said' (Monier-Williams, 1997: 38). Anuvad, with its focus on subjective ways of explanation, hence provides a direction for what is called the theory of sense (théorie du sens) (Seleskovitch and Lederer, 1984), based on 'listening to the sense', or 'deverbalising' the text through translation to capture and render the sense in a different lexicon. But yet again, to what extent can the subjective sense be derived while the rest is ignored? For me, one way to answer this is to follow the principle of the necessary degree of precision, advocated by Hans Hönig and Paul Kussmaul (1982), according to which the appropriate sense can be determined by the required function of the translational activity in a specified context: 'there has to be a cut-off point where translators can safely say "This is all my readers have to know in this context"' (Hönig, 1997: 11). This principle of necessary is further founded on the notion of the cultural turn (Snell-Hornby, 1990), which includes culture and politics based on specific ideology in translation.

The translation involved in this endeavour is aimed at highlighting non-normative expressions and thus is bound to bear the marks of interminable rereading and rewriting, arising from my critical difference and resulting in a manipulation of the text to make the nonnormative visible in the texts, a translation that shares the politics of translation of a postcolonial or feminist/queer translator (Godard, 1990: 91). Tejaswini Niranjana has informed us of a need for an interventionist approach (Niranjana, 1992: 173) that in a speculative manner aims at illustrating how 'In the interests of constructing a unified national identity that will challenge colonial domination, the discourse of nationalism suppresses the marginal and non-elite peoples and struggles' (ibid.: 166). My translation thus aims at an 'afterlife' of the source text, based on the reproduction and renegotiation of the targeted culture, relocating the source text at the 'inter'/'in-between'/'third' space, thereby eschewing the politics of polarity that comes from the others of our selves. Such a translation 'makes it possible to begin envisaging national anti-nationalist histories of the "people"' (Bhabha, 1994: 38–39). Since the primary motive of the work is to create a 'contact zone' (Pratt, 1992: 6) between cultures formerly separated but coming together through translation and writing, I am more interested in considering translation as 'deverbalising' in a needs-based framework of necessity, designed by a cultural and political drive of unmasking queernormativity. My translation process is mainly about how my engagement relied on 'deep listening' and, thereafter, transposing interlingually while looking for layers of meaning beyond and beneath words. I am not much bothered with the problem of maintaining the authenticity of the original, since the notion of being original has been under serious interrogation:

> Each text is unique, yet at the same time it is the translation of another text. No text can be completely original because language itself, in its very essence, is already a translation—first from the nonverbal world, and then, because each sign and each phrase is a translation of another sign, another phrase.
>
> (Paz, 1992: 154)

Translating the tribal world provides a different notion of history apart from chronological historicising. Through the history of imagination as revealed by the stories, I have tried to understand and translate the imagination, which in turn provides a justice which the 'mainstream' does not—through the language of the outsider—because it is not the lack of imagination but the lack of language that hampers one's voicing of resistance (Moraga, 1983: 166).

The translations of others that I have taken into consideration,[13] including my own, which I have done with the help of Indigenous people from each of the communities—well versed in that particular tribal language and in the languages that I understand, namely Bangla, Nepali and English—are creative but not subversive. The oral storytelling of the Totos, Rabhas, Limbus and Lepchas has been translated and written into English with care: so that the hermeneutic content remains the same. This has been ensured by engaging in the entire translation process many people from the tribal communities. Writing these tribal tales down in translation would also provide the possible foundation for 'textual communities' (Stock, 1987: 90–92). Such textual communities may further provide a possibility of forming alliances (maybe what Benedict Anderson (2006) calls imagined communities) for new kinds of political solidarity.

Transgression and the nonnormative

To be regarded as a competent social agent, one has to go through the disciplining of the body/desire/emotion through a routine-based control designed by the state (Giddens, 1991: 57). The ones who provide resistance, getting otherised as the deviant, outsider or outcast constitute the nonnormative in the 'mainstream'. The poststructural/postcolonial theories have exposed the 'normatised' body/orientation as a cultural construct rather than as a natural entity. This argument is based on the claim that the multiplicity of meanings inscribed on and infused in bodies are the outcome of the agencies of power in a culture whose people want to fortify their ideologies as 'normative'. Thus, the 'normal' bodies are those that become the embodiments

39

of the ideas of those who hold power in a culture. Hence, the corporality of the body is a cultural site in which devious political ideologies are deftly imposed with the expectation that the 'correct'/'sanctioned' desires can be generated. Accordingly, subtle hegemonic mechanisms operate through the apparently unified or noncontradictory bodies marked with the desires which are marked as 'normal'. As a corollary to this, an investigation into the 'abnormal' bodies with 'unnatural' desires may have the effect of subverting a power structure.

For a queer, nonnormative individual situated at and censored by the 'mainstream', the way to resist against the surveillance of the 'mainstream'/state is to look for alter-spaces of sanction and acceptance as opposed to contestation and censoring. These tribal folk literatures depict ample nonconformist queer desires and queernormative relationships that can serve as major weapons against the otherising discourse of 'abnormality' and against the nonnormative gaze that is cast on queer desire/orientation and transmitted by 'mainstream' majorities. The tribal folktales, by celebrating abject bodies/transbiology/magic real transgressions and producing an 'imagining deviance' (O' Neill and Seal, 2012), validate the assumption that by revealing 'that which was previously considered natural and commonsense' (Creswell, 1996: 10); the margins can indeed give us clue about the politics of 'normality'.

The term 'queer', by focusing on the lives and perspectives related to sexualities/orientations/bodies/expressions beyond the 'mainstream's' accepted notion of the norm, 'marks the excess of something always unassimilable that troubles the relentlessly totalizing impulse informing normativity' (Dinshaw et al., 2007: 189). Scrutinising the 'structures of feeling' (Williams, 1977) related to gender, sex and sexuality, queer theory engages with 'the political ramifications, the advantages and dangers, of culturally "fixed" categories of sexual identities and the ways in which they may . . . be performed, transgressed and queered' (Goldman, 1999: 525). By bringing nonnormative issues like incest, erotic grandmothers and other taboos together with queer issues, this book attempts to extend the scope of queer studies, since the general sense of the term 'queer' is 'that which is puzzling and confusing' (McGillis, 2003: 88).

These tribal folk literatures with their riddling of the tales of queer transgressive implications or other counternormative, counterhegemonic queer alliances take us into a culture whose norms qualify the nonnormative of the dominant mainstream. By applying contemporary queer frames to these folks, all full of transbiological and magic real transgressive devices and unspeakable desires and inclinations, the focus shifts from the normative to the tales' internal struggles: multiple complex desires and their performative temperaments. The worlds in folk literature, featuring human and nonhuman at once weird and wonderful, are obviously imaginative. However, as Jack Zipes observed, imaginative worlds can generate fresh approaches:

'Folk and fairy tales . . . are not static literary models. . . . Their value depends on how we actively produce and receive them in forms of social interaction which leads toward the creation of greater individual autonomy' (Zipes, 1979: 177).

For attaining a greater individual autonomy, the censored queer of the 'mainstream' can engage in a perverse reading (Zimmerman, 1993) of the tribal literature through a queer lens in order to enter into the folktales' world of enchantment that helps 'mainstream' queers forget, even if temporarily, the oppression of the real world and imagine alternative potentialities. These tribal folktales, like fairy tales, combine the ambiguous, ambivalent and magic with the real and thereby allow the marginalised to think of a possible space where nonnormative queer people are invited to participate in the realm of queernormative enchantment. Often beneath the apparent story of conforming, there is tremendous tension and conflict in the subplot which challenges 'mainstream' normativity. Tiffin has rightly observed that even if the folktales' 'basic principles . . . are those of human existence, the world in which such principles are enacted is significantly different from the real, so that normal expectations are completely transcended' (Tiffin, 2009: 13). By transcending the 'normal', again as labelled by the dominant culture, we can argue that these tribal cultures open possibilities for rising above and thereby demolishing the stereotypical sociocultural expectations which get continuously promoted by the 'mainstream'.

What is often considered to be nonnormative from the standpoint of the 'mainstream' is by and large quite admissible in the tribal world. The aims of my work are to reveal the marginality of the reading self, labelled as nonnormative by the dominant culture, and to underscore the politics of a perverse reading of these tribal folktales, attempted by a queer reader located at and excluded by the 'mainstream'—all with an urge to cultivate a sense of belonging through intimacy with the non-phobic tribal world. The word 'nonnormative' has also been used to highlight the tribal inclusion of the expressions that get excluded as queer transgressive by a 'mainstream' culture. The upsurge in queerphobia[14] immediately after the decriminalisation of consensual same-sex sex in India reveals how the dominant nontribals are still trapped in a bonsai culture of stunted growth, where the 'mainstream' either imagines everyone to be a mirror image of the 'majority' or is conscious of differences and yet still otherises people.

Transgression denotes the attitude of surpassing boundaries. Any constraint imposed on conduct—taboos imposed from the outside or the self-imposed restriction as the internal response to moral policing—brings the plausible prospect of transgressing the limits. In these tribal folklores, the queer transgressive bodies/expressions are at once the outcome of and the response to the emerging stereotypical patterns of inhibitions. The transgressive pull to exceed is therefore, in a way, the recognition as well as the completion of prohibition. Queer transgression is not a plea

41

for disorder; rather, it is the revelation of the chaos and the often-futile but mandated chase towards a necessitated order. Contextualising transgression within the framework of moral transitions, Jervis has observed that

> Transgression . . . involves hybridization, . . . and the questioning of the boundaries that separate categories. . . . What it does do, though, is implicitly interrogate the law, pointing not just to the specific, and frequently arbitrary, mechanisms of power on which it rests—despite its universalizing pretensions—but also to its complicity, its involvement in what it prohibits.
>
> (1999: 4)

From the viewpoint of the sovereign—that is, an unbounded potential of human possibility—the contemporary tribal society, with the interfering 'mainstream' struggling to link ethnic communities with the majoritarian customs and beliefs, must be compelled to gradually narrow down its perception of normal human functioning. Even then, the elements of fantasy in the folk literature show the kind of 'hybridisation' that Jervis (1999) mentions. Durkheim in his conceptualising of the 'sacred' and the 'profane', acknowledged the tension resulting from the distinctive survival of 'objects-in-thought' and 'objects-in-reality', the 'actual' and the 'imaginary', or rather the 'social interest'/'social institutions of public knowledge' and the 'personal interest'/'potential of individual consciousness', which become the decisive ground for a queer transgressive impulse: 'The sacred is par excellence that which the profane should not touch, and cannot touch with impunity' (Durkheim, 1971: 40). The organic bond in a society, which seems to be stronger in a tribal society like that of the Totos or the Rabhas, nevertheless, in a mode of transition, cannot be fully based on the determinism of the 'scared' (often the borrowed one from the 'mainstream' to replace the 'primitive'/endogenous) but rather must be based on the interpretation of it through the 'profane'. Because of the rigidity of the prevalent governmental rules, which propels the transitory tribal societies towards blurring and distorting the boundaries/categories of conduct that results from the death of the old (sacred) and from the immaturity of a newer (sacred) outlook, people become free to transgress with the choice of the 'profane'.

It appears that, subsequently, the social bond of morality and the societal structure would be under threat. But herein enters the importance of transgression as a means of holding primeval intimacies together within the transitory socioethical structure. The transition of a simple tribal society to a complex/altered one, often influenced by the 'mainstream' vision of progress through exposure to industrialism/technology and the removal of traditional/customary stances, finds a parallel in the demise of childhood and movement towards the twilight of crypto-adulthood and quasi-childhood of adolescence.[15]

Kojève has shown how the self can look for its liberation through transgressive desire—to desire/want is to engage the self-consciousness of the subject with/in relation to the thing-like-ness of objects, excluding the self: 'Desire is what transforms Being, revealing to itself by itself in (true) knowledge, into an "object" revealed to a "subject" by a subject different from the object and "opposed" to it' (Kojève, 1969: 3–4). Nietzsche, in his plea for the 'overman' (1885) has also recommended celebrating the desire of the individual by revolting against the defending and conciliatory politics of order. For Nietzsche, one needs to have a will to power by asserting the subjective desire/determinations through the rejection of the values of others; this again becomes just another plea for transgression. Nietzsche in *On the Genealogy of Morality* (1887) writes about how morality is always a historical construct resulting from the moralities' undergoing evolution. Thus, a sign of morality needs to be scrutinised in order to disclose its intentions and transgressions.

Bataille, as an icon of transgression, emphasises positioning transgression always in relation to prohibition: 'The experience of transgression is indissociable from the consciousness of the constraint or prohibition it violates; indeed, it is precisely by and through its transgression that the force of a prohibition becomes fully realized' (Suleiman, 1990: 75). Bataille, Freud and Foucault have separately asserted that the awareness of our limits lies mainly in the sphere of human desire and sexuality. For Bataille and Foucault, transgression derives meaning from the discovery of a limit to be broken, without which transgression is left without any significance:

The play of limits and transgression seems to be regulated by a simple obstinacy: transgression incessantly crosses and recrosses a line which closes up behind it in a wave of extremely short duration and thus it is made to return once more right to the horizon of the uncrossable.

(Foucault, 1977: 34)

The moment when transgression and prohibition collide, they celebrate the mutual exposing of prohibition's essential frailty and transgression's imminent fatigue. The transgression–prohibition relationship, according to Foucault, is as simple as the flash of lightning and as complex as the spiral that holds them together (ibid.: 35). Foucault's 'limit' is similar to taboos, where taboos get entangled with transgression. As Freud tried to understand the human impulse of defiance primarily through the realm of 'libidinal' sexuality, so too did Bataille try with eroticism:

The transition from the normal state to that of erotic desire presupposes a partial dissolution of the person as he exists in the realm of discontinuity. . . . The whole business of eroticism is to destroy the self-contained character of the participators as they are in their normal lives.

(Bataille, 2001: 17)

As a critique of reason, Bataille further criticised taboo which compels human being to correspond to the world with the 'normatised' rationality like 'a shudder appealing not to reason but to feeling, just as violence is' (ibid.: 64). Criticising the hierarchical divide between the sacred and the profane, Bataille seems to celebrate the human being's inner fascination for all that is restricted (ibid.: 68). The refuting of taboo that enables the expression of the erotic is often conveyed with the metaphors of violence, like murder or torture:

Cruelty and eroticism are conscious intentions in a mind which has resolved to trespass into a forbidden field of behaviour . . . for these contagious domains are both founded on the heady exhilaration of making a determined escape from the power of taboo. . . . Cruelty may veer towards eroticism.

(ibid.: 80)

Hence, in the folk stories, we find the instances of burning toad skin, destroying a pumpkin or murdering someone's wife's sister as violent steps to transgress into the realm of forbidden eroticism. The folktales with images of incest/prohibited sex, bloodshed and necrophilia, which intertwine sexuality, death and violence, illustrate the transgressive escalation out of regulatory dominance, resulting in a joyful anguish which is quintessentially erotic: 'And nowhere is this contradictory, heterogeneous combination of pleasure and anguish more acutely present than in the inner experience of eroticism, insofar as this experience involves the practice of sexual "perversions", as opposed to "normal" reproductive sexual activity' (Suleiman, 1990: 75).

Bataille's notion of excess energy as the outcome of the general economy produced by the Marxist deployment of wealth cannot be altogether utilitarian but rather can be used only sans goal or meaning, through an erotic-cum-violent economy of unproductivity that transcends the use value. Kristeva writes that

The logic of prohibition, which founds the abject, has been outlined and made explicit by a number of anthropologists. . . . And yet Georges Bataille remains the only one, to my knowledge, who . . . links abjection to the inability to assume with sufficient strength the imperative act of excluding.

(1982: 64)

Thus, in Bataille, who talks of a utilitarian consumption and of a 'sovereign' consumption as ends in themselves, we have the justification for the erotic, violent and queer nonutilitarian sexualities that one comes across in the folktales. The excess or the surplus, accumulated in the sacred realm of prosperity/well-being/joy/righteousness/morality/virtue, according to Bataille, in a transgressive mode has to be unloaded, expended, exhausted and exonerated through a profane notion of 'gift', so that the accumulation of energy does not result in a scenario where all is lost but rather where 'sovereignty' is attainted through 'the glorious expenditure as the possibility for a mingling of the most sacred and the unspeakably profane in their common transgression of the restricted economy of utility' (Gallop, 1981: 11). The urge for sexual sovereignty results in a collapsing of the hierarchies of the 'correct', 'commendable' and 'true' and incorporates the 'filthy', 'untidy', 'obscene' and 'weird' (ibid.).

The use of grotesque in the folktales becomes an important tool for celebrating fantasy and the bizarre with the motif of transgressing the division between true and weird, human and nonhuman and classes/configurations of men and their gestures: 'the grotesque tends to operate as a critique of a dominant ideology which has already set the terms designating what is high and low' (Stallybrass and White, 1986: 43). The 'carnival', popularised by Bakhtin, has become a useful vehicle to read the social, 'so that we can go beyond patterns of lived experience to explore the structures of independence of individual and community, order and chaos, the sacred and the profane' (Chaney, 1994: 39–40). With the transition taking place in sociocultural norms, the protagonist of the folklore has to be in a masquerade with the 'pumpkin' or live with a real-dead-wife, because, as informs Foucault, they can no longer cling to the identification of a faint individuality with the solid identities of the past but can partake in 'unrealisation' through the excessive choice of identities, almost in the form of a concerted carnival (Foucault, 1977: 160–161). A dialogic interaction that removes the divide of high and low, through the affluent cacophony of uninhibited dialogue, brings out the carnivalesque:

> This temporary suspension, both ideal and real, of hierarchical rank created during carnival time a special type of communication impossible to everyday life . . . frank and free, permitting no distance between those who came into contact . . . and liberating from norms of etiquette and decency. . . . A special carnivalesque . . . was formed.
>
> (Bakhtin, 1984: 10)

Such carnivalesque gets manifested with the transgressive celebration of the grotesque body of the pumpkin's getting married to the king's daughter, in a dialogic interaction, breaking down the standardised notion of a class/ norm divide. 'Carnival was the true feast of time, the feast of becoming, change and renewal. It was hostile to all that was immortalized and completed' (ibid.: 10). Regarding the celebration of the body, Jervis says, 'The body comes to be the central carnival image; it is a symbol of "the people", i.e. of the social body. Hence the physical body is characterized as huge, ever-growing, ever-renewed, just like society itself' (Jervis, 1999: 19). In the carnival or mode of carnivalesque, the individual/human body, social body and the entire body of knowledge are interchangeable, permitting us to transition from one to another—defecation, dissociation, deconstruction. It allows us not only to move from the centre to the margins, to crumble down the relation between signifier and the signified and opt for another meaning—thereby enabling us to transgress via irony, interference or even exploration—but also urges us to effectively behave in a new way to deal with the altered social relations, on account of the denunciation of traditional schemas of classification. In an authentic carnival mode, one overthrows the restrictions imposed on the everyday existence and fatefully desire the undesirable. Echoing Freud's position on taboo, Featherstone wrote, 'In effect the Other which is excluded as part of the identity-formation process becomes the object of desire' (Featherstone, 1992: 283).

Folktale as a genre of folk literature: definition, collection and selection

Folklore denotes the corpus of the group-specific knowledge that constitutes what Gary Alan Fine termed 'idioculture'—that is, a system of knowledge related to a particular community (Fine, 1982: 47). Storytelling is a major aspect of 'idioculture', through which the members of the group

> announce to each other that they 'belong' together. . . . Narrator and audience build community together, and as the position of narrator changes into that of listener, the communal role of stories is made evident to all by their lived experience as actor and audience.
> (Fine, 1987: 231–232)

The term 'folk literature' has been used as synonymous with folklore narratives available as written text. Anything in print can be treated as literature (Dundes, 1965: 35). In this context, it is relevant to introduce Archer Taylor's opinion that the most attractive aspect in the study of folklore 'arises when one regards folklore as literature and asks the questions that a literary historian might ask' (ibid.: 38). According to the folklorists, there can be three major forms of folk narratives: 'myths', narrating stories about immortal characters; 'legends', narrating stories about quasi-historical individuals with extraordinary merits; and 'folktales', narrating stories about common people as protagonists.[16] This book, which aims to deal with the common rather than the exceptional or the invented, will mostly focus on the genre of 'folktale' and may occasionally cite the other narrative genres of folk literature as cross-references.

Although folktales deal with common people by including a variety of other subgenres like fables and fairy tales, along with jokes and novellas, they often narrate some occurrences that are unusual but not fanciful. Folktales are more or less mimetic, in that even the animal fables and fairy tales, illustrating the wishful desire/dream, depict 'magical or marvellous events or phenomena as a part of human experience' (Jones, 1995: 9) or 'use personified animals to depict otherwise realistic human behavior' (ibid.: 10). From this observation, it can be argued that the worlds of magic/fantasy/wonder in folktales needs to be treated as coded embodiments of magic real possibilities. The apparent nonrealistic subgenres of folktales address the real questions of ordinary individuals faced in everyday life but through heuristic techniques: they indeed express suppressed/unconscious desires, or rather queer desires. Folktales, as documentations of evident as well as plausible queer desires can be considered mimetic representations of the subsistence of the common mass once we accept the observations made by Antoine de St. Exupery: 'It is only with the heart that one see rightly; what is essential is invisible to the eye' (ibid.: 12).

The study of tribal folk literature cannot be undertaken without any first-hand knowledge of the oral practices.[17] The extensive fieldwork that I conducted, capturing through in-depth interviews the oral narratives of the tribal narrators and closely following a qualitative methodology, resulted in the present collection of folktales. The fieldwork resulted in the collection of 26 folktales from each community. I decided to restrict this study by selecting from my collection only those tribal folktales that resemble the tales that were already published by previous researchers. This mode of selection is the consequence of my anxiety over what is termed 'fakelore'. 'Fakelore' implies the bulk of artificial reproductions delivered under the claim that are part of authentic folklore (Dorson, 1969: 60). Since my collected/translated material has not been published, it is difficult for me to separate, if at all, the folklore from the 'synthetic product claiming to be authentic oral tradition but actually tailored for mass edification' (Dorson, 1976: 5). Thus, to overcome the problem of possible fakelore in my collection, only those tribal folktales that bear a resemblance to the previously published folktales have been selected.[18] Studying the folklore in literature and culture involves two basic steps: identification, which is objective and empirical, and interpretation, which is subjective speculation of the identified folklores (Dundes, 1990: 51). This study, therefore, is mainly a work of interpretation of queer expressions in a dialogic mode conducted by a nontribal queer ally.

Methodology of interpretation

The first question that I asked myself while thinking of doing this work was, as a student of literature, am I eligible enough to enter the domain of sociocultural study of folklore? The criticism of Alan Dundes against the folklorists who try to create a false binary between the methods of studying folklore in literature and that of studying folklore in culture pacified my anxiety. The methodology of studying folklore in literature, according to Dundes, is similar to that of studying folklore in culture (ibid.).

This sociocultural study of the nonnormative (queer) expressions was based on the conviction that folktales reveal more than the mere literary idioms of the community: '[Folktale] is, in a very real sense, their ethnography which, if systematized by the student, gives a penetrating picture of their ways of life' (Herskovits, 1948: 418). Richard Bauman wrote that 'Folklore is a function of shared identity' (Bauman, 1971: 32). The incongruous and perplexing elements in folktales, while illustrating the communities' manifold ways of life through shared identity, display the efforts of the individuals towards the gratification of the suppressed sexual desires by escaping in the zone of fantasy, away from 'biological limitations as a member of the genus and species' (Bascom, 1965: 291).

Hence, the purpose of this study is to assess tribal folk literature as a projective system (Bascom, 1965: 292). In psychology, projection refers to externally attributing tabooed tendencies that actually lies within the self to another individual or the environment (Dundes, 1980: 37). This projection can be deconstructed by interpreting the symbols used in folktales. The connotative meanings of symbols may differ and are not universal; as Dundes remarks, 'symbol employed in any one given folkloristic (con)text may be related to a general system of symbols' (ibid.). The interpretations of the use of symbols in the folktales can most significantly express the shared queer identity of tribal groups: 'A relationship between human individuals and selected cultural elements—the symbols—is the essential feature of a collective identity' (Spicer, 1971: 796).

For Max Weber, ethnic groups are formed by 'those human groups that entertain a subjective belief in their descent because of similarities of physical type or of customs or both' (Weber, 1968: 389). This work focuses on those symbols and customs of the four tribal communities, reflected in their folktales, which are relevant to discussions on sexuality, since 'sexual identity is one of the first types of identity to be socially recognised' (Dundes, 1989: 16). Tribal folktales deal with identity confusion regarding sexuality through their extensive use of transbiology and magic realism, which in turn gives indications about how Indigenous peoples often desire to make alterations in sexual identity/orientation/act. These queer articulations emerge from inside out of the stories and have not been reversed from outside in by the researcher. There is every possibility of multiple revisions/distortions in the

48

folkloristic data regarding the queer asseverations, but the importance lies in the alterations' having been initiated by people in the tribal communities.[19]

To assess this projection in folktales, we thus need to adopt a methodology that can interpret queer customs cloaked under symbolic and fantastic dimensions. But the popular method of structural analyses will not work here. Alan Dundes considers semiotics, an overused but inadequate tool for studying folklore: 'In short, however useful semiotics may be for honing tools of description and classification in folkloristics, it has yet to prove itself in the study of the meaning of folklore' (Dundes, 1980: 35).

The suitable methodology adopted for this study is instead an interdisciplinary approach of anthropological interpretation, psychoanalytical interpretation and ethnopoetics. Ethnopoetic interpretation explores literary devices, like magic realism, that even non-literary societies use in their art. Psychoanalytic interpretation helps to deconstruct the elements of fantasy and symbolic-metaphorical expressions in terms of mainly Freudian or Jungian ideas to reveal the ambivalent take on the queer emotions and customs resulting from the transitory confrontations. The anthropological interpretation of the folktales directs the ethnopoetic and psychoanalytic interpretations towards understanding 'family tensions, unconscious wishes, and interpersonal dynamics that often stand in direct contrast to observed behavior' (Dundes, 2005: 264), thereby providing clues about the inner mindscape of queer Indigeneity, despite the pressures of 'governmentality' to conform through transformation.

The common accusation against psychological analysis of tribal folktales is that of being reductionistic. But reductionism, as the hallmark of most of the natural sciences, cannot be estimated as good or bad. We should not dismiss psychoanalysis as a merely reductionist approach without trying to understand the merit of the proposed psychological pattern that would contribute to reaching fresh revelations. After all, even non-psychoanalyst researchers of folktales have ended up producing tale types, motif numbers or structural slots which are equally reductionistic (Dundes, 1897: x).

The most crucial aspect of the methodology is whether the use of Western theories is valid when applied to interpreting Indigenous literature. The study of Indigeneity, or nativism, as a contemporary discipline cannot exist separately from an interdisciplinary mode. Nativism today is rather a deconstruction of 'Aboriginalism' (Attwood, 1993), which resulted in distancing the First Nations from the rest, and for such a deconstruction of 'Aboriginalism', one needs to link the study of Indigeneity with the Western perspectives, often to challenge them, rather than to maintain the segregation which might produce 'an oddly parochial formulation of the discipline' of tribal/Indigenous study (Andersen, 2009: 81). The Indigenous study must be founded on the consciousness of 'Indigenous *density* (rather than difference)' (ibid.: 82). Following Robin Kelley's argument, once the wrapping of the commodified Indigeneity in terms of the difference in 'the surface, the skin, the viscosity, the mask' is unpacked, Indigenous people can discover in the 'density' of their Indigenous being 'a more profound complexity, greater clarity and the potential for emancipation' (Kelley, 2005: 10).

To counter the hegemonic representations of Indigeneity which margin-alise the density of Indigenous people, Indigenous studies, following the arguments of Moreton-Robinson, must use all the available epistemolo-gies, not only those which distance Western perspectives from the study of Indigeneity. Maintaining a conscious gap between the Western epistemolo-gies and Indigeneity, which is apparently protective, is actually a perception grounded on a notion of inferiority: 'Buried within this assumption is the idea that we are incapable of change or developing strategies for survival that enable us to extend on the multiple subject positions we have created through kinship and community politics' (Moreton-Robinson, 2004: 87). What is important today in the study of Indigeneity is the recognition of a 'cultural interface' as 'the intersection of Western and Indigenous domains' (Nakata, 2002: 285). As Jace Weaver has rightly observed, 'in dealing with the totalizing systems that we know as native cultures, each view from tradi-tional disciplines is limited and partial' (Weaver, 2007: 235), and therefore, an interdisciplinarity of all Western and of all endogenous methodologies and epistemologies needs to be used in Indigenous studies, to appreciate Indigenous density rather than mere difference.

Western theories are often seen as barriers for the decolonising efforts of Indigenous scholars. However, it must be understood that decoloniality actu-ally implies a resurrection of 'decolonial knowledge making' that is possible only when Indigenous studies '[reassert and draw] in concepts and mean-ings from Indigenous knowledge and systems of thought and experience of the colonial' (Nakata et al., 2012: 124). Works have already been done where the emancipatory component of Western critical theory has been used in Indigenous studies (e.g., Freire, 1972; Horkheimer, 1993). Thus, rather than Mignolo's call for epistemic disobedience (Mignolo, 2009), of delink-ing Indigenous studies from Western epistemologies, I keep more faith with Wiredu's recommendation for an epistemic awakening (Wiredu, 1995), as a way to link the lens of Western theory with the perspectives emerging out of Indigenous experiences. Ultimately, it is the 'middle voice'[20] that helps any researcher/reader to be aware of the limitation of any individual understand-ing, with the acceptance that there always remains a middle space between one's limited way of comprehension and other possible ways.

A 'coming community': connecting the subcultures of resistance

Why is there an irresistible desire to get connected with an-other world? Bataille argues that the solidarity between the individual and the community takes place 'through rents or wounds' (Bataille, 1985a: 251). As a debarred queer of the Third World, I do not find it difficult to understand the wound and the struggle of the Fourth World. The sharing of wounds marks the beginning of an endeavour to connect, through dialogic communication, these two subcultures: queer and tribal. In the 'other' community, one finds an imperative that contests the common discourse from which one is excluded (Lingis, 1994: 11–12). The 'surfaces of the other', surfaces the suffering, appeal to the self to extend sensitivity to 'other', not to 'order the course and heal the substance of the other but to feel the feeling of the other' (ibid.: 31). Addressing the 'suffering' someone is an appeal to an-other for what is not available to oneself in one's own environment. Hence, the desire to get connected with the Fourth World comes from the consciousness that it has an element to embrace and empower nonnormative queer people of the Third World: 'We appeal to the others to help us to be at home in the alien elements into which we stay' (ibid.: 122).

This intimacy between the queer Third World and the Fourth World would result in a bond of two subcultures of resistance through a belonging without any appropriated/hybrid identity but rather with a belonging in its being *such as it is*. This togetherness without a plea for common identity, but founded on a dialogic continuum retaining the singularity of the Third World and Fourth World intact, would result in the formation of a 'coming community' and its 'coming politics': 'The novelty of the coming politics is that it will no longer be a struggle for the conquest or control of the state, but a struggle between the state and the non-state (humanity)' (Agamben, 2009: 84). For a Third World non-Indigenous person, the mode of coming community can be the best option of togetherness with the Fourth World Indigenous community; this attitude with the stress on singularity minimises the notion of motivated intrusion, unlike that of the capitalist agency of market in the tribal space of which ethnic communities are nowadays most suspicious. Hybrid identity as an outcome of transition may happen due to the presence of the tradition of Other/an-other, yet in the coming community, the approach should be premised at least on a bond predicated on 'being-thus' as opposed to 'being-such' for a togetherness (ibid.: 'Appendix'). Jean-Luc Nancy expressed a similar view of intimate belonging: 'all loves . . . are superbly singular' (Nancy, 1991: 99). For Nancy, even love, which is predominantly seen as shared encounter/relation, actually remains a singular passage of opening of the one to another, thereby exposing the singularity of a being in its community and thereafter the singularity of 'Being' itself. The intimate formation of the coming community rejects all forms of 'conditioned' belonging, through the realisation of the singularity of 'Being', by communicating in an empty stateless space of not being identical. This realisation, posed with a singular unity, is nevertheless challenging, because

> What the state cannot tolerate in any way, however, is that the singu-
> larities form a community without affirming an identity. . . . Whatever

51

singularity, which wants to appropriate belonging itself, its own being-in-language, and thus rejects all identity and every condition of belonging, is the principal enemy of the state.

(Agamben, 2009: 85–86)

The coming community, according to Nancy, can be best evoked through writing:

Community without community is to come, in the sense that it is always coming, endlessly, at the heart of every collectivity. . . . The call that convokes us, as well as the one we address to one another . . . can be named, for want of a better name, writing, or literature.

(Nancy, 1991: 71)

The chief aspiration behind this work is that this writing on the tribal literature would accelerate communication between the queer Third World people and the Fourth World people, since communication with a 'depth perception' as opposed to 'surface sensitivity' is the only way to silence not the interlocutor 'other' but rather the outsider: the neocoloniser state (Lingis, 1994: 71). The formation of a community between these two subcultures is premised on the hope that amid 'the work of the rational community, there forms the community of those who have nothing in common, of those who have nothingness . . . in common' (ibid.: 13).

Notes

1 According to Jose Martinez Cobo,

Indigenous communities, peoples and nations . . . form at present non-dominant sectors of society and are determined to preserve, develop and transmit to future generations their ancestral territories and their ethnic identity, as the basis for continued existence as peoples in accordance with their own cultural patterns, social institutions and legal systems.

(Cobo, 1986: 1)

2 "Supreme Court Dismisses Petition Seeking Civil Rights for Homosexuals", *Business Standard*, April 15, 2019. www.business-standard.com/article/pti-stories/sc-dismisses-plea-seeking-civil-rights-for-homosexuals-119041500965_1. html Accessed on August 25, 2019.
3 "India Abstains from Voting for LGBTQ Rights at UN Human Rights Council", Geeta Mohan. *India Today*, New Delhi, July 12, 2019. www.indiatoday.in/india/story/india-united-nations-lgbtq-rights-1567935-2019-07-12 Accessed on August 25, 2019.
4 Endogenous ethnography (i.e. ethnocultural study by Indigenous people alone) has the danger of '[p]resumptions of a common frame of reference and shared identity [that] can . . . complicate the anthropologist's task by leaving cultural notions implicit, making her work to get people to state, explain, and situate

the obvious' (Weston, 1991: 14). Seteney Shami observed that 'The indigenous anthropologist does not come into the field with all the knowledge and experiences generated by the various and complex structures of societies' (Shami, 1988: 135).

5 Bimalendu Majumder's book on Toto, which is related to my work, was published in 1991. All the other books, as anthologies of tribal folktales that I am using for this study, were published at a later stage.

6 Expressions like 'inner texture', 'intertexture' and 'social and cultural texture' are used by Vernon K. Robbins in his books *Exploring the Texture of Texts* (1996a), pp. 7–94, and *The Tapestry of Early Christian Discourse* (1996b), pp. 44–191.

7 For the concept of the reoralisation of a text, see Mills (1990).

8 The Latin historians continued this practice. Tacitus, for instance, omits certain details while exercising his independence and illustrating his interpretative tendency. For references and discussion, see Syme, 1958: I, 189.

9 See Tuplin, 1993: 36–40.

10 For instance, Dhaniram Toto had to use Bangla script while writing his books in the Toto language, due to the unavailability of Toto script. In 1997, the government of West Bengal awarded Dhaniram for his literary endeavours. Toto script was developed under his leadership in 2015, comprising six diphthongs, nine vowels and 22 consonants.

11 A parallel can be traced even in ancient Athens. The students of Thucydides who practiced written/documentary history were the so-called political dissenters, as pointed out by Ober (1998): Xenophon, Plato, Aristotle, and other critics of Athenian democracy.

12 Early philosophers like Plato equated writing with orality, rendering writing as a metaphor for memory: 'It appears to me that the conjunction of memory with sensations, together with the feelings consequent upon memory and sensation, may be said as it were to write words in our souls' (Plato, 1963: 39). Aristotle, while differentiating the seeing of an object in its presence from the seeing of a representational image of something else, regarded memory as reading the image and regarded remembering (often manifested through orality) as an internal visual perception that resembles the act of reading a written document. New coinages like 'oral writing' or '*oralitéécrite*' (written orature) have also focused on the interrelation between the oral and the written.

13 For example, Majumdar, 1991, 2008; Saha, 2015; Tamsang, 2008; Doma, 2010; Kotturan, 1976; Pappadis, 2001.

14 For example, see "Transgender Community Face Increasing Violence Since 377 Ruling" by Vartika Rastogi. *The Citizen*, September 17, 2018. www.the citizen.in/index.php/en/NewsDetail/index/7/15000/Transgender-Community-Face-Increasing-Violence-Since-377-Ruling.

15 A similar notion gets conveyed through Turner's elaboration of 'liminality' as

> a term borrowed from Arnold van Gennep's formulation of rites de passage, 'transition rites'—which accompany every change of state or social position . . . marked by three phases: separation, margin (or limen . . . though cunicular, 'being in a tunnel', would better describe the quality of this phase . . . its hidden nature, its sometimes mysterious darkness), and reaggregation.
>
> (Turner, 1974: 232)

16 For the classification, see Jones, 1995: 7–8. I do not agree with the kind of distinction made by Dan Ben-Amos in his article 'Folktale', where he considers

that myths are true, legends are supposed to be true and folktales are inherently untrue. However, he arguably contradicts his differentiation: 'Myths are about supernatural beings that exist beyond the boundaries of human time and space'. For details, see Dundes, 2005: 255–256.

17 I am thankful to the University Grants Commission, New Delhi, for sanctioning a major research project on collecting and translating the tribal folktales of the Lepcha, Limbu, Toto and Rabha communities. I must also acknowledge the support that I received from the Indian Institute of Advanced Study, Shimla, without which I could not have completed the interpretations.

18 See note 13 for the published anthologies of folktales that I used as references.

19 Commenting on the kaleidoscopic patterns of the variability of the folktales, Christine Goldberg suggested that the variations by the contemporary folk tellers matches those of their predecessors' 'dilemmas about consistency vying with variability' (1986: 164). She concluded the article with the affirmation that 'Tales are not monuments, but both are artifacts deigned to meet the needs and aspirations of those who maintain them' (ibid.: 172).

20 'Middle voice', according to Hayden white, indicates a 'posture that is neither subjective nor objective, neither that of social scientist with a methodology and a theory nor that of the poet intent upon expressing a personal reaction' (White, 1999: 37). This, for me, is a call for being aware of the limitations of any work, because there are multiple other ways of comprehension and a call for understanding the benefit of trying to fit into a middle space, between a limited individual understanding and the possibilities of otherness.

3

'WANDERING BETWEEN TWO WORLDS'

'Mainstream' ethos, transgression and narratives of the anarcho-dissidence in Toto

[W]e must bear in mind that folk and fairy tales per se have no actual emancipatory power unless they are used actively to build a social bond . . . social interaction . . . agitatorial cultural work, etc.

(Zipes, 1979: 21)

The magic in the tales (if magic is what it is) lies in people and creatures being shown what they really are.

(Opie and Opie, 1974: 14)

Folktales cannot bring revolutions. Nevertheless, they have the emanci-patory potentials to raise crucial questions related to globalisation versus homogenisation, industry versus empire, Indigenous autonomy versus the corrective agencies of the state and a tribal alter-modern ethos versus domi-nant norms of repressive modernity. Freud maintained that the 'poets and philosophers before me discovered the unconscious. What I discovered was the scientific method by which the unconscious can be studied' (Trilling, 1951: 34). Hence, psychoanalysis can be best considered when it is con-nected to literature. A deconstructive reading of Indigenous literature, spe-cifically of the issues that are excluded by the contemporary 'mainstream', is the only way to get the marginalised rid of anxieties and inhibitions.

Storytelling is an imaginative craft, and 'Imagination is the organizer of mediation . . . the [mental] labor process through which natural drives, consciousness and the outer world are connected with one another' (Richter and Merkel, 1974: 18). Imagination is thus historical and alterable. It can be used not only as compensation for absence but also as a 'criticism of life'. Folktales, in spite of the happy endings, mirror through the elements of fantasy the contradictions that stem from the exclusions that occur for peo-ple who don't assimilate into the 'mainstream'. Erasing the binary between fantasy and the existential world, the tribal folk literature, with an 'uplifting of time' (Zipes, 1979: 101), allows time to appear timeless in a refutation of rationalised time, which represents regulatory modes of early capitalist and administrative invasions and thereby creates a desired utopia to represent self-determination through the timelessness of the folktales.[1] The fantastic and the magical in the folktales illustrate the yearning of the Fourth World to restore their societal Indigenous ethos, delinked from the constitutive hierarchy of 'mainstream' modernity. In a situation where the dominant culture, equated with an 'advanced knowledge', becomes repressive, the imaginative elements of folktales need to be revisited as counter-perspectives of subverting 'reason'/'enlightenment' and as tools as against the mere projection of a utopia. These elements present the capability of tribal folk to decide their lives on their own terms as the sovereign makers of their own history.[2]

The Toto community, like any other previously secluded tribal communities, is in a phase of transition due to the socioeconomic trespassing of the 'mainstream' in its ethnoscape. The 'mainstream' is the carrier of the ideology that is sanctioned by the state as normative, and the tribal people, at the interface of the limited range of consumable identities that are sold to them, find themselves hanging in between an irreversible past and an impossible future. The Indigenous geo-space of the Toto, hitherto representing a range of autonomy, is slowly being transformed by the presence of state agencies. Transformation of the tribal rural/forest spaces cannot be separated from the issues of the consequent changes in their daily existence/customs/practices (Pinder, 2005: 3). Colonialism further creates a hierarchy of civil knowledge over the Indigenous and accelerates the conflict between the civil state and the state of nature: 'For the principal task of civilisation, its actual raison d'être, is to defend us against nature' (Freud, 1961: 58). This conflict results in the tribals' becoming victims of the false assurances of individual freedom and social equality supposedly offered by the agents of neoliberalism.

The option that remains as a counter to the 'moralizing revenge of the powerless' (Brown, 1995: 61) is that of an 'imagining revenge' (Nietzsche,1969: 36). The folktales, as indicators of tribal anarcho-dissidence, become portals of retaliation through the help of magic and fantasy, which also serve as modes of propagating the community's endogenous ethos. With the rapid change brought out in their surroundings, the Toto people, with their inheritance of traditional Indigenous modernity, find themselves positioned between ethnic modernity and 'mainstream' modernity, 'one dead,/The other powerless to be born/With nowhere yet to rest my head' (Arnold, 1999: 85–86). The sense of dangling in between the two 'unreachable' worlds is accompanied by an awareness of displacement and denial. The Toto folktales that contain magic real devices convey the resistance aimed at the changing power dynamics owing to the neocolonial encroachment of the state: 'the fantastic reveals that which must be concealed so that one's internal and external experience may be comfortably known, so that one may get along day to day in the communal world' (Olsen, 2004: 290). The 'mythopoeic reality'[3] manifested through the mechanisms of 'estrangement' or 'defamiliarisation' in the tribal stories, where nothing seems to be true yet everything seems true, is actually an ironical way to 'confront [audience] with inescapable, perhaps unpalatable, truths about the human condition ... and then to posit alternatives which address the particular injustices, inequalities and oppressions with which the [composer] takes issue' (Filmer, 1992: 3).

Anarchism as a critique of borders and hierarchies, resembling the queer antistatist agenda of refusing to behave as a progenitive citizen and inspired by Foucault and Deleuze, along with the anti-identity argumentation of Butler, aims at constructing anarchist expressions resisting the formal parameters of thought and practice, provided by neocolonial or neoliberal notions of democracy (Heckert and Cleminson, 2011: 7). Since 'any attempt to build a society where people are comfortable with themselves and each other *must* include a radical reorganization of sexuality' (Heckert, 2004: 101), the Toto people often find themselves under constant surveillance of sexual reformatory mechanisms, against the traditional queernormative understandings of their alter-makeup as humans: 'we are in a struggle with the government, and the government is in a struggle with us' (Foucault, 1997: 167). Under the cloak of enchantment and the uncanny, one can discover in these tribal folktales the (post)anarchist approach that 'prioritises the value and necessity of difference over identity' (Heckert, 2011: 200) in order to conceal one's distinct identity and begin the continuous process of becoming *not* oneself, as a force of resistance (Newman, 2001: 159). Therefore, the use of transbiology in Toto folktales functions as a 'creative power of freedom, ontological opening ... [that] constructs value from below' (Negri, 1999: 86). The anarcho-dissidence in Toto folktales attracts the dissident 'mainstream' queer person to participate in an anarchist 'perverse reading' of these tales as an effort for a relationship, with the consciousness that 'the state is a condition ... a mode of human behaviour; we destroy it by contracting other relationships, by behaving differently' (Landauer, 1973: 226). The study of coded ideas of noncompliance in the Toto folktales is an endeavour to relate with the struggle of the tribal world against the repressive norms and fractional laws imposed on them by the state and thereby participate as an ally in their resistance against subjectivation. Judith Butler has rightly remarked that when majoritarianism aided by

> law becomes an instrument of state violence. . . . Then one has to engage forms of 'disobedience'. . . . one has to become what Althusser called a 'bad subject' or a provisional anarchist, in order to unbind the law from the process of subjectivation.
>
> (Heckert and Cleminson, 2011: 98)

These select Toto tales were collected during my fieldwork with my companion translators; interestingly, these also appear in Bimalendu Majumdar's monograph. There are mainly two reasons for taking the published stories into account: to address the question of authenticity and to address the question of the continuity. The folktales which appear in Bimalendu Majumdar's monograph are in some sense authentic, since they have been proven to not be fakelore. Secondly, dealing with the stories, which seem not to have been altered[4] for at least the past 25 years, partly makes my task easier insofar as addressing the issue of the ongoing culture of transmission of the folktales among tribal people, most importantly among the majority of the people who do not know English[5] and therefore nullifying any possibility for the tellers to come across the tales in printed forms and translated forms.

This study, moreover, is not about identification but rather about interpretation. I have chosen to look for the historical moments of alter-modernity in the folktales that illustrate 'non-normativity', as understood by me as a queer man who represents the culture of an-other, while at once being otherised by the culture that I represent. Hence, I look for the queernormative moments of past that are relevant for my dialogic understanding of the modern self through an-other. Understanding 'Folklore as autobiographical ethnography, as a mirror of culture' (Dundes, 1980: 38) helps us to understand the cultural invasions of the dominant 'mainstream' and the consequential homogenisation of the tribal sociocultural practices through the strategic use of projective materials devised by Indigenous people as a mechanism of revealing their resistance. The major task, therefore, is to identify the psychological motifs of the projections by decoding such metaphorical usages. Treating projections as literalisations of metaphors and symbols is a possible way of deciphering the psychological content of folklore (ibid.: 45). For this purpose, the Toto folktales have been categorised under three broad themes:

- From leading grandmother to misleading witch.
- Dissident intimacies.
- Evil as emancipation.

As tropes of the past, this thematic division enables us to outline the non-normative tribal focus and a trajectory of the 'mainstream's' engineered normativity by relying on Hayden White's metahistorical conviction that literature and history are 'almost indistinguishable' in that they 'overlap, resemble, or correspond with each other' (White, 1978b: 121).

From leading grandmother to misleading witch

The Toto community had hardly been phobic towards the erotic. So far as sexual intimacies were concerned, both men and women have been allowed to experience premarital eroticism, which even today continues but in secrecy, due to the presence of the normatising agents of the 'mainstream': counselling nongovernmental organisations with their welfare manuals of medical discourse for producing docile bodies, preaching missionaries terrifying them about the sins of flesh and vigilant administrative agents of the state offering assurances of money for conformity.

Counter to the 'mainstream' sexual discourse where the state/law treats sexuality merely as reproductive and therefore compels it to be confined within a procreative institution (turning even live-in heterosexual relationships into an almost institutionalised construct), in Toto society, marriage would have taken place only after the woman was sure that she had conceived. The institution of family was seen from a utilitarian standpoint, but not sexuality. The pleasure aspect of eroticism was always acknowledged in Toto culture, assuring space for nonreproductive intimacies. Even in the near past, unmarried pubescent girls were free to choose their provisional partners among the guests who arrived at their dwelling, and the young unmarried Toto boys were exposed to sexual life by being intimate with either the widows of their elder brother or/and with young grandmothers (except their own grandmothers) with whom they shared a casual relation (Roy Burman, 1962). After coming into contact with the 'mainstream' culture through the intermixing with the neighbouring Rajbangshis, Bengali and Nepali folk, the Toto censored this system, though youths seem too often to get intimate with such grandmother figures, secretly.

The folktales of this section reveal the ambivalent apprehension regarding the queer grandmother–youth sexual intimacies that have emerged out of the normatising efforts of external agencies, and Indigeneity is unable to entirely overcome the appeal of the suppressed tribal ethos embedded in the collective unconscious. Under this theme of grandmother–youngster erotic queer intimacy, four Toto folktales have been selected—*The Pumpkin Prince*,[6] *The Orphan Boy*, *The Story of Two Orphans* and *The Witch Mother*—to show how the prevalent Indigenous relationship, through the inhibited interference of the normative gaze, is being transformed into a marginalised exception, resulting in intricate psychological conflicts due to the suppression of this nonnormative relationship, as revealed through these tales.

Tale 1: The Pumpkin Prince

Once upon a time, there lived an old couple. The grandfather and grandmother after cleaning up a patch of the jungle around their house sowed some pumpkin seeds. But to their disappointment, only a single pumpkin tree grew up and produced just one pumpkin. The old couple preserved the single pumpkin to consume in future. One day, when the grandmother was about to eat the pumpkin, it began to plead her not to cut it but preserve it so that it could take care of the old couple, and it promised to do the farming on their behalf. From that day onwards, the cultivation was done by the pumpkin. He also took great care of the grandparents. The pumpkin proposed one day to visit the king's house so that he could make one of the king's daughter his wife. The grandparents wished him luck. Reaching the king's house, the pumpkin found that the daughters of the king were busy washing their dishes after having their meals. He proposed to the eldest daughter of the king. But the eldest daughter rejected him because he was a mere pumpkin. The middle one also rejected him on the same grounds. Ultimately, when the youngest one arrived before the pumpkin, the pumpkin proposed to her: 'Can you come with me to my house and live with me?' The youngest of the king's daughters accepted the proposal, and both of them started moving towards the pumpkin's house. The king's daughter saw a mango tree on the way and asked the pumpkin to bring her some mangoes. Climbing up the tree, the pumpkin asked the king's daughter to spread a piece of cloth for collecting the mangoes. All of a sudden, the pumpkin burst into pieces by jumping on the cloth. The wife began to weep since she thought that she had lost her husband. Suddenly, a handsome prince came out of the pumpkin. Finding such a beautiful bridegroom, the king's daughter was delighted. Thereafter, they started living joyfully by enjoying their wealth. Eventually the king's daughter gave birth to a son. The eldest and the middle daughters of the king were very angry and jealous when they came to know about all of these. They even started repenting for the mistake of rejecting the pumpkin. One day, the eldest sister came to the youngest sister's house. Offering to take the lice off her head, the king's eldest daughter took the youngest sister by the side of a river. The eldest sister suggested that the youngest one remove her clothes in order to take a bath in the river. The moment the pumpkin's wife removed her clothes, her eldest sister pushed her into the river. The youngest daughter of the king drowned and died. Dressing herself with the clothes of the pumpkin's wife, the eldest sister came back to the pumpkin's house. Although the difference was not recognized by the pumpkin prince, the son refused to drink milk and continued to cry throughout the night. In the early morning, the apparition of the deceased wife came to breastfeed her son. The son refused to drink from the disguised wife and went on crying throughout successive nights. The child's behaviour created a suspicion in the pumpkin's mind. That night, he checked his wife closely and discovered that although there were many similarities with his real wife, she appeared to be not exactly the same one. The whole night, he remained awake. He found out that early in the morning the real wife appeared and started weeping while feeding her son. Soon the pumpkin prince understood that the woman who was staying with him was not his real wife but her eldest sister, who had killed the king's youngest daughter in order to stay with the pumpkin prince as his wife. He got hold of his real wife while she arrived to feed her son and insisted that she reveal the truth. After hearing all that had happened, he asked the youngest sister of the disguised wife to wait in an adjacent room. The false wife came to serve breakfast, and the pumpkin prince asked her to dig a deep hole in the courtyard so that he could plant an areca nut tree. Accordingly, the disguised wife dug a big deep hole. The pumpkin prince tied up the false wife's hands and legs and pushed the disguised wife into the pit. He buried her whole body by filling up the deep hole with mud, and only the head of the false wife remained unearthed. He brought the real wife out of the room and beheaded the eldest sister of the real wife with a single stroke of his *patang* (sword). Thereafter all of them lived happily, accumulating more wealth in due course.

The projection of ephemeral sexuality[7] through the folktale enhances the possibility of a queer reading of *The Pumpkin Prince*. The offbeat engagement of the tale, a triangular intimacy between the human, nonhuman (apparition of the dead wife) and plant in the domain of erotic desire,[8] renders it a refuge of ephemeral sexuality. The reference of transbiology in the tale exemplifies the queer antiassimilationist-cum-antiseparatist characteristics of being 'transitive—multiply transitive'.[9] That there happens to be just a single pumpkin which the grandmother has managed to acquire for consumption points out that queerness needs to be seen as a preference. The atypical bond, suggested by 'consumption', which is a symbolic representation of copulation,[10] between the pumpkin and the grandmother is cut off once the king's youngest daughter agrees to marry the pumpkin. He remains no longer a mere pumpkin (in a satirical resemblance of the mainstream notion of an 'insufficient/useless man') and instead develops into a 'prince'.[11] The venture of normatising, conversely, remains incomplete despite the pumpkin's attempt of fitting into the heteronormative institute of marriage and reproduction. Hence, a replacement of cohabitation must be made: from older grandmother (the ethno-traditional norm but a taboo for the 'mainstream') to an elder sister (suggesting the historic censorship of tribal norms by labelling them as primitive by the 'mainstream'). Having killed the king's eldest daughter and uniting with his former wife, an endeavour of restoring the normativity has been apparently undertaken. Nevertheless, the interesting paradox that surfaces is that what has to be revived is the 'magical' that used to be ushered in by his love for the grandmother disguised as a pumpkin and not as a normative human being. After the pumpkin's short performative interphase of living as a pumpkin prince with a human wife so that the role of the 'reproductive agent' as a normalised man can be enacted, the preferred nonnormativity is attained in the form of the compensatory apparition, disguised as his real but dead wife, in order to match the pumpkin prince's 'inextinguishable' queerness and thereafter live happily ever after.

The tale underscores the fact that in a changed tribalscape, the desired queer life can be lived only under the disguise of a pumpkin. However, the enactment of a fleeting normative life illustrated by the pumpkin's death and the emergence of the heteronormative man ultimately pave the way for the tale to move further towards the desired regaining of the nonlife/afterlife where the reeled adaptation of the real life, troubled with the politics of the 'mainstream' normativity, can be ratified and where the queer desire symbolised by the 'in-between' pumpkin prince's blissful settlement with his real-dead wife can be restored. The coalescing of weirdness with the probable, through the return of the dead, marks an element of the uncanny. The sense of the uncanny, that causes panic combined with risk, is analogous to the sensation created while encountering the return of the most familiar:

> this uncanny element is actually nothing new or strange, but something that was long familiar to the psyche and was estranged from it only through being repressed . . . something that should have remained hidden and has come into the open.
>
> (Freud, 2003: 148)

The depiction of a communicating pumpkin highlights nonnormative transgression and anxiety, which conveys that the portrayal of the fantastic is an outcome of the regulatory forces creeping into Toto society, and thus, in due course, brackets the Indigenous queer normal as a 'normal-deviant' (Goffman, 1990). The use of transbiology validates this claim. The 'ghostly' existence of a tribal nonconformist, compelled to role-play as per the homogenising dictates of the majoritarian kleptocracy, is candidly elucidated by the folktale's uncanny end of the pumpkin prince's joyful cohabitation with his phantom wife, while yearning relentlessly for the resurgence of the repressed desire for the grandmother, which finds its eventual eruption in the craving for the demise of the normative agent. The uncanny, hence, is not the incident of death but its return, which echoes the well-known saying that 'the mail carrier always rings twice'. Death's return needs to be comprehended in terms of what has been killed, either by actual action or in deliberation. The incapability of the pumpkin prince to distinguish between his real wife and her eldest sister, which is central to the awareness that his real wife is dead, is arguably an example of projective inversion (Dundes, 1980: 51). The projective inversion has allowed the tabooed desire of the tribal protagonist, in getting rid of his wife through murder for the sake of the restoration of his queer grandmother fixation, to be deliberately trans-posed as the product of an usual rivalry of a jealous elder sibling. The latent necrophilia is regarded as an outcome of the anxiety of being rejected by a woman, which the protagonist of the tale faced earlier when he pursued the eldest and the middle daughters of the king, and it unveils the crucial inca-pability of the pumpkin prince to maintain a long-term straight identity.[12]

Tale 2: The Orphan Boy

There was an orphan boy once upon a time. He was given shelter by a villager, who assigned the boy with the daily duty of taking the villager's cattle for grazing but didn't offer the orphan boy ade-quate food. One day while taking the cattle out for grazing, the boy felt very hungry but could not manage to get any fruit or tuber in the forest. He started crying, and shortly thereafter an old woman appeared. Hearing about his hunger, the woman pointed at a red cow of his herd. She said, 'The moment you hit the right horn, you will get flattened rice, and to get molasses, hit her left horn'. She then vanished into the forest. The orphan boy followed her instruc-tion and ate to his heart's content. Moreover, finding a piece of cloth, he assembled the leftover food and kept it hidden in the cav-ity of a tree before returning back to the house. Meanwhile, a crane came and ate up the food from the cavity. Coming for the food, the next day, the boy could not find any food left but discovered a crane flying away from the tree. He realised that the crane had eaten up his food and started chasing the crane for three days and three nights. Finally, the crane surrendered and said, 'Please don't kill me. Come to my house, and I will offer you food and clothing. Tie some mustard to my tail, which will drop as I fly, and you can follow the track to reach my house'. Collecting a handful of mus-tard from the nearby village, the boy followed the crane by walking an entire day and an entire night. The next day, he ran into a house at the end of the forest. Inside the house he found the same old woman who had helped him to get food out of the red cow. Learn-ing that the orphan was going to the crane's house, the old woman said, 'The servants of the crane's house would not allow you to enter the house by the main door. So take the back door on the right side. Inside the room of the crane, you will see a small phial, which you must acquire from the crane'. Walking for three days along the way as directed by the old woman, he reached the crane's house. The servants, expectedly, didn't allow the boy to enter. He took the back door and found the crane sitting on a beautiful elevated platform, and the crane asked the boy to wish for anything for himself. The boy asked for the phial, and the crane offered it to him, by asking him not to open it before reaching his house. Three days passed while the boy was walking back towards the village, and every day, the weight of the phial seemed to increase. Unable to resist his curiosity, he opened the cork of the phial, to discover a beautiful girl sitting in it. He tried to close the mouth of the bottle with the cork, but the girl resisted him. Soon she came out and pleaded, 'Take me to your house as your wife'. Overwhelmed with joy, the orphan asked her to wait there till he could gather the villagers and get married before taking her home. The girl sat on the branch of the tree. Suddenly an ogress appeared, and after killing the girl, the ogress sat on the tree, disguising herself as the girl. The boy returned and took the ogress as his wife to the village, where he built a house for both of them. The boy sowed a seed of sweet pumpkin by the side of the house. Soon the ogress became pregnant. The pumpkin vine too started spreading out the leaves and bore a fruit just above the main door. The vine touched the ogress every time she went in and out of the house. This annoyed her so much that she uprooted the vine, along with the fruit, and threw it off. Soon a pamelo tree emerged out of the same place where the pumpkin had grown, and a fruit sprouted. In the meantime, the ogress gave birth to a son. One day while she kept the son under the shade of the tree, the pamelo fruit fell and hit the son, and he was killed. Out of rage, the ogress wife went out to call people and cut down the tree. None agreed to cut the tree down. Finally she herself chopped the tree down and threw it off. One day the old woman visited the orphan boy, asking for a pamelo fruit. He said that it was cut down and thrown outside. Yet the old woman managed to gather a fruit from the remains of the tree and took it home in her basket. One day a beautiful girl came out of the pamelo. It was none other than the lady of the phial. She asked the old woman to bring some beetle leaves and areca nuts, along with an earthen pot, from the market. Every day the girl started chewing the beetle leaves and spat them into the earthen pot till it became full. With the old woman, she visited the orphan's house and poured the sputum out into the house. In the evening, the old woman summoned the boy to tell him about the ogress wife. She advised him to kill the ogress wife. Returning home, the orphan found that his house was wet with a pool of blood. He could not differentiate the sputum from actual blood. Being convinced that his wife was an ogress, he sought advice from an old woman. The old woman said, 'Tell your wife that you are planning to buy lots of areca nuts, which need a large pit, to be stored and processed. Then once it is over, you ask the wife to peep into it to check its depth. As she does so, cut her head and throw her body away into the pit and cover it with earth'. The orphan boy did as the old woman directed him. Finally the old woman came with the beautiful woman and said, 'This is who you brought from the crane's house. The ogress killed her, and you had wrongly accepted the ogress as your wife. Now take your real wife'. The orphan boy came to his house with the beautiful wife and lived happily ever after with no shortage of anything in his life.

The grandmother fixation continues in *The Orphan Boy* and shows the orphan protagonist's queer incapacity for heteronormative conjugality, similar to the ensuing homoeroticity of a man with a mother fixation. Since the protagonist is an orphan boy and not a pumpkin, enough caution has been taken to curtain queerness from the vigilant gaze of the 'mainstream'. Negating the image of the dependent human child crying out for human care, the orphan boy, unlike most of the folklore orphans, suffers hardly from shelter, clothing or melancholia but quintessentially from hunger, where the food, metaphorically, gets equated with sexuality. Expectedly, the old woman appears to teach him the tactics of satiating his appetite. Avoiding the normative line of milking the cow, the old woman trains the boy to incorporate, in his response to hunger, sensual gratification by hitting the cow with an erotic violence to content himself through a magical trick. Although magic references to reality are permissible by tribal consensus, their allusive gambit is beyond the command of the statist 'mainstream'.

The cow, with its assumed milking, suggests a latent consciousness of a suckling child's oral aggression.[13] The deliberate rejection of the usual milking, that would have depicted the old woman as a motherly figure nourishing the child in a metaphoric milking with an unconscious sexual intent, foregrounds the conscious amorous nature of the old woman and reveals the essential sensual context of hunger together with the violence of eroticism. The cow thus becomes the replaced agent of the grandmother, who traditionally served the food to young Toto boys, but this is increasingly 'vanishing' under censoring normative regimes. The old woman thus disappears, only to return by means of another of her agents. The crane, as a possible agent of the old woman (representing the erotic grandmothers), appears only to bring the boy away from the old woman, who taught him how to respond to his appetite.

In the Toto world where the traditional tribal practice is in severe expurgation, the orphan boy cannot dwell with the old woman. Hence, he is asked to get a phial from the crane's house. A girl's emerging out of the uncorked phial and the orphan boy's wish to marry her results from his earnestness to abide by the grandmother's instruction. The girl inside the phial offered by the crane, one of the old woman's agents, symbolises not a free individual with subjective agency but rather a shadow grandmother.

The boy's ambivalent struggle with his queer inclination vis-à-vis his grand-mother fixation has been paradoxically expressed: on the one hand, he is allowed to get the phial from the back door, symbolising that the desire for the would-be wife is not innate but strategic, and on the other hand, by disobeying the crane's order of meeting the girl only after returning to the house—that is, only in the presence of the heedful old woman—he exposes his inability to be a part of any normative relationship in the presence of his grandmother.

The queer motif wins over the normative, since the girl is ultimately killed. The compulsive heteronormativity that is foisted on tribal queer people by nontribal agencies is portrayed by his marriage with an ogress, which best renders the heteronormative institution as ghostly as it can be for an Indigenous queer. The imaginative tale of a happily married life with the ogress wife and a son fails to sustain itself for long. The pamelo tree can be again seen as the grandmother's agent. Just like the crane, her association with the pamelo tree can be established in retrospection. Given that her agent girl, who was killed by the ogress, revives out of the pamelo that the grandmother gathered from the orphan boy's house, it is not difficult to understand that the pamelo that killed the orphan boy's son was the result of the counter-magic of the old woman[14] against the magical ogress, who tried to trap the orphan boy within domestic normativity. Finally the grand-mother finds the resurrected pamelo girl, with her nonnormative connotation implied by transbiology, useful in getting rid of the ogress wife—who is an 'ogress' for a queer tribal orphan since she has 'burdened' him with a normative domesticity. The queer orphan boy kills the ogress wife to live happily with the amorous grandmother and a nonnormative wife. Treating the rebirth of the dead girl as metaphorical depiction of necrophilia further underscores, as a repressed drive for a same-sex relationship, that the boy will live with no shortage of anything in his life, since the grandmother is present, as are the desired men whose presence has been strategically erased out of the text by turning it into an impossible tale of no other man and, thereby, a possible account of viable queerness.

The 'cover story' of living with a dead/ogress wife, along with a purpo-sive subtext of blankness that is created by depicting the single male char-acter with his magic real wife as an empty signifier, shows how the tribal epistemic situation that permitted homosexuality to be talked about is forced to be reconstructed under 'mainstream' pressure through omission, silence and evasion. The tribal homonormativity that is subtly made visible by the complete invisibility of any other male characters smartly equates 'mainstream' homophobia with an unfeasible absurdity. The overt depic-tions of the transgressive talking crane, monstrous wife and end of institu-tionalised reproductive futurism are the added modes, effective enough to ridicule and resist the normatising panic through the assertion of a normal nonconformist.

Tale 3: The Story of Two Orphans

Once upon a time in a village, an epidemic broke out, and both the husband and the wife died. Their children—an elder daughter and a son—became orphans. The girl used to work in the neighbouring houses, helping them in fetching water or in the jhum cultivation and in doing so managed to gather food for both of them, or else she used to gather wild fruits and vegetables from the forest. The sister grew up into the most beautiful young girl of the village, while the brother was only eight years old. She was helped by her brother in her works. One day she said to her brother, 'I am going to the neighbouring village. You stay here and don't worry about me'. One winter passed and another winter arrived while the boy kept on waiting, thinking that the sister would turn up. But she did not return. Finally he decided to go in search of her. The entire day he walked. In the evening, he found himself in front of a house of an old woman, staying on her own. Seeing the orphan boy, the old lady offered him shelter for the night, asking him not to travel further in darkness for there was a forest nearby. The old lady offered him such good food that he could have never afforded for himself. She gave him such warm woollen blankets that he had never enjoyed before. He slept in repose. The next morning, the old woman proposed to guide the boy in finding his sister and showed him her house. But the boy changed his mind: 'I want to stay with you, grandmother. I do not want to go looking for my sister now'. The woman was also hoping for the same. Further, gratifying the unarticulated wishes of the woman, he said that that he would do works for her like fetching firewood from the forest and collecting grass. The old woman bought a pair of pigs for him that multiplied within a few years, and they earned a good amount by selling them off, with which they reconstructed a nice house for themselves. One day he decided to move out in search of a wife, reassuring the old woman that he would come back and stay with her. She agreed, persuading him not to be too late. After a day-long walk, he reached the village of his elder sister. Meeting her after such a long time, he narrated all that had happened to him till his current quest for getting a woman for himself. The elder sister said, 'I will find a woman for you. You stay with me tonight, and tomorrow we shall start looking'. The brother went to the elder sister's place. But he found that she was not as caring as she had been before. For example, she gave him breads made of bran meant for the pigs. The boy could not eat those. In the morning, the sister queried if he would like to stay longer. But he said, 'I cannot eat what you have served. I will move out today in search of my wife'. The elder sister taunted him by saying, 'Nobody will give their daughter in this village to you, because you could not eat the bran-made bread yesterday'. The boy asserted that he would rather not look for a woman among the villagers who were bran eaters. Again he walked through the day and before the sunset he arrived before the king's house. The king had three daughters, but no son. Seeing the boy from a distance, the eldest sister, who was playing with the other two sisters in front of the house, ran to inform the king about the arrival of a stranger boy. The king thought that he might be a possible son-in-law and asked her to call him inside. Hearing from the orphan that he was searching for a wife, the king said, 'I will give one of my daughters provided that you render your service to my family for three years before getting married'. The orphan boy agreed to the proposal and started staying there while helping in cultivation, growing crops, and collecting fruits from the forest, and he even looked after the cattle and pigs. Every day, he used to mark on the pillar of his house to keep a proper count of the days. After the end of the third year, he requested the king fulfil the promise. The king arranged for a grand feast to celebrate the wedding of his eldest daughter with the orphan boy. The orphan didn't have a house of his own, but he immediately decided to go back to the grandmother's house. The king said, 'Now I will not forbid you from going back to your house'. The next day, he started walking with his wife towards the village of the grandmother. But it was already dark when he reached a village by the side of the forest. So he decided to stay through the night in a deserted hut. A fox appeared in the second half of the night, asking, 'Who is in the hut?' Hearing from the boy about his plan of returning to the grandmother, the fox informed him that she had been dead and that now the woman whom he would find there was in fact a witch, who should have been killed before he would stay there with the wife. The fox then chalked out a plan for them. Following the plan of the fox, the orphan and his wife reached the grandmother's house, where the witch greeted them genially, and they too pretended not to have recognized her as a witch. He shared the food that he carried from the king's house with her. In the afternoon, with the help of his wife, he dug out two big holes in the courtyard. As per the direction of the fox, they set fire near the forest in the evening, and then rushing in front of the house, they started shouting, 'All the women of the house get out straight away. The king's soldiers are approaching'. Hearing this, the moment the witch came out, she fell into a hole. Instantly, they covered it with earth. Finally the witch was killed. Thereafter, the orphan boy and his wife, along with many children, lived happily ever after.

The Story of Two Orphans is a folktale with an oxymoronic tragic happy end. The entire conflict regarding what was once normal but recently projected as nonnormative in the Toto subculture finds literary expression through what Tolkien calls 'Eucatastrophe' (Tolkien, 1990), or the catastrophe that is finally twisted into an encouraging turn at the end. Throughout the folktale, there is an undercurrent of the orphan boy's nonnormative inclination—first towards the elder sister and then towards the older grandmother, both of which need to be buried in order to fit into institutionalised heteronormativity of the dictatorial 'mainstream'.

The use of winter as a synecdoche to represent the year suggests the lack of warmth from which an eight-year-old boy has been suffering while waiting for the elder sister. The fact that after two years, which marks the onset of adolescence, he starts out on an expedition in search of the elder sister hints at his incapacity for any other intimacy that is quite expected from an adolescent boy, abandoned by his immediate kin. The boy's entry into the grandmother's dwelling where he gets 'food' and a 'warm' bed is quite an expected one, from the perspective of the Toto custom of grandmother–youth intimacy. The latent incest also surfaces at the end of the search, with the boy's entry into the erotic non-'mainstream'.

The transgressive eroticity of the relationship can be better understood if we contrast the boy's building of a new house for the newfound partner with his former asocial temperament. The boy turns into an adult, and as per Toto norm, he is supposed to look for a woman who can be his wife. The orphan boy thus moves out to seek out a young woman, assuring of his return to the old woman, who also wants him to come back soon. The search for the young woman culminates in his running across his lost sister. Caught up in a circular web of nonnormative desire, the boy seems to oscillate from one transgressive desire to another. However, the boy's overcoming the fixation of the elder sister confirms the colonial enforcement of the incest taboo. The sister's offering of bran-made breads, generally used to feed pigs, to the brother and the brother's bracketing of her as one among the villagers of bran eaters show the ambivalence resulting from the sister's natural 'appetite' and 'lack of restraint' regarding kindred intimacy as opposed to the tabooed notion of uncleanness that has been installed in the brother's psyche.[15]

Yet Indigeneity is tough to regulate, and the tribal nonnormative self gets revealed despite the schematic 'mainstream' norm, such as in the sister's utterance: 'Nobody will give their daughter to you in this village'. This antagonism might also offer a hypothesis for the plausible resentment against incest in the transmuted Totopara, which might have compelled her to distance herself from her brother while she was an adolescent and he a budding body of eight. Interestingly, the orphan boy gets spotted by the eldest sister among the king's daughters, as another replacement of the boy's love for his elder sister, to whom he gets married only after a gap of three years. This delaying of marriage can be seen as a projective inversion by which the boy's reluctance has been substituted inversely as the king's hesitation. This is proven by the desperation of the boy who instantly gets reminded of his transgressive association with the grandmother immediately after his entrance into institutionalised heteronormativity. The next day, the newly wedded couple starts returning to the old woman. The 'mainstream' feels threatened at the perceivable reiteration of that which it wants to prohibit. A strategic fox visits the boy in late-midnight to inform him that the old lady in the grandmother's house is actually a witch who needs to be destroyed before the boy can start his conjugal life. The orphan boy, in the most unconvincing way, seems to have been convinced of his normative duty of disconnecting himself from the conventional Toto intimacy altered as a taboo.[16] The orphan boy follows the instruction, with full realisation that it comes from a *fox* that approaches in the *dark*. The folktale thus again uses projective inversion to show that the proposed conviction of the orphan boy is actually the inversion of his compulsion, resulting from the normative prescription of the despotic governmental agencies. The tribal desire for an old woman is displaced by turning it into a taboo, as manifested by the schematic progression of, first, changing the grandmother into a witch and, second, burying her. The (corporal) burial of the desired grandmother, who has to be mutated into a witch, within the same domestic space where there has to begin a coaxed normatised living, ironically reinforces the 'mainstream's' limitation in preventing the mutinous eruption of the nonnormative desire buried (psychologically) deep in the Toto collective unconscious.

Tale 4: The Witch Mother

A long time back, a man in a village lost his wife when the daughter and the son were infants. He was an affluent man, but soon the food that he had stored was all exhausted, since he could not work and had to just look after the children. He was against remarrying because he worried that the stepmother would not treat the kids well. He asked his neighbours if they could take care of his children so that he might work and get some food, but none of them agreed to take charge of the kids. All of them suggested that he remarry. The man, apprehensive of further confusion on the arrival of a new woman, continued to gather wild fruits and tubers from the forest to feed his children. After some time, the daughter grew up. She said to her father, 'You can go out and work. I can take care of my brother for a few days'. Bringing a fair number of tubers for the kids to survive, the man happily left his house in search of work, saying, 'I will return after seven days and seven nights'. He walked through the forest during the day, and while it was dark, he found himself walking round the same place. Actually, he was possessed by a witch, who was not allowing him to move further. It was nighttime, and the surroundings became dark. Suddenly he could make out fire in the distance, and following the direction of the fire, he walked to discover a hut. Inside the hut, he found large quantity of grains stored in the rooms. In the kitchen, he found a beautiful woman who was crying, sitting near a fire. The man asked her why she suffered. The woman said, 'I have become an orphan, and I don't have anyone to look after me'. The man said, 'If you are prepared to take care of my son and daughter, then I can take you home as my woman'. The woman agreed willingly: 'I will give them motherly love and serve them food'. At that time, a parrot yelled, 'It's all fake. She is a witch'. The man wondered who it was. The woman suggested, 'It is a wicked bird who speaks nonsense whenever it finds a man'. They had their food and slept. The next morning, packing food for the children, the man and the woman started walking back to his home, while the parrot appeared once again and screamed: 'Don't take this witch with you'. The woman tried to kill the bird, but it flew away. At home, the children were happy to see their father back, along with a new mother. For some days, they enjoyed the food that he had carried, and all of them had lovely time. Soon the food was exhausted, and the man had to go out to work, leaving the children under the guardianship of the wife. The wife actually was looking for the right moment. She never liked the children. She started engaging them in domestic works. She also asked them to fetch water by giving them cracked bamboo pipes. The entire day the children tried to store water in their pipes, but through the pores, the water leaked out. As it was getting late, they began to weep. A crane that was resting by the side of the lake asked them about their agony. Understanding their crisis, the crane made suggestions: 'Take some mud and close the holes. Then you can carry water, and your mother will be pleased'. To the contrary, the new mother was very annoyed. She rebuked them for the delay and gave only a few tubers to eat. The next day, handing over a sword (*patang*) that had no sharpness, she ordered the kids, 'Go and collect firewood from the forest. I need wood from the trees that are alive, and the wood should be dry'. Spending almost the entire day, they could not find a tree that was alive yet dry. They started crying once again. Just then a woodpecker appeared, and after listening to their trouble, it arranged the firewood for them. The new wife of their father was more furious and astonished in finding the children back with firewood as she had demanded. She gave them handful of wild tubers. The next day, she sent them to the forest to collect the eggs of wild hens. The children didn't know where to get the wild hens. Roaming all round the day, they could not even collect a feather of the hens. Soon it was dark, and they lost their way in the jungle. They saw fire burning at a distance. Following the glow, they came ultimately to the hut of an old couple. The old couple welcomed the kids, and listening to their suffering, the couple said, 'Oh poor babies. Stay here till your father returns'. They stayed there amid plenty of food and care, yet they missed their home. In the meantime, the man came back, and the new wife told him, 'The wicked children must have gone to the forest despite my regular warning'. That moment, the parrot cried out, 'Witch, witch. Look for your kids in the forest'. The new wife was actually a witch who had killed the daughter of the old couple residing in the forest and was staying as the wife of the children's father. The witch tried to kill the bird but failed in all her attempts. Giving a lemon to the man, the bird continued to utter, 'Eat this and then place your hand on the wife's head. Her reality will be revealed'. The woman ran to escape from the man. The bird asked the man to follow. The man ran fast to follow the flying bird. Ultimately they reached the front of the hut of the old couple. The witch wife fell down in front of the hut, and the moment the man touched her hair, he found the witch woman being transformed into another woman. The old couple rushed out of the hut and screamed out of their happiness: 'Oh our daughter'. The bird recounted to them the details of what had actually happened. After that, the man started living happily with the daughter of the old couple along with his children. Even the parrot became a family member.

The Witch Mother is a cleaned-up folktale where the adult Toto man can no longer choose to fall for a grandmother figure, but in the 'mainstream' normative mode, an almost arranged marriage has to get married to the adult daughter of the old woman. Yet the fantastic hybrid/in-between creatures, like the parrot, the witch as becoming woman and the woman as unbecoming witch, in their apparent defamiliarisation[17] allude to a story whose relevance goes much beyond the tale.

The widower protagonist, performing queer androgyny, engages in 'good-enough mothering' (see Donald Winnicott, 1953) of his two kids, by taking care of the household and disengaging himself from the 'mainstream' role of the working/earning man. The neighbours pressure him to remarry. But his anxiety against marriage hints at his liking for performing the feminine, which further suggests a latent homosexual inclination. Queering of kinship is best done by rendering heterosexual relationships as perilous or even fatal (Greenhill, 2008: 150), and the folktale, in the major part of its plot, seems to function as a critique of a remarried normative life. The remarriage has brought misery to the two kids to the extent of endangering their lives. The primordial Toto desire for the grandmother returns, however, in a chastised form of a nonerotic redeemer. The queer assumption is further validated by the fact that although the man remarries twice, in both the cases, he comes across magic real wives: first the witch as a becoming woman and then the resurrected dead woman as an unbecoming witch. Since 'make-believe [is] really another way of talking about the reality of things' (Wilson,1990: 214), the reality that one can trace behind the man's pseudo-normatised conjugality can possibly be that of a discreet queer leaning. The implied necrophilia, deducible through the man's marriage with a restored dead woman who's also a metamorphosed witch, validates the speculative homoeroticity. In the new regulative human ontology, as perceived by tribal people, where body has to be desired only within a functional heterosexual boundary, the counteraction of queer Indigeneity is best expressed through transgressing that functional boundary.

Representing the human through their nonhuman status, the totemic nonhuman creatures often symbolise some remote codes/estimations of conduct/desire that are undergoing vigilance, in the transitional society. The animals and birds in folktales often add an allegorical dimension to the folktales in the form of a 'structured system', creating 'a continuous parallel between two (or more) levels of meaning in a story' (Baldick, 1990: 5). The talking animals and the talking birds represent the collapse of language as means of genuine communication due to a prevailing state of 'emergency' characterised by a lack of human relationship—a lack that is the marker of a closely knit simple society being slowly replaced by its transformation into a complex postindustrial/techno one. It also conveys (the disillusionment/discomfort at) the rapid curtailment of tribal social values, established wisdom and knowledge from previous eras, after contact with the 'mainstream's' fastidious reverence for technology, biology and particular religion. From the transformed realm of existence, the once natural, for the tribal individual, might appear as anthropomorphic. The abundant presence that one can feel of the 'animalising' in Toto folktales also reveals the bio-centricity as well as the compulsion of the teller/composer/performer to revisit this biological history in order to frame the biological imagination through what Lawrence calls a 'blood consciousness', 'instinctive knowledge' and 'species intensity' (Norris, 1985: 191) as one's resistance against the altered social condition of a regulated/institutionalised compulsive heteronormativity. In this folktale, the warning parrot—guiding the male protagonist against the witch wife, revealing the hidden misdeeds of the witch in the manner of a comradeship and finally opting to live with him—also adds a parallel dimension of nonnormative eroticity to the apparently normative text. The parrot as a metaphor has often been connected with 'fire', 'revealer of the secrets', 'healer', and 'erotic love'.[18] In this folktale, the parrot represents all four symbolic connotations. As a beacon bearer for the man, guiding him towards his goal, it represents fire; it plays the 'revealer of secrets' by revealing not only the offences of the witch mother but also the homonormative insight that he might have been hiding from the redefined self; it might have been healing the man's wounds of repressing his ingrained homosexuality; and opting to be the companion of the tribal man, resisting to give up his Indigenous queer-continuum, the parrot becomes the projection of erotic love. The bird's identification of the lonely woman as a witch; its repetitive plea to the man to make him alert, with the implicit intention of resisting the marriage; the witch woman's attempts to kill it without success; and, most importantly, its appearance only as a companion of the man, in contradiction to the crane and the woodpecker, who appear to assist the kids in distress, turns the parrot into a queer 'thing with feathers' (Tatar, 2004: 122), flying into a story of liberation for an Indigenous gay man to ascertain the possible in excess of the real.[19] The homonormativity can be established as counternormative, not in the transformed tribal world monopolised by the heteronormative instruments, but elsewhere; however the bird's choice to cohabit with the man brings the elsewhere home, through flights of fantasy. Fantasy alone holds the freedom to imagine the normatised self and 'other' as the normal otherwise. The ending of the folktale also offers a sense of an end of the reproductive futurism induced by normatisation, for unlike the other tales, although the man is wedded to the grandmother's magic real daughter, there is no narrating of their producing of 'many children' in order for them to live happily ever after. The man is happy because the folktale ends with the assurance of a counternormative, counterhegemonic queer alliance: 'Even the parrot became a family member'.[20] Thus, as a metanarrative, the folktale argues for the possibility of another 'crooked' account, parallel to the straight story of two kids, a wedded couple and an non-amorous grandmother.

Dissident intimacies

The tribal folktales of disgruntlement concerning the 'mainstream' civilising schema are not mere preposterous inventions but rather the outcome of experiences.[21] A psychoanalytic reading of the Toto 'structures of phantasy' (Abraham, 1913: 72), as reflected in their tales, helps us take a historical view of the wishes made in prehistoric times.[22] A queer reading not only elucidates folktales as documentation in the form of fantasies by an individual compelled to repress the Indigenous body idiom but also expounds on the tribal dissident desire to sustain the erotic collective that was gradually stigmatised and treated as abject by the 'feeling rules'.[23] The three tales categorised under the title of 'Dissident intimacies'—*The Naked Orphan, Seven Brothers and One Sister* and *Wild Hen and Her Son*—masking the undercurrent of deviant desires with magic real instruments and apparently normatised plot, impart a metahistoric trajectory of external repression and internal repercussions through phantasy. This helps in filling the gap between the present-day fallout of historical fabrication and prehistoric truth.[24]

Tale 5: The Naked Orphan

There was a time long back when an orphan man used to stay with his son and daughter. Removing his clothes, one day he started to play and shout near the king's waterfall. The daughters of the king found him playing and they went to inform the king of his presence near their waterfall. The king thought that he might have been a possible bridegroom and asked the daughters to call him inside. Seeing the naked orphan, the king proposed that the orphan choose any one of his two daughters as his woman. The orphan opted for the youngest one. Putting the clothes on, he took permission from the king and started returning to his house, along with the king's youngest daughter, who was crying out of the premonition that the orphan must have been a very poor fellow. Reaching his house, the king's daughter, however, was happy to find the house a good one with ample cattle heads and food. Three days later, the couple went to the king's house for the betrothal ceremony. Being uneasy, the orphan returned with the wife, inviting the king to visit his place. The king visited him, accordingly, in the evening, along with the elder daughter, and was very pleased to see the house full of abundance. The king arranged for the wedding, and once it was over within a few days, he asked the son-in-law and his youngest daughter to accompany him. The orphan stayed back while his wife went to the father's house, along with her elder sister. The orphan then started preparing his own food and arranged his own bed all by himself. One day when he woke up in the morning, he found breakfast was already being prepared. He thought not to sleep in the night, but soon fell asleep. Yet early in the morning, he woke up to find someone going out of the house after preparing the food. He caught her and found that she was none but his newly married wife. She described how her elder sister, being jealous of her marriage to the wealthy orphan, killed her by pushing her into the king's water pool. The orphan started sweating out of rage and told her to stay with him. He called the elder daughter of the king and thrashed her hard. The king too didn't allow the elder daughter to step into his house. Thereafter, the orphan stayed with the younger daughter of the king as his real wife and led a peaceful life ever after.

The title of the Toto tale, *The Naked Orphan*, is provocative. The fact that the person, despite having a son and a daughter, was abandoned like an orphan hints at his unease with the heteronormative family. His nakedness becomes the criterion for eligibility to be considered by the king as his would-be son-in-law. The daughters do not respond to the man's nakedness, but the king then and there concludes that he is a credible bridegroom. This queer measure of the king staying with his two daughters, where the queen is absent, can be regarded as a projective inversion where the homosocial king tries to fulfil his nonnormative longing to remain connected with the naked man by asking him to take any of his daughters. The man stays naked during his communication with the king till he starts for his home, only to return to the king after three days. He feels uncomfortable and decides to leave the king's house. This uneasiness can be the outcome of homophobia, and the conflict in the tribal queer is manifested by his in-betweenness as well as desirability, indicated by his asking the king to visit him before leaving the king's place. The king comes to him that evening. He does not come alone, but with the elder daughter as an agent who, again in the mode of projective inversion, executes his desired mission of annihilating the heteronormativity of the orphan man. The orphan man in the expected queer trajectory prefers the real deceased wife and thrashes the elder sister before she is thrown out of the house. The hostility again highlights the antipathy towards and wrath against normatisation. In the same way, by driving the elder daughter out of the house, the king with the forlorn status becomes the perfect match for the orphan, who is now left with a phantom wife as the only remainder of his performative heteronormative episode. The story thus hints at the togetherness of two males with two kids, which indeed for two tribal queers, as the story suggests, is a happy gay family for a peaceful life.

Tale 6: Seven Brothers and One Sister

Once upon a time in a village, a sister used to stay with her seven brothers. Apart from the youngest one, all the six brothers were married. One day when the seven brothers left the village for the bartering trade, the six wives planned to kill the sister. On the seventh day, when the brothers were supposed to return, the six jealous wives, on the pretext of removing the lice from her hair, took the youngest sister by the edge of the river and pushed her into deep water, where she drowned. On the way towards their home, the eldest among the brothers heard a yelling voice while crossing the river. Addressing the voice, he said, 'If the voice is from someone outside the family, please come to the fold of my garment on the right side, else if the voice is of some family members, then come to the garment fold on left side'. But no one retorted. All the six brothers experienced the same. But only when the youngest one addressed the voice did a bird suddenly appear and enter the pocket-like fold of his garment on the left side. The youngest brother thought of gifting the exceptionally beautiful bird to his sister. Entering the house when the brothers looked for the sister, the wives started giving various false excuses. One said that she had gone to fetch water; another said that she had gone to play. Keeping the bird at home, the brothers left to look for the sister. In the meantime, the wives killed the bird and cooked it. On their coming back home, the wives informed their husbands about their cooking and eating the bird. While the youngest brother was about to eat, the pet cat approached him for some rice and promised to provide him with a bone of the bird. Being fed with some rice, the happy cat vomited out a piece of the bird's bone on a heap of ash and asked the youngest brother to preserve that bone, after which he wrapped it in cotton. The youngest brother followed the instruction only to discover that each day the shape of the bone was changing bit by bit till it took the full shape of the youngest sister. Finally, the sister emerged out in her full form and narrated the entire incident of the brutality of the six wives on the seven brothers. The brothers drove their wives, after thrashing them hard, out of the home. Then they all got married later on again and began to live separately. The sister also got married to a young good man. After she died, her soul turned into a parrot.

The mute avoidance of any specificity is a hallmark of all Toto tales which deal with subsequent prohibitions.[25] The normative principles dumped upon the tribal culture by the 'mainstream', as a manipulative transition from what has been officially propagated as 'animal man' to 'civilised man', is based on the negation of Indigenous sensuality/sensibility. Consensual adult incest, not necessarily always aimed at reproduction, involves the recreational aspect of sex which the 'mainstream' rigorously tries to deny in its associating compulsive reproducibility with sexuality, making it fully utilitarian and thereafter banning all other intimacies as illicit. Consensual adult incest among the ethnic community also demonstrates the endogamous strategy of what Clifford Geertz calls the theatre state (Geertz, 1980) tactics of Indigeneity by which incest as a coherent practise could announce the ethnic superiority of the tribes over the nontribals: 'surely recurrent in human history, our innate alertness to the emotional complexity of incest can be turned to precise political ends' (Wolf and Durham, 2005: 156). Hence, for the hegemonic settler colonialism, incest had to be negated by regulating it as a taboo in order to counter tribal individuality. This radical negation is best expressed through an obsessional drive for what has to be avoided, especially as a response to the eruption of incest as a taboo. The tribal tales highlight an insurgence against imposed obscenity, on the basis of the premise that 'the prohibition is there to be violated' (Bataille, 2001: 64). A study centred on normatising regulations can illustrate how the levied incest taboo has been recast either as a reviving Indigenous desire that can never be overcome but handled with composure or to be calculatingly transported to the realm of nonhuman as projective inversion.

Seven Brothers and One Sister tracks the detour of tabooed adult incest through discomfort. The incestuous liking of the youngest brother for the sister is obvious not only for the fact that he is unmarried but rather because of the fact that only when he has addressed the voice, the bird, as the metaphorical memento of the sister does enter his pocket at the very left side, symbolic of the human heart and its connotative desirability. Further, his attempt to 'eat' (the confluence of food and sex in folktales has already been laid out) the bird, in which the cat intervenes to stop him,[26] registers the natural propensity to engage in incest.[27] The sister has to be dead, because the Toto brother, in the course of a structured transition, needs to be dissociated from nature and needs to conform with culture through the tabooing of incest and a prescriptive social contact with the nontribal world in the form of exogenous marriage, which necessarily weakens endogamous tribal cohesion, represented by the separate homes for each married brother.[28]

The cat is a trickster, yet it fails to curb the incestuous drive. Like an imperishable phoenix, the desired sister emerges out of the ash. The seemingly normative end ironically hints at the fragility of the aversion. The incest seems to be successfully removed only in relation to a magic real, dead-yet-alive sister, allowing space for the desire to be retained for the real one. The rebirth of the sister in the form of a parrot, which has already been established as a metaphor of transgressive desire in the previous tale of *The Witch Mother*, further emphasises the Toto resistance, with the possible return of the domesticable parrot to the desiring youngest brother. The desire turned into a taboo that cannot be practised, due to the imposed exogamy, however, is made public through the parrot's harmonies of protest.

Tale 7: Wild Hen and Her Son

A long, long time ago, at the very outset, when there was no human being on earth but only water and forests everywhere, there lived a wild hen and an old cock, as the world's primordial creatures, in the dense forest. There was plenty of food for them, and they were living very happily, by earnestly loving one other. In the morning, they would visit the forest for food and return in the evening. However, the happiness did not last for long. One day, the wild hen started laying eggs and the husband was happy that they would have a number of children to help in the work as well as look after them in their old age. While the hen started incubating the eggs, the cock went to the forest to bring food for the hen. One day, the husband left for the forest but never returned. The wife kept on waiting but in vain. Similarly, all her attempts to hatch the eggs were futile. At last, one egg hatched, and a baby cock emerged. Time passed, and the boy grew up. He asked the mother about her father. She recounted how the father vanished into the forest. The boy went in search of the father in the forest but could not find him. Returning to the house, he told his mother, 'Father must have been eaten up by the forest animals'. Remaining silent for some time, the mother said, 'Since now, none but we exist alone, we need to have children. From today onwards, there would remain no relation of mother, father, brother, sister among us'. Since then, they began to stay as husband and wife and gave birth to a number of offspring.

The Toto folktale *Wild Hen and Her Son* begins where *Seven Brothers and One Sister* ends. In a more vigorous mode of affirmative abjection, it celebrates the 'mainstream' equation that links tribalism with wildness: the mother wild hen as an Indigenous anarcho-dissident contumaciously enters into an incestuous coupling with her grown-up male progeny. Because the son is grown up, he is not robbed of the agency which one generally comes across in a stereotyped portrayal of incestuous relationships among mothers taking advantage of minor sons. This situation negates the axiom of abuse promulgated by the tabooed 'mainstream', time and again adding a paedophilic overtone to mother–son incest. The wild hen and her son exhibit incest as a consciously decided participation.

On the basis of Uexküll's ethology as biological ontology (Uexküll, 1985), Jesper Hoffmeyer has talked about the message-bearing 'intentionality' of animality. According to him, organisms are potential embodiments of anticipatory power, by which they exhibit the 'aboutness' of their body in relation to their environment (Hoffmeyer, 1993). In the period of an indoctrinated tabooing of incest, a political shifting of incest from human to the untamed nonhuman plane of the wild hen and her son, as becoming-animals, reminds us that 'Becoming-minoritarian is a political affair' (Deleuze and Guattari, 1988: 292), and the folktale demonstrates that the tribal community had attempted to deviate from majoritarian power through becomings, which 'always imply a deterritorialization out of the molar regime (Subject or State) that blocks the molar capacities to generate affect and to be affected in a great number of ways' (Beaulieu, 2011: 77). The talking hen and talking cock, as becoming animals, reveal the dissidence against shrewd modifications imposed on Toto outlooks regarding their notion of relationships: with themselves, with other bodies and with the inverted environment.

Evil as emancipation

Convinced that evil is 'in the eye of the beholder', Ronald Paulson has declared that 'evil is a cultural construct' (Paulson, 2007: xiii). The 'mainstream' notion of evil is essentially the cultural imperialistic design of the neocolonial 'national bourgeoisie that took the baton of rationalization, industrialization, and bureaucratization in the name of nationalism, [that] turned out to be a kleptocracy' (Appiah, 1991: 349). A deconstructive reading of the folktales—*The Story of Itspa and Her Uncle Pidua Coming of the Rivers* and *Why the Totos Take Beef*—reveals that the tribal community has taken a neotraditional turn to the treatment of evil so that the Totos are able to oppose both the 'mainstream' aesthetics of modernism and the usurping politics of modernisation that has been imposed on Indigeneity.

Tale 8: The Story of Itspa and Her Uncle Pidua

Once upon a time, in the north there was a hill named Badu with a stream flowing at its foothill, which was the abode of the deities like Itspa and the rest. The entire place was so densely covered with forest that even during the daytime one would feel scared to visit the place on account of the demons. Even the animals and birds were afraid of the evil spirits and demons who resided there. Pidua, who is also known as Moishing, is a deity who is enormous in shape, almost like a black bear. Being stubborn, he was beyond the control of the parents, even right from his boyhood. That ultimately detached him from the family, and he turned into a vagrant. Meanwhile, Sainjani (Itspa), the daughter of Pidua's elder brother, reached adolescence, and her body was in full bloom like the full-flooded hill stream. Her hairs resembled the black bats of the forests. She roamed around with her female companions like a peacock roaming around the jungle. One day while Sainjani was gathering fruits and tubers in the Ti-tring forest, she got trapped by a ghost who used to misguide people, and consequently, she was isolated from and was all alone. Wandering all alone, she was by a river bed with a small water pool. Being thirsty, she tried to drink water from the pool, and that was the very first moment when she saw her shadow, cast on the pool water. She got so captivated by her own beauty that she fancied taking a bath in the river in order to enhance her prettiness; accordingly, she undressed herself. Just then, a strong wind blew over the forest, and Pidua arrived with the storm. He had no notion of Sainjani, as he was disconnected from his family. Looking at the beauty of Sainjani, he failed to resist his temptation, so he jumped on Sainjani to ravish her. However, coming to her senses within a short while, she realized what had been actually happening to her. Being a daughter of a god, she was a brave girl who could easily defeat and finally cut off Pidua's head with her *patang* (sword). Sainjani's father appeared on the scene; having informed by friends that she had been lost in the forest, he was on a search for her. He was shocked to hear the entire incident and introduced the daughter to his brother, by asking Sainjani to forgive her uncle and transplant his head. Despite being sorry for her uncle, Itspa said that since she could hardly trust Pidua, she wanted him to promise that he would never try to play mischief on anyone in future. Pidua's head was still talking, and he agreed to her proviso. Itspa transplanted his head, but in a reversed position so that Pidua could never look directly at anyone, because she was still apprehensive of his misconducts. Pidua then and there left the place, along with his supporters, while Itspa and her father went back to the heavenly habitat on the hilltop of the Badu.

Itspa, in *The Story of Itspa and Her Uncle Pidua*, is the supreme god of the Totos. Being intersex, Itspa is sometimes referred to as Sanja (he god) and sometimes, Sainjani (she god). Itspa is the deity (head) of a clan that used to be primarily food gatherers,[29] and due to the transition initiated by the presence of the nontribal agricultural communities, the clan is also partially exposed to agriculture (Majumdar, 1991: 128). In the altered Toto world-view, Itspa becomes the epitome of 'culture' by internalising the 'civil' traits of the alien 'mainstream', while Pidua, the head of nomadic hunting clan, is the epitome of nature which is instinctive and therefore, from the nontribal invaders' point of view, discourteous. The enforcement of a framed binary of good and evil on the basis of the dichotomy between the embodiments of the culture (propagated by governmental and non-Indigenous agencies) and the nature (connoting the Indigeneity which is often seen by the 'mainstream' as uncivilised and uncultured) is clear. For the non-Indigenous agricultural community, sex is the utilitarian act of providing offspring and thereby revered from the stance of a fertility cult. For the hunting clan, sex is free from any motif of a functional dimension added to it and thereby unregulated. Moreover, as has already been discussed, premarital sex has been a common practice in Toto society. Hence, Pidua's arrival just before the nude Itspa has been schemed, following a much-acknowledged Toto norm where it has been a regular practice for a young Toto girl to be intimate with anyone who approaches her.

The unsought imposition of nonnormativity on non-'mainstream' desire instigated from the *outward* (resulting in sullying Pidua as evil) as opposed to the yearning for desire that has yet to be labelled as evil from *within* is conveyed by Itspa's initial spontaneous response. She is said to have come to her normatised senses, however, only after having spontaneously involved with the docketed 'evil' of relishing the pleasant sensual delight with Pidua for some time, before she could remind herself of the imposed norms that cannot be violated. The figure of Itspa's father as the transgressive tribal man, who is ready to forgive Pidua, becomes the representative of the tribal resistance against all that has been framed as evil by the state. He seems to understand that the evil in the form of the Indigenous Pidua is only a weak creature that needs the help and prayer of the tribal community as supports

81

against the 'mainstream' biopower.[30] The restoration of Pidua's head is symbolic of the failure of the corrective/functional/restrictive governmental directive of annihilating the projected evil over that which has been accepted as natural. Even Itspa, knowing well that Pidua won't change, transplants his head. The reverse transplanting is again figurative: Pidua, the signifier of that which has been categorised as evil, is the desire that can never be overcome by the tribal group; hence it has to be prudently admitted but never accepted. Itspa's impromptu intimacy with Pidua, tagged as evil, and her later choice of reviving him, knowing well that his promise for reparation can hardly be trusted, highlight the 'radical' character of evil as a component of human nature, which 'implies the propensity in the human being towards evil' (Coeckelbergh, 2004: 344) and validates the Kantian notion that this radical evil depends not on the nature or will of human beings but on 'a free power of choice' (Kant, 2009: 59).[31] By the emancipatory choice of enlivening Pidua, Itspa actually chooses to deny the index of evil that has been tagged with every Toto ethnocentric outlook, which is contradictory to the dominant mindset of the 'mainstream'.

Tale 9: Coming of the Rivers

There was a time long ago when even though there were no rivers or streams on earth, there were enough water pools on top of the hills as well, due to which no one suffered from water scarcity. One day Pidua, after hiding the water into the belly of the hills, pushed the clouds away from the sky. The people prayed to Itspa Shainjha for rescue. Trying to trace the disappeared clouds and water, he asked the hills and jungles, who had the gift of speech. But both lied to him and didn't help him. Then Itspa asked the moon, to which the moon suggested he ask the sun, since sun travels the path all through the day more frequently than the moon. On being questioned, the sun hinted at the bellies of the hills. Itspa, who was shivering with wrath, hit the hills with his sword and the water stored inside them, came spouting out in the form of rivers and streams. Owing to their falsehood before Itspa, the forests and the hills lost their power to speak.

As an instance of inverse projection, Itspa the god figure, in *Coming of the Rivers*, becomes the symbol for the cultural imperialists, thereby suggesting a rise in the stern regime of censorship by this transformational shift. The god figure in the ironic image of Itspa is made to represent the intolerance of the neocolonial state. The folktale begins with the description of the self-sufficiency of the Totos on account of their natural resources, namely water. Pidua, the preset evil, hides the water as one of the vital natural resources from being exploited by the colonisers. Playing the strategies of the invaders, the internal coloniser in the form of the god figure Itspa is shown to have fooled the tribals by pretending to be their redeemer: the Indigenous lot comes to the exploiter disguised as protector for help. Recognising the latent capitalist motive, the benefactors of Indigeneity in the form of hills and jungles, symbolising the exact topography of Totopara, decide not to assist the god figure and instead become the supporters of Pidua. However, after receiving assistance from the sun, reminding us of Bataille's sun/anus allegory,[32] the true colour of the camouflaged god figure gets exposed through the act of extracting water from Toto resources and thereafter by victimising the custodians of Indigeneity by turning them into subalterns—unable to protest against or speak about the essential evil of the pseudo-good god figure, intimately associated with the power equation of authority.[33] The hill and the forest choose not to help the god-like avatar of capitalism but the evil Pidua, which shows the Totos' consciously counter-equating evil with emancipation: 'evil is due to human freewill' (Mackie, 1990: 33).

Tale 10: Why the Totos Take Beef

The Totos were not beef eaters in ancient times, and they never killed cows. However, they were compelled to do so after an incident. Once, the Totos during one of their hunting sessions killed an animal which they thought to be a sambar (deer). They seasoned it with rice and iu (traditional liquor), and before going to sleep, the mondal (chief) took a bamboo pole and hung the head of the animal on it, to be consumed the next day. Early at dawn, the head priest and mondal summoned the community for an urgent gathering, where mondal recounted his dream, in which Itspa took offence for not offering him the food that they had hunted. Itspa demanded that the mondal offer him the next day the same animal that they had hunted the previous day. Hearing this, people brought down the head that they had hung on the pole, only to discover with utter shock that what they had thought to be a sambar was actually a cow. But since it was the order of the deity, they had to perform the religious ceremony, and that was when the Toto people started offering beef both to the deities and to themselves. The king of Coochbehar, having heard about the sacrificing of the cow, which was prohibited, expelled the Totos from his kingdom. They were given refuge by the king of Bhutan for some time and, thereafter, they returned to Totopara.

If in the former folktale, Itspa gets projected as the replaced icon of the malevolent invaders, then in *Why the Totos Take Beef*, Itspa becomes the tribal agency of rebelling against prohibitions. Although the Totos say that they had been nonconsumers of beef in the past, the mistake of treating the cow as a sambar hints at their narrating antiquity in a way to placate Hindutva imperials.

It is interesting to recall that Marquis de Sade dismantled 'civilisation' as a conspiracy by which the weak 'mainstream' tries to shackle the strong non-civil 'natural' by naming it as 'evil'.[34] Mondal, being the head and, thereby, the representative of the group, however, fails to suppress the transgressive desire for the prohibited/evil which surfaces in his dream. Freud and Oppenheim have assured us that the narrators of dreams in folk literature often use a pretext of premonition[35] to hide their awareness of the fulfilment of their hidden wishes (Freud and Oppenheim, 1958: 25). To counter the coloniser king's order, Mondal, as the spokesperson of tribal transgressive desire, politically insets the desire of the tribal deity Itspa, who demands the consumption of beef that was prohibited as evil by the empire-building non-tribals. Mondal easily gets the mass sanction in normalising that which was once-prohibited through the sacrificial offering of beef to the deity. Finally, the Totos' desire for the nonnormative transgression, labelled as evil, triumphs over the fear of the sovereign, who expels them only to find their coming home after a short refuge in Bhutan.

C. Fred Alford's *What Evil Means to Us* concludes that evil is 'not a state of mind, but a state of world' (Alford, 1997: 15). Evil, according to him, is 'no-thing' (ibid.: ix)—that is, 'the nothingness we dread' (ibid.: 15), the nothingness that results from 'the loss of self, loss of meaning, loss of history and loss of connection to the world itself' (ibid.: ix). Alford's existential notion of evil shows that evil is more experiential. Even merely being human is to keep up a correspondence with evil: 'doing evil is an attempt to transform the terrible passivity and helplessness of suffering into activity' (ibid.: 3). Placing Indigeneity in a paranoid-schizoid position where the tribal community dreads its 'doom at the hands of malevolent external persecutors who seek to destroy' them (ibid.: 40), the Toto folktales confirm that the tribal people choose to be party to the 'mainstream' notion of evil, and as an 'evildoer', Indigeneity nevertheless tries to claim its authority over the gaze of the domineering Other.[36]

Towards a sexual democracy

Raymond Williams has cogently defined culture as the manifestation of a collective pluralist move of heterogeneous people where every individual participates in the structuring and restructuring of a culture, through multiple contacts and amendments under pressure, which ultimately endeavours for common expression in arts and learning, often made and remade by the individuals of the collectivity (Williams, 1989: 4). Culture, hence, is the indicator of plurality and revisions. The Toto folktales—ranging from the assertive nonhuman, eloquent about the queer transgressive desire, to the exhaustive use of fantasy, transbiology and magic realism—bring out the gradual

muting of the plural voices of alternative sexuality/eroticism under a growing transitional/neotraditional society, where multiple modifications in the
narrative have to be made on account of the increasing pressures exerted by
an 'other' culture coming into contact with a suppressive authority.

The Toto tribal tales, despite multiple revisions, can be seen to have
approved queer desire as an accepted Indigenous trait and non-heterogeneity
as an approved tribal norm. Toto as an ethnic tribe is destined, like all other
Fourth World communities, to be the centre of the 'inclusive' nation-building agenda of the Third World state. Such inclusion is in the end exclusion-
ary. As a sexual minority of the Third World, one can easily relate to the
counternormative tribalism that is reflected in the Toto folktales and that
strives for a sexual emancipation. As opposed to the 'chronomyopia'[37] of
governmentality, emerging out of the overestimation of the colonial documented time as history, where queerness is viewed as an unusual peril to be
sociopolitically victimised, the remaining larger portion of undocumented
history of the pro-queer ethnocentric outlook of these Indigenous tribal
communities, like the Toto, needs to be unfolded as the ground for claiming sexual democracy. For queer people now, it appears to be an accepted
maxim that the only way to look for legitimisation is to consider 'the personal as political'. But for the personal to fully develop, by the reorganisa-
tion of a queerphobic social order, the political has to be motivated towards
'the possibility of the *radical democratization* of the personal' (Giddens,
1992: 182), which intimately depends on the emancipation of sexuality.
The queer reading of the Toto tales by an anarcho-dissident non-Indigenous
ally in this book is an attempt to initiate the dialogic collaboration towards
democratising desire and sexuality.

Notes

1 For a deconstructive reading of the utopian function of folktales, see Bloch,
  1987.
2 Gert Ueding suggested that the unreal elements of folktales intend 'to tear the
  affairs of human culture from the superstructure and sort them out from that
  ideology which legitimates and glorifies a society with false consciousness' (Ueding, 1976: 1, 22).
3 I borrowed the term from the title of a book by Masud Zavarzadeh, *The Mythopoeic Reality: The Postwar American Nonfiction Novel*, which is a similar study
  of 'a zone of experience where the factual is not secure or unequivocal but seems
  preternaturally strange and eerie, and where the fictional seems not all that ficti-
  tious, remote and alien, but bears an uncanny resemblance to daily experience'
  (1976: 56).
4 The version that I found in my fieldwork is almost similar to Bimalendu Majumdar's English translation of Toto tales, published in 1991.
5 None of the storytellers whom I interviewed knew English.
6 For an alternative reading of the tale, see Chakraborty (2020b).
7 Munoz observed that 'queerness has existed as innuendo . . . fleeting moments,
  and performances' (Muñoz, 1996: 6).

8 The grandmother's attempt to 'eat' the pumpkin is a gastronomic metaphor for a latent sexual motif of 'appetite'.

9 See Sedgwick, 1993: xii, where she states that

> something about *queer* is inextinguishable. Queer is a continuing moment, movement, motive—recurrent, eddying, *troublant*. . . . The queer . . . is transitive—multiply transitive. The immemorial current that queer represents is antiseparatist as it is antiassimilationist. Keenly, it is relational, and strange.

10 'Throughout the cultures and epochs, metaphors of consumption act as a major symbolic vehicle to both convey and shape concepts of sexuality, agency and gender identity' (Andrievskikh, 2014: 137).

11 The hyperbole suggests a counter-discourse, against viewing queer as incomplete, depicting queer as superior over a mere commoner.

12 According to Jonathan P. Rosman and Phillip J. Resnick, the following is one of the psychodynamic events which can lead to necrophilia: 'He (usually male) is very fearful of rejection by women, and he desires a sexual object who is incapable of rejecting him' (1989: 161).

13 Melanie Klein has asserted that for a child, the mother's breast that is the primary source of gratified pleasure becomes the target of the fantasies, manifested through the child's oral aggression, which are 'of a definitely cannibalistic nature': 'In his imagination the child attacks (the mother's body), robbing it of everything it contains and eating it up' (1975: 293).

14 The old woman comes to the orphan boy's household for the first time and asks for a pamelo even though the tree was destroyed by his ogress wife. This again proves that the pamelo tree must have been one of the agents about which she has prior knowledge.

15 In many tribal cultures, the pig is the symbol of an unrestrained desire that is both sensual and courageous. However, from the nontribal majoritarian perspective, pig mostly stands for uncleanness.

16 Fox, as the symbolic projection of 'sly', arriving in 'darkness' represents the dubious hegemonic mechanisms of the state. Perhaps the governmental agencies and their intrusion in Toto ecology have been metaphorically revealed as the fox, unascertained by its hidden approach in the dark for hindering the heterogeneity of the tribal sociocultural praxes under the pretext of facilitation.

17 For Shklovsky, defamiliarisation is equivalent to either a euphemistic use of elucidating dissonance in the apparently harmonious contexts or parallelism, which, according to him, is 'to transfer the usual perception of an object into the sphere of a new perception'. Thus, for him, the nonhuman creatures acting like human beings, in the mode of defamiliarisation, actually throws different light on outlawed social and moral issues (Shklovsky, 1988: 26–27).

18 Parrot, according to the Amahuaca of Eastern Peru, has stolen fire from the giant Yowashiko for humankind to survive. In Afro-Caribbean folklore parrot is shown as revealer of secrets and bringer of messages. The Yanomami people of the Amazonian basin treat the feathers of parrot as a healing piece. In the Hindu image of Kamadev, the god of erotic love, a parrot is shown to be carrying him while he shoots his arrows of desire. See Cassandra Eason (2008) for details.

19 According to Sedgwick (1993: 8), queers often take the identity of storytellers and fantasists for self-description. Here the narrator as a fantasist storyteller augments the surety of being queer.

20 Although the title of chapter 6 in Radhika Govindrajan's book (2018) is 'The Bear Who Loved a Woman: The Intersection of Queer Desires', focusing on the tales of women–bear intimacies, Govindrajan has mainly tried to emphasis how women express their sexual needs and try to have control over their sexuality by retelling these tales. But there is no discussion on the possibility, if at all, of any same-sex desire.

21 According to Jung, 'The primitive mentality does not invent myths, it experiences them. Myths are original revelations of the preconscious psyche, involuntary statements about unconscious psychic happenings, and anything but allegories of physical processes' (1963: 73).

22 'The race, in prehistoric times, makes its wishes into structures of phantasy, which as myths reach over into the historical ages' (Abraham, 1913: 72).

23 Jung has rightly observed that

> fantasies (including dreams) of an impersonal character . . . have their closest analogues in mythological types. We must therefore assume that they correspond to certain collective (and not personal) structural elements of the human psyche in general, and, like the morphological elements of the human body, are inherited.
>
> (Jung, 1963: 74)

'Feeling rules' denote the rules that govern collective nature and the means of displaying the expected/inherited emotions.

24

> [T]he primal phantasies . . . are a phylogenetic endowment. . . . all the things that are told to us to-day in analysis as phantasy . . . were once real occurrences in the primaeval times of the human family, and that . . . phantasies are simply filling in the gaps in individual truth with prehistoric truth.
>
> (Freud, 1916: 370–371)

25 'Therefore there exists an aspect of the transition from animal to man so radically negative that it remains unspoken' (Bataille, 2001: 215).

26 The cat is often associated with malice and is a symbol of bad luck in India.

27 Citing how people instinctively, and not because of any fear of legal penalties, try to move their hands away from fire, Frazer, while explaining how law often forbids what people instinctively try to perform, remarked that

> Instead of assuming, therefore, from the legal prohibition of incest that there is a natural aversion to incest, we ought rather to assume that there is a natural instinct in favour of it, and that if the law represses it . . . because civilized men have come to the conclusion that the satisfaction of these natural instincts is detrimental to the general interests of society.
>
> (Frazer, 1910: 97–98)

28 For Lévi-Strauss, culture, by its punishing rules, polices the natural 'incest-inclining' as a taboo. See *The Elementary Structures of Kinship* for details.

29 Itspa has been shown as going to the forest with the women, to gather food.

30 Agamben argues that

> the devil is the only weakest of creatures. . . . not only can it not do us harm, but on the contrary it is what most needs our help and our

prayers. It is, in every being that exists, the possibility of not-being that silently calls for our help (or, if you wish, the devil is nothing other than divine impotence or the power of not-being in God).

(2009: 31–32)

31

[T]here is in the human being a natural propensity to evil. . . . This evil is *radical*, since it corrupts the ground of all maxims; as natural propensity, it is also not to be *extirpated* through human forces, for this could happen only through good maxims- something that cannot take place if the subjective supreme ground of all maxims is presupposed to be corrupted.

(Kant, 2009: 59)

32 In 'The Solar Anus', Bataille seems to make a crucial dark parody of the sun. The point of analogy between sun and anus seems to be made on the basis of the sun's role in eliminating harvest and giving rise to drought, similar to the excretory function of anus. For details, see Bataille, 1985b. In the article 'Bataille's "The Solar Anus" or the Parody of Parodies', Leslie Anne Boldt-Irons suggests that sun in 'The Solar Anus' becomes the parody of the elevated status, which the mainstream demands, as opposed to commonality (in this context the tribalism), as described by Bataille (Boldt-Irons, 2001: 362).

33 In *The Lucifer Effect* (2007), Zimbardo has illustrated how evil is intimately associated with the power equation of authority.

34 See the introduction to *Oxford World's Classics: The Marquis de Sade, The Crimes Of Love*, where David Coward argues that from the novels of Sade, it is clear that the prohibitive rules of a society pervert the natural order by criminalising the instincts on the basis of which nature operates through human beings:

> Civilization is a conspiracy of the weak, who invented religion, morality, law, . . . to shackle the strong. In so doing they have meddled with the necessary indifference of nature which they name Evil, and to it have preferred the Good, which is an illusion
>
> (Sade, 2005: xxii)

35 As per the opinion of Freud and Oppenheim, the symbolism involved in the dreams narrated in the folklore coincides with that accepted in psychoanalysis. They further state

> that a number of these dreams are understood by the common people in the same way as they would be interpreted by psychoanalysis—that is, not as premonitions about a still unrevealed future, but as the fulfillment of wishes, the satisfaction of needs which arise during the state of sleep.
>
> (1958: 25)

36 The gaze of the 'other', according to Sartre, is 'a limit of my freedom . . . it is given to me as a burden which I have to carry without ever being able to turn back to know it, without even being able to realize its weight' (Sartre, 1989: 262). One has to invalidate the active gaze of the 'other' to assert the existence of the self. Sartre argues that 'the Other has to make my being-for-him being so far as he has to be his being' (ibid.). This establishes that the autonomy and subjectivity of others demands the loss of integrity of the self. Sartre's notion of the gaze of the subject finds its match in Alford's idea of the evildoer who exercises the authority of the self to claim power over the 'other'.

37 Chronomyopia, as Robin Fox has elucidated, refers to one's fixation that prompts one to overrate the present by labelling the familiar as 'history' at the cost of

> relegating more than 99 percent of human existence to 'prehistory'—a mere run-up to the real thing. It would be more logical to label hominids up to, say, the invention of tools, as 'past man', those from thence until the Neolithic revolution as 'present man' and immediate humans as 'late man'.
>
> (Fox, 2011: 16)

4

DISCORD AS DEFILEMENT

Consensual incest in Limbu folktales and 'mainstreaming' the feminine

Any stigma, as the old saying is, will serve to beat a dogma.
(Guedalla, 2007: 150)

Disagreement clearly has not to do with words alone. It generally bears on the very situation in which speaking parties find
themselves.
(Ranciere, 1998: xi)

The Limbu community, on the basis of the ethno-religious views, where
the only supreme goddess of Yumanism[1] is Tagera Ningwaphuma whose
cosmic consciousness and eternal 'motherhood' give rise to all other crea-
tions, privileges the feminine as the principium reality. The radical element
in Yumanism lies in its hierarchical trinitarianism, where both the First
Reality, Tagera Ningwaphuma, and Yuma Sam, her daughter-cum-heir and
the second person in the Trinitarian order, are female deities to be followed
by the third Person, Thoba Pa-Sam or Hang-Sam, the masculine component
originating out of the primordial womanhood. Hence, Yumanism teaches
the Limbu, unlike most of the 'mainstream' religions of India, to provide the
feminine with the foremost agency of even defying the grip of the masculine.
This essential difference of beholding the feminine disposition with a high
esteem is indeed in discord with the patriarchal denigration of womanhood
that is often central to the 'mainstream' socioreligious stance.

Adding more discomfort to the 'mainstream' moral patrol, the Limbu
woman seems to violate most of the 'mainstream' codes of good conduct
prescribed for an 'ideal *devi* in the house' by the patriarchy. Although Limbu
society is not free from taboos, the interesting part lies in the fact that the
characters in Limbu folktales who often transgress the taboos are mostly the
defiant women, unlike the 'mainstream' projection of Indian men, who seem
to be the sole dynamos in challenging taboos while the 'mainstream' women
(contrary to the Western discourse of the rebellious Eve) are always conscious
of and concerned with reinforcing tabooed convictions—for example, Sita

and Savitri are the icons who are supposed to be revered by 'mainstream' majoritarian Indian women and not the nonconforming Draupadi.

The study of select Limbu folktales would enable us to understand how, like the totem father of Freud, the 'mainstream', after trespassing into the Limbu domain, has been suffering from moral panic that has initiated it to engage with the task of 'civilising' the mountain tribes by solidifying taboos among its discontents. Unlike the structuralists' semiotic framing of motifs, Wilhelm Dilthey's poetics (1887) aimed at understanding the 'inner experience' of the 'mental life' treated motif as the dominant symptom of the circumstances of life: 'Several motifs are operating with a larger poetic work. Among them one must have the dominant motivating force toward the establishment of a unity within the entire work' (Rickman, 1976: 89). This study of the selected Limbu folktales reveals one motif—that is, feminine prowess as the major transgressor of the taboo in a dual capability: feminine transgression in some of the Limbu tales, following Dilthey's poetics, functions as a situation of life having the potential to become art, while the other Limbu tales reveal that with the entry of the alien culture of the 'mainstream', the motif has already gone through artistic emendation.

Incest among the adults and the woman question

The daughter of the god in the Limbu folktale *Death by a Flower* reaffirms that 'The law only forbids men to do what their instincts incline them to do' (Freud, 1950: 160). In Limbu myths, incest as a taboo often appears to be counterfeit—as if it is a limitation that has been imposed only to be transgressed. Not only are the mythic couple in Limbu *Mundhums* (myths) involved in incest,[2] but it seems to be almost impossible for the martinets to regulate this couple. The Limbu myth of the 'Origin of Incest', 'Lungdhung kai phekma', describes the inbreeding of 17 offspring by Sutchhuru Suhangpheba and his sister Tetlara Lahadongna. The sun and other distant bodies decided to separate them. All the children were placed on a sieve. The eight sons who moved down the sieve stayed with the mother; the remaining nine sons followed the father; and a daughter who was halfway through the sieve became a tree. Being disconnected after promising never to be united again, Sutchhuru Suhangpheba named himself Sodhung Suhangpheba, and Tetlara Lahadongna started calling herself as Thillilung Thamdenlungma. Many years later, when Sodhung Suhangpheba had already remarried, to Laoti Phungphahangma, he suddenly came across his former sister wife. Both of them failed to resist their urge and made love several times (facing the east, north, south and west) in various places—on the marshy land, treetop, heap of firewood, stone walls, by the lake—giving birth to evils like diseases and spirits of misfortunes, along with divine species like crabs and reptiles, which, according to the myth, are supposed to be the messengers of celestial beings (Subba, 2012b: 110–117). The sister[3] of the tribal tale *Death by a Flower* seems to suggest that 'It is absurd to be proud of one's ancestors; it is better to be an ancestor oneself' (Freud, 1965: 470).

Tale 1: Death by a Flower

Once upon a time a god had a son and a daughter. He sent them down to the earth. Having grown up together, the sister longed to marry the brother. By the virtue of possessing the divine mind, the brother came to know about the secret desire of the sister and without further ado married another woman who soon gave birth to a son. This made the sister very jealous. One day the wife found her sister-in-law swinging the baby's cradle with her foot and spelling out an evil chant. The wife complained about this to her husband, who became furious enough to kill the sister. The wife restrained him, because killing the sister with a weapon is considered to be a sin. She gave him an idea of hitting the sister with a deadly flower, when she would ask for a flower in the community dance. Accordingly, he called people for singing and dancing and offered all ladies natural flowers, except his sister. When the sister insisted on having one, he struck her chest with the poisonous flower that infected her and finally killed her. The brother bribed the people not to inform the father about his burning of the sister's body, and then and there, he started cremating her. However, the god-father, after getting the smell of the daughter's smoke up in the sky, came down only to find out about his daughter's jealously, which was caused by the baby. He wanted to kill the baby, but the baby wanted some sacrificial offering before his death. As per the wish of the baby, the god-grand-father gave a pig to the baby as a sacrificial offering to be offered in the puja. As soon as the pig was offered, the grandson died.

In this folktale, the sister almost follows the footsteps of her mythic ancestor, Irere Idhuknama. According to one of the Limbu *Mundhums*, the god Sodhung Lepmuhang and his second wife, Laoti Phungphahangma, conceived a twin son and daughter, who developed incestuous inclinations inside the womb. After they were born as Pajoiba Tendhumyangba and Irere Idhuknama, they were shifted to another world of human existence, Ketchhuwa Upanga Pangbhe, because of their incest. When they grew up, Irere Idhuknama and Pajoiba Tendhumyangba gave birth to Langerekpa and Namgerekpa, two sons, as the consequence of their relationship. Later, Irere Idhuknama suggested that the brother should also bring a woman for exogamous conjugality. Pajoiba Tendhumyangba brought women from all four directions before the sister, but none of them agreed to marry him, since they could easily detect the jealous displeasure of his sister. Then he went to the underworld to find Lupli Adenhangma, the daughter of the serpent king and the jealous sister watched him swearing his troth to the serpent princess. The marriage took place in the presence of the god-father Sodhung Lepmuhang. Soon the couple gave birth to a son, whom they named Lapoti Laphungyangba Nampoti Namphungyangba. The baby was kept under the custody of Irere Idhuknama, and his parents had to leave for the field to work. One day while Lupli was working in the field, milk started oozing out of her breast, and she ran to her baby. Back home, she found that the jealous sister-in-law was swinging the crib by her feet in sheer disdain while cursing the baby as 'a bastard child of obscure parentage, becoming huge day by day, weeping with no reasons, indecent like the promiscuous mother' and whatnot. Lupli complained to her husband, and Pajoiba confirmed the validity of his wife's annoyance by returning home early the next day. He was so agitated that he was about to kill his sister. But Lupli stopped him and gave him a better idea. Accordingly, Pajoiba brought both harmless and harmful flowers from the hill. Following Lupli's advice, he started distributing the harmless flowers among the neighbouring women. Irere, as expected, wanted a flower from the brother. Pajoiba struck his sister's bosom with all the poisonous flowers, and she soon died.

Since there was no concept of observing the rituals after death, Irere's soul could not find the destination and as an apparition came to her sons and ordered them to ask her father, Sadhung Lepmuhang, to guide her towards her ultimate destination. The god-father, being informed of his daughter's death, also came to know about the conspiracy of his son and daughter-in-law. He killed all of them, including the grandson, out of rage. But soon he realised that the child was innocent, so he blessed the grandson with a boon of becoming a part of divinity. He also felt miserable that all his children were dead. Tears started rolling down his cheeks, and that gave rise to the death ritual in the form of the ceremony of tears that cleanses grieving people (Subba, 2012b: 101–104). Both the mythical sister and the folktale sister have suffered due to their claim for consensual incest. Reading the folktale in the light of the two myths would enable us to understand the gradual inversion of a traditionally accepted norm into a nonnormative taboo culminating out of the infiltration of the pre-empting 'mainland' culture.

Adult incest, as a taboo, is commonly prohibited in what is commonly known as the North Indian 'mainstream' culture. In the myth of the 'Origin of Incest', the injunction on consensual incest by the intruding outlanders[4] is metaphorically conveyed by disapproval from 'sun and the other distant bodies' of the Indigenous prevalent practice. The desire is nevertheless tough to be erased. Therefore, despite a promise of separation that the 'distant bodies' had compelled them to pronounce, Sutchhuru and Tetlara, changing their names, reconciled as a sign of protest against the taboo and made an effort to reinforce the tribal ethos that provides liberty to an adult in the matter of sexual orientations and preferences. Internalising the 'mainstream' tabooed notion of incest as an evil, they are shown as giving rise to ill effects, in contrast to the inbreeding of 17 normal sons.

However, a counter-narrative of resistance can be traced against the defiling gaze of the 'mainstream' through the saga of giving birth to those who are traditionally associated with divinity—crab and reptiles. In the second myth, the mainstream notion of privileging exogamy over endogamy that had emerged out of a colonial bio-medical discourse where consanguineous marriages were believed to produce unfit children seemed to be propagated unmitigatedly.[5] The fact that a Limbu woman conjugally related to her brother and yet after giving birth to two sons was indoctrinated to look out for an exogamous marriage shows that the mechanisms of the 'mainstream' had already started colonising even the private tribal space.

The tension emerging out of the conflict between the traditional Indigenous norms and the imposed normativity through settler colonialism is replaced, in the mode of projective inversion, by the rivalry between two women over one man, since the issue of polygamy is much more familiar and a lesser crisis for the patriarchal 'mainstream' than that of an incest. The folktale *Death by a Flower* bears lesser marks of the 'savage mind' than its corresponding myth, where the 'civilising' of the sister has been accomplished, as a part of the 'mainstream' endeavour of pushing the Indigenous 'nature' to the domain of 'culture',[6] by portraying her as a spinster, as opposed to her nonnormative mythic counterpart. However, by depicting that the god-father has smelled of her daughter's flesh (reminding most of us of the 2006 German fantasy thriller 'Perfume: The Story of a Murderer' directed by Tom Tykwer, where body odour is strongly associated with erotic fantasy), an incestuous, erotic dimension is subtly added. This subtle alteration in the myth by the oral performers of the folktales prove that orality, despite being creative, is never subversive in the sense that the social function of storytelling remains intact (Ricard and Veit—Wild, 2005: 178).

Tale 2: Four Brothers and a Sister

There was a time when a king had four sons, and he was worried that none of the sons would be able to give birth to future generations due to the lack of a daughter. However, when the queen got pregnant, he said that in case she gave birth to a girl, he would kill all his sons because he would not need them anymore. Hearing this, the queen started weeping when her youngest son Lagerick asked her, 'What makes you sad mother?' He made her son promise not to inform the king about the secret that she was ready to share with him. She then told Lagerick about what the king had planned if she would give birth to a daughter. The son shared the secret with other brothers and they thought of running away to the forest. The mother suggested that she would fly a red flag on the rooftop if a daughter was born, else a white flag, seeing which they might return to their father's house. A few days passed, and the brothers saw a red flag. They understood that the mother had given birth to a sister. They moved further away and built a small house for themselves. After five or ten years, the daughter one day discovered some men's clothes and went to her mother, asking about the owner of the clothes. The mother revealed the truth to the daughter. She was very annoyed and started moving towards the forest in search of her brothers. Finally, she found a small house and a man staying inside. Being interrogated, she said, 'I have come to find my four brothers, the youngest being Lagerick'. The man happily introduced himself as Lagerick. They were too glad to be united. However, Lagerick remembered suddenly of the brothers' plan to kill anyone who would come in search of them. He hid the sister when it was time for the other brothers to return home. When they returned, Lagerick informed them of the sister's pursuit, and the other brothers cancelled the plan, because they too were happy to find the sister. In the meantime, the sister thought of offering flower garlands to each of the brothers. The moment she plucked the flower for the garland, the brothers turned into crows and flew away. The sister started crying and went on searching in the forest. She suddenly came across an old lady who asked her about her problem. After hearing everything, she said to the sister, 'If you want to see your brothers, do not cry or laugh in front of any old woman for the next three years'. The girl thought, 'It is impossible not to talk to old woman approaching me for assistance for three years. I will better hide myself by living on the tree'. For almost three years, she lived on the tree. All of a sudden, a king who was passing by saw the beautiful girl on the top of the tree. He carried her down and took her on his horse to the palace and married her. But the girl didn't utter a single word. The mother of the king said, 'I think she is a witch. Better get rid of her by drowning her in a big pot of boiling water'. Accordingly, the king tied her to a big pot. Just when he was about to pour the boiling water, a gust of wind blew and four crows appeared. Immediately the crows were transformed into the four brothers. The brothers untied the sister and guaranteed to protect her in the event of a crisis.

This Limbu folktale, *Four Brothers and a Sister*, is significant for two important reasons: first, by depicting the rivalry between the father and the sons regarding the possession of the woman in the family, it reveals the practical utility that is central to the motif of imposing a taboo on incest, and second, the emergence of the incestuous desire, symbolically conveyed by the sister's quest for her brothers and the consequential offering of garlands to them, confirm that the desire runs in an undercurrent all through the Limbu culture, despite the ban imposed by the 'mainstream'. Reversing the murder motif of the brothers against the totem father, this folktale, which seems to have been popularised only after foreign inhibitions started spreading roots even in the Limbu tribalscape, portrays a father who treats his sons as his rival regarding the possession of the forthcoming girl in the family and thereby reaffirms Freud's conviction that since 'an incestuous love choice is in fact the first and regular one', a taboo has to be implemented; after all, 'it has a practical basis as well' (Freud, 1953: 220–221). The possibility that the first part of the folktale must have resulted from a 'mainstream' prole-gomenon's inserting it at a later stage is further strengthened if we add that, contrary to the woman-centric narrations in traditional Limbu folklore, the practical utility of turning incest into a taboo is mainly aimed at protecting the unity of men—even at the cost of the desire of the female and ignoring the question of the pleasure principle of the women—exactly in the mode of the male-centric provisos of the 'mainstream' patriarchy.[7] Yet even if the major part of the story of the tale is the outcome of the interpolation of the 'mainstream', the prime focus still centred, in the counterculture of Limbu orality, on the yearning of the sister for her brothers.

The entire argument about the imposition of the taboo on consensual incest by the 'mainstream' can be refuted on the basis of the arguments put forward by scholars like Edward Burnett Tylor, Leslie White and Claude Lévi-Strauss,[8] according to which an Indigenous group by its preference for alliance formation through exogamy must have strategically decided to forgo endogamy through incest, by turning it into a taboo. The taboo on incest is explained as the necessary invention to achieve precise political ends. Bataille has argued that incest as a taboo originated in the men's wilful resolution to sacrifice their rights on their own women and give them away, on the basis of exchange to form alliances and thereby, as said Lévi-Strauss, accelerate a movement from nature to culture.[9]

Feminist critics often agree with the sacrifice and gifting, because for them, incest, even among adults, is the site for the operation of patriarchal power exercised over the most immediate and accessible women.[10] But in case of Limbu tribalism, the imposition of a taboo on incestual desire can never be an *endogenous*[11] turn. The main reason behind this supposition is the dominant position of women in the Limbu cosmic and worldly out-looks. Limbu myths and folktales illustrate women's desire for consensual incest. In the folktale *Death by a Flower*, the sister exercises her free will, despite the resistance of her brother, who immediately makes arrangements for an exogamous marriage in order to escape the tabooed relationship the moment he comes to know of her incestuous desires. In *Four Brothers and a Sister*, the sister again takes the initiative in finding her brothers and, as an expression of her suppressed erotic desire, wishes to offer garlands to each of them. The threatened brothers immediately fly from her ominous presence in the metaphorical depiction of the flying crows, which symbolise bad omens. Hence, the Limbu folktales demonstrate that the Indigenous culture used to provide tribal women with the agency and power to exercise and assert her preference for incest.

Arguing for a biosocial study of incest as a taboo and viewing it as social reproduction, Schneider proposed that since incest as a concept varies from one culture to another, the definition of incest has to be culture-specific (Schneider, 1976: 149–169). For the Limbus, incest is seen mainly as inbreeding by the brother and sister, where the process is mostly initiated by the sister.[12] The heteropaternalism[13] that had trespassed into the Indigenous domain of the Limbu community under the pretext of 'mainstream' governmentality[14] must have been hyperactive in turning the tribal practice into a taboo. The ending of the folktale *Four brothers and a Sister* explicitly depicts the loss of the feminine Indigenous right to desire and the repression resulting from the prohibiting of incest. If the brothers seem to have decided to reject incestuous endogamy in order to form exogamous political alliance, then what happens to the desiring sister?[15] The decision of the brothers to sacrifice their right on the sister is not a selfless one, but rather, it is directed towards group alliance, which in turn reduces the sister to a gift object that needs to be exchanged.

The taboo imposed on incest in Limbu culture has resulted, initially, in muting the voice of Limbu women, revealed in the silence of the sister, regarding their erotic desire and sexual preferences. She is then taken away (in exchange) by a strange man, symbolised by the king, which ultimately reduced the traditionally empowered woman to a subjugated captive, with no rights and liberty of her own; instead, she is to become the pathetic female icon of misery and infliction, like the female victims of 'mainstream' patriarchy. The king's attempt to murder the sister, in collaboration with her in-laws, is a symbolic manifestation of metastasising the culture of the abuse against women among the indigenes by the infringing nontribal neocolonisers, reminding us of the regressive 'mainstream' practices like dowry menace and Sati.[16] Devouring the image of a daring tribal woman, the prohibition of consensual incest as a taboo has recast the Limbu adult woman into the 'mainstream' shade of a helpless woman who is never allowed to actively desire but who can only passively depend on men for her protection.[17]

The Limbu folktales, thus, evidently bring out the essential androcentrism of the taboo, imposed on consensual incest: while *Death by a Flower* prohibits incest on account of the notion of group alliance, the folktale *Four Brothers and a Sister* conveys the anxiety from incest over group harmony—though both concerns are for the benefit of men. However, in *Four Brothers and a Sister*, the rebel sister unmasks the essential duality of a taboo against incest for the sake of familial unanimity through an avoidance of things that are related to the danger of sexual desire.

The family, paradoxically, has to play the foremost role in the revelation and deployment of sexuality so that the girl is made to become a woman by the realisation of feminine attributes, which includes the body, desire and sexual orientation. But the sexual awakening that takes place in the familial ambience by a sexualising of the family space is essentially incestuous, which therefore needs to be suppressed as a taboo. The suppression itself makes the individual more conscious of the repressed desire. In the tale, this sexual consciousness is symbolised through the metaphorical discovery of the sister of her brothers' clothing, which compels the secretive family to address sexuality. The puzzled daughter of the folktale interrogates the mother and searches for the object of her interest till her curiosity is satiated. But this satisfaction also results in the full understanding of desire that is essentially incestuous and that therefore, as a taboo, needs to be repressed. But like any form of repressed desire, it slips out, and the tabooed desire gets prominently exposed not only to the desiring self but also to the brothers, from whom the incestuous desire is supposed to be hidden. Hence, despite the juridico-discursive power of the statist 'mainstream', the Limbu folktale *Four Brothers and a Sister* proves that incest in the tribal culture is disavowed and solicited[18] as if it had been refashioned as a taboo only to provoke an Indigenous feminine transgression in a counternormative mode.

From defiant to defilement

Defiant characters, who are also bracketed as perverts, demonstrate their affinity for 'radical pluralism' (Giddens, 1992: 179) as means of establishing the nonconformist self.[19] As an alternative, radical pluralism seeks to suggest guidelines for sexual options, without making claims for any coherent moral principles. The radicalism lies in the pluralism which recognises 'normal sexuality' as just one among several options: 'Subjective feelings, intentions and meanings are vital elements in deciding on the merits of an activity. The decisive factor is an awareness of context, of the situation in which choices are made' (Weeks, 1985: 219). The sexual pluralism of the defiant Limbu women illustrates the Foucauldian possibility of overcoming the dominance that the ministered version of a 'mainstream' sexuality exerts on the Indigenous lives and brings to light the instant objections that such a move towards liberation entails. The defiant female figures of the tribal folktales, in utter disagreement with the infiltrating 'mainstream', have been gradually associated, symbolically, with defilement (Ricoeur, 1967) by the biopolitical[20] engagements of the squatters. The assertive women who, on the basis of the Limbu mores, have refused to project themselves as victims or as survivors of incest were thereupon strategically strained by a sudden label of defilement, intensifying the tabooed imposition of impurity and evil on their nonnormative longings.

In the folktale *Brother-Sister Marriage*,[21] of the Koch-Rabha tribal community from the neighbouring Cooch Behar district, the Rabha mother, an archetype of traditional Rabha matriliny, insists on arranging a marriage between her son and stepdaughter on the basis of her optimistic matrimonial prospects and thorough knowledge of Rabha marital regulations, while the stepdaughter, as one who has internalised the 'mainstream' patriarchal taboo, dies by suicide in order to prevent marrying her half-brother and thus being stigmatised. Because the Rabha society follows matrilineal heritage, the children inherit the *gotra*,[22] or family lineage of the mother. Hence, as per the Rabha tradition, the stepdaughter would not embody the family pedigree of the mother's son, as she would be representing the line of family pedigree of her own mother. But with the 'process of patriarchalization' (Raha, 1989: 12), first through the 'Hinduization of the primitive tribes . . . being integrated into its lower strata and becoming regarded by the Hindus as out-caste' (Grigson, 1938: 277) and later by their gradual conversion to androcentric Christianity, 'as part of a struggle to establish a new sense of self and to construct a salient new identity as Rabhas, a practice of identification based on reflexive agency, but not grounded in conscious choices or strategies' (Karlsson, 2000: 152), the matrilineal traits have been replaced by patriliny, where the Rabha habitus becomes a 'subject to interested human manipulation' (Moore, 1994: 53) of portraying difference as defiled. The return of the sister as an apparition and acting as the wife of her half-brother, however, reveals the crucial in-betweenness arising out of a call for ancestral Rabha-ness and neo-Sanskritisation. Yet the ending of the Rabha tale as an achievement of Rabha acculturation slashes the defiant through defilement.

Tale 3: Losing a Daughter

Semewa was a young girl who lived with her mother a long time ago. One day the mother collected some mushrooms from the forest and put them in the sun, asking Semewa to watch carefully so that no one could steal the mushrooms. The sun was so strong that the mushrooms shrank into tiny wrinkles. The mother came back and was terribly upset by the condition of the mushrooms. She suspected that her daughter might have done something. Although Semewa denied having committed any mischief, the mother called her a liar and hit her with a sweeping broom so hard that the daughter eventually died. The next day, when the mother gathered some fresh mushrooms and put them in the sun, she found that the mushrooms automatically shrank. She was so full of guilt that she started weeping. Thereafter, running into the forest she began to search for her dead daughter by calling out 'Semou, Semou', the daughter's nickname. Thereafter, she turned herself into a suffering bird of the jungle, and one can still find her in the form of the Semewa bird, yelling, 'Semou, Semou'.

Paul Ricoeur in *The Symbolism of Evil* listed the three basic facets of evil: defilement, sin and guilt (Ricoeur, 1967: 18). Defilement, indicative of strain, constitutes the initial schema of evil, where one discovers the self as the victim of some sudden reversal with no proper clue of the reason behind it, except that 'a quasi-material something that infects as a sort of filth, that harms by invisible properties, and that nevertheless works in the manner of a force in the field of our undividedly psychic and corporeal existence' (ibid.: 25–26). The mother's eternal pursuit for the daughter by hymning her name, like the general practice of chanting the name of a lover in their physical absence by the beloved, provides hint about the mother and the daughter as covertly fixated. Dorothy Dinnerstein wrote that a woman with her inborn lesbian-continuum is destined to suffer from a dilemma between homoerotic affection with 'filial-romantic-gratification' and heterosexual carnal passion: 'To realise that one is a female, destined to compete with females for the erotic resources of males, is to discover that one is doomed to renounce one's first love' (Dinnerstein, 2002: 8). Hence, given the phallic connotation of mushrooms, the shrunken mushrooms can signify the girl's unsatisfiable fecundity due to her consciousness of the innate urge for same-sex erotic gratification directed towards her mother. The Indigenous mother has to be displaced by the 'mainstreamed' one, and accordingly, she is made to view her incestuous daughter as a symbol of defilement. Defilement gives rise to the suspicion about the surfacing of some 'precategorical evil',[23] resulting in the policing of the symbolic exposition of evil through the imperatives of purity, obedience and punishment. 'With defilement we enter into the reign of terror' (Ricoeur, 1967: 25), as defilement empowers one to regulate others by symbolically demarcating the elements of discord as impure/strained and ultimately impute them with law and punishment. Accordingly, the normatised mother kills the daughter in order to punish her incestuous bent. However, the mother's late understanding of her daughter's passion as essentially intrinsic makes her repent with a reciprocal longing and, taking the form of a Semewa bird, as a counter-strategic imitation of the 'mainstream' mode of associating eroticity with singing birds like the nightingale, she sings the nickname of her dead daughter forever.[24]

Tale 4: The Story of Two Brothers

Wandering through the forest, a woman became thirsty once upon a time. She found a water-filled stone and drank the water. After walking for some distance, she again became thirsty and drank from a log that was filled with water. Some time passed, and she suddenly discovered herself to be pregnant. It was also discovered that the water that she drank from the stone was in fact a tiger's urine and that of the log was the urine of a man. She was hence made pregnant by both an animal and a human being. Consequently, she gave birth to a boy and a tiger as twin brothers. The more they grew up, the tiger kept on finding ways to eat the man brother. The man, though he always took care of the tiger brother, finally found no other alternatives left, apart from killing the tiger in order to save his own life. Both of them went to a jungle. The man climbed up the ninth branch of a Simul tree while the tiger sat on the eighth branch. Then he proposed that tiger brother close his eyes and open his mouth as wide as possible so that he could jump right into the tiger's mouth and allow the tiger to eat him. The tiger followed the instructions. The man, with the sole arrow left with him, shot straight into the tiger's widened mouth. The tiger fell down and was dead. This made the mother happy, and she threw flowers for the well-being of her human son. The man, however, climbed down the tree and de-skinned the tiger to make a Limbu drum called *Chya-brung*. Then, along with the mother, the man brother performed the tiger-style dance with the drum in honour of the dead tiger brother's vigour.

The Story of Two Brothers is another Limbu tale that serves as a site of contention between the tribal norm and 'mainstream' normativity. Revealing the once-prevalent practice of polyandry among the Eastern Himalayan tribes, this Limbu folktale depicts the woman's multiple partners in the symbolic narrativising of her pregnancy from a man and a tiger.[25] The folktale speaks to what Lévi-Strauss termed an 'anthropophagic' strategy of 'eating up' the strange Others in such a way that they are absorbed by the eating body so that their distinctiveness as nonconformists is lost. Substituting copulation with that of drinking urine illustrates the tabooed notion of defilement imposed on polyandry by the ' "anthropoemic" formula of "vomiting" and "spitting out" those "unfit to be us", either isolating them by incarcerating them inside the visible walls of the ghettos or the invisible (though no less tangible for this reason) walls of cultural prohibitions' (Bauman, 2000: 176). The urine, as the metaphor of the expelled object of desire, becomes Kristeva's 'abject', which at once invokes abhorrence and obsession, abomination and jouissance.[26] Fooling the tiger brother by its human sibling only to kill him in order to make the mother happy represents a metahistorical event—that is, how under the pressure of the dominant governmental discourse, the tribal adherence to their liberal sexual norms that had paved the way for feminine recalcitrance has been erased.

Tale 5: The Papoo Fish

There was a time long ago when a grandmother was the sole guardian of a boy whom she looked after till he grew up into a man and got married. The boy then thought of keeping the grandmother

101

away from him. He took her and left her inside a cave in the jungle. After some days, he visited the cave and found her alive. So he took her to a riverside and abandoned her. However, returning after several days, the man found that the grandmother was clutching a big rock with her hands and was still alive. He asked her if she was hungry, and the grandmother nodded her head to imply that she was indeed very hungry. Then the man said, 'Show me with your hand how much food you need'. The moment the grandmother opened her palms, she slipped into the river. But instantly she was transformed into a papoo fish with the grey plaits of her hairs turning into the silver plaits which one can see at the back of the papoo fish.

The Papoo Fish narrates the story of a deprived grandmother's 'becoming' of the fish; the Limbus do not eat the papoo fish, because they believe that it carries the tabooed ancient spirit. The sociocultural spirit that has been strained as a taboo by the state agencies is again allied to the alternative image of Indigenous womanhood as opposed to the 'mainstream' Brahmanical one. In the 'mainstream' Hindu tradition, old people in general and the old women in particular, as per the Vedic prescription of the Four Ashrams, were supposed to renounce worldly attachments and live a secluded life as *Vanaprastha* and *Sannyasa*. Seen as unproductive burdens on the family, old women, usually widows, are often forced to live a forlorn life of misery.

The spirit of the Limbu grandmother in the folktale is just the opposite. Despite the tabooed imposition on the tribal convention, like that of the Totos, the boy fails to overcome the tremendous pull of an ancient yearning and returns to the grandmother. The Limbu grandmother, disregarding the 'mainstream' code of abject old age, expresses her 'hunger' for food (in folklore, food is often used as a symbol for sexual appetite) and life. Violating the 'mainstream' cultural norm of femininity that is associated with advanced age, the tribal grandmother, with her projection of preserving a youthful power in her body as manifested by her durability, resembles the popular transgressive figure of a MILF.[27] Under the regime of assimilative surveillance, the normatising agencies make the rebellious old woman sink deep into the river so that the exclusive trait of discordant desire can be washed away. The grandmother's passage from a radical female to a prohibited fish, nevertheless, metaphorically documents the rendering of the alternative tribal femininity of discord[28] into a tabooed defilement.

The normatised turn

The folktale *The Serpent Queen*, although popular among the Limbus, is hardly a tale of the Limbu community; rather, bearing all the marks of the 'mainstream' transformative agencies, it is a tale *for* them.

Tale 6: The Serpent Queen

There was a time when there was a queen who would change lovers each day, by appointing a man as the king for the day, and the next morning, that man would be found dead. Being appointed as the king became the saddest event of a man's life, and everyone thought that in the near future there would be no single living male left. Eventually a clever man got appointed as the king. At night, he wrapped a banana tree in a blanket, placed it on the bed and hid himself, at which point he witnessed how a snake came out of the queen's nose and bit the banana tree. He repeated the trick the next day, and the moment the snake emerged out of the queen's nose to bite the banana tree, he killed it with his *khukuri*, the small curved sword. Thereafter, none of the kings were killed.

The narrative's political use of the 'marvellous' addresses the subjugation of women by projecting a woman's body as baleful. This transformed tale depicts the 'false consciousness' of 'the premature harmonizing of the social contradictions' (Bloch, 1987: 117). The repetitive killing of men by the empowered woman, in the form of the queen, is a generative device of making the projection appear like a timeless reality.[29] The folktale has been transformed into a 'warning tale' by the tactful use of the 'marvellous' as reflected in the phantasmic association of fear with the female body. The growing estrangement of the 'mainstream' from the tribal must have resulted in the political deployment of the 'marvellous' in schematically portraying the present (Limbu tradition) as dangerous and thereby rationalising the transfigurations as an assurance of a safe, better future.[30] The 'mainstream' 'marvellous' reconstruction of the Limbu female body aims to expel desire by representing empowered Indigenous womanhood as cataclysmic.[31] Killing the fantastical snake, which ensures the protection of kings from challenges posed by a woman, ultimately foregrounds the craftiness of men in supplanting Limbu gynocentrism through the 'mainstream' enforcement of patriarchal authority in a mode of 'a wish-fulfillment of which the body is the chief subject and object' (Seifert, 1996: 42).

Tale 7: Losing a Father

Sometime in remote past, a son was walking with his father in the jungle. The father went into a bush to relieve himself when a tiger came from behind and ate him. The son kept on waiting, but his father didn't return. Because it was getting dark, he returned to his home and informed his mother: 'I think Father has disappeared into the forest. He went into the bush but never returned. A bird, instead, followed me home from the forest'. The mother went out to see the bird, which was sitting on the weaving loom. All of a sudden, it turned into a needle. The mother told the son, 'This is your father'.

If the folktale *The Serpent Queen* has shown how the 'mainstream' has reoriented the social, moral and ontological differences into a likelihood through the transmutation of the female body and by effectively estimating feminine signs of discord as defilement, then *Losing a Father* seems to show that the normatising efforts have succeeded in turning feminine nonconformity into a taboo. The Limbu mother and the son in every way resemble the mother hen and the son of the Toto folktale *Wild Hen and her Son*. Like the father cock, the father in Limbu tale *Losing a Father* is lost in the forest, and the son fails to find any trace of his survival. Hence, it can be predicted that in an archetypal pattern, this Limbu tale resembling the Toto plot would have naturally moved towards a consensual incest between the two adults initiated by the Limbu mother (reminding us, as Ramanujan [1991] has pointed out, of the mother–son erotic intimacy as one of the major common motifs in Indian regional folktales), like the mother hen. But like civilising the assumed savage, the father has to be restored as a patriarchal agent of surveillance. The bird is too feeble an image to describe the paternal agency. The father thus becomes a needle to represent the violent 'mainstream' gaze that would nail down 'the fearful danger'[32] if Indigeneity were ever to dare to transgress the taboo imposed on gynocentric adult incest. The 'khukuri' in the previous tale and the 'needle' in this tale are instruments of reformation and thus expose the essential ferocity that is often veiled with the projected 'welfare', under the pretext of which the governmental disciplinary agencies introduce managerial tactics to intervene in the independent living of tribal people. These statist agencies strive to highlight the social/reformative at the cost of making the political subject—like Indigeneity—lose its spatial association and sovereign moorings (Cruikshank, 1999).

The gynocentric apostate

Romance within the family steered by a woman, as narrated in the Limbu folktales, holds the danger of 'the pervasive moral authority of the majority'[33] that understands incest to be a domain of exhibiting patriarchal power. As Gramsci has rightly observed, the folklore worldview lies often 'in contraposition . . . to the "official" conception of the world' (qtd. in Byrne, 1982: 71). Luigi Lombardi Satriani also affirms that folklore offers an 'alternative culture' against the dominant culture (Satriani, 1974). The Limbu folktales contain a predominant gynocentric subculture that opposes the regular patriarchal pre-eminence. At the backdrop of a changed consumer, homogenised world, one needs to endeavour to put folklore to 'political use'

(Cirese, 1076: 67), through what Clara Gallini calls the refunctionalisation of traditional folklore forms (Favretto and Itcaina, 2017), in order to bring out the cultures of contestation between the liberal tribal society and the illiberal majority.

Refuting the generalised notion of addressing adult incest as an androcentric tool that renders women either as victims or as survivors, these Limbu folktales reveal how the prohibition against consensual adult incest has instead turned the matriarchal Yumanist genealogy of tribalhood into a reorganised state of custody. Hence, the taboo attached to adult incest in the Limbu context needs to be understood in the light of the 'mainstream' perversion[34] of a hegemonic, 'maleist'[35] imposition that has facilitated giving women away as objectified gifts for political alliances among men. This psychoanalytic study of the Limbu tales, focusing on the inversion of the sexual hierarchy by Limbu women in relation to adult incest, has pointed out that 'these pleasures, which we lightly call physical' (Colette, 1982: 72), are actually crucial sites to prove how eroticity, like our notion of gender, is also political.[36] Reaffirming that 'If human nature is historical, individuals have different histories and therefore different needs' (Ignatieff, 1984: 135), the incestuous preferences of adult Limbu women prove how correctly Emma Goldman identified 'mainstream' or 'state' life as 'unfit' for women, since nothing can enable the 'state' to get rid of its tabooed notion of 'impurities' connected with women.[37]

Notes

1 The way of life of the Indigenous Limbu tribes, which is based on traditional faith, is called Yumanism. For details, see Subba, 2012a.

2 The Lepcha myth of origin, is also a saga of transgressing the incest taboo by the first Lepcha brother, Fadongthing, and his sister, Nuzaongnyoo, despite the warning given by the creator father, Itboo-Deboo, of the disaster if they cross the boundary. For details, see Tamsang, 2008: 3–4.

3 Ramanujan (1991), while representing the various prominent motifs of the folktales from different parts of India, translated a 'mainstream' Rajasthani folktale, *Brother's Day*, where the motif is to highlight the selfless sacrifice of both the brother and the sister out of their mutual protective feeling for one another, without any sexual undercurrent.

4 We learn from Foucault that imposing laws on the nonconformist 'other', through prohibition, obedience and punishment and by censoring alternative discourses of the 'other', provides the 'mainstream' with a sense of privilege of being capable of exercising power. He also warned us about the essential weakness of such negative reformation: 'Power would be a fragile thing if its only function were to repress, if it worked only through the mode of censorship, exclusion blockage and repression . . . exercising itself only in a negative way' (Foucault, 1980a: 59). The folktale *Death by a Flower* reveals both the imposition of incest as a taboo, like a law on Indigeneity, and the tribals' revolt not to succumb to the imposed rule, thereby exposing the fragility of this power.

5 Foucault strongly argues that, on the basis of some scattered bio-medical reports, the prohibition against incest as a universal taboo is a recent imposition:

> Incest was . . . widely practised among the populace, for a very long time. It was towards the end of the 19th century that various social pressures were directed against it. . . . the great interdiction against incest is an invention of the intellectuals. . . . If you look for studies by sociologists or anthropologists of the 19th century on incest, you won't find any, apart from 'some scattered medical reports', despite which 'the practice of incest didn't really seem to pose a problem at the time'.
>
> (Foucault, 1988: 302)

Alan H. Bittles used recent data to show how the notion of biological degeneration, associated with inbreeding, is not a scientific one: 'Assessed in terms of completed family size, a recent meta-analysis was unable to identify any overall adverse effect of inbreeding on fertility, and in a large majority of the constituent studies consanguineous couples actually had more children' (Wolf and Durham, 2005: 45). He has also reminded us that 'in Roman Egypt, full brother-sister unions accounted for 19.6 percent of marriages in the city of Arsinoe, with a further 3.9 percent of marriages between half siblings' (ibid.: 47). Leslie White, without any ambivalence, concluded that 'Inbreeding as such does not cause degeneration; the testimony of biologists is conclusive on this point' (White, 1948: 417).

6 Leslie White and Claude Lévi-Strauss believe that by turning incest into a taboo, the group actually transcends from the state of animal 'nature' to the realm of civilised 'culture'. This shows how 'mainstream' anthropologists, despite being progressive, fail to overcome the hierarchical notion of the natural as savage and the cultural as civilised and therefore as something superior that needs to be imitated.

7 Freud explains the taboo as an implementation for the benefit of men:

> Sexual desires do not unite men but divide them. Though the brothers had banded together in order to overcome their father, they were all one another's rivals in regard to the women. . . . Thus the brothers had no alternative . . . but . . . to institute the law against incest, by which they renounced the women whom they desired and who had been their chief motive for dispatching their father.
>
> (Freud, 1950: 144)

8 Edward Burnett Tylor suggested that 'among tribes of low culture there is but one means of keeping up permanent alliances, and that is by means of intermarriage' (1889: 267). Leslie White wrote that

> Cooperation between families cannot be established if parent marries child; and brother, sister. A way must be found to overcome this centripetal tendency with a centrifugal force. This way was found in the definition and prohibition of incest. . . . The leap was taken; a way was found to unite families with one another, and social evolution as a human affair was launched upon its career.
>
> (1948: 425)

Claude Lévi-Strauss, almost echoing White, observed 'that the prohibition of incest provides sufficient guarantee that a network of alliances, resulting in all other respects from free choices, will not compromise social cohesion' (1969: xxxix).

9 For details, see *Eroticism: Death and Sensuality*, 1987.

10 Ward believes that '[in] the incestuous family we find the most powerless of females, a girl-child, has become the sexual possession of the Father, the king in his castle lording it over his concubine' (1984: 193). Dominelli has also viewed incest as an authoritarian exercise of power that is 'practised by individual men who wield tremendous authority over the individual girl' (1986: 9).

11 'Endogenous' usually means all that which originates from within the specific ideas, values, practices, attributes, institutions and knowledge which have distinct relevance to a given society (Maruyama, 1981).

12 Apparently, this sister–brother incest may seem to resemble what Deleuze and Guattari has termed 'Schizo-incest', which 'takes place with the sister, who is not a substitute for the mother' (Deleuze and Guattari, 1986: 67); but the essential difference lies in the fact that the Limbu incest, which seems to be instigated mostly by a woman, does not correspond to the fallacious trait of Schizo-incest, which, according to Dana Polan, seems to treat a woman as a 'succouring aid to the adventuring male in his quest to go beyond limits' (ibid.: xxvi).

13 Heteropaternalism refers to 'the presumption that heteropatriarchal nuclear-domestic arrangements, in which the father is both center and leader/boss, should serve as the model for social arrangements of the state and its institutions' (Arvin et al., 2013: 13).

14 Freud wrote in *Totem and Taboo* that the taboo of incest is mostly the outcome of an anxiety: 'they are afraid precisely because they would like to, and the fear is stronger than the desire' (1950: 31).

15 The image of a desiring sister, preferring to have the brother back rather than her husband and son, is conveyed even in a Lepcha folktale *The Invaluable Brother*:

> Once upon a time there was a village that was attacked by the robbers and the villagers, while chasing them, came across three men in a field whom they mistakenly captured as disguised robbers. Those three men were handed over to the king's men by the village people. A few days later, the king heard that a woman was crying for 'something to get covered'. Accordingly, he asked the ministers to give her clothes. The ministers approached her but returned to the king to relay that the woman was looking for a husband. The curious king sent his men to bring the woman to him. The clever woman stated, 'A husband is the real covering for a woman, without whom even ornaments fail to cover up her nakedness. Hence I want my husband to cover myself'. The king, who was pleased by the prompt reply, asked her about her relationship with those prisoners. She answered that they were her husband, son and brother. The king then said, 'I can release any one of them. Whom do you want?' The woman replied, 'Your grace, I can acquire another husband and give birth to another son but since I am an orphan, I cannot have another brother of my own. So I will prefer to get my brother back over the other two'.

16 Sati refers to the malpractice that was once prevalent in India, where Hindu widows were burnt alive with the dead bodies of their husbands.

17 This reminds us of the dictates of *Manusmriti*, where a woman is shown to be always in need of a man as her protector: a father, a husband or a son.

18 Foucault seems to be aware of this ambivalence. For him, incest 'being constantly solicited and refused', acts as 'an object of obsession and attraction, a dreadful secret and an indispensable pivot'. It is evinced as that which 'is strictly forbidden in the family insofar as the latter functions as a deployment of alliance . . . a thing

that is continuously demanded in order for the family to be a hotbed of constant sexual incitement' (Foucault, 1981: 109).

19

> What used to be called perversions are merely ways in which sexuality can legitimately be expressed and self-identity defined. Recognition of diverse sexual proclivities corresponds to acceptance of a plurality of possible life-styles, which is a political gesture.
>
> (Giddens, 1992: 179)

20 The term has been used by following Audrone Zukauskaite's elucidation of biopolitics as a divisive categorisation of people on the basis of 'appropriate bodies'/'improper bodies' as citizens/noncitizens, person/nonperson and human/nonhuman. For details, see Audrone Zukauskaite, 2016.

21 *Brother-Sister Marriage:*

> It was of many years back when in a forest there was a large lake and a small Koch-Rabha village by its side. In that village a widow used to live with her son and her stepdaughter. With much difficulty she could make both ends meet, but as time passed the kids grew up and stepped into their youth. The brother turned into a young man of great skill in farming, fishing and cattle rearing. The half-sister became a good home-maker, with expertise in weaving and cooking. The widow, scrutinising the beauty and calibre of her stepdaughter, planned for a good future for her son, by getting him married to his half-sister. Quietly, she went to the head priest, and after telling him about their different *gotras* by explaining to him the differences in their matrilineal familial pedigree, she asked if there would be any problem in getting them married. The priest said that since the line of matrilineal order is different, there is no barrier on the basis of the customary law. The Rabha mother started making preparations for the wedding without intimating the brother and the sister, since she wanted to surprise them. On the day of their marriage, the sister came to know from one of her friends about her stepmother's plan. Discreetly she took a boat and came right at the middle of the nearby lake. The stepmother started calling her back: 'Please row back to the bank, my child'. But the stepdaughter replied, 'If brother becomes a husband, then no one will consider me to be good'. Having said this, she sank into the lake with the boat. The priest then announced that he must have said something wrong in an intoxicated state, and from then onwards, even marriage between half-brother and half-sister has been treated as detrimental. Some days passed, and the mother suddenly discovered that someone was doing all the household chores that she had expected from her daughter-in-law. While her son went out for his work and she took the cattle away for grazing, someone had come and cooked the food, washed the clothes and even prepared the bed to sleep. One day the mother pretended to take the cattle out but returned unnoticeably only to find her dead stepdaughter doing all the work. The mother came out of her hiding place and touched the apparition, who immediately turned into a kite bird and flew away, never to come back again.

22 This means family genealogy traced from a common source.

23 Echoing Ricoeur's designating of defilement as primordial evil, Alford viewed defilement as 'precategorical' evil which ensures 'the loss of boundaries, the way in which inside and outside are no longer distinct' (Alford, 1997: 60).

24 The Lepcha folktale *Sweet Potatoes* features an identical plot, with an undercurrent of eroticity associated with food and the hungry orphan siblings, where an orphan brother and his sister are compelled to enter the forest (symbol of 'unruly sexuality' in *Psychology and Alchemy*, 1969) in search of food. The brother, who has gone weak and pale due to starvation, repeatedly cries for 'kew, kew', meaning sweet potatoes (again a sexual symbol) in the Lepcha language. The sister, while digging deeper into the earth, goes on uttering 'kyon, kyon', to reassure her brother, saying 'I will give you, I will give you' in her Lepcha dialect. In the process, both of them die and are transformed into the bird that the Lepchas call 'kew-kyon' to forever remind the people of the hungry siblings (Kotturan, 82–83).

25 A similar Lepcha folktale, one that features both incest and polyandry, has been scripted as Namsamay and His Magic Drum in *Legends of the Lepchas: Folk Tales from Sikkim* (130–136), according to which Khappura Nellongdimma Teegenjonga, tired of her search for the brother, becomes terribly thirsty. Suddenly she happens to find two small ponds. Drinking from both the ponds, she quenches her thirst and resumes her quest. Soon she reaches Tibet, where she makes a small hut for herself. One night in her dream, she hears a loud voice of God telling her that she has mistaken a tiger's urine and her brother's urine as rain water in the two ponds. As a consequence, she will give birth to a baby with a tiger nature and another with a human nature. Accordingly, she becomes a mother of twin boys. The one with his nature as a tiger soon threatens to kill the mother if she does not allow him to eat his human brother. The mother shows the trick of killing the tiger son to her human son. Finally, the good/human son kills the evil/tiger son, and the mother and the human son, in a paradoxical brutal means, eat the meat of the tiger son/brother.

26

> Urine, blood, sperm, excrement then show up in order to reassure a subject that is lacking in its 'own and clear self'. The abjection of those flows from within suddenly become the sole 'object' of sexual desire—a true 'abject' where man, frightened, crosses over the horrors of maternal bowels and, in an immersion that enables him to avoid coming face to face with an other, spares him the risk of castration. But at the same time that immersion gives him the full power of possessing, if not being, the bad object that inhabits the maternal body. Abjection then takes the place of the other, to the extent of affording him jouissance.
>
> (Kristeva, 1982: 53–54)

27 'The "milf" fantasy combines the sexual knowledge of the experienced older woman with the danger of doing something forbidden. For some males, the turn-on involves the idea of sex with someone who's acted like a mother to them' (qtd. from Lowen by Dearey, 2014: 110).

28 Discord, seen from the perspective of these assertive Limbu women, seems to suggest, similar to Ranciere's concept of 'disagreement' (Ranciere, 1998), a concern not just for any fixed set of demands to be made but more importantly for who gets to make demands. Discord in these Limbu tales, following Ranciere's idea of 'disagreement', is essentially centred on the issue of the possible equality of women, as the ones who are making their demands.

29 Susan Stewart wrote that repetition is truly possible only outside the everyday life. Commenting on the generative power of repetition, she observed that

> What is repeated is what is, a parameter defined in spite of time. . . . If repetition in fictions is an aid to our sense of closure, giving us a sense of

return to a beginning, it is because repetition is always involved in giving
integrity to what is repeated.

(1978: 121)

30 'The merveilleux is capable of reproducing familiar realities, but also of revealing their incoherences and suggesting, in however schematic a way, a different
future' (Seifert, 1996: 23).

31

In expressing desire, fantasy can operate in two ways: . . . it can tell of,
manifest or show desire (expression in the sense of portrayal, representation, manifestation, linguistic utterance, mention, description), or it can
expel desire, when this desire is a disturbing element which threatens
cultural order and continuity (expression in the sense of pressing out,
squeezing, expulsion, getting rid of something by force).

(Jackson, 1981: 3–4)

32

The Kangaroo is a harmless animal, the word shit is a harmless word.
Make either into a taboo, and it becomes most dangerous. The result of
taboo is insanity. And insanity, especially mob insanity, mass insanity, is
the fearful danger that threatens our civilisation. . . . If the young do not
watch out, they will find themselves, before so very many years are past,
engulfed in a howling manifestation of mob insanity, truly terrifying to
think of. It will be better to be dead than to live to see it.

(Lawrence, 1994: 420)

33 Richard S. Randall argues that 'The pervasive moral authority of the majority is
a basic problem of democracy' because, 'implicit in its great ethical force is the
idea that the majority is right, that it governs . . . because its policies are wise'
(Randall, 1989: 166).
34 Jacques-Alain Miller claims that 'perversion is when you do not ask for permission' (Miller, 1996: 316).
35 Stephen M. Whitehead uses 'maleist' as a synonym for androcentrism: to
'describe a male-centred view of the world, one which, by definition, posits
female, girl/woman, feminine as marginal, partial, and for ever relational to
male' (Whitehead and Barrett, 2001: 365).

36

Like gender, sexuality is political. It is organized into systems of power,
which reward and encourage some individuals and activities, while punishing and suppressing others. Like the capitalist organization of labour
and its distribution of rewards and powers, the modern sexual system
has been the object of political struggle since it emerged and as it has
evolved.

(Rubin, 1999: 171)

37 For a detailed study of Emma Goldman's anarcho-feminist critique of the state,
see Haaland (1993).

5

STAGES IN THE PROSCRIPTION OF HOMOEROTICITY

Lepcha folktales and mythistory

The past is a foreign country: they do things differently there.

(Hartley, 2002: 17)

The truth has become an insult.

(Adichie, 2008: 178)

The burden that the past tends to impose on us through outmoded forms of moralities, authoritatively projected as the continuum of a monolithic tradition, calls for serious reconsideration. Queerness in Indian history, mostly chronicled as a recent derivative of the 'nonnative queer modernities' (Morgensen, 2011: 20), is the outcome of misrepresentations disseminated by colonialism. The colonial heteropatriarchy, on one hand, eliminated all non-heteronormative Indigenous desires, kinship and ultimately Indigenous culture by creating what Sherene Razack termed a 'white settler society' (Razack, 2007: 8), while on the other hand, made the 'queers appear definitively not Native—separated from, yet in perpetual (negative) relationship to, the original peoples of the lands where they live' (Morgensen, 2011: 21). This study, as an effort in de-minoritising the Indigenous homosexual experience, is an attempt to identify the moments of expurgation by 'working on historical questions through the reading of [folk] literature' (Sedgwick, 1985: 137). To get rid of present 'mainstream' prejudices regarding homosexuality, the past has to be reviewed responsibly. Queer activism against present-day homophobic anxiety cannot be done without trying to excavate the alternative historical queernormative norms of the undocumented time when desires other than heterosexuality were not censored. History is 'a consciousness of chaos', a 'will to form' a 'suprahistorical' (White, 1973: 355), and perspective is crucial to delivering the future and the present free from the shackles of the 'ironic perspective' of a suppressive historicity. Strongly following the maxim that 'One can study only what one has first dreamed about' (ibid.: epigraph), an 'anti-ironic' metahistorical realism[1] has to established regarding the queer Indigenous past by the creative use of mythistory.[2]

Perceiving historical myths and fables/folktales not as whimsical fabrications but as foundational narratives, mythistory purports to consider these stories as historical documents—'social charters'—of what those tellers of primordial mythical time that precedes historical time experienced and desired to experience. According to the exponents of mythistory, the personal-cum-national identity of a community cannot be understood without recognising the myths and folklore as historical sources capable of providing us with historical truths. These narratives have been accepted as the most secured symbolic means of protecting the authority of the community against colonisers' attacks on the validity of unique Indigenous perspectives and praxes. Mythistory is thus 'a useful instrument for piloting human groups in their encounters with one another and with the natural environment' and for the historian who plays the role of a 'truth-seeking mythographer'.[3]

We learnt from Hayden White that the purpose of history is to make the strange familiar, which according to Coleridge is also the function of literature. Treating the folktales as the 'fictions of factual representation' (White, 1976), this chapter explores the 'moralizing impulse' (White, 1980: 26) characteristic of narrative discourse. Adding a plurality of meaning to our past by rendering 'the meaningless meaningful' (Ibid., 1966: 134), the past must be studied in a mode that Benjamin termed 'messianic', to show how the past, far from being already fulfilled, has been waiting for a sense of reconceptualised fulfilment (Pensky, 2004: 193–195).

The proclamation of sexual rights, against the majoritarian propagation of homosexuality as a 'sexual wrong' against the Pan-Indian backdrop, should emphasise that 'when we struggle for rights we are not simply struggling for rights that attach to my person, but we are struggling to be conceived of as persons' (Butler, 2005: 69). The Lepcha folktales have been studied in a new light of psychological infusion of mythistory for mining some broken bits of past, in the form of four distinct phases of decline, which allow us to understand how we have been forced to forget some portion of our own history: on the schematic erasure of homosexual desire and sexual preferences. Mythistory—emerging as the discourse that treats the 'poetic logic' (Vico, 1984: 401) of fictional narratives as the outcome of both individual and collective historical memory—attempts to reveal the extortive transformation of moral values and sociocultural ordering of the past, retrospectively. Since 'there is no such thing as politically innocent historiography' (White, 1978a: 24), history, from the perspective of mythistory, becomes a subjective 'poetic creation' (Vico, 1984: 401) of the past. This is based on considering folktales and fables as oral heritage that is 'always co-incident with history' (Gourgouris, 2003: 43), as part of an 'attempt to recreate the life and thought of the remote past through a new combination of human faculties' (Mali, 2003: 9) of imagination and interpretation. Perceiving literature as 'humanity's deepest psychic reservoir' (Gourgouris, 2003: 43), mythistory paves the way to 'perform the relation of the political to the *poietic* in our own social-historical moment' (ibid.: 10).

The four Lepcha folktales, *Two Friends and the Devil*, *The Luckless Punshohang*, *The Orphan Boy and the Giant* and *Two Brothers*, hint at the four distinct stages in the gradual proscription of homoerotic preferences in the Lepcha landscape. The first two Lepcha tales which hint at the prevalent homoerotic Indigenous relationships have similar plots to those under the titles of *Two Friends* and *The Luckless Punshohang* in the 1976 anthology of Lepcha[4] folktales by George Kotturan. In the recent 2008 anthology by Tamsang Lyangsong, these two explicit tales of homoeroticity were omitted.

The schematic savaging of the once-civilised Lepcha tribal world—a nonrepressive society that allowed space for homoerotic alliances—by the homophobic colonial regime can be charted out through a sequential reading of these four folktales. The Lepcha image of men, as a stark antithesis to the hypermasculine European notion of manliness, is best expressed in the folktale *All about Adventure*.[5] This tribal tale features the satiric plea for what John Stoltenberg termed 'refusing to be a man' (John Stoltenberg, 1990). This Lepcha folktale, along with highlighting an alternative, Indigenous masculinity, also makes quite clear the extent of shock that the colonial state machinery suffered from this tribal alter-masculinity,[6] which, as a consequence, must have hastened the colonial 'civilising' agenda with an immediate procedure of detraditionalisation[7] with the help of Christian missionaries, propagating the prohibition of 'demonic' carnal desire in general and homosexuality in particular.

Indigenous gay relationships and colonial angst

The friendship of the two boys in the Lepcha folktale *Two Friends and the Devil* who used to meet in the early morning and spend the entire day away and aloof from their houses, in togetherness as bird collectors, typically follows the pattern of friendship among the gay people who tend to build a community.

Tale 1: Two Friends and the Devil

One upon a time, there lived two young friends from two different villages. They used to catch birds and sell them to earn their livelihood. Every day in the morning, one friend from his village used to travel to the other friend's village, and together they used to climb up on the mountaintop to watch and trap birds from the trees. One day, the one who used to come to the friend's village proposed that they meet on the mountaintop, the next day. Accordingly, he reached the mountaintop, and sitting on the branch of a tall tree, he kept waiting for his friend. Suddenly he felt that someone was approaching him. Thinking that it was his friend, he asked: 'Why are you so late?' A voice answered, 'It's difficult. How did you climb up the tree?' The boy looked back and discovered that it was a devil and not his friend. That was why he didn't know how to climb up. Suddenly the boy saw that the devil took his friend's head out of his bag. 'Come and taste a little of my cucumber', invited the devil. The boy was terrified to see the bleeding head of his friend. But he got an idea. He threw a bundle full of his trapped birds far away. The moment the devil went to get the bag, he climbed down and ran back home. However, the boy was so shocked and sad that he ultimately died just like his friend.

That these two boys are not from the same village points to homoeroticity, because unlike being together as a community of villagers, an individual looks out for a friendship of homophily beyond the immediate circuit in order to relish the norms that 'stimulate and develop' his understanding of the non-heterosexual identity more adequately in '[their] unchosen community of origin' than in '[their] original community of place' (Friedman, 1993: 252). The two boys from two different villages resemble the networked people of a gay community who migrate and meet a part of their involvement in understanding 'the political relevance of friendship' (Arendt, 1968: 24). The absence of any cross-sex friendship, which is a characteristic feature in all of the four Lepcha folktales, suggests that the Indigenous space did 'allow homoerotically inclined individuals to develop ties of varying closeness with one another' (Vanita and Kidwai, 2000: 198).

In a repressive persecution of queer people, who may not fit into the frame of a useful procreant, the Indian state has for a long time striven to erase homosexual desire by criminalising it, until the recent decriminalisation of same-sex relationships, although the 'mainstream' continues to project it as non-Indian and a mere imitation of foreign attributes. This gives birth to a binary of 'twoness' that splits the normatising 'mainstream' and nonconforming sexualities into a power struggle of polarised opposition, resulting in either resistance against or submission to the demands of the other as the only possibility.

The next step for which the present sexual minority in India has been waiting is a movement towards a 'third' space of recognition. It is surprising to see that the sociocultural acceptability for which the Indian queer community has been fighting and waiting used to thrive in queernormative Indigenous Indian spaces. The Lepcha boyfriends reveal how in the form of the mountaintop where two friends used to meet every day, a space of 'thirdness' (Benjamin, 2004) did exist as a cocreated, legitimate tribal space. The Lepcha naming of their mountain villages, like Tadong, which originated

114

from the Lepcha phrase *tao dong*, meaning a search for the uncommon/ unusual, also provides evidence of the actuality of a tribal 'third' space. The unusual or uncommon is related to matters that are corporeal and not transcendental, because there are other places specified for such spiritual endeavours, like Ghoom, which derives from the Lepcha word *Gom*, meaning a place to meditate to attain salvation, or Rumtek, from Lepcha *Rum-Tek*, meaning a place to offer prayers to the gods.

The 'thirdness' in this tale symbolises the Lepcha mental space of acknowledgement, as opposed to today's homophobic subjugation, through a recognition of non-heterosexual sexual orientations. The tribal tale, depicting the liberty that the two Lepcha boys used to have in terms of their undisturbed involvement with same-sex intimacy, exhibits that, apart from the dutiful socioeconomic role-performances, there had also been a freedom of choice in the Indigenous domain for 'a willingness and a capacity for friendship's surprising one-to-one relations' (Little, 1989: 154) as a democratic and human progressiveness towards accommodating differences.

The unwillingness of one of the boys to enter into another's village alerts us to an upcoming impediment. The boy's initial mistake of considering the devil to be his friend reminds us of the colonial tactics of pretending to be a facilitating friend. The bleeding head of the tribal boy, killed, cut and carried by the devil, is the metaphorical representation of the brutal colonial violence in its savage deracinating of the homophile ethnic ethos in the name of 'civilising' Indigeneity with Victorian Christianity.[8] The devil's motive for mutilating the murdered body in the form of separating the head and carrying it as an exhibit cannot be understood unless the queer tribal body is related to the eradicative raid of the Lepcha body politic by colonial captors,[9] importing homophobia as one of the major outcomes of their Victorian 'fanatical purity campaign' (Bhaskaran, 2002: 16). Seen as a sin from the conservative Christian perspective, the tribal homoeroticity for the usurping reformers could have been depolluted only with images of slaughter and disfigurement.[10]

As 'signatory to the very charter of fiction' (Stewart, 1984: 51), death has been unavoidably associated with gender and sexuality.[11] Bronfen and Goodwin have shown that the concerns of gender/sexuality and death, seen as two possible axes of enigma and repudiation in relation to heteropatriarchal subjectivity and culture, pop up in the cultural discourses like 'the blind spot the representational system seeks to refuse even as it constantly addresses it' (1993: 20).

The politics behind the demonstration of the separated head can be grasped on the basis of the Foucauldian idea of biopower: 'biological existence [to be] reflected in political existence' (Foucault, 1981: 142). The 'devil' with the tribal head, as an outcome of the 'numerous and diverse techniques for achieving the subjugations of bodies and the control of populations' (ibid.: 140), represents the policing authority of the state apparatus in 'the administration of bodies and the calculated management of life' (ibid.). The removed head embodies brutality as an essential component of colonial bio-power in the forceful regulation of the Lepcha body in the name of disciplinarian techniques, so that the Indigenous population can be compelled to succumb to the dominator's propagated notions of being 'normal' and 'healthy'. The body of the tribal boy was not sexed until his head was cut off; the isolated head is the signifier of an insinuation to affect the queer-accommodating ethnoscape with an invested determination for normatising sex.[12] The indication of death, as an instrument of command that removes a body, branded as 'perverse', from the sexual economy, therefore must be taken not just as the symbolic beginning of the colonial oppression over the tribal territory but also as a metaphor of the permanent loss of the sexual-heterogeneous ethical values and determinacies like homophilia.[13]

Signifying 'repugnance' or 'the (primordial) object of disgust' (Hegarty, 2000: 58), death, for Bataille, in a two-way mode of repulsion and attraction which he calls 'abjection', also allures humanity with a desire for what is been excluded. According to Bataille, an 'aura of death is what denotes passion' (ibid.: 20). The most noteworthy utterance in *Two Friends and the Devil* is the seductive invitation of the devil that resembles Bataille's notion of the tangled confusion regarding sexual pleasure and taboo: 'Come and taste a little of my cucumber'. After an initial pause of bafflement, one can understand the phallic implication of this apparently unrelated expression, by recognising the devil as the colonial abuser-seducer. Edward Said points out that 'the Orient was a place where one could look for sexual experience unobtainable in Europe' (1978: 190). The devil's passion, highlighting the transgressive temptation of the imposer of the taboo, depicts life as a 'primary impulse' towards an 'explosion' that often touches upon death.[14] The devil's statement also proves that homophobia is actually an offshoot of a latent homosexuality.[15] This Lepcha folktale, retrospectively, points at the greater 'permissiveness' that homoeroticity acquired in an ethnic climate, where the two tribal boys could prefer an alter-masculine life of 'irresponsibility, self-indulgence and an isolationist detachment from the claims of others' (Ehrenreich, 1983: 169) within the tribal habitus.[16]

Two Friends and the Devil, as a tragedy of the two tribal male friends, on account of the violent trespassing and the consequent distorting of the Lepcha 'field'[17] by the colonial 'devil' under the camouflage of modernising, is a mythistoric narration of the demolition of tribal ecosystem and the sub-version of the liberated norms that were sensitive to the endogenous 'rules' framed out of a 'collective intentionality' (Searle, 1995: 13) peculiar to the Lepcha habitus. It also chronicles the inimical rejigging of the Indigenous liberal state into a 'moralizing state' (Moore, 1995: 4) of moral fixity. The detached tribal head becomes the epitome of the homophobic 'structuralist constructivism' or 'constructivist structuralism' (Bourdieu, 1989: 14) by the invaders, who severed the Lepchas from their ethnic habitus (embodied history) by depriving the homoerotic Indigenous person of their agency. The subsequent homophobia among Indigenous people needs to be seen as the internalisation of the *subjectivist* (Bourdieu, 1977) vision that fails to uncover the violent 'constructs of the constructs'[18] beneath the recent social temper.

Structuring of the closet

The next Lepcha folktale, *The Luckless Punshohang*, marks the changes inserted into the tribal ethos of world making,[19] to reproduce a spurious version of homophobic Indigeneity.

Tale 2: The Luckless Punshohang

Once upon a time there was a house of two brothers—the baby brother and luckless Punshohang, the elder one. It was a time when the holy people came and drew away all the devils except a single devil family, who remained in a cave. One day the parents of the two brothers went to work in the field by leaving the baby with Punshohang. Punshohang did not know that there was a devil family who stayed in a nearby cave. Finding the house empty, the mother devil came and took Punshohang to her cave. She locked him with her children devils before going out for her nocturnal work. When the father and mother devils left, Punshohang was afraid: 'I think these children are going to kill me and eat me'. He started crying. The children came and licked up his tears. This made Punshohang annoyed, and he began to cut the devils left and right with his knife. The parent devils returned with food early in the morning. The children devils ate, but Punshohang could not eat their food. That day again during the night the parents went out, leaving the children devils locked inside the cave with Punshohang. Punshohang again began to cry, and the children devils licked his tears. He again became mad and started cutting the children left and right with his knife. This made him so exhausted that he fell into a deep sleep. While he was sleeping, the children devils woke him up. Giving him the key, they showed him the way to escape. Punshohang ran back to his house. He told his parents about all that had happened to him. However, he died that day.

It is a tale that reveals the second phase of the prohibition of tribal homoeroticity in the form of turning same-sex intimacy into a closeted devilish act in 'caves'. A series of questions come to the mind regarding Punshohang and his relation with the children devils. Why did the mother devil take Punshohang alone and not also his infant brother? What is the reason behind the gender ambiguity of the children devils? What is the nature of Punshohang's 'cutting' the children with his knife in a congenial way that the parent devils returned only to find the children unscarred, unalarmed and willing to stay with him at night?

Devils, as textual representations of *'unlicensed* difference' (Bauman, 1992: xvi), tend to display 'clearly the markings of deviant sexualities and gendering' (Halberstam, 1995: 4). The folktale provides metahistorical evidence of how with the coming of 'the holy men', the dissident queer people of the soil who resisted sexual engineering were bracketed as devils by the imperial rationality that devaluated the raw tribal unconventionality. Hence, labelled as a devil, the tribal mother should have been aware of the heretical sexual demand of her children, which could only be satisfied by a grown-up boy with a tenacity for nonconformity. The kidnapping of Punshohang as not being postulated on normative heterocentricity was a likely reason for the gender ambiguity of the children devils given that it took place in a developing heterosexist state, where abduction, as an extension of the Lepcha custom of elopement for initiating a heteronormative marriage, was the apt available means of providing a partner for vulnerable homosexual Indigenous people. If Punshohang was chosen for the queer children devils to fit and perform as the same-sex 'doubles', then why did he cry? His fear can be best understood in terms of Angela Connolly's psychoanalytic reading of an encounter with an abject person in the form of devil as chancing upon 'limits, differences, evil and death' (Connolly, 2003: 410). Anxious due to the return of what had been repressed as nonnormative, Punshohang was possibly terrified by the gay children devils the first night due to an 'uncanny horror' that initiates in the self a longing for a participation into what has been proscribed as the devil Other and for the urge to suppress the devil for an egotistical pleasure of masterhood.[20] Punshohang's ambivalent use of a metaphoric knife, which was used to hit the devils without hurting them, links to his uncanny horror emerging from his repressed alternative tribal sexuality that was no longer permissible in the hegemonic domain of foreign settlers. Punshohang's cutting the children devil with his knife and their act of licking the tears from his cheeks are sexual allegories.

In an intimate provocation for belonging, by transgressing the limits drawn by the state agencies, between the normatised self and the devil Other, the 'filthy' skin of the insubordinate tribals tagged as 'devils' touched the altered skin of the closeted tribal gay who has been left with the only chance of cherishing his homoeroticity in a cave full of strangers.[21] Punshohang's initial fear during the second night, followed by a repose that denotes sexual satiety, represents the 'sublime terror'[22] that enables the individual to reconcile, by overcoming the instituted boundary, with the abject/devil Other as their own mirror image of the desires stereotyped as 'perverted' by the coercive mechanisms of the majoritarian 'mainstream'. The children devils' act of letting Punshohang go back to his house, again, as a mythistory of the transformation in the nature of the homoerotic Indigenous bond on account of the imported, tabooed prejudice against same-sex intimacy, illustrates that the stable relationship between the two gay boys in the sexual democratic tribal world of *Two Friends and the Devil* has been distorted to pave the way for a clandestine, polyamorous encounter as the only choice for a discreet, closeted tribal homosexual like Punshohangin. *The Luckless Punshohang* marks the beginning of the vitiated scenario where a queer Indigenous man can meet strangers to have sex in a cave and, thereafter, come out straight.

The death of the gay boy, at the end of both this tale and the previous one, serves a significant purpose, which can only be comprehended once we again are reminded that, as 'biological concepts that are linked inviolably', death and sexuality need to be treated together (Trites, 2000: 122) in order to view 'death epochs' (Ariès, 1985: 1) as historical shifts in the relationship between the self and the changed cultural configuration of power. What these deaths symbolise can be best understood by recognising death as a signifier of 'a people's own power' in proclaiming the primacy of a natural drive over a scripted culture.[23] The plots of *Two Friends and the Devil* and *The Luckless Punshohang* as mythistory verify how—with the schematic expurgation of the Indigenous libertinism in 'natural' heterogeneous sexuality, causing a denial of 'eroticism'—Indigenous sexuality was gradually denounced as perverse. The boys in both these Lepcha tales, who died abruptly with no suggestion of homicide or malady, seem to adopt suicide as a voluntary, sovereign choice to quit rather than merely survive in 'an entirely profane world' where nothing is left 'but animal mechanism' (Bataille, 1988: 128). These deaths figure as a crooked substitution of the acknowledged and the living (as here and now to nowhere) by the unfamiliar and the dead.

The gay anguish at the negation of 'the promise of life implicit in eroticism' opened the way for an anguished queerness through passage into 'the sensuous aspect of death' (ibid.: 2001: 59). The suicide of these homosexuals must not be regarded as denoting all about death itself but rather must also be about their assertive control over their own lives by resisting colonising control and by denying normatising agents' establishing dominion over the defiant body and marginalised desire—through the empowered realisation that 'death is power's limit, the moment that escapes it' (Foucault, 1981: 138). As the counternormative 'abnormal' and 'unhealthy' weapon that could defy the administration of desire through a calculated management of the body, death, in the form of a choice made by these homoerotic tribals, triumphantly celebrates 'an incurable deviancy. . . . nothing else is as offensive as this' (Baudrillard, 1993a: 126).

Becoming a man: identifying with the oppressor

Halberstam (1995) shows how the monster/giant serves as a metaphor for the fear of all that must be expelled, by classifying them as foreign, impure and perverse: in this case, to replace a sexual egalitarianism with a sexual hierarchy.

Tale 3: The Orphan Boy and the Giant

Once upon a time, there lived a starving orphan boy. He went to his uncle and got some *chi* [fermented beer] and *zo* [rice] to eat. Putting on new clothes, he took his uncle's cattle for grazing. Upon his return, he was provided food by his uncle. However, the boy was not satisfied and went on demanding more food, again and again. Finding him to be greedy, the uncle asked the boy to leave his house immediately. The boy became very sad. He came across a spring where he placed his *vore* [a snare used to catch birds] and hid himself in a bush nearby. But every time he came to check the *vore*, he found it empty. He was angry and wanted to see who was taking his catch. Suddenly he heard some noise of someone approaching him. But it was not a usual human sound. Being frightened, he pretended to be dead. Looking through his eye slits, he found that a giant was coming towards him. The giant was happy to see a bigger game caught up in the snare. Taking the boy on his hand he said, 'Hmm, today I got quite a big bird'. Looking at the boy, he asked: 'Are you alive or dead?' The boy was too frightened to answer. He rather stayed motionless as if he were dead. Thinking that he was dead, the giant carried him on his shoulder and climbed on a huge rock mountain. Again he examined the boy and asked whether he was alive or dead. Not getting any reply, he opened the door inside the rock cave and placed the boy in a corner and then rested on the huge bed. Waking up after some time, he rang a bell, and plenty of food, treasure and *chi* appeared before him. After this, he again checked the boy, and finding him dead, he left the bell on his stone shelf and went out for his work. The boy took the bell and slowly came out of the room and ran back home as fast as possible. Reaching his house, he rang the bell and immediately huge heaps of food and wealth appeared in front of him. Soon he became rich and lived happily thereafter.

The Lepcha folktale *The Orphan Boy and the Giant* features a starving boy who could not help but join the homosocial company of the giant homosexual Other. The mask of faking 'death' as the product of his internalisation of homophobia signals the third phase of changing the Fourth World people into a 'correct' and 'functional' (McHoul and Grace, 1993: 17) normatised role. The boy's pretending to be dead must have emerged out of an 'ago-nized sexual anaesthesia', resulting from the 'male homosexual panic'[24] (Sedgwick, 2002: 161). That the Lepcha boy was starving, despite his uncle's offering him with food, suggests the 'hunger gaze' (Lawson, 2011) of the homosexual tribal male, starving because of the anorexic undernourish-ment of his sex-starved queer body. The starved tribal body becomes the embodiment of the colonial eschewing of the Lepcha gay body beneath its projected 'creative virtue' of the civilising of Indigenous people. The tale reveals that by subtracting the 'most terrible suffering' of an outlawed tribal homosexual from the imperial-cum-fetishistic mission of reinventing Indige-neity into a 'multiplicity of formalizations' (Badiou, 2007: 143), the reality of an Indigenous queer identity was inverted into a supreme fiction of the unreal giant for posterity.

From the queernormative space of 'thirdness' in *Two Friends and the Devil* via the closeted gay in *The Luckless Punshohang*, this tale, *The Orphan Boy and the Giant*, focuses on the orphan Lepcha boy's essential 'life-in-death' in a transformed realm of homosexual panic where his camouflaging the body as a corpse becomes 'an image of otherness that is also, paradoxically, the image of self' (Schwenger, 2000: 400). The orphan boy's pretending to be a cadaver turns out to be the mythistoric representation, as 'object's aftermath', of the Indigenous queer made to be viewed as an image of the dead—'present in absence'—like 'that which comes later, which is left over and allows us still to have the object at our command when there is nothing left of it' (Blanchot, 1982: 260).

The Lepcha boy reveals his unusual greediness, to the extent of an esti-mated abnormality, due to which his uncle throws him out of his house. Being a marginalised tribal gay in an inverted ambience of homophobia, the tribal orphan fails to resist the temptation of a homosocial intimacy with the gay Other. Yet internalising the official mandate to view the gay Other as a demonised giant against whom a 'civilised' man ought to take a pivotal stand, he decides to feign death. The fear of emasculation by the gender policing of the colonisers keeps the Indigenous orphan thoroughly alert so that, by mimicking the model of masculinity, he would never dare to expose his homosexuality in his quest for accumulating the imported cultural sym-bols which denote manhood and a promise of materialistic success. The giant repetitively asks him if he is alive, but the orphan plays his role well. Corpsing his gay body, the Lepcha boy finally demonstrates his efforts for acclimatising to a colonial notion of masculinity in his relentless test to prove before the rest of the men, including himself, that he has been successful in mastering the homophobic share of the masters. The tribal boy's loss of his homoerotic self, however, is compensated by his becoming of a wealthy man as a result of his imitation of the hegemonic masculinity.[25] Being empow-ered, with food and wealth through the exploitation of the nonnormative giant, the Indigenous boy emerges as the rectified model of a renovated

Indigenous person whose normativity is rightly demonstrated by his feigned announcing of the death of homoeroticity, which, in consequence, would bring the approval of manhood from the colonial other men.[26] The Indigenous queer body's being identified as a cadaver, in an internalised mode of echoing the homophobic panic of the oppressor, functions as a defence against the possible humiliation of getting labelled as an insufficient man.[27] The homosexual body as a copse demonstrates how, by inscribing every law on the subject bodies,[28] racial domination operates through the domination of the grotesque native men, otherised on the basis of their differences, until the dissentient body fulfils the bureaucratic agenda of being 'disciplined', thereby 'communicating' with the colonial idea of a rationalised manhood, by the means of 'mirroring' the hawk-eyed scheme for docility.[29]

This Lepcha folktale focuses on the sociocultural reconstructing of the tribal in the form of an orphan boy transmuting himself into a successful, wealthy man by his fitting into the colonial frame of manhood. The orphan boy's endeavour of deracinating the deviant tribal—otherised as a giant—through the contrived proclamation of the deadened end of Indigenous homoeroticity, documents the metahistory of silencing queer Indigeneity as unbecoming of a man. The majority of the Indians, as obedient pupils and aspiring neocolonisers, have been continuing this colonial lesson of a masculinity that exploits and otherises Indigenous nonconformists, in a mode of denying the existence of a prehistoric queer Indigeneity.

Hate story: foreignising homoeroticity

A particular theme in the domain of folktales acquires a specified meaning by its repetitive use. The storytellers, while experiencing the theme through subsequent renditions in a recurring retrospective mode, ultimately turn the theme into a motif of history.[30] Hence, the repetitive coupling of two boys as friends in Lepcha folktales, to emphasise the issue of 'choosing one's company' on the basis of a definite standpoint on close same-sex relationships, turns the theme of male intimate bond into a homoerotic motif.[31] Studies on intimate friendships have generally drawn the conclusion that most close friendships contain an erotic element, which is usually repressed as an embarrassment (Seiden and Bart, 1975). Best friends are seen to come together in a similar way as the lovers are drawn towards one another.[32] Living together as same-sex friends is a physical process where their bodies play a significant role in binding themselves to each other.[33] Foucault pointed out that the social censoring of male friendship is correlated with the diabolising of homosexuality.[34]

Tale 4: Two Brothers

A long time back, there were two brothers: the rich younger brother and the poor elder brother. The younger brother was close to his friend. Ignoring the elder brother, he used to take care of his friend affectionately. The younger brother one day said, 'Dear friend, let's go to the forest to collect red berries', and they went to the forest. Climbing up the tree, the younger brother started eating the berries, and the red juice oozing out of the fruit marked him red. Calling out to his friend, he tumbled down the tree, 'O! I'm falling'. Climbing down the tree, the friend found the younger brother lying on the ground and smeared in red colour. He said, 'You are no way related to me. Why should I look after you? Rather I will inform your brother. Let him come and take care of you'. He left the place without attending the friend. The elder brother, however, rushed to the spot. Looking at his younger brother, he lamented: 'My brother, you have forgotten your own brother and have neglected me. You have showered all your love and affection on such an undeserving man'. As he was about to lift the younger brother to carry him home, the younger brother opened his eyes and said, 'Brother I am fine. Nothing has happened to me'. He got up and went back home with his elder brother. From that day, the friend was no more a friend, but the two brothers were always together, loving and caring for one another. This is the reason why the Lepchas believe that nothing is more important than the love of one's own kin.

Regarding the prohibited friendship between two Lepcha men—unlike *Two Friends and the Devil* and *The Idiot*[35] (a folktale from the 1976 volume of Kotturan, in which through the portrayal of an idiot brother blood relation was depicted as insufficient, and as a corollary, this has made room for effective bonds outside immediate kinship)—in *Two Brothers*, the concluding points definitely seem to refer to the moment of foreignising the homoerotic subculture of Indigenous friendship: 'From that day, the friend was no more a friend, but the two brothers were always together, loving and caring for one another. This is the reason why the Lepchas believe that nothing is more important than the love of one's own kin'. Realising that they could no longer feel at home in a deterritorialised tribalscape, 'from that day' the queer male friends, having dramatised—like a play within a play—the plotted hatred regarding a same-sex relationship as a savage affair of the forest, returned straight with an elder brother into the regulated family lifestyle of a reterritorialised unhomely house.[36]

The elder brother's antagonistic attitude from the beginning of the tale, due to the younger brother's expressive caring of his friend, hints at the social discomfort regarding the open demonstration of strong friendship, in a domain of misshapen tribalism where stigmatising all possibilities of homoeroticity as effeminate had already been in progress, signalling the foreignisation of the prevalent homoeroticity among this Indigenous people with the installation of the racial hypermasculinity as the only legalised model in the Lepcha territory. The younger brother's performative death thus signals the 'social death' (Patterson, 1982) of the Indigenous queer, resulting from the colonial mission to alienate non-heteronormativity from Indigeneity.

A deconstructive reading of the normatised return of an Indigenous queer, however, throws a different light on the conventional notion of the 'normative mainstream' family and brotherhood. From the sons of the totem father fighting among themselves, *Two Brothers* shows how a brotherly bond has been appropriated for sexual reform that aims to replace homoeroticity with a brotherly sublimation of a generalised, inherited relationship.[37] Moreover, the incident of forcing the boy into a 'mainstream' family set-up helps to demystify the often-transmitted, mythologised image of a natural, ineluctable drive towards the comfort of 'kinship, love and having nice things together'.[38]

The anxiety of the poor elder brother at his rich younger brother's attachment to a male friend finds its replication in the writings of English scholars like J. Millott Severn.[39] The inhibition of the younger brother's friend against touching his buddy, as if it has to be considered as an untouchable body that can be touched and taken care of only by his own brother, unveils the mythistory of touch aversion, which in the long run has given birth to homophobic touch isolation. After their undoing of homo-amorous male solidarity, the younger brother and his friend would then be dragged, perversely, into heterosexual role-playing. The fact that the brother had to depend on a mere sham to find proof of his friend's genuineness, creates, owing to the lack of procedural fairness, serious doubt regarding the sincerity of the entire trial. Nevertheless, with the friendship coloured as foul, the folktale becomes a metahistorical narrative of how an Indigenous same-sex friendship of possible eroticity is displaced—never to be practised.

The disenchantment of the younger brother mirrors the legitimation of an uncontested colonial standard of propriety. The homoerotic nonutilitarian love of the wilful tribal subject, idly busy in bird watching or simple fruit tasting, became uncultured the moment when its purposelessness was injected with sense, meaning and design. Motivated by a colonial (to be continued by the neocolonisers) urge for a reculturalisation (under the pretext of humanisation and rationalisation,), the naturality of gay wondering males as celebrated in the folktale *Two Friends and the Devil* was decimated by the time the Lepha storytellers began to concoct *Two Brothers*. *Two Brothers* also hints at quite an advanced stage of colonial expansion in the Lepcha land, on account of which the younger brother could exemplify the reparation of a gay Indigenous person who had already been metamorphosed into a hapless object, and thereafter, by his mastering the colonial gay aversion, he had to be brought back to the house of his straight, normative brother.

Reinventing erotic geographies

The reconceptualisation of a 'normatised' sexual identity is often intimately associated with the reconfiguration of a homoerotic tribal space, and the Lepcha folktales reflect the reordering of the location for gay intimacy on the mutilated Lepcha sexual geo-space. A genealogy of how the differing sexual citizens were putrefied as noncitizen devils can be best understood in terms of human geography: the setting, as an eroticised topography, serves to provide, in Stephen Pfohl's term, ' "vernacular" erotic geographies' (1993). Understanding the politics of remapping is important to exposing the revisions brought in the Indigenous space in relation to queer eroticity by the cultural imperialism of a racist state. With the variations taking place against the backdrop of the flow of time, reflecting 'the forms of the most immediate reality' (Bakhtin, 1996: 85), these Lepcha folktales, seen through the lens of a chronotope,[40] add details to the 'chronotope of passage' (Gilroy, 1993: 4) in tribal homoeroticity.

From being together all through the day, as depicted in *Two Friends and the Devil*, the tribal homosexual in *The Luckless Punshohang* is forced to be at ease with his sexuality only within a clandestine closeted cave, in darkness. The nocturnal setting marks the change brought in the tribal outlook, in its viewing of homoeroticity as a nonnormative style of living.[41] The mythistoric transformation of the spatial expressions—from that of the open mountaintop in *Two Friends and the Devil* to a confined cave in *The Luckless Punshohang*, via the migrated land of the giant in *The Orphan Boy and the Giant* to the ultimate forest, symbolising exile, in *Two Brothers*— hint at the negative transformation taking place in the sociopolitical and cultural Lepcha geo-space, which had further forced Indigenous gays to compromise their lives. The fixing of the younger brother of *Two Brothers* into the designed normative order, as a corollary, provides a model of strategic repression for posterity—resulting in the contemporary rejection of providing certainty about Indigenous homoeroticity, by calumniating it as a contingent identity[42] of the past. The rearrangement in the setting of the Lepcha folktales, in the mode of regression, traces the mythistoric trajectory of obliterating queer Indigenous people. Revealing the changing lines of boundaries and borders drawn on nonconformist Indigeneity, the inimical altering of the backdrops in these tribal tales reaffirm that 'space is a pressing matter and it matters which bodies, where and how, press up against it' (Probyn, 1995: 81). Illustrating the contrast 'between *being what one was and making oneself what one should be*' (Bauman, 1992: xiii), the transporting of the homoerotic Lepcha boys from the open mountaintop to the forest of banishment symbolically highlights the adverse direction towards which the altered space ushered in the tribal homoerotic body. The ultimate end of the Indigenous gay body seems to rest on the ability of pretending to be a corpse. However, as Butler observed, death seems to be a 'compensatory curse' in relation to the blessing of a prohibited love. The 'death', symbolising a libertine compensation[43] for Indigenous homosexual desire, stands for 'the telos of male homosexuality, its genesis and its demise, the principle of its intelligibility' (Butler, 1992: 359). The Lepcha folktales, exposing the invented moral obligation bestowed on a power-laden space and emerging as a conscious mythistoric counter-scripting of tribal queer metahistory— out of the realisation that an identity not scripted for the future becomes a contingent identity—need to be disseminated intellectually[44] as a significant counternormative defence against the contemporary prognosis of homosexuality as a non-identity in 'mainstream' India.[45]

Notes

1 Hayden White observed that one needs to reconstruct history in the way one wishes to see the future: '[W]e are free to conceive "history" as we please, just as we are free to make of it what we will' and for transcending

> the agnosticism which an Ironic perspective on history, passing as the sole possible 'realism' and 'objectivity' to which we can aspire in historical studies, foists upon us, we have only to reject this Ironic perspective and to will to view history from another, anti-Ironic perspective.
>
> (1973: 433–434)

2 For a detailed introduction to mythistory, see Joseph Mali (2003).
3 McNeill blended his conviction that 'Truth about human behaviour is an unattainable goal' (McNeill, 1986: 8), which at the best can be detectable through the multiple versions of 'truths' critically disseminated by historians, with his belief that societies seek to organise their notions of the past in a similar way to their having confidence in mythical truths. This enabled him to show that the historical truths like that of the myths are ever evolving and are inevitably under the threat—similar to that of the myths—because of the tension that while for some people (who share and support the historical assumptions and particularities) the historical truths publicised by historians are genuine facts, for some others these are doubtful, like the myths. Moreover, like scientific truths, historians' achievement of truths evolve across generations and in the process are amendable (the manner in which 'the versions of the past acceptable today' seem to be more accurate than that of the historical truths put forward by the historians of earlier generations). Hence, McNeill concludes that what has been generally accepted as historical truths are mythistories, and all histories are in fact historiographical 'myth-making and myth-breaking' histories (ibid.: 9).
4 Kotturan (1976) argues in his introduction that these tales are of Lepcha origin.
5 The following is a retelling of the folktale *All about Adventure*:
   There was a prosperous settlement once upon a time in a remote mountain valley. There was enough water, and the soil was so fertile that the people in the village never suffered from any shortage of food. Even then, the young men who were under the impression that every man should have some adventure in his life were not happy with their smooth life. They were hardly satisfied with the regular sowing, harvesting, singing and dancing. They thought of going to some faraway place for real adventure. Forming a group, the men planned to visit the king. The villagers prayed for their smooth journey and safe return. The

elderly people thought that these youngsters would make them feel proud by proving themselves as worthy men of adventure. The young men started moving towards the capital, which was quite a distant town. On their way, the village girls offered them garlands, which made them proud like the pumpkins. After some time, looking at the birds, they said, 'It's a pity that we cannot fly'. Some of the men said, 'We need to be brave for that' and started to climb a tree. They were so high that they forgot about the ground below and jumped from the tree as if they could fly like the birds. The others saw them fall down and die one after another. The others said, 'They are martyrs. They were brave enough to prove that flying is for the birds'. The remaining men continued to move towards the capital. Reaching the palace, they went to meet the king: 'O good king', they said, 'we have come from a distant village to find adventure. Please tell us what we can do for you'. The happy king said, 'I am pleased to see you young enthusiastic men. You can take care of the palace garden'. After some days, the men began to complain: 'Have we come here to do gardening? We could do this in our village'. They lost interest and decided to return to the village. The king, thanking them for the service, gave them a bag full of butter, salt and an ox head. Each of the men felt excited thinking of the village people, singing and dancing together. They were soon tired and hungry and decided to eat, but the problem was that they were men who didn't know how to cook, since at home, food was served by their women. Opening the bundle that the king had gifted them, they mistakenly treated the salt as rice and put the entire bulk in a pot full of water. They thought that the butter was flour, ready to be baked, which they placed on an iron plate over the fire. Meanwhile while washing the ox head, it slipped and fell into the river. Suddenly they found that all the salt got mixed into the water and the butter, which they thought to be flour, melted down. Sadly, they were starving all the way back, though they learned an important lesson.

6 Alter-masculinity suggests that 'Men need to develop their "feminine side" and reclaim emotions, dependency needs, passivity, fluidity, playfulness, sensuality, vulnerability and resistance to always assuming responsibility' (Goldberg, 1979: 254).

7 Detraditionalisation has been used in the sense of rejecting the 'inclusion' of unique Indigenous subcultures and instead appropriating it in the dominant culture.

8 The Lepchas have often been dismayed by the Christian 'exclusivist attitude' (Longkumer, 2010: 85) that induces them to value their identity as religious converts more dearly than their ethnic identity. Given the early exposure of the Lepchas to Buddhism in Sikkim, resulting from the activity of Lhatsun Namka Jigme (1597–1650), it is not difficult to imagine that the conversion to Christianity would have been viewed as the entry of the devil: 'A Buddhist Lepcha villager of Nampatan stated: "They call us Satan. This causes tension. They do not accept different beliefs"' (Bentley, 2007: 64).

9 '[A]t most times and places in pre-nineteenth-century India, love between women and between men, even when disapproved of, was not actively persecuted. As far as we know, no one has ever been executed for homosexuality in India' (Vanita and Kidwai, 2000: xviii). The otherising of the queer is comparatively a new phenomenon in India, since it has its origin in the colonial regime where the heteronormative gaze of the colonisers has projected homoeroticity as 'special oriental vice' (Bhaskaran, 2002). Macaulay, in his keenness to civilise South Asians with British Victorian moralities, also contributed to the labelling sodomy and any other man–man acts of eroticity as 'unnatural' and therefore criminal offences (Kugle, 2002: 37).

10 The missionary invasion started in 1841 with the arrival of Reverend William Start in Darjeeling. He translated the Bible into the Lepcha language and had it published (Wylie, 1854). Later, Reverend William Macfarlane certified that 'The Lepchas seem to be the most hopeful people for us in the hills' (Perry, 1997: 42). One of the Lepcha Christians stated his views regarding the Anglicisation of the tribal world:

> Forgetting our own age-old customs and ways of life, the beginnings of which are lost in antiquity, now among our Christian kinsmen there is a definite trend to display with pride, like the proverbial peacock, the plumes of Western culture in almost everything that is displayable. Moving outside more often than not, suit, hat and tie proclaim that the person is a Christian convert.
>
> (Foning, 1987: 294)

11 Scholars like Laura E. Tanner, Elisabeth Bronfen and Kerry Mallan have worked on the depiction of death in literature and its relation with the societal power dynamics related to gender and sexuality.

12 Judith Butler rightly observed that 'the body is not "sexed" in any significant sense before its determination within a discourse through which it becomes invested with an 'idea' of natural or essential sex'; rather, it 'gains meaning in discourse only in the context of power relations' (Butler, 1997: 117).

13 Death, according to Baudrillard, 'ought never to be understood as the real event that effects a subject or a body but as a form in which the determinacy of the subject and of value is lost' (1993a: 5).

14 By imposing a taboo, which can 'curse gloriously whatever it forbids', life, according to Bataille, exists only as a difference between taboo and transgression: 'Life is a swelling tumult continuously on the verge of explosion' (2001: 59).

15 Adams et al. write that 'individuals who score in the homophobic range and admit negative affect toward homosexuality demonstrate significant sexual arousal to male homosexual erotic stimuli' (1996: 444) and argue that homophobia is 'associated with homosexual arousal that the homophobic individual is either unaware of or denies' (ibid.: 440).

16 Habitus, according to Bourdieu, is 'society written into the body, into the biological individual' (1990: 63). According to Dagmang, habitus signifies both 'the social habitus of a certain group of people and the personal habitus of an individual'—that is, 'the generalised and habitual schemes of thought, appreciation and action' that would become a part of one's 'second-nature ability':

> Their predispositions or determined typical ways of looking or viewing at things, ways of evaluating taste or values, ways of approaching an event or problem through action, prefigure everything that a group or a person may think, appreciate or do.
>
> (Dagmang, 2010: 72)

17 'Field' refers to

> what Goffman calls the 'sense of one's place'. It is this sense of one's place which, in interactions, leads people whom we call in French '*les gens modestes*', 'common folks', to keep to their common place, and the others to 'keep their distance', to 'maintain their rank', and to 'not get familiar'
>
> (Bourdieu, 1989: 17)

18 Social reality has been studied as a collage of multiple 'constructs' by Schutz (1962: 59): 'Thus, the constructs of the social sciences are, so to speak, constructs of the second degree, that is, constructs of the constructs made by the actors on the social scene'.

19 'To change the world, one has to change the ways of world-making, that is, the vision of the world and the practical operations by which groups are produced and reproduced' (Bourdieu, 1989: 23).

20 As per Connolly, the uncanny horror resulting from an otherised image of a devil, offers 'the possibility of an unconscious participation in guilty pleasures through the identification with the monster and its subjectivity' and 'the super-egoical pleasure of control over and repression of the monster as the dark shadow double of the ego consciousness' (2003: 419).

21 Skin, as Anzieu argued in *The Skin Ego*, is the substance on which individuality gets scripted according to the response of the self to the dominant sociopolitical discourses. Sara Ahmed argued that different skin, in sustaining separateness or fluidity, signals resistance or eagerness for intimacy and belonging (2005: 104–106).

22 Connolly categorised 'sublime terror' as 'an "unlimiting" of the imagination, an increase in consciousness and a capacity to accept ethical guilt about our abject desires' through which the self resolves the boundary between the 'monster' or the devil, seen as the self's Other, on the basis of the recognition that 'the perverse and psychotic desires of the monster are a mirror image of our own perverse desires and the perversity of our own community and culture, based as they are on mechanisms of sacrifice and of scapegoating' (2003: 419–420).

23 'Death—not in the abstract, but people dying and the processes by which they die—may signify by turns a monarch's sovereignty, a people's own power, and the primacy of biology over culture' (Bronfen and Goodwin, 1993: 5).

24 Homosexual panic refers to an unyielding unacceptance of homosexuality by a man who is not 'able to ascertain that he is not (and his bonds are not) homosexual' (Sedgwick, 1985: 88).

25 'The hegemonic definition of manhood', according to Michael S. Kimmel, 'is a man *in* power, *with* power, and *of* power. We equate manhood with being strong, successful, capable, reliable, in control' (2005: 30).

26 David Leverenz rightly observed that 'ideologies of manhood have functioned primarily in relation to the gaze of the male peers and male authority' (1991: 769).

27

> Men become depressed because of loss of status and power in the world of men. It is not the loss of money . . . which produces the despair that leads to self-destruction. It is the 'shame', the 'humiliation'. . . . A man despairs when he has ceased being a man among men.
>
> (Gaylin, 1992: 32)

28 'There is no law that is not inscribed on bodies. Every law has a hold on the body' (De Certeau, 1984: 139).

29 For details about the typology of body use, see Arthur W. Frank, 1991. He shows how, on the basis of 'regimentation', 'consumption' and 'recognition' as being normal, the body is dominated, using rationalisation as an alibi.

30 During storytelling, it is through 'repetition' that 'events . . . are experienced a second time in the form of suffering by memory operating retrospectively' by which 'action . . . establishes its meaning and that permanent significance which then enters into history' (Arendt, 1968: 21).

31 According to Arendt, one's standpoint is best expressed through 'choosing one's company': '[O]ur decisions about right and wrong will depend upon our choice of company, with whom we wish to spend our lives' (1982: 113).

32 Lillian B Rubin wrote that 'More than others, best friends are drawn together in much the same way as lovers—by something ineffable, something to which, most people say, it is almost impossible to give words' (1985: 179).

33

> Living together, as male friends were expected to do unless married, is a very physical process. The phrase 'one soul in two bodies' suggests the importance of the body as that which allows men to bind themselves to each other.
>
> (Culberston, 1996: 164)

34 Foucault, in an interview, elaborated on the interrelatedness between the anxiety over same-sex friendship and homophobia:

> For centuries after antiquity, friendship was a very important kind of social relation: a social relation within which people had a certain free-dom . . . as well as very' intense emotional relations. . . . sex between men became a problem—in the eighteenth century. . . . As long as friendship was something important, was socially accepted, nobody realised men had sex together. You couldn't say that men didn't have sex together—it just didn't matter. . . . Well, I'm sure I'm right, that the disappearance of friendship as a social relation and the declaration of homosexuality as a social/political/medical problem are the same process.
>
> (Rabinow, 1998: 170–171)

35 The following is a retelling of the folktale *The Idiot*:

There lived two brothers once upon a time. The elder one was strong but stupid, while his younger brother was weak but intelligent. One day, both of them started for Tibet to sell quinine. They walked for 30 kilometres and felt very tired. Since it was already very dark, they could not see anything around, except a huge tree. They thought of spending the night, sleeping under the shel-ter of the tree. The elder brother, before going to sleep, went in search of water. Soon he came across a tiger that was busy eating a deer. The foolish brother, mistaking the tiger for a big cat, threw a large stone for fun. Returning to his younger brother, he stated amazingly: 'O my brother, I saw a big cat eating a big deer'. The younger brother became curious to see the big cat that could eat a fully grown deer. When both of them reached that spot, the tiger had already run away into the forest. So they found only the deer lying dead. The younger brother said: 'Let us carry the deer to cook and eat it ourselves'. Accordingly, carrying the deer to their shelter, they made a fire to cook a nice curry. The tiger, in the meantime, got the smell of the deer curry and arrived at the cooking spot. The tiger started demanding his share from the younger brother, telling him that it was the tiger's prey. But the younger brother didn't want to share the curry. Soon a fight began between the tiger and the younger brother. Being not at all strong, he asked help from the elder brother, who was, however, concerned only about the curry: 'I am least bothered about you', he said, 'You fight but don't dare touch my curry'. The weak brother was on the verge of defeat. But being clever, he secretly toppled the curry and shouted, 'Look brother. The tiger has thrown your curry on the ground'. The idiot brother became furious. Catching hold of the tiger's tail, he swung it round in such a way that the tail got detached from the tiger's body. It ran away into the forest out of fear. The two brothers resumed their journey towards Tibet.

36 'The home is where people are offstage, free from surveillance, in control of their immediate environment. It is their castle. It is where they feel they belong' (Saunders, 1989: 184).

37 In *Hymns to Progress*, Havelock Ellishas couches brotherly love, unlike a possible homoerotic male to male relationship beyond the immediate family circuit, as a safe, enriching bond of noneurotic intimacy: 'Onward, brothers, march still onward,/March still onward hand in hand;/Till ye see at last Man's Kingdom/Till ye reach the Promised Land' (Goldberg, 1926: 99).

38

> It is the belief that kinship, love and having nice things together are naturally and inevitably bound up together that makes it hard to imagine a world in which 'family' plays little part. This mythologised unit must be picked apart, strand by strand, so that we can understand its power and meet the needs of each of the separate elements more fully.
>
> (Barren and McIntosh, 1982: 159)

39 In 1898, Severn wrote that

> Excessive Friendship has brought disgrace and ruin upon many an otherwise good character. It causes its possessor to seek company simply for the sake of being in it, whereby their time is wasted and they become a natural prey to the dishonest, tricky, unscrupulous, and vicious, who may take advantage of and link them into all sorts of obligatory concerns ruinous to their pockets and their morals.
>
> (76)

40 'Chronotope', as per Bakhtin's definition of the term, refers to 'the intrinsic connectedness of temporal and spatial relationships that are artistically expressed in literature' (1996: 84).

41 'Being queer means leading a different sort of life. . . . it's about the night' (Alcorn, 1992: 21–22).

42 Contingent identity refers to a marginalised personal identity of misrecognition, whose apodictic 'historical origin' of nonconformism has been politically projected as a chance (mis)happening of the past. Seen from a racial perspective, homosexuality, as an Indigenous alternative norm, became a problem of effeminacy for colonisers, who treated it as an artificially 'man-made', contingent, delegitimised phenomenon. For details, see Bauman, 1992: 1–25.

43 The imagining of death as sensual compensation for suspended sexuality finds a poetic parallel in the following lines of Thom Gunn's 'In Time of Plague': 'My thoughts are crowded with death/and it draws so oddly on the sexual/that I am confused/confused to be attracted/by, in effect, my own annihilation' (2007: 59).

44 The role of the modern intellectual, according to Foucault, is not to endeavour towards any conclusive exploration but to expose the power mechanisms as formative influences:

> The intellectual no longer has to play the role of an adviser. The project, tactics and goals to be adopted are a matter for those who do the fighting. What the intellectual can do is to provide instruments of analysis and at present this is the historian's essential role . . . in other words, a topological and geological survey of the battlefield—that is the intellectual's role.
>
> (Gordon, 1980: 42)

131

45 For a brief account of the prevailing queerphobia in India, see Paola Bacchetta's 'When the (Hindu) Nation Exiles Its Queers', where she discusses xenophobic queerphobia and queerphobic xenophobia:

> xenophobic queerphobia, . . . [is] a particular form of queerphobia that justifies itself by constructing the self-identified Indian queer as originating outside the self-same nation. In this logic, Hindu nationalists claim that queerdom is 'not Indian' and that the British brought homosexuality to India. . . . In turn, queerphobic xenophobia will signify a particular type of xenophobia in which queerdom is assigned (often metaphorically) to all the designated Others of the nation regardless of their sexual identity.
>
> (1999: 143–144)

6

MANLY WOMEN, WOMANLY MEN

Genderqueer in select Rabha tales

I was and still am convinced that being a man is not the same as being masculine (and therefore very unfeminine).

(Februari, 2013: 21)

When I was 5 or 6 years old, I began to say to myself that whatever anyone said, if I was not a boy at any rate I was not a girl.

(Ellis, 1900: 235)

A 'chronic revision' of the local activities 'in the light of new information or knowledge' (Giddens, 1991: 20) is necessary to liberate Indigenous cultural particularities from the homogenising trend of globalisation. This can be done by tracing modernity through the relics of fuzzy tribal identities, as opposed to the fixed and invented/imposed identities of colonisers. If the word 'culture' stands for 'the meanings which people create, and which create people' (Hannerz, 1992: 1), then the most important question that arises is about the 'agency' of people applying their own meanings to the term. In a contemporary Indian context, an official ethnic identity has emerged out of the mere conservation of the colonial construction through appropriation. Any attempt to appreciate how the locals would have used their agency to view themselves differently must be based on the readings of Indigenous folk traditions studied through a non-'mainstream' lens, focusing on the 'the tension between equality as sameness with normativity' and 'equality as freedom for difference from the norm' (Weiss, 2008: 89). A queer reading of the select Rabha tribal tales would result in emphasising the traditional balladeer's cherishing of Indigenous freedom in retaining the antinormative differences from the 'mainstream', along with the modernity of the oral tales, in performing genderqueer identity through the feminine demeanour of men and the masculine demeanour of women. Genderqueer, just like androgyny,[1] signifying a fluid dissolving of the gender binary, refers to a playful, interchangeable use of attributes that eventually leads to 'sexual indifference'—an elimination of the gender poles and the favouring of *appearance* over *being* (Baudrillard, 1993a: 20, 23). Genderqueer, then, can be seen as an umbrella term for 'the dissolution of once stable polarities of male and female, the transfiguration of sexual nature into the artifice of those who play with the sartorial, morphological or gestural signs of sex' (Felski, 1996: 337). Many tribal folktales, as storehouses of a genderqueer archaic memory, help us to unlearn the gender/sexuality differences in a 'return of the repressed',[2] thereby provoking us to reflect on the complementarity of sexes against the heteropatriarchal transforming of it into a hierarchical reality. In the following Rabha tales, the genderqueer performance of manly women and womanly men 'serves as the expression of a range of sexual identities, social possibilities and imaginative freedoms' (Hargreaves, 2005: 10). Even if the genderqueer individuals of the Rabha tales are mostly lacking in 'realness', their absence in the contemporary manipulated tribalscape suggests a 'nonexistence' in the real that, paradoxically, leaves relics in the real (Zupancie, 2012).

Feminine masculinities

The Helpless Kartika, as a Rabha adaptation of the myth of the bachelor Kartika prevalent in the northern part of India, depicts the effeminising of the macho god of South India with two wives, who, even according to the folk versions popular in North India, is supposed to have left the family on account of his mother's doting on her other son, Ganesha, and thus neglecting him.[3]

Tale 1: The Helpless Kartika

Kartika is the son of Mahadev Shiva and his wife, Parvati. One day, Shiva got permission from Parvati and arranged Kartika's wedding with Usha, a beautiful and respectable goddess. Parvati, even though she gave Shiva consent, was not happy. The marriage date drew near, and Mahadev started making arrangements for the journey to the bride's house, which would take three days to arrive and three days to come back. Performing all the rituals, Kartika, Shiva and the bridegroom party started for the bride's house. Reaching halfway, Kartika discovered that he did not have the wedding ring. He thought that mother Parvati must have forgotten to give that to him. Asking everyone to wait for him, he returned to pick up the ring. Reaching home, he found that Parvati was cooking rice in a huge earthen pot and meat on a large frying pan. He asked Parvati why she was making such a huge arrangement when hardly anyone else was around. Parvati replied that after getting married, Kartika would bring the bride along with him, and the wife would then never allow the mother-in-law to eat to her heart's content. Hence, she was trying to satiate all her desires before Kartika would return with Usha. Hearing this, Kartika became very sad and said, 'I promise in the name of my father that I will undertake whatever you ask me to do in order to make you happy'. Parvati happily stated, 'I am attracted to you. Your beauty surpasses the beauty of all the gods and goddesses. I want you to satisfy my carnal yearning.' Kartika closed his eyes and covered his ears with his hands. In a terrified voice he asked, 'How is it possible? Isn't this a sin?' Parvati reassuredly replied, 'Why should it be a sin when you have grown up? Why shouldn't one be allowed to taste the harvest that one had seeded?' She reminded him of promising in the name of Shiva to do anything to please her. Finding himself helpless, Kartika urged, 'I have one condition. Take me to a place where there is no creature to see us and bad mouth us for our deed'. Parvati took him to a far-off place which was thoroughly desolate. The moment they were about to make love, a peahen came out of nowhere, followed by a peacock. Kartika got up and said, 'You have failed to fulfil the condition, mother. I cannot keep my promise as well'. Parvati, agitated by her unsated desire, cursed the peahen: from then onwards, she would never get sexual satisfaction. Since then, according to the Rabha belief, a peahen becomes pregnant by swallowing the tears and sweat of a peacock. Parvati also cursed Kartika with impotency, and because of that, he has to stay as a bachelor.

This widespread Rabha tribal tale affirms that 'There is great value in pulling these words from the no- longer conscious to arm a critique of the present' (Muñoz, 2009: 19). Inverting a tale of alienation between mother and son into an incestuous one, the Rabha tale also inverts the 'mainstream' conception of Kartika, an ascetic manly warrior god who represents power and strength, into a feeble, terrified person. Contrary to the 'assertiveness norm' and 'tough value' of masculine culture,[4] which holds that 'caring and gentleness are only for women' (Hofstede, 1998: 103), Kartika displays defencelessness and bewilderment. His gesturing of closing his eyes and covering his ears display a 'modesty norm' and 'tender values' associated with the feminine (ibid.). However, Kartika's timidity is balanced by his assertive rejection of Parvati on account of her failure to fulfil his precondition for erotic intimacy. Providing a sharp contrast to his former 'infantilised' personality of a man desperately in search of a refuge from disrepute,[5] Kartika performs maleness in his determined declaration, 'I cannot keep my promise'. Refusing to 'neither opt to assimilate within *the binary* structure nor strictly oppose it', Kartika as a representative of a genderqueer individual disidentifies by means of 'a strategy that works on and against dominant ideology' (Muñoz, 1999: 11). Disidentification ensues through the unlearning of norms, thereby creating an in-betweenness where the 'binaries begin to falter and fiction becomes the real' (ibid.: 20). This ensures the queering of the gender binary. Kartika's effeminacy in being initially subjugated by Parvati and his eventual overpowering of her make the genderqueer Kartika the nonnormative transgressor who can 'walk both sides of the gender fence' (Pittman, 1996: 4). This popular Rabha remembering of a radically revised genderqueer tale highlights how 'normativity attempts to close off prior critical and sexual universes' by cleaning up the struggles of the past 'into historic quests for legitimacy and evaluating legitimacy through how well we surrender claims to sex and sexual heterogeneity' (Dinshaw et al., 2007: 193). This Indigenous adaptation of a 'mainstream' tale also shows the tribal resistance against the 'kind of structurally embedded amnesia [and] astrategic forgetting'(Doyle, 2008: 210) that makes genderqueer appear as gender dysphoria.

The following Rabha folktale, *Love Story of Seuji*, once again features a nostalgic return to the old days of the sages from whom the Rabhas often trace their origin, as a search for the lost genderqueer space and time which can, nevertheless, carve out a memory that is counterfactual to currently divided gender realities.[6]

Tale 2: Love Story of Seuji

A long time ago, there lived a man who, having fathered a son named Anteswar, gave up worldly attachments and became a sage. However, he asked his wife and son to remember him in times of crisis. One day when Anteswar had fallen sick, his mother went into the forest for medicinal leaves. Coincidentally the mother of another girl, Seuji, who was also unwell, came in search of medicine, and both mothers decided that their kids would get married to one another once they had grown up. Unfortunately, Anteswar's mother suddenly expired, and an elderly spinster of the neighbourhood stared taking care of Anteswar. Then the day arrived when Seuji's mother approached Anteswar to marry her daughter, as per the promise made by her and his late mother. The spinster, although she was much older, got attracted to Anteswar, who grew up to be a handsome young man. On the day of marriage, she, having good knowledge of witchcraft, took the shape of the bride and got married to Anteswar. At night, when she re-established her real identity, he became sad and started planning to get rid of her in order to marry the real Seuji. One day, he proposed his wife to go to the river to remove the rust from his sword and lice from their hair. While the wife got busy in removing lice from her head, Anteswar, with a single stroke of his sword, beheaded her. The detached head, however, did not die and came rolling towards him. Anteswar became scared, so he climbed up a tree. The head started climbing too. He then began to ask help from his saint father, who sent his disciple for his son's protection. But the head attacked the disciple and defeated him. Then the saint father sent a wild boar that ultimately smashed the head and saved Anteswar. In a while, he got wedded to Seuji. Both of them were happy to be together after such a long waiting, but Seuji was often scared of the catastrophe that might befall as a curse for killing the former wife. One day she was so worried that she told the entire event to her mother and her maternal uncle. The maternal uncle became agitated after listening to Anteswar's duplicity. He stared chasing after him in a great fury, and Anteswar started running fast to escape from the uncle. Seuji also joined Anteswar, to save him from her uncle's frenzy. She understood that her uncle had created magical grasshoppers to tempt Anteswar. She alerted him not to eat those raw and went to fetch fire from a neighbour's house to roast the grasshoppers. When she came back, she found that Anteswar had disobeyed her instruction and was lying dead after having consumed the magical grasshoppers. Seuji fainted and remained unconscious for a long time. Recovering her senses, she found herself in her mother's place. She lamented and mourned for months. But as she was a beautiful girl at the peak of her youth, it was not possible for her to stay alone for long. She got involved in a clandestine affair with a man and became pregnant. When she informed the man of her pregnancy and asked him to marry her, the man became panicky. He knew that since he was from a warrior's clan, the society would not allow him to marry Seuji, who was a descendant of a sage's clan. In utter disgrace, the man jumped into the river. Seuji too jumped into the river to save him, but because of her pregnancy, she had gained weight and therefore she too sank deep into the river. This is how Seuji's love story came to an end.

Anteswar and the second man in Seuji's life, in sharp contrast to Seuji and the neighbourhood spinster, get effeminised by their lack of most of the traits that are regarded as masculine.[7] Anteswar had to use subterfuge to behead the first wife which reveals his martial inadequacy in comparison to the wife who has proficiency in handling the armours of magic. Anteswar's subordinate muscularity is further exposed by his frightfully running away from the detached head of the first wife. The head of Anteswar's elderly wife, chasing him even after being removed from her female body reminds us that 'The primordial intentional act is the motion of the body orientating itself with respect to and moving within its surroundings' (Young, 1990: 148) and disrupts the restrictions and inhibitions associated with the woman's speciality and motility in that she transcends space through the placing of her head in aggressive motion within it, which is otherwise seen as a gesture of a 'male's ontological security' (Whitehead, 2002: 189).

The authority that the disconnected female head exerts on the living Anteswar further emasculates him. Not only on the basis of his physical strength but also due to his lack of perceptual power, Anteswar is infantilised when compared to the woman like Seuji. Since manly behaviour is defined in contrast to both childish and feminine features, Anteswar's 'child-like' noncompliance and 'womanish' panic makes him an unmanly gender-queer male.

The second man in Seuji's life, as an ironic descendant of a warrior's clan, seems to be also an unmanly male who, rather than playing the conventional role of an aggressive man destroying all the barriers of the societal norm to determinately live an independent life, becomes distressed at the presumption of a local opposition and jumps into the river for a pusillanimous escape. Both Anteswar, representing the lineage of a sage, and the man from the warrior's clan, however, highlight that in an unperturbed tribal society, 'femininity-in-masculinity' has usually been an admissible trait, as opposed to the colonial gaze, which conceives of 'femininity-in-masculinity' 'as the final negation of a man's political identity, a pathology more dangerous than femininity itself' (Nandy, 1983: 8).

Tale 3: Creation of Liquor

Many years ago, in seven Rabha villages, there lived seven headmen. One day a sage appeared in the dream of all those seven headmen. The sage said, 'Tomorrow morning I will send a gift under the Shimul tree for your betterment'. The next day, the seven heads of the seven villages assembled under the Shimul tree in the morning, to find seven elephants standing in a queue. The Rabha headmen were confused because they had no sense of the purpose of those elephants. A Tibetan man was passing by them. Seeing the elephants, he offered them seventy rupees and bought those seven elephants. Now owning the elephants, he said, 'I will make them carry logs from the forest and throw them on the river in order to make boats and sell them to the people of the flooded land to make profit in lakhs'. The Rabha headmen looked at one another in disgrace. Dividing seventy rupees among themselves they returned to their respective villages. At night, the sage again appeared in their dream. Rebuking them for their stupidity, he said, 'Tomorrow morning again I will send another gift for your benefit under the Shimul tree'. The next morning the seven Rabha headmen rushed to the spot and found seven horses standing in a row. They were in utter bewilderment since they could not make out how those horses were advantageous for them. Just then a Bengalee man, walking by them, looked at those seven horses and offered a deal of thirty-five rupees for all the horses. The Rabha men gladly took the money in exchange of the gift sent by the sage. The Bengalee, while leaving the place, uttered, 'I will soon become a rich man by earning through seven horse carts'. At night, again in their dream, the sage appeared shouting at them in fury. Then he said, 'Tomorrow I will send money for you morons. Come under the Shimul tree early in the morning'. The seven Rabha headmen leisurely reached the place to notice that the sage had already started showering money on them. The seven headmen had carried with them only small handbags. They were very happy to accumulate whatsoever little amount they could put into the small handbags. A Marwari man was walking past the Shimul tree. Seeing the showering of cash, he started putting the notes in his bag and shirt-pockets. Since there was a lot more lying on the ground, he wrapped himself with banana leaves and removing his dhoti he packed all the money into it. That night although the sage appeared in the dream of the seven Rabha headmen, he didn't seem to be agitated. Rather pleasantly he said, 'I have tried by all means. But there is nothing more that I can do for your development. I will now try to make you happy. Tomorrow gather under the tree, and you will be happy to see my gift.' The next morning the seven Rabha headmen found a huge earthen pot under the Shimul tree. Removing the lid, they found it to be filled with some sweet-smelling liquid. They were so intoxicated by the aroma that they could not resist the temptation of tasting it. The more they drank, the more they desired and finally they fell asleep. Waking up, they found a profound sense of tranquillity in their mind. The seven headmen called all their villagers and they enjoyed the drink. Then all of them thanked the sage and asked him to teach them the process of making the delicious drink. From then onwards, the Rabha people learnt the procedure of making their unique liquor, which they called *chwako* or *chwakwat*.

Beneath the apparent sarcasm in *Creation of Liquor*, there is a deep-rooted alternative approach to the notion of development and masculinity. The tribal identity of a Rabha man has been affirmed through negation. Unlike a Tibetan man, for whom commanding elephants to carry logs guarantees monetary gain as a sign of development; a Bengalee man, whose notion of progress lies in a monetary profit by controlling horses as cart pullers; or even a mainstream Marwari man, whose idea of advancement is proportional to surplus capital stock, the seven Rabha headmen lose all three chances for material affluence only to be given mental bliss. The seven Rabha men thus exhibit a tribal resistance against the so-called virile preference for command, control and capital and preference for repose, indulgence and merrymaking. According to Diana Fuss, this unstabilising of gender roles is the first step towards a gender-based identity politics of equality.[8] This Rabha tale of genderqueer men can be seen as tribal resistance against gendered modernity, which is essentially masculine in its overemphasis on reasonableness, competitive individuality and progress at the cost of passion and social bonds.[9] Each Rabha headman avoids the snare of conforming to what it means to be a 'real' man.[10]

The headmen's choosing liquor is a symbolic preference for a community property that is at once socialist and democratic. These genderqueer Rabha village heads, contriving the model of a possible 'socialist gender' through their antipathy for both capital and gender control, as an antithesis to those who ' "possess" gender as a commodity', act as not only 'critiques of gender roles but also socialist critiques of how those gender roles [support] capitalism' (Clark, 2007: 19). This 'socialist gender' is a prerequisite for 'sexual socialism' (Shively, 1991: 258).

Tale 4: The Lazy Gallant

This happened a long time ago. In a Koch village, there lived six brothers. The first five brothers worked hard, while the youngest one was lazy. He would sleep all through the day. In the evening, idly he would roam around playing his *dotara* (a two-string musical instrument) or at the most catch a few birds since he could not eat rice without meat. People used to call him, jokingly, the lazy gallant. The five brothers did all the laborious work, like cutting logs and raising the cattle, and their wives did all the household chores, like cooking and weaving. The five brothers and the four wives were annoyed with the lazy gallant. Only the eldest sister-in-law was affectionate; she used to weave him clothes and serve him the major amount of meat and rice every day. The elder brothers tried their best but could not mend his sluggishness. Finally, one day they came to the conclusion that it was better to get rid of him than to continue with him by serving the largest portion of meat without any output. They planned to stab him that night after dinner. The eldest among the wives came to know about the plan and warned the lazy gallant not to sleep in his bed. He slept in another room, keeping a huge pillow covered with a blanket on his bed. The five brothers came to the youngest brother's room and stabbed the pillow. Thinking that the lazy gallant was dead, they went off to sleep. The next day, to their utter surprise, they found their youngest brother alive. The promised to kill him that night. But the idle boy's eldest sister-in-law, advising him to spend the night in the animal shed, put stones and bricks on his bed and covered them with a bed sheet. The brothers returned, and after dinner entered the lazy gallant's room. They hit the stones and bricks with their swords thinking that it was their youngest brother. The next morning the eldest brother's wife suggested the lazy gallant to stay away from the house for some days. He carried his *dotara*, clothes, a fair amount of food supplied by the eldest sister-in-law and entered the forest. All through the day, he just played his *dotara*. In the evening, he felt that someone was touching his shoulder. Turning back, he found a beautiful girl sitting behind him. The girl introduced herself as a princess who had to leave her house due to the murderous plan of her stepmother and on the way became attracted to the beautiful notes of his *dotara*. She proposed the lazy gallant to marry her. They were married and lived well with no work for some days, surviving on the food packed by the eldest brother's wife. Soon there was no food left. The lazy gallant asked his wife to visit his eldest sister-in-law for help. The eldest brother's wife was glad to meet the wife of the lazy gallant. She instructed the youngest brother's wife to burn part of the forest and sow the seeds of maize and rice, which she had packed and handed over to the princess. According to her direction, the lazy gallant and his wife learnt jhum cultivation and lived happily ever after.

In *The Lazy Gallant*, the youngest brother's genderqueer behaviours result in his withdrawal from practising skills like woodcutting and cattle raising that are supposed to be vigorously laborious and thus masculine, because of his engagement with alternative, non-masculine habits like slumbering, catching small birds and playing *dotara*. Underlying the common belief that 'knowledge and social values are associated with the elders' and 'uncertainty and ignorance are associated with the junior generation' (Jackson, 1978: 346), the politics that the folktale often exposes is that of 'a formal contrast between status position on the one hand and personal capability on the other' (ibid.: 349). Contrary to the seven headmen of the previous Rabha folktale, the five elder brothers of this tribal tale, who seem to be all for an externally standardised 'status position' in their performing stereotypical masculinity and their mimicking the colonial desire of erasing effeminate men,[11] represent the new adults who internalise the effeminophobia of the colonisers.[12] And the last-born son represents 'the reversed mirror image of the rejected norm' (La Barre, 1970: 40) and a minor yet steady tribal resistance against colonisation. The elder brothers' attempts to kill the unproductive youngest brother also show how the colonisers have installed the capitalist notion of counting worth on the basis of the productive value. Devastating what Shively calls 'sexual socialism', capitalism seems to have forced tribal men to perform a standardised masculinity which ultimately prohibits not only non-heteronormativity but intimacy in total (Shively, 1991: 258). In contrast to the seven headmen, the five

Rabha brothers underscore that the ethnic space of differences has been slowly appropriated by the 'mainstream' on the basis of 'those justifications of modernity—progress, homogeneity, cultural organicism, the deep nation, the long past—that rationalize the authoritarian "normativising" tendencies within a culture in the name of national interest' (Bhabha, 1990: 4). The genderqueer headmen of the preceding Rabha folktale, unlike the five brothers who appear to be the forerunners of present-day people of the transformed society, might have their roots in the then prevailing Rabha matriliny, which further proves that an atypical, sovereign imagination is after all part of 'place-based imaginations' (Dirlik, 1999). The matrifocal tribal notion of a fluid gender role in conventional Rabha society has been deliberately replaced by patrilineal models as non-Indigenous culture, along with the

> Christian religion, brought by colonialism, [that] carried rigid gender ideologies which aided and supported the exclusion of women from the power hierarchy. . . . The rigid gender system meant that the roles are strictly masculinized or feminized; breaking gender rules therefore carries a stigma.
>
> (Amadiume, 1987: 185)

The youngest brother's dependence on women in the form of the sister-in-law and wife, both for his physical and emotional sustenance yet again makes him appear as a degraded male devoid of 'mainstream' manhood.[13] However, the genderqueer sixth brother displays a tribal nonconforming attitude that does not consider manliness to be played in an oppositional relation to femininity in front of other males as well as himself, which is rather an outcome of fearing femininity in oneself.[14]

This androgynous genderqueer behaviour, however, should not be seen as an exclusive concept functioning in only the Rabha traditional world, but rather, it is prevalent in Asian philosophical traditions, where one often finds an urge to achieve an androgynous state of the soul. For example, Taoist mysticism features the often-quoted lines of Tao Te Ching: 'He who knows the male, yet cleaves to what is female/Becomes like a ravine, receiving all things under the heaven/(Thence) the eternal virtue never leaks away' (Needham, 1956: 58). Nonetheless, by only playing a *dotara*, which seems to be economically unproductive and therefore valueless according to colonialism and capitalism, the youngest brother's final development into a prosperous man, married to a princess and possessing sufficient harvest, highlights that the folktale privileges Rabha genderqueer behaviour over colonial stratifications. Opposing the popular macho doctrine of building one's own fortune through hard work, this Rabha tale, asserting the success of a passive man, indicates that 'good fortune can only come if it is not sought' (Dundes, 1962: 173). The last-born son's performing of 'androgyny offers to redeem masculinity by feminizing it' (Hargreaves, 2005: 100) and offers the basis of a radical challenging of an imposed gender ideology. The lazy gallant, as an unmanly man who succeeds in meeting the conditions of becoming the hero of the tale, shows that genderqueer behaviour fills the vacuum often created by the 'antimale feminist critiques of masculinity' (hooks, 2004: 166), which fail to encourage anything positive in masculinity. Opposing the tenets of patriarchal masculinity, the lazy gallant performs a 'feminist masculinity' that, replacing the old perception of strength as 'power over', 'defines strength as one's capacity to be responsible for self and others' (ibid.: 117).

Manly femininities

An exploration of the genderqueer behaviour of Rabha women should include *Love Story of Seuji*. The neighbouring spinster who takes care of Anteswar can be considered genderqueer, and with a manful obstinacy, she manages to attain the object of her longing. Transgressing the romantic belief that 'The girls have a dream, the boys a desire' (Anderson, 1990: 113), the spinster deploys the masculine gambit of wining the sexual object more for control than for developing a relationship based on love.[15] The fact that she is shown as the practitioner of witchcraft further makes her a 'gender blender'.[16] Witchcraft as genderqueer behaviour makes the practising woman a 'gender blur' (Blum, 1998: 45) who does not construct alternative sets of determined categories in opposition to the gender binaries but blends and blurs them into a multiplicity of a wavering 'inchoate self'.[17] The fact that the spinster, who later becomes aggressive in marrying Anteswar against his will, was the only one to affectionately shoulder the burden of nurturing the orphan Anteswar also makes her a perfect genderqueer for whom identity is 'provisional and contingent' (Jagose, 1996: 76), or a 'proliferation' (Butler, 1990: 46) of 'a flexible space for the expression of all aspects of non-(anti-, contra-) straight cultural production and reception' (Doty, 1993: 3). The genderqueer behaviour of the tribal woman in this folktale, 'encourages a distrust of all determinisms' with the motif of stimulating people to reconfigure themselves by 'select[ing] new identities, slip[ping] in and out of roles in protean fashion' (Nye, 1998: 3).

The Rabha women's exercising their free will in choosing their partners, in manlike firmness, can again be found in the folktale *Mothers and Daughters*.

Tale 5: Mothers and Daughters

Once upon a time, there were two sisters who went to a sage in the forest with the hope of having children. The saint, knowing that it was a sacrilege, could not resist the temptation. Attracted by

143

their beauty, he satisfied their craving and once again submerged himself in deep meditation. The sisters left him, and in due course of time, each of them gave birth to a daughter. The two daughters grew up as passionate, adventurous and reckless girls. One day the two young girls saw two young brothers, and having learnt the art of enchantment from their mothers, they turned themselves into earthen pots. Instantaneously the two young men were attracted to those pots and thought of carrying the pots back to their house. On the way, however, the pot fell down from the elder brother's hand. To his surprise, he found that blood oozed out of it, and the molten clay turned into a bird that flew away in the sky. Back home, the younger brother was astonished to find a young beautiful girl come out of the pot and do all the household works. The two brothers held her and pressed her to introduce herself. She recounted the entire story: 'Both of us wanted to marry you two. Since the elder brother killed my elder sister, I am here to marry the younger brother', she concluded. The elder brother became jealous of his younger brother's fortune. He decided to kill the younger brother in order to marry the beautiful girl. Accordingly, he took his younger brother to the forest and left him deep inside the jungle from where it was not possible for the younger brother to return to the house. The beautiful girl had a pet parrot. She sent the parrot in search of her beloved, and the elder brother was shocked to see that his younger brother had returned. The next day, when both the brothers went to the forest for work, the elder one forcefully tied the younger one to a tree just in front of a snake den. The girl, with her magic, came to know of the elder brother's evil plan and immediately sent her pet dog, which set the younger brother free, scared the snakes away and brought the younger brother back home. The next day, the elder brother set the forest on fire and pushed his younger brother into it. The girl came running, but it was too late. By the time she reached the spot, the younger brother was already dead. She started weeping out of grief. Her mother and her mother's sister came rushing to her. Hearing about the elder brother's misdeed, they created a magical river on the way to the elder brother's home. The river flooded into his house to drown the wicked brother. With his death the mothers succeeded in avenging the daughters' loss.

The customary tribal sexual liberty has helped the two sisters to get themselves pregnant by a single sage. Following the sexual self-determination of their mothers, even the daughters decide on their own to marry the two brothers. Although the sisters do not take recourse to the defiant/antagonistic seduction of the spinster in *Love Story of Seuji*, the art of a masqueraded seduction initiated by women is a reversal of a patriarchal trap (as suggested by feminists) that men often set to subjugate women. By their magic real transformation into earthen pots, the two sisters, challenging the deterministic notion of body as biologically unbending, posit their genderqueer bodies as 'contested terrain [upon which] the interplay of text and physicality [render] a body in process, never fixed or solid, but always multiple and fluid' (Price and Shildrick, 1999: 4). The manner in which the wife of the younger brother succeeds, by sending her parrot and dog on time, in saving the life of her husband, who appears wobbly compared to her competences, again highlights her genderqueer feminine concern as well as manly confrontation that in effect, while substantiating androgynous behaviour as a more gender-liberal principle also corroborates that 'it is in those works where the roles of the male and female protagonist can be reversed without appearing ludicrous or perverted that the androgynous ideal is present' (Heilbrun, 1974: 10). Although the younger brother gets murdered, yet the fact that the two mothers take revenge, by killing the chief cause of the daughters' desolation, confirms that 'Women are better men than men' (Februari, 2013: 92). The genderqueer behaviour of the two mothers, as the representatives of the originally matrilineal Rabha society, offers a model for decolonising[18] colonial gender stratification, which in turn challenges 'the contemporaneity of the non-contemporaneous' (Bloch, 1991: 106).

The Manly Woman has the most potential to challenge the present-day 'invisibilisation' of the genderqueer.

Tale 6: The Manly Woman

Long ago, there was a young woman. Her name was Maaykawn. She was fearless, courageous and full of strength like a man. For that reason, people used to call her a manly woman. Like a man, she could cut wood with an axe. She was efficient in doing all manly work. She would assist men in their jhum cultivation and walked on the road like a boy. The village women used to refer to her as an ox-like virile women while talking among themselves. Due to her macho attire and attitude, she was almost past her youth and yet unmarried. The men were afraid to mingle with her. She also hardly socialized with other women. After everyone left, she would go to the river and bathe all alone. One day a woman arrived, carrying her little boy on her back, when Maaykawn was taking a bath after everyone had left the riverside. She requested that Maaykawn take care of her boy until she was finished washing her clothes. Maaykawn kept the baby with her for some time. Then the woman came back, she invited Maaykawn to visit her place and have food with her. But Maaykawn said, 'No, I do not want to come and eat in your place. I am a single woman. It's not a good thing to visit an unknown woman and eat with her. I helped you because you

are also alone like me. But I cannot accompany you.' Failing to
have earned Maaykawn's trust, the woman with her son went into
the forest towards home. The next day, she again appeared with
her son and a big pile of clothes. After washing those, she said to
Maaykawn, 'Look today I have so many clothes to carry home.
How will I carry the child? Please help me today.' Maaykawn felt
that it would have been bad not to help her. She carried the clothes
while the boy was with the mother. As she walked faster, she reached
the woman's house much before her. Entering the house, she was
surprised to see all forbidden food in the room. Then she understood that the unknown woman must have been a witch. Quickly
she came out and returned to her village. Maaykawn understood
that living single alone is bad, since by staying all alone, one would
tend to develop all sorts of corruption like that forest woman.

Maaykawn, being a woman and daring like a man, makes people acknowledge her as a degendered manly woman, positioning herself outside the
predefined boundaries of oppositional gender constructions.[19] Her genderqueer activities, including efficiently doing all the work that is purportedly
for men, challenges and dismantles the 'division between the sexes' which
appears 'to be "in the order of things", as people sometimes say to refer
what is normal, natural, to the point of being inevitable' (Bourdieu, 2001:
8). Maaykawn, both in her gender-bending getup and gesture (her boy-like
walking on the road), also defends the notion that genderqueer behaviour
refers to both individual traits and a performance. Scholars have often
opined that gender identity is more grounded upon a 're-presentational'
exposition of gendered behaviours, so it is a matter of depiction rather than
a psychological configuration.[20]

Her genderqueer mannerisms provide a nonnormative ground for alienation.[21] The specific reference to cutting wood with an axe or assistance in
jhum cultivation shows that, apart from the gendered occupations, 'Specific jobs are even more gender-segregated' (Lorber, 1994: 195). However,
it is perhaps Maaykawn's macho attire that must have provoked the other
women to call her an 'ox-like virile woman'.[22] This apparently comic cat-
calling earnestly bears the seed of a politics of panic which tries to portray
a single woman as a possible 'corrupt' individual and a probable 'witch'.
Maaykawn as a woman in a man's outfit not only declares herself as a
masterless individual but also refuses to accept a subordinate position.[23]
Maaykawn's aping of man makes her perfectly androgynous: although
on the social level, this usurped manliness asserts masculinity as a desired
attribute, while on the personal level, her appropriating of man's function
enables her to disregard men as no longer serviceable for her.[24] Thus, for
the governmentality, the only way to replace the traditional matrifocal
Rabha viewpoint—though the gender binary unfailingly creates empty and

overflowing categories[25]—with that of 'mainstream' patriarchy is through propaganda of fear that finally results in the demonising of a single, independent masculine woman. 'Mainstream' programmes of 'transformatisation' that have forced Maaykawn to admit the faultiness of living life as single again reveal a superseding manhood and a masculinism that naturalises male domination in order to justify it.[26] Nevertheless, as a suggestive remedy for 'mainstream' patriarchal domination, the Rabha genderqueer behaviour in the folktale needs to be considered a positive political action against strict categories of manly and womanly.

From the 'mainstream' position, domesticity becomes a gendered, partitioned space where women need to achieve 'romantic love; feminine nurturance, maternalism, self-sacrifice' and the men should characterise themselves with 'masculine protection and financial support' (Barrett, 1988: 205). Contrary to this 'mainstream' idea of domesticity, the Rabha folktale *Saving the Man* features a genderqueer wife who slaps and hits her husband and thereby saves him from being exterminated.

Tale 7: Saving the Man

Once upon a time, there was a newly married couple. The girl's parents visited her in-laws and invited the newly wedded couple as a part of the ritual. The wife was happy, and she did the packing. Eating rice water, she went to sleep so that the next day early in the morning, she, along with her husband, would leave for her parent's house. In her sleep, she dreamt that while her husband was eating a fish in her parents' house, a fish bone got struck in his throat and he died. She woke up and found that her husband was sleeping peacefully by her side. Again in her sleep she dreamt that while her husband was cutting banana leaves, he was badly hit by a banana trunk on his chest, and he died then and there. The wife could not sleep and was panicky throughout the night. But she didn't say anything to her husband, and both of them started for her parents' house early in the morning. In the afternoon, while taking a bath in the river Torsha, the husband, caught a big Boroli fish, which his mother-in-law cooked and served him for lunch. Since the wife had the memory of last night's bad dreams, she was sitting by his side. Almost immediately the husband seemed to have choked while the wife slapped him hard, and the rice and fish bone came out of his mouth. The new son-in-law felt humiliated on being smacked by his wife in front of his mother-in-law. However, he thought not to create a scene and silently finished his lunch. His mother-in-law then asked him to cut some banana leaves for dinner. The wife immediately recollected the previous night's dream. She followed him to the forest. Straightaway hit by a banana trunk on his chest, he,

147

almost unconscious, fell to the ground. The wife started punching him on his back, which made him recover his full sense. Finding his wife hitting him in the presence of the in-laws, he felt embarrassed. Feeling insulted and thinking that his wife was maltreating him, he started to pack his luggage in order to move out of his house. The wife then told him about her dreams. The man felt ashamed and stayed happily with his wife, ever after.

The wife's sudden dreaming of the forthcoming menace is quite an acknowledged occurrence[27] that must have made her worry. Her feminine anxiety for her husband and her husband-like protection of him from perils are genderqueer behaviours and '[offer] possibilities of the other, possibilities of change and transformation, and possibilities for freedom and emancipation that go beyond the constraints of biological sex and socially ascribed genders' (Linstead and Pullen, 2006: 1303). The husband's annoyance at her crossing the limits of her gender allotted role, on one hand, brings out the limitation of rigid heterosexuality[28] and, on the other, encourages the androgynous performing of a Rabha genderqueer woman as 'an archaic and universal formula for the expression of wholeness, the co-existence of the contraries, or *coincidentia oppositorum* . . . . symboliz[ing] . . . perfection . . . [and] ultimate being' of desired equilibrium (Eliade, 1975: 174–175). The husband's immediate reaction of being disrespected and mistreated can be best explained by the stereotyped image of a self-supporting man.[29] Finally, the genderqueer characteristics of the tribal wife reflected in this folktale—her taking charge of her husband's safety both at home and the world beyond—challenges the 'diacritical construction, both theoretical and practical', which, as an important feature of the 'mainstream', makes the two gender roles appear as 'socially differentiated from the opposite gender (in all the culturally pertinent respects), i.e. as a male, and therefore non-female habitus or as a female and therefore non-male habitus' (Bourdieu, 2001: 24).

Indigenous trans identity

The changes in the originary totemic, matrilineal space with its gender-fluid queering into a heteropatriarchal domain[30] have mainly resulted from colonial and neocolonial influences on the genderqueer tribal domain, like the hetero-masculine institution in the form of church or homophobic, patriarchal spokespersons like present-day Hindu frontrunners. Manis Kumar Raha writes about how the surrounding non-Indigenous people have 'compelled the village Rabhas to involve intimately into the Hinduization', while in the case of the forest Rabhas, 'they have embraced [Christianity] in recent years only for certain benefits, mainly economic' (Raha, 1989: 320). In post-independent India, the same colonial ideal of maintaining queer/straight and pathological/normal binaries in the name of preserving a 'natural' order and revolutionising all other traditional nonnormative notions has been adopted in building the modern nation-state.[31] Genderqueer behaviour in these traditional Rabha folktales can be seen as the manifestation of the tribal urge to 'go beyond the both imperatives of essentialism and social constructivism' of gender and sexual identity through an espousal of a 'trans identity' (Nagoshi et al., 2014: 185) that embraces all who don't to fit into the colonial/statist delineations of femininity and masculinity and, thereby, provides a means of reconciling a contradiction by acknowledging 'the tension between self-experiences and societally defined identity embodiment and between self-determined and societally determined identity construction' (ibid.: 186).

As an alternative to what Foerst (2004) rightly pointed out—that is, the tendency in all the -*ologies* in most societies to favour *logos* as the foundation of veracity and disfavour *mythos* as myth-making inventiveness of the narrator/storyteller—this trans identity of the genderqueer tribal people affirms the significance of the knowledge disseminated through these folk narratives as valuable for addressing the contemporary complications arising out of the sex/gender dichotomy. The *resistance identities* of the genderqueer Rabha folktale characters, 'that are in positions/conditions devalued and/or stigmatized by the logic of domination' and that counteract *legitimising identities* 'introduced by the dominant institutions of society to extend and rationalize their domination vis-à-vis social actors', open the door for *project identities* of posterity 'when social actors, on the basis of whatever cultural materials are available to them, build a new identity that redefines their position in society and, by doing so, seek the transformation of overall social structure' (Castells, 1997: 8), perhaps through a retreat that follows the model of the traditional genderqueer Rabhas. As a step towards a collective struggle against the discriminations by the coloniality of the 'mainstream', the genderqueer behaviour of both unmanly male and unwomanly female characters in these Rabha folktales surely seem to indorse that '*the personal is what makes the political possible*' (MacInnes, 1998: 135).

Notes

1 Androgyny generally suggests an in-between co-equal existence of masculine and feminine attributes. Genderqueer may not suggest a proportionate becoming but a fluid exchanging of the characteristics that are constructed as masculine and feminine in a way of dissolving the binary. Genderqueer embodies the non-static performing of femininity-in-masculinity and masculinity-in-femininity. The lack of equal proportion, unlike in androgyny, which ensures a sense of completeness, also enables genderqueer to get rid of the androgynous narcissism of being complete in oneself.

2 'It is therefore not so much the "advent" of an androgynous nature that we are becoming aware of but more its "return" . . . "the return of the repressed"' (Badinter, 1989: 167).

3 This folktale resembles the Marathi version of the folktale revolving round the theme of mother–son incestual relationships, titled *Mother Marries Son*, documented by Ramanujan (1991), where the goddess Satwai, while writing the daughter's fate on her forehead, ends up writing that she is destined to marry her son. Folktales with similar motifs can also be found in Konkani, Tamil and Kannada.

4 Having studied 14 countries, including India, it has been concluded that there is a general tendency in India to appear more 'masculine' than the men actually are. For details, see Hofstede, 1998: 112.

5 According to the observation made by Barry Adam, 'Shame is not an originary experience; it is an attitude demanded of the inferiorized' (Adam, 2009: 304). Kartika's embarrassment is exposed by his plea to escape from disgrace: 'Take me to a place where there is no creature to see us and bad-mouth for our deed'. This shows that his manhood has been inferiorised by Parvati.

6

> Memories enable more than survival; they are imaginative ways to disrupt and transform conditions that make survival necessary. Like utopias, memories craft a world that stands as a counterreality to the lacking or painful present, creating narratives of 'the past' so as to challenge the inevitability of dominant constructions of 'reality'. The space- off and timeout of memory afford a critical distance from which to evaluate present conditions that lead to alienation and yearning as we picture alternatives that challenge the inevitability of those conditions and imagine other social arrangements that transform 'reality' into a more livable (relation to) time and place.
>
> (Castiglia and Reed, 2012: 12)

7

> We typically expect men to be strong, independent, and competitive, and to keep their emotions hidden. These are features of the male gender role. By contrast, we typically expect women to be caring, emotionally expressive, polite, and helpful: features of the female gender role. . . . A masculine trait is self-confidence; a masculine behaviour is aggression. . . . A feminine trait is emotional; a feminine behavior is helping someone.
>
> (Helgeson, 2001: 4–5)

8

> Such a view of [sexual] identity as unstable and potentially disruptive, as alien and incoherent, could in the end produce a more mature identity politics by militating against the tendency to erase differences and inconsistencies in the production of stable political subjects.
>
> (Fuss, 1989: 104)

9

> Modernity is commonly viewed as a masculine phenomenon, in which the male ideals of rationality, competitive individualism, progress, and order are promoted and valorized in comparison (and through contrast) with the supposedly female ideals of emotion, social bonds, continuity, and 'tradition'.
>
> (Hodgson, 2001: 8–9)

10 According to Bourdieu, stereotyped

> Manliness, understood as sexual or social reproductive capacity, but also as the capacity to fight and to exercise violence (especially in acts of revenge), is first and foremost a *duty*. Unlike a woman, whose essential negative honour can only be defended or lost, since her virtue is successively virginity and fidelity, a 'real' man is someone who feels the need to rise to the challenge of the opportunities available to him to increase his honour by pursuing glory and distinction in the public sphere.
>
> (Bourdieu, 2001: 50–51)

11 For details, see Krishnaswamy, 1998; Sinha, 1995.

12 Mrinalini Sinha in *Colonial Masculinity* writes that 'the colonial authorities had injected a powerful new dimension in the self-perception of "effeminacy"' among the people in India, which made them conscious of trying to have 'redeemed their "manliness"' (1995: 93) mostly by their mimicry of the colonial standards of hypermasculinity.

13 *Englishman* propagates that Indian men 'are notoriously destitute of manliness' and are often 'cowardly in their treatment of the weaker sex' (*Englishman*, April 26, 1883. 2). In the opinion of J. Munro, 'The training of natives from their childhood, the enervating influence of the zenana on their upbringing, early marriage' are mostly responsible for the deficiency of 'those manly and straightforward qualities which under other conditions are found in Englishmen' (Sinha, 1992: 100).

14 In most 'mainstream' men, 'Manliness, it can be seen, is an eminently relational notion, constructed in front of and for other men and against femininity, in a kind of fear of the female, firstly in oneself' (Bourdieu, 2001: 53).

15

> To the young man, the woman becomes, in the most profound sense, a sexual object. Her body and mind are the object of sexual games, to be won for his personal aggrandizement. Status goes to the winner, and sex is prized not as testament of love but as testimony to control of another human being.
>
> (Anderson, 1990: 114)

16 The term 'witchcraft' derives from the word 'wic' or 'wicca', meaning 'wise one'. According to Christopher Penczak, 'Wicca was used to refer to male practitioners and wicce to female practitioners'. However, Penczak also mentions that the witches generally 'reclaim all these roles and traditions', as both male and female, and the fact that the modern restoration of witchcraft is usually denoted as wicca further makes the genderqueer identity of witch androgynous (Penczak, 2003: 3).

17

> [T]he recognition that the standards established by contemporary western categories of gender, sex and sexuality are socially constructed does not eliminate the impact of these categories. It does, however, serve as an invitation to construct alternative categories. The goal is not to exchange one empirically underdetermined set of categories for another empirically underdetermined set of categories. Instead the goal is the proliferation and multiplication of categories.
>
> (Marinucci, 2010: 35–36)

151

18 'Decolonizing means reinscribing the suppressed, the ruinous, in the present' (Sanjines C., 2013: 24).

19 According to Stone, genderqueer people 'speak from outside the boundaries of gender, beyond the constructed oppositional nodes which have been predefined as the only positions from which discourse is possible' (Stone, 1991: 351).

20 'The body gives rise to language, and that language carries bodily aims, and performs bodily deeds that are not always understood by those who use language to accomplish certain conscious aims' (Butler, 2004: 199).

21 'Gender norms are inscribed in the way people move, gesture, and even eat' (Lorber, 1994: 23).

22 'Clothing, paradoxically, often hides the sex but displays the gender' (ibid., 22).

23 'When women took men's clothes, they symbolically left their subordinate positions. They became masterless women, and this threatened overthrow of hierarchy was discursively read as the eruption of uncontrolled sexuality' (Howard, 1988: 424).

24

The male trappings were used as armor—defensive and aggressive. It . . . attacked men by aping their appearance in order to usurp their functions. On the personal level, it defied men and declared them useless; on the social level, it affirmed male . . . to assert personal needs and desires.
(Warner, 1982: 155)

25

'Man' and 'woman' are at once empty and overflowing categories. Empty because they have no ultimate, transcendental meaning. Overflowing because even when they appear to be fixed, they still contain within them alternative, denied, or suppressed definitions.
(Scott, 1988: 49)

26

Masculinism takes it for granted that there is a fundamental difference between men and women, it assumes that heterosexuality is normal, it accepts without question the sexual division of labour, and it sanctions the political and dominant role of men in the public and private spheres.
(Brittan, 1989: 4)

27

In fact, a majority of narratives about female visionary experiences are based on the sudden and *spontaneous* arising, either in sleep or while awake, of very intense, vivid visionary dreams without the dreamer necessarily making any attempt to seek such a vision.
(Irwin, 2001: 95)

28 Monica Sjoo and Barbara Moor rightly observe that

Creative women and men in all ages have found rigid heterosexuality in conflict with being fully alive and aware on all levels—sexual, psychic and spiritual. . . . It is as if, on all levels of our being, we are split into one half, and forbidden the other. We are split against ourselves, and against the 'self' in the other, by this moralistic opposition of natural polarities in the very depth of our souls.
(1987: 67–68)

29 'Often our very sense of male identity is sustained through our capacity for *not* needing the help of others' (Seidler, 1992: 1).
30 'My first few field trips among both forest and village dwelling Rabhas in both Jalpaiguri and Cooch Behar districts, proved my hypothesis that the Rabha society was moving from matriliny to patriliny' (Raha, 1989: 5).
31 'Governmental officials and public health experts have employed science speak and the "language of truth" in order to colonize ever more spheres of human life, including sex, and to manage ever smaller details of citizens' everyday existence' (Fruhstuck, 2014: 18).

7

QUEER INDIA AS NEO-BAHUJAN
Towards a possible assembling

[W]hat is happening, actually, is that we are remembering who we are and that our identities can no longer be used as a weapon against us.

(LaFortune, 1997: 222)

I am all races because there is the queer of me in all races.
(Anzaldúa, 1987: 102)

The taboo imposed on the queer community has been prevailing in contemporary India as a present past that is tried to be transmitted into the future through a constant regulating and replicating of 'correctness'.[1] In the current neoliberal capitalist scenario in India, with socialism being turned into a token principle of the Constitution's preamble, it is not surprising that same-sex bonding is viewed as an 'institutionalized irrationality' (Lasch, 1977: 144). The procreative sexual drive, propagandised as the individual's sensible hunt for economic ends, is conceived of as profitable and therefore rational in the imagined rationality of capitalism. Apart from this tough capitalist logic, people who refuse to be disciplined by the state are put under 'indefinite discipline: an interrogation without end, an investigation that would be extended without limit to a meticulous and ever more analytical observation' (Foucault, 1995: 68). Queers in India have lost their jobs, family supports and ultimately their lives for being caught up in 'disciplinary' mechanisms, and even after the decriminalisation of consensual same-sex relationships, the instances of discrimination against the queer community have hardly declined, due to which sexual minorities in India have been unable to recover from perturbation and fear.[2] I hope that the psychoanalytic study of these folktales has succeeded in tracing out a tribal-based tradition of knowledge about what is now called queer sexuality. This queering of the tribal folktales should also be able to challenge the post-independent trend of Indigenous Indian scholarship that has mostly failed to rescue itself from the imperatives of Brahminic alignment and its positioning as always an Indigenous of the Western.[3]

The tribal characters in the Toto, Rabha, Lepcha and Limbu folktales challenge gender stereotypes and seem to recommend 'the construction of an erotics that decenters genital sexuality and de-essentializes gender' (Weeks, 1945: 186), eventually to evoke new forms of 'intricate interdependencies' (Radway, 1999: 8) among all who represent the nonnormative. 'Queer' represents the uncannily defamiliarised selves who exist differently in different cultures and parallelly alienated in similar ways in other cultures. The 'queer of me' as a scary body (Anzaldúa, 1987: 77), therefore, can be politically made functional to become an 'interface' for the 'inter-faces' of 'our multiple-surfaced, colored, racially gendered bodies [to] intersect and interconnect' (ibid., 1990: xvi) on the basis of all that has been abjected by the dehumanising 'mainstream', towards an ever-ongoing hybridisation.

Turning away from Darwin's overemphasis on competitive struggle towards Kropotkin's notion of 'mutual aid' as the 'instinct of human sociability',[4] the gay, lesbian, bisexual and transgender people who find themselves positioned in the 'mainstream' as the major victims of the 'mainstream' need to relate their awareness as sufferers with the Dalit tribals, who are also made to suffer by the neocolonial state and, in so doing, identify as 'neo-Bahujan'. The Bahujan movement, through the formation of a 'samaj' (collectively) to fight against the oppressive Hindus who practised discrimination, was initiated by Kanshi Ram following the empowering ideologies of Ambedkar. It aimed at an emancipatory togetherness for the scheduled castes (bringing together even the untouchable castes), scheduled tribes, other backward class and religious minorities. And it emphasised 'the need to reach beyond the Dalit milieu' (Jaffrelot, 1998: 35). Hence, the Dalit consciousness of becoming the Other of the Hindu Right and its fortification of a 'masculinized nationalism' can assist sexual minorities in coming out as a neo-Bahujan, since Bahujan is 'no longer just a Dalit' (ibid.) by birth but rather a political category. Dalit scholars[5] have revealed that the category of Dalit, apart from drawing affinities between the people of lower castes, tribes and backward classes, also 'can be both a destabilising identity and an identity that allows for the assemblage of alliances among all afflicted' (Peacock, 2020: 123). Insights about the resistance against subalternity from Dalit studies can offer 'the real possibility of solidarity between Dalit and gay rights groups' through the larger recognition that Dalit is a fluid identity of fortifying 'authentic lines of affinity between others who do not belong and who fall in between' (ibid.: 124) in the neocolonial nation-building process.

The futurity of queer Indian people, who are often marked with 'no future'[6] in contemporary Indian society, due to the country's denying them civic rights and due to their lack of ample protection against harassment, is no different from the bleak future of Indigenous communities, who also need to

> question the value of 'no future' in the context of genocide, where Native peoples have already been determined by settler colonialism to have no future. If the goal of queerness is to challenge the reproduction of the social order, then the Native child may already be queered.
>
> (Smith, 2010: 48)

Treating queer as a coalition of the nonconformist identities beyond the incoherent, state-organised boundaries and believing strongly that 'The past is always contingent on what the future makes of it' (Grosz, 2001: 104), this queering of the select tribal folktales envisages a queer hybridisation that may sanction an in-betweenness for tribals and nontribal queers to cocreate a mental space of 'thirdness' (Benjamin, 2005–6: 119) as an existential 'product of crossbreeding' (Anzaldúa, 1987: 81), out of the realisation that 'it is the multiplicity and interconnectedness of our identities that provide the most promising avenue for the destabilization and radical politicalization of these same categories' (Cohen, 2005: 45). Relying upon a 'moral third',[7] a thirdness as the capacity of listening to multiple voices of others who seem to be voicing even some parts of the self, can play a part in a collaborative, intersubjective struggle against past experiences of denunciation. This thirdness is 'not to be understood primarily as the intervention of an other, but rather requires the "one in the third", the attunement and empathy that make it possible to bridge difference with identification, to infuse observation with compassion' (Benjamin, 2002: 50). It is also crucial to overcome the binary between the 'doer' and the 'done to', which, when sustained, becomes a powerful strategy of the state to rule by distancing different yet equally marginalised identities.

In 'The Ballad of East and West', Rudyard Kipling wrote that 'Oh, East is East and the West is West and never the twain shall meet'. This is the claim of the sexual fundamentalists in India who consider queer a non-Indigenous colonial ingress. This nonnormative study of the traditional tribal tales through a modern queer lens, with a plea to bring out 'a process of rebirth, searching for new paths for future development', has ultimately been devoted to focusing on Indigenous communities' arrival at transmodernity, which is founded on the 'unsuspected cultural richness, which is slowly revived like the flames of the fire of those fathoms buried under the sea of ashes from hundreds of years of colonialism' (Dussel, 2010: 14). The modernisation of postcolonial India has been based on the formulation of a 'state-centric Indian nation', but it has also given birth to a 'rebel consciousness' (Roy, 2005: 2176). The antinormative queer rebel victimised by the 'mainstream' ultimately looks forward to an intersectionality with Indigeneity on the basis of the shared, single dimension of otherisation, under the assurance that 'the intersection of identities takes place through the articulation of a single dimension of each category' (McCall, 2005: 1781). Ultimately, this bond of intersectionality with the wretched of the 'mainstream' 'can also lead to post-ethnic consciousness where ethnic groups are not just interested in maintaining boundaries but in a boundary-crossing inter-cultural dialogues and communication' (Kumar, 2014: 96) that form interconnected communities of the marginalised, working towards resistance and transmodernity.

Differentiating 'the popular', as the multitude of 'all defenceless, dispossessed, and aggrieved members' from the privileged, the protected and rightful notion of 'citizenship' as a 'unique historical we', Vidal suggests that 'the popular', 'whatever their racial, ethnic origin or social status, have right to full solidarity' (Vidal, 2009: 32). This solidarity can be founded upon an 'amphibious' politics of belonging, one that can be 'adopted to both lives or both ways of life' of marginal 'mainstream' queer people and queer Indigeneity and, in so doing, can reliably develop each of them into 'more than one cultural tradition and that facilitates communication between them' (Mockus, 1994: 37). Mockushas further maintained that this amphibian intersectionality would ensue 'soft boundaries' through which the 'amphibian borders' of the diverse culture would crisscross and 'obey partially divergent systems of rules without a loss of intellectual and moral integrity' (ibid.: 39).

The intersectional/intercultural connection of victimised 'mainstream' queer people with the 'peripheral' tribal societies, equally oppressed by the suppressive state regimes and neoliberal interests, is possible in my own experiences, through a 'mainstream' queer's performing of what the German hobbyists who follow multiple aspects of a Native American lifestyle call 'practical ethnology' (Graham and Penny, 2014: 169). The 'going native' of the repudiated 'mainstream' queer is meant not to annihilate the non-Indigenous identity but rather to enhance a politics of belonging in the form of a 'communitas' of the 'ex-centrics', so that the murky existence of otherised 'mainstream' queer people is illumined with the non-tabooed 'light of pure anteriority' (Cioran, 1970: 48). The 'performance turn' initiated by scholars like Kenneth Burke, Erving Goffman, John Austin and Judith Butler paved the way for an affordable 'performativity' of a 'surrogate Indigeneity' (Graham and Penny, 2014: 182) by contested 'mainstream' Indian queer people, one that would ensure a processual recounting of interactions and an assertion of a 'disidentification' with an ever-shifting identity.

The Supreme Court of India's valorisation of consensual same-sex relationships was indeed a step towards decolonising queer lives; however, there are many hurdles yet to overcome. The resentment[8] against Transgender Persons' (Protection of Rights) Bill 2019, which violates various provisions—like a transgender person's right to self-identification and determination to either choose or refuse sex reassignment surgery—provided by the Supreme

Court's 2014 NALSA (National Legal Services Authority of India) judgement reveals that there are many other aspects yet to be critically considered to achieve complete sexual decolonisation.

One aspect of decolonising the queer Indian community is that of striving for endogenous acknowledgement by illustrating how queerphobia was imposed by the Western colonisers on an autochthonous queernormativity. I hope that this particular aspect of decolonisation has been addressed well by the revelation of queernormative Indigenous past through the queering of select tribal folktales. There is, however, another aspect of decolonisation regarding the queer community in India, one that must combat the anti-other outlook of both the majoritarian 'mainstream' and the neocolonial state towards sexual minorities. I argue that a queer–Indigeneity alliance, as proposed in this book, is imperative to more effectively fight against internal colonialism.

The present Indian right-wing government aspiring to turn India into a 'Hindutva' nation seems to treat Indigenous people with special attention only when it comes to what Nirmal Kumar Bose (1941) called the 'Hindu method of tribal absorption'. Otherwise, tribals are continuously made aware of their Dalit status by the neocolonial state's control over tribal regions (Guha, 2007) through a nexus comprising industrialists, administrators of forests, the military, the police and all other (predominantly nontribal) agents of the state that operate by 'raiding villages, stealing properties and grain, sexually abusing women, brutally killing some Adivasis, and detaining and torturing others' (Kennedy and King, 2013: 21). These 'others', who can be identified as non-Indigenous allies (e.g., Binayak Sen and Sudha Bharadwaj, among many others), have also been victimised by the state for helping tribal people in their struggle to resist their loss of rights over their lands, forests and even traditional ways of life. Understanding the exploitation 'in the context of a neocolonial political economy in which the state cares more about the minerals lying below the ground than the adivasis living above it' (Kennedy and King, 2011: 1642), the tribals are terribly aware of their Dalit position. Their distress is surely getting worse with the loss of equalities and democratic rights[9] following the rise of the Hindu Right in India, which Ambedkar accurately predicted:

> If Hindu Raj does become a fact, it will, no doubt, be the greatest calamity for this country. . . . [It] is a menace to liberty, equality and fraternity. On that account it is incompatible with democracy. Hindu Raj must be prevented at any cost.
>
> (Ambedkar, 2014: 359)

On the other hand, there has been a strategic 'masculinization of Indian politics' (Kinnvall, 2019))—evident in the Bharatiya Janata Party's (BJP) populist references to Narendra Modi's '56-inch chest' as firmly 'able

and willing to bear the harshest burdens in the service of Mother India'
(Shristava, 2015: 334)—aimed at redefining India as a 'masculinist nation'
where more aggressive males are required to protect the motherland. This
refashioning of the 'nationhood', on the basis of a gendered privileging
of 'masculinity', is surely going to aggravate the crisis for queer people in
India with the possibility of being otherised for not being macho enough
as per the standards of right-wing manliness or not feminine enough to
deserve fair treatment from protective hypermasculinity. The neocoloniality of India as reflected in the mandate of providing specified evidences in
order to be acknowledged as an Indian citizen by the National Register of
Citizens (NRC)—along with the passing of Citizenship Amendment Act,
2019 (CAA), in Parliament—has adversely affected both the Dalit tribals
(and accordingly, despite the fact that the North East Indian states either
completely or partially are excluded from the new Act, there have been
widespread protests against CAA and NRC in the states of tribal majority)[10]
and dispossessed queer people in terms of their incapability of producing
the required documents. '[Q]ueer people are the persecuted minorities'[11]
and should be protesting against Citizenship Amendment Act and National
Register of Citizens. Indian queer people who have been abandoned by their
families and left with no documents to authenticate their citizenship need to
politically identify as 'neo-Bahujan'. Reconsidering Dalit as not exclusively
a birth-based natural identity, queer Indians should forge an intimate bond
with the Dalit Bahujan tribals by politically positioning themselves as neo-
Bahujan in order to fight against a common adversary. Inspired by the Marathi writer Arjun Dangle's view that, 'Dalit is not a caste but a realization'
(1992: 264) and by K. Satyanarayana's assertion that Dalit is a democratic
identity based on 'diverse self-identifications and positions of the marginalized castes, genders and other minorities' (2020: 27), the queering of the
tribal tales in this book is an attempt to strengthen the sexual minority's
politics of becoming Dalit.

As a non-Indigenous queer located in the 'mainstream' but mostly otherised by it, my coming out as a neo-Bahujan aimed at a politics of intimate belonging has been assisted by the discovery of queernormative liberal
spaces (as reflected in the tribal folktales) of acceptance among Indigenous
people and by a shared experience of marginalisation due to the recolonisation of the reimagined and masculinised Hindu Right nation. I hope that
the discovery of queer-friendly Indigenous people in this queer reading of
the tribal folktales will pave the way for queer Indians to befriend tribal
Bahujans through a politics of becoming Dalit and for the emergence of neo-
Bahujan as an identity anchored in a conscious choice 'of loving others who
are equal in their Otherised state of "statelessness"' (Chakraborty, 2020a:
2). This is the first step towards an assemblage for annihilating the Dalit
wretchedness, by both the tribal Dalit Bahujan and queer people emerging as neo-Bahujan through a politics of becoming Dalit, based on shared

experiencing of discrimination (in the hands of the Hindu Right majority's rhetoric of a populist and hypermasculine nationalism) that contribute to the evolution of the Dalit consciousness.

Resistance against domination has to be 'learnt' by a 'practised' interaction that is based on one's *conscious choice* of loving the other: 'The moment we choose to love we begin to move against domination, against oppression. The moment we choose to love we begin to move towards freedom, to act in ways that liberate ourselves and others' (hooks, 1994: 298). Chasing a dream provoked by Deleuze, that 'Difference must leave its cave and cease to be a monster' (Deleuze, 1994: 29), there has been an intense struggle in concretising queer aspirations in some tangible form, which in turn would make my marginal life a bit more bearable, with a hope for a good life.[12] The search has resulted in my stepping into the 'queer heterotopias'[13] of these tribal folktales, which has facilitated envisaging 'a sign of an actually existing queer reality, a kernel of political possibility within a stultifying heterosexual present' (Muñoz, 2009: 49). My personal experiences during the fieldwork convinced me of a potential intimacy among queers and tribal communities through the forming of 'plural singularities'[14] on the shared commonalty of discrimination by the state. This 'political project' which is a precondition for the emerging of the 'multitude', has already evolved among Indigenous and the Indian queer communities in the form of the struggle for dignity. The consciousness that transforms 'I want' into 'I am entitled to' (Pitkin, 1981: 347) is essentially that of dignity,[15] which can further vitalise the 'multitude' of Indigenous people and queer people, urging them to declare, 'I have the right to have rights' (Arendt, 2000: 37), assisting in developing 'greater common habits, practices, conduct, and desires' (Hardt and Negri, 2004: 218). This visualising may be utopian, particularly when the issue related to the civil rights of queers in India appears to be lying on uncharted territory. Even today, Indian queer people are deprived of most of the civic rights. Let individuals, who are standing on my opposite side, view it in terms of moral, legal and normative disputes. I would rather stick to an anticipative, futuristic, utopian possibility. I do not hope for an immediate 'return of the plebeian' in the form of a 'human wave that over-whelmed the institutions of the state' (Gutierrez et al., 2000: 162) for the sake of the 'rehabilitation of the customs and traditions of the oppressed' (ibid.: 177) by the multitude of the marginalised. I only hope that this endeavour of mine permits me to usher in a tribal queernormativity out of the 'waiting room of history' (Chakrabarty, 2000: 8) so that the marker of an 'import'/'outsider'[16] is soon replaced by endogenous acknowledgements.

Notes

1 See, for example, "Shock and Outrage Won't Stop Indian Parents Forcing Queer Children into 'Conversion Therapy'", Taran Deol, *The Print*, May 20, 2020.

https://theprint.in/opinion/pov/shock-and-outrage-wont-stop-indian-parents-forcing-queer-children-into-conversion-therapy/425439/; "Homophobic Attack Leaves Hyderabad Man with an Injured Leg", By Donita Jose, *The New Indian Express,* July 29, 2019. www.newindianexpress.com/cities/hyderabad/2019/jul/29/homophobic-attack-leaves-hyderabad-man-with-an-injured-leg-2011001.html Accessed on June 12, 2020.

2 "Why India's Laws Are Still Not LGBT+ Inclusive". Ketaki Desai, *Times of India*, September 2, 2029. https://timesofindia.indiatimes.com/india/why-indias-laws-are-still-not-LGBT+-inclusive/articleshow/70948616.cms; "A Year After SC's Sec 377 Order, LGBT+ Community Waits for Inclusive Laws". Ambika Pandit, *Times of India*, August 31, 2019. https://timesofindia.indiatimes.com/india/a-year-after-scs-sec-377-order-LGBT+-community-waits-for-inclusive-laws/articleshow/70917432.cms Accessed on April 9, 2020.

3 For details, see Agarwal, 1995.

4 Kropotkin suggests in his *Mutual Aid* that

> Sociability is as much a law of nature as mutual struggle. Of course it would be extremely difficult to estimate, however roughly, the relative numerical importance of both these series of facts. But if we resort to an indirect test, and ask Nature, 'Who are the fittest: those who are continuously at war with each other, or those who support one another?' We at once see that those animals which acquire habits of mutual aid are undoubtedly the fittest.
>
> (2006: 5)

5 See, for example, Guru (1998). Even Sharan Kumar Limbale wrote that 'Dalits do not belong to one nation or one culture only, they are found everywhere in different forms. They are relegated to the periphery by the dominant forces of the society and remain excluded from the mainstream culture' ("An Interface with Sharan Kumar Limbale" by Neha Kanaujia. http://researchscholar.co.in/downloads/75-neha-kanaujia.pdf Accessed on June 16, 2020).

6 City dwellers might find this as an overstatement. However, in the rural areas, being queer is still considered a disease or a sin. For instance, see "What It Means to Be Gay in Rural India", by Vikas Pandey. *BBC News*, New Delhi, September 6, 2018. www.bbc.com/news/world-asia-india-45430953; "Queer Question in Rural India: Mainstream Cinema & Other Realities", by Mohd Usman Mehandi. *Feminism in India*. April 24, 2020. https://feminisminindia.com/2020/04/24/queer-question-rural-india-mainstream-cinema/Accessed   on June 6, 2020.

7 According to Jessica Benjamin,

> The moral third refers to those values, rules, and principles of interaction that we rely upon in our efforts to create and restore the space for each partner in the dyad to engage in thinking, feeling, acting or responding rather than merely reacting.
>
> (2009: 442)

8 See "Why India's Transgender People Are Protesting Against a Bill That Claims to Protect Their Rights", by Ajita Banerjie. *Scroll.in*, November 26, 2019. https://scroll.in/article/944882/why-indias-transgender-people-are-protesting-against-a-bill-that-claims-to-protect-their-rights.

9 Prunima S. Tripathi correctly predicted the fading of Modi charisma among the tribal people in Jharkhand, which was well reflected in Jharkhand state election results in 2019, when The Jharkhand Mukti Morcha and Congress alliance won

the majority seats. See "Jharkhand Tribal Resentment", *Frontline*, May 8, 2019. https://frontline.thehindu.com/cover-story/article27056694.ece.

10 Roluahpuia (Feb. 20, 2020). "Peripheral Protests: CAA, NRC and Tribal Politics in Northeast India". www.law.ox.ac.uk/research-subject-groups/centre-crimi nology/centreborder-criminologies/blog/2020/02/peripheral Accessed on April 20, 2020. Also see "Citizenship Amendment Act (CAA), and the Tribal Community (Adivasi)", in *Round Table India* (18 December 2019) where Jawar Bheel has explained why "CAA and NRC should also be opposed for being anti-adivasi". http://roundtableindia.co.in/index.php?option=com_content&vie w=article&id=9773:citizenship-amendment-act-caa-and-the-tribal-community-adivasi&catid=119:feature&Itemid=132 Accessed on April 20, 2020.

11 See "'Queer People Are Persecuted Minorities': Women, LGBTQ Community March Against CAA, NRC", Mudita Girotra, *The New Indian Express*, January 4, 2020. www.newindianexpress.com/cities/delhi/2020/jan/04/queer-people-are-persecuted-minorities-women-lgbtq-community-march-against-caa-nrc-2084928.html Accessed on April 21, 2020.

12 Sara Ahmed wrote that

> We need to think more about the relationship between queer struggle for a bearable life and aspirational hopes for a good life. Maybe the point is that it is hard to struggle without aspirations, and aspirations are hard to have without giving them some form.
>
> (2010: 120)

13 According to Angela Jones, 'queer heterotopias are places where individuals can challenge the heteronormative regime' (2009: 1).

14 'The multitude is composed of an internally different, multiple social subject whose constitution and action is based not on identity or unity (or much less, indifference) but on what it has in common' (Hardt and Negri, 2004: 100).

15 A lack of approval of one's identity, according to Arendt, can rob one of basic human dignity:

> a human being in general—without a profession, without a citizenship, without an opinion, without a deed by which to identify himself—and different in general, representing nothing but his own absolutely unique individuality which, deprived of expression within and action upon a common world, loses all significance.
>
> (1994: 302)

16 Recently, while opposing a plea in support of recognising gay marriage under the Hindu Marriage Act, the Solicitor general Tushar Mehta has told the Delhi High Court, on behalf of the government, that same-sex marriage is against Indian culture. See "'Same-sex marriage is not a part of our culture', says top govt law-yer, opposes plea in Delhi HC". Apoorva Mandhani, *The Print*, September 14, 2020. https://theprint.in/judiciary/same-sex-marriage-not-a-part-of-our-culture-says-central-govt-opposes-plea-in-delhi-hc/502232/ Accessed on September 15, 2020.

BIBLIOGRAPHY

Abraham, Karl. *Dreams and Myths: A Study in Race Psychology*. New York: Journal of Nervous and Mental Disease Publishing Company. 1913.

Abramowski, Luise. "Die 'Erinnerungen der Apostel' bei Justin". In Peter Stuhlmacher (ed.), *Das Evangelium und die Evangelien. VorträgevomTübinger Symposium 1982* (WUNT, 28). Tübingen: Mohr Siebeck. 1983. pp. 341–353.

Adam, Barry D. "How Might We Create a Collectivity That We Would Want to Belong To?" In David M. Halperin and Valerie Traub (eds.), *Gay Shame*. Chicago: University of Chicago Press. 2009. pp. 301–311. Print.

Adams, Henry E., Lester W. Wright, Jr., and Bethany A. Lohr. "Is Homophobia Associated with Homosexual Arousal?" *Journal of Abnormal Psychology*, Vol. 105, No. 3 (1996), pp. 440–445.

Adichie, Chimamanda Ngori. *Half of a Yellow Sun*. London, New York, Toronto and Sydney: Harper Perennial. 2008.

Afzal-Khan, Fawzia, and Kalpana Seshadri-Crooks, eds. *The Pre-Occupation of Postcolonial Studies*. Durham and London: Duke University Press. 2000.

Agamben, Giorgio. *The Coming Community*. Trans. Michael Hardt. Minneapolis: University of Minnesota Press. 2009.

———. *Infancy and History: Essays on the Destruction of Experience*. Trans. Liz Heron. London and New York: Verso. 1993.

Agarwal, Arun. "Dismantling the Divide Between Indigenous and Western Knowledge". *Development and Change*, Vol. 26, No. 3 (1995), pp. 413–439.

Ahmed, Sara. *The Promise of Happiness*. Durham: Duke University Press. 2010.

———. "The Skin of the Community: Affect and Boundary Formation". In Tina Chanter and Ewa Plonowska Ziarek (eds.), *Revolt, Affect, Collectivity: The Unstable Boundaries of Kristeva's Polis*. Albany: State University of New York. 2005. pp. 95–111.

Alcorn, K. "Queer and Now". *Gay Times*, May 1992. pp. 20–24.

Alford, C. Fred. *What Evil Means to Us*. Ithaca, NY and London: Cornell University Press. 1997.

Amadiume, Ifi. *Male Daughters, Female Husbands: Gender and Sex in an African Society*. London: Zed Books. 1987.

Ambedkar, B.R. "Pakistan or the Partition of India". In Vasant Moon (ed.), *Babasaheb Ambedkar: Writings and Speeches*, Vol. 8. Mumbai: Education Department. Maharashtra Government. 2014.

Andersen, Chris. "Critical Indigenous Studies: From *Difference* to *Density*". *Cultural Studies Review*, Vol. 15, No. 2 (September 2009), pp. 80–100.

Anderson, Benedict. *Imagined Communities: Reflections on the Origin and Spread of Nationalism*. Rev. ed. London: Verso. 2006.

Anderson, Elijah. *Streetwise: Race, Class and Change in an Urban Community*. Chicago: Chicago University Press. 1990.

Andrievskikh, Natalia. "Food Symbolism, Sexuality, and Gender Identity in Fairy Tales and Modern Women's Bestsellers". *Studies in Popular Culture*, Vol. 37, No. 1 (Fall 2014), pp. 137–153.

Anzaldúa, Gloria E., ed. *Making Face, Making Soul/Haciendo Caras: Creative and Critical Perspectives by Women of Color*. San Francisco: Aunt Lute. 1990.

———. *Borderlands/La Frontera: The New Mestiza*. San Francisco: Spinsters/Aunt Lute. 1987.

Anzieu, Didier. *The Skin Ego*. Trans. Chris Turner. London and New Haven: Yale University Press. 1989.

Appadurai, Arjun. "Number in the Colonial Imagination". In Carol A. Breckenridge and Peter van der Veer (eds.), *Orientalism and the Post-Colonial Predicament*. Philadelphia: University of Pennsylvania Press. 1993.

Appiah, Kwame Anthony. "Is the Post- in Postmodernism the Post- in Postcolonial?" *Critical Inquiry*, Vol. 17, No. 2 (Winter 1991), pp. 336–357.

Archibald, Robert R. *A Place to Remember: Using History to Build Community*. Walnut Creek, CA: Altamira Press. 1999.

Arendt, Hannah. "The Perplexities of the Rights of Man". In Peter Baehr (ed.), *The Portable Hannah Arendt*. New York: Penguin. 2000.

———. *The Origins of Totalitarianism*. New York: Harcourt Books. 1994.

———. *Lectures on Kant's Political Philosophy*. Ed. Ronald Beiner. Chicago: University of Chicago Press. 1982.

———. *The Life of the Mind*. San Diego: Harcourt. 1981.

———. *Men in Dark Times*. San Diego: Harcourt Brace Jovanovich. 1968.

Ariès, Philippe. *Images of Man and Death*. Trans. Janet Lloyd. Cambridge: Harvard University Press. 1985.

———. *Un Historien du dimanche*. Paris: Editions du Seuil. 1882.

Arnold, Matthew. *The Works of Matthew Arnold*. New York: Wordsworth. 1999.

Arvin, Maile, Eve Tuck, and Angie Morrill. "Decolonizing Feminism: Challenging Connections Between Settler Colonialism and Heteropatriarchy". *Feminist Formations*, Vol. 25, No. I (Spring 2013), pp. 8–34.

Attwood, Bain. "Introduction". In B. Attwood and J. Arnold (eds.), *Power, Knowledge and Aborigines, Journal of Australian Studies*. Melbourne: La Trobe University Press. 1993. pp. i–xvi.

Bacchetta, Paola. "When the (Hindu) Nation Exiles Its Queers". *Social Text*, No. 61. Out Front: Lesbians, Gays, and the Struggle for Workplace Rights (Winter 1999), pp. 141–166.

Badinter, Elisabeth. *The Unopposite Sex: The End of the Gender Battle*. Trans. Barbara Wright. New York: Harper and Row. 1989.

Badiou, Alain. *The Century*. Trans. Alberto Toscano. New York: Polity Press. 2007.

Bakhtin, Mikhail M. "Forms of Time and of the Chronotope in the Novel". *The Dialogic Imagination: Four Essays by M. M. Bakhtin*. Ed. Michael Holquist. Austin: University of Texas Press. 1996. pp. 84–258.

———. *Problems of Dostoevsky's Poetics*. Ed. and Trans. C. Emerson. Minneapolis, MN: University of Minnesota Press. 1984.

———. *Rabelais and His World*. Trans. H. Iswolsky. Bloomington: Indiana University Press. 1984.

Baldick, Chris. *The Concise Oxford Dictionary of Literary Terms*. Oxford: Oxford University Press. 1990.

Ballhatchet, Kenneth. *Race, Sex and Class Under the Raj*. London: Weidenfeld and Nicolson. 1980.

Barren, M., and M. McIntosh. *The Anti-Social Family*. London: Verso. 1982.

Barrett, Michele. *Women's Oppression Today: The Marxist/Feminist Encounter*. London: Verso. 1988.

Bascom, William R. "Four Functions of Folklore". In Alan Dundes (ed.), *The Study of Folklore*. Berkeley: University of California. 1965. pp. 279–298.

Bataille, Georges. *Eroticism*. Introduction. C. MacCabe. London: Penguin. 2001.

———. *Ilcolpevole*. Trans. A. Biancoforte. Bari: Dedalo. 1989.

———. *Inner Experience*. Trans. Leslie Boldt. New York: State University of New York Press. 1988.

———. *Theory of Religion*. Trans. Robert Hurley. New York: Zone Books. 1988.

———. *Eroticism: Death and Sensuality*. Trans. Mary Dalwood. London and New York: Marion Boyars. 1987.

———. "The College of Sociology". In Allan Stoekl (trans.), *Visions of Excess: Selected Writings. 1927–1939*. Minneapolis: University of Minnesota Press. 1985a.

———. "The Solar Anus". In Alan Stoekl (ed. and trans.), *Visions of Excess: Selected Writings, 1927–1933*. Minneapolis: University of Minnesota Press. 1985b.

Baudrillard, Jean. *Symbolic Exchange and Death*. Trans. Iain Hamilton Grant. London: Sage Publications. 1993a.

———. *The Transparency of Evil: Essays on Extreme Phenomena*. Trans. James Benedict. New York and London: Verso. 1993b.

Bauman, Richard. "Differential Identity and the Social Base of Folklore". *Journal of American Folklore*, Vol. 85 (1971), pp. 31–41.

Bauman, Zygmunt. *Liquid Modernity*. Cambridge: Polity Press. 2000.

———. *Intimations of Postmodernity*. London and New York: Routledge. 1992.

Beaulieu, Alain. "The Status of Animality in Deleuze's Thought". *Journal for Critical Animal Studies*, Vol. IX, No. 1/2 (2011).

Becker, Howard S. *Outsiders: Studies in Sociology of Deviance*. New York: The Free Press. 1966.

Behadad, Ali. *Belated Travelers: Orientalism in the Age of Colonial Dissolution*. Durham and London: Duke University Press. 1994.

Bell, D., and J. Binnie. *The Sexual Citizen: Queer Politics and Beyond*. Cambridge: Polity Press. 2000.

Bellah, Robert N., Richard Madsen, William M. Sullivan, Ann Swidler, and Steven M. Tipton. *Habits of the Heart: Individualism and Commitment in American Life*. New York: Harper and Rowe. 1985.

Benjamin, Jessica. "Psychoanalytic Controversies: A Relational Psychoanalysis Perspective on the Necessity of Acknowledging Failure in Order to Restore the Facilitating and Containing Features of the Intersubjective Relationship (the Shared Third)". *The International Journal of Psychoanalysis*, Vol. 90, No. 3 (June 2009), pp. 441–450.

———. "Two-Way Streets: Recognition of Difference and the Intersubjective Third". *Differences: A Journal of Feminist Cultural Studies*, Vol. 17, No. 1 (2005–6), pp. 116–146.

———. "Beyond Doer and Done to: An Intersubjective View of Thirdness". *Psychoanalytic Quarterly*, Vol. 73 (2004), pp. 5–46.

———. "The Rhythm of Recognition: Comments on the Work of Louis Sander". *Psychoanalytic Dialogues*, Vol. 12, No. 1 (2002), pp. 43–53.

Benjamin, Walter. *GesammelteSchriften*. Ed. Rolf Tiedemann and Hermann Schweppenhäuser, Vol. I–VII. Frankfurt: Suhrkamp. 1972.

———. "The Task of the Translator". Trans. H. Zohn. In L. Venuti (ed.), *The Translation Studies Reader*. London and New York: Routledge. 1969. pp. 75–82.

———. "Über den Begriff der Geschichte," English Translation: "Theses on the Philosophy of History". In H. Zohn (trans.), *Illuminations. Essays and Reflections*. New York: Schocken. 1968.

Bennett, David, and Homi K. Bhabha. "Liberalism and Minority Culture: Reflections on 'Culture's In Between'". In David Bennett (ed.), *Multicultural States: Rethinking Difference and Identity*. London and New York: Routledge. 1998. pp. 37–47.

Bennett, W. Lance. "Storytelling in Criminal Trials: A Model of Judgement". *Quarterly Journal of Speech*, Vol. 64 (1978).

Bentley, Jenny. "'Vanishing Lepcha': Change and Cultural Revival in A Mountain Community of Sikkim". *Bulletin of Tibetology*, Vol. 43 (2007), pp. 59–79.

Berger, Peter, and Hansfried Kellner. "Marriage and the Construction of Reality". *Diogenes*, Vol. 46, No. 1 (1964).

Beteille, A. "The Concept of Tribe with Special Reference to India". *Journal of European Sociology*, No. 27 (1986).

Bhabha, Homi K. "Framing Fanon". Foreword to Franz Fanon. In Richard Philcox (trans.), *The Wretched of the Earth*. New York: Grove Press. 2004.

———. *The Location of Culture*. London and New York: Routledge. 1994.

———, ed. *Nation and Narration*. London: Routledge. 1990.

Bhaskaran, Suparna. "The Politics of Penetration: Section 377 and the Indian Penal Code". In Ruth Vanita (ed.), *Queering India: Same Sex Love and Eroticism in Indian Culture and Society*. London: Routledge. 2002. pp. 15–29.

Bilgrami, Akeel. "Secularism, Nationalism and Modernity". In R Bhargava (ed.), *Secularism and its Critics*. New Delhi: Oxford University Press. 1998. pp. 380–417.

Blanchot, Maurice. *The Space of Literature*. Trans. Ann Smock. Lincoln: University of Nebraska Press. 1982.

Bloch, Ernst. *Heritage of Our Times*. Trans. Neville Plaice and Stephen Plaice. Berkeley: University of California Press. 1991.

———. *The Utopian Function of Art and Literature*. Trans. Jack Zipes and Frank Mecklenburg. Cambridge: MIT Press. 1987.

Blum, Deborah. "The Gender Blur". *Utne Reader*, September–October 1998.

Boldt-Irons, Leslie Anne. "Bataille's 'The Solar Anus' or the Parody of Parodies". *Studies in 20th Century Literature*, Vol. 25, No. 2 (Summer 2001), pp. 354–375.

Bose, Nirmal Kumar. "The Hindu Method of Tribal Absorption". *Science and Culture*, Vol. 7 (1941), pp. 188–194.

Bourdieu, Pierre. *Masculine Domination*. Trans. Richard Nice. Cambridge: Polity Press. 2001.

———. *In Other Words: Essays Toward a Reflexive Sociology.* Trans. Matthew Adamson. Stanford, CA: Stanford University Press. 1990.

———. "Social Space and Symbolic Power". *Sociological Theory*, Vol. 7, No. 1 (Spring 1989) pp. 14–25.

———. *Outline of a Theory of Practice.* Cambridge: Cambridge University Press. 1977.

Brittan, Arthur. *Masculinity and Power.* Oxford: Basil Blackwell. 1989.

Bronfen, Elisabeth, and Sarah Webster Goodwin. "Introduction". In Sarah Webster Goodwin and Elisabeth Bronfen (eds.), *Death and Representation.* Baltimore: Johns Hopkins University Press. 1993. pp. 3–25.

Brown, Wendy. *States of Injury: Power and Freedom in Late Modernity.* Princeton, NJ: Princeton University Press. 1995.

Brundage, W. Fitzhugh. "Introduction: No Deed but Memory". In *Where These Memories Grow: History, Memory and Southern Identity.* Chapel Hill: University of North Carolina Press. 2000. pp. 1–28.

Bruner, Jerome. *Actual Minds, Possible Worlds.* Cambridge: Harvard University Press. 1986.

Butler, Judith. "On Being Beside Oneself: On the Limits of Sexual Autonomy". In Nicholas Bamforth (ed.), *Sex Rights: The Oxford Amnesty Lectures2002.* Oxford and New York: Oxford University Press. 2005.

———. "Imitation and Gender Insubordination". In D. Carlia and J. DiGrazia (eds.), *Queer Culture.* Upper Saddle River, NJ: Pearson. 2004.

———. *The Psychic Life of Power: Theories in Subjection.* Stanford, CA: Stanford University Press. 1997.

———. "Sexual Inversions: Rereading the End of Foucault's *History of Sexuality, Vol. I*". In Domna C. Stanton (ed.), *Discourses of Sexuality: From Aristotle to AIDS.* RATIO: Institute for the Humanities. Ann Arbor: University of Michigan Press. 1992. pp. 344–361.

———. *Gender Trouble: Feminism and the Subversion of Identity.* London and New York: Routledge. 1990.

Byrne, Moyra. "Antonio Gramsci's Contribution to Italian Folklore Studies". *International Folklore Review*, Vol. 2 (1982), pp. 70–75.

Byrskog, Samuel. *Story as History—History as Story: The Gospel Tradition in the Context of Ancient Oral History.* Boston, Leiden: Brill Academic Publishers. 2002.

Casey, Edward S. *Remembering: A Phenomenological Study.* Bloomington: Indiana University Press. 1987.

Castells, Manuel. *The Power of Identity.* Oxford: Blackwell Publishers. 1997.

Castiglia, Christopher, and Christopher Reed. *If Memory Serves: Gay Men, Aids and the Promise of the Queer Past.* Minneapolis: University of Minnesota Press. 2012.

Chakrabarty, Dipesh. *Provincializing Europe: Postcolonial Thought and Historical Difference.* Princeton, NJ: Princeton University Press. 2000.

Chakraborty, Kaustav, ed. *The Politics of Belonging in Contemporary India: Anxiety and Intimacy.* London and New York: Routledge. 2020a.

———. "Memories of a Queer Sexuality: Revisiting Two 'Toto' Folk Tales". In Rajeev Kumaramkandath and Sanjay Srivastava (eds.), *(Hi)Stories of Desire: Sexualities and Culture in Modern India.* New Delhi and Shimla: Cambridge University Press and Indian Institute of Advanced Studies. 2020b. pp. 96–115.

———. *Indigeneity, Tales and Alternatives: Revisiting Select Tribal Folktales*. Shimla: Indian Institute of Advanced Study. 2017.

Chaney, D. *The Cultural Turn: Scene-Setting Essays on Contemporary Cultural History*. London: Routledge. 1994.

Chattopadhyay, Tapan. *Lepchas and Their Heritage*. New Delhi: B.R. Publishing Corporation. 2013.

Cicero, M. Tullius. *Rhetorica ad Herennium*. Trans. Harry Caplan. Cambridge: Leob Classical Library. 1954.

———. *DeInventione*. Trans. H.M. Hubbell, Vol. 2 (LCL). London: William Heinemann and Cambridge, MA: Harvard University Press. 1949. pp. 1–345.

Cioran, E.M. "Encounter with the Void". Trans. Frederick Brown. *Hudson Review*, Vol. 23, No. I (Spring 1970), pp. 37–48.

Cirese, Alberto Mario. "Concezione del mando, filosofiaspontanea e istinto di classenelle 'Osservazionisulfolclore' di Antonio Gramsci". In A.M. Cirese (ed.), *Intellettuali folklore, instinto di classe*. Torino. 1076.

Clark, K., and M. Holquist. *Mikhail Bakhtin*. Cambridge, MA: Harvard University Press. 1984.

Clark, Laurel A. "Beyond the Gay/Straight Split: Socialist Feminists in Baltimore". *NWSA Journal*, Vol. 19, No. 2 (Summer 2007), pp. 1–31.

Climo, Jacob J., and Maria G. Cattell, eds. *Social Memory and History: Anthropological Perspectives*. Walnut Creek, CA: Altamira Press. 2002.

Cobo, Jose Martinez. "The Study of the Problem of Discrimination Against Indigenous Populations". Document E/CN.4/Sub.2/1986/7/Add.4. Geneva: Office of the United Nations High Commissioner for Human Right. 1986.

Coeckelbergh, Mark. "Can We Choose Evil? A Discussion of the Problem of Radical Evil as a Modern and Ancient Problem of Freedom". In Daniel E. Keen and Pamela Rossi Keen (eds.), *Proceedings of First International Conference on Considering Evil and Human Wickedness*. Oxford: Inter-Disciplinary. 2004. pp. 339–353.

Cohen, Cathy J. "Punks, Bulldaggers, and Welfare Queens: The Radical Potential of Queer Politics?" In E.P. Johnson and M.G. Henderson (eds.), *Black Queer Studies: A Critical Anthology*. Durham: Duke University Press. 2005. pp. 21–51.

Colette, S.G. "The Ripening Seed". In H. Alderfer, B. Jaker, and M. Nelson (trans.), *Diary of a Conference on Sexuality*. New York: Faculty Press. 1982.

Collins, Patricia Hill. "Learning from the Outsider Within: The Sociological Significance of Black Feminist Thought". In M.M. Fonow and J.A. Cook (eds.), *Beyond Methodology. Feminist Research as Lived Research*. Bloormington: Indiana University Press. 1991.

Connolly, Angela. "Psychoanalytic Theory in Times of Terror". *Journal of Analytical Psychology*, Vol. 48 (2003), pp. 407–431.

Corso, Raffaele. *Folklore: Storia, Obbietto, Metodo, Bibliografia* (Classic Reprint). London: Forgotten Books. 2018.

Creswell, Tim. *In Place/Out of Place: Geography, Ideology and Transgression*. Minneapolis and London: University of Minnesota Press. 1996.

Croce, Mariano. "Homonormative Dynamics and the Subversion of Culture". *European Journal of Social Theory*, Vol. 18, No. 1 (2015), pp. 3–20.

Cruikshank, Barbara. *The Will to Empower: Democratic Citizens and Other Subjects*. Ithaca, NY: Cornell University Press. 1999.

Culberston, Philip L. "Men and Christian Friendship". In Bjorm Krondorfer (ed.), *Men's Bodies, Men's Gods: Male Identities in a (Post)Christian Culture*. New York and London: New York University Press. 1996. pp. 149–180.

d'Azevedo, Warren L. "Uses of the Past in Gola Discourse". *Journal of African History*, Vol. 3, No. I (1962), pp. 11–34.

Dagmang, Ferdinand D. *The Predicaments of Intimacy and Solidarity: Capitalism and Impingements*. Manila, Philippines: De La Salle University. 2010.

Dangle, Arjun. *Poisoned Bread: Translations from Modern Marathi Dalit Literature*. Bombay: Orient Longman Ltd. 1992.

De Boeck, Filip. "Beyond the Grave: History, Memory and Death in Postcolonial Congo/Zaire". *Memory and the Postcolony: African Anthropology and the Critique of Power*. London: Zed Books. 1998. pp. 21–57.

de Campos, H. *Deus e o diablo no Fausto de Goethe*. San Paolo: Perspectiva. 1981.

De Certeau, Michel. *The Practice of Everyday Life*. Berkeley. University of California Press. 1984.

Dearey, Melissa. *Making Sense of Evil: An Interdisciplinary Approach*. New York: Palgrave Macmillan. 2014.

Deleuze, Gilles. *Difference and Repetition*. New York: Columbia University Press. 1994.

Deleuze, Gilles, and Felix Guattari. *A Thousand Plateaus: Capitalism and Schizophrenia*. Trans. B. Massumi. London: Athlone Press. 1988.

———. *Kafka: Toward a Minor Literature*. Trans. Dana Polan. Minnesota: University of Minnesota Press. 1986.

Dilthey, Wilhelm. "Die Einbildungskraft des Dichters: Bausteine fur einePoetik". *GesammelteSchriften*, Vol. VI (1887), pp. 103–241.

Dinnerstein, Dorothy. "Higamous-Hogamous". In Christine L. Williams and Arlene Stein (eds.), *Sexuality and Gender*. Oxford: Blackwell Publishers. 2002.

Dinshaw, Carolyn, Lee Edelman, Roderick A Ferguson, Carla Freccero, Elizabeth Freeman, Judith Halberstam, Annamarie Jagose, Christopher Nealon, and Nguyen Tan Hoang. "Theorozing Queer Temporalities: A Roundtable Discussion in Queer Temporalities". Ed. Elizabeth Freeman. Special Issue, *GLQ: A Journal of Lesbian and Gay Studies*, Vol. 13, No. 2–2 (2007), pp. 177–195.

Dirlik, Arif. "Place-Based Imaginations: Globalisation and the Politics of Place". *Review: Fernand Braudel Center*, Vol. 22, No. 2 (1999), pp. 151–187.

Doma, Yishey. *Legends of the Lepchas: Folk Tales from Sikkim*. New Delhi: Tranquebar Press. 2010.

Dominelli, L. "Father-Daughter Incest". *Critical Social Policy*, Vol. 16 (1986).

Dorson, Richard M. *Folklore and Fakelore: Essays Toward a Discipline of Folk Studies*. Cambridge, MA: Harvard University Press. 1976.

———. "Fakelore". *Zeitschrift fur Volkskunde*, Vol. 65 (1969).

Doty, Alexander. *Making Things Perfectly Queer: Interpreting Mass Culture*. Minneapolis: University of Minnesota Press. 1993.

Doyle, Vincent. " 'But Joan! You're My Daughter!' The Gay and Lesbian Alliance Against Defamation and the Politics of Amnesia". *Radical History Review*, Vol. 100 (Winter 2008), pp. 209–221.

Dundes, Alan, ed. *Folklore: Critical Concepts in Literary and Cultural Studies. Volume III*. London and New York: Routledge. 2005.

————. *Essays in Folklore Theory and Method*. Madras: Cre-A. 1990.

————. *Folklore Matters*. Knoxville: The University of Tennessee Press. 1989.

————. *Interpreting Folklore*. Bloomington: Indiana University Press. 1980.

————, ed. *The Study of Folklore*. Berkeley: University of California. 1965.

————. "The Binary Structure of Unsuccessful Repetition in Lithuanian Folk Tales". *Western Folklore*, Vol. 21 (1962), pp. 165–174.

————. *Parsing Through Customs: Essays by a Freudian Folklorist*. Madison, WI: The University of Wisconsin Press. 1897.

Durkheim, E. *Elementary Forms of the Religious Life*. London: George Allen & Unwin. 1971.

Dussel, Enrique. "Transmodernity and Interculturality: Philosophy of Liberation". Paper presented at the International Symposium on 'Learning Across Boundaries'. University of Luxembourg, June 2010.

Eason, Cassandra. *Fabulous Creatures, Mythical Monsters, and Animal Power Symbols: A Handbook*. Westport, CT and London: Greenwood Press. 2008.

Ehrenreich, Barbara. *The Hearts of Men*. London: Pluto Press. 1983.

Eisenstein, Zillah. *Against Empire: Feminisms, Racism, and the West*. London and New York: Zed Books. 2004.

Eliade, Mircea. *Myths, Dreams and Mysteries*. New York: Harper and Row. 1975.

Ellis, Havelock. "Sexual Inversion in Women". In *Studies in the Psychology of Sex*, Vol. II. New York: Random House. 1900.

Esposito, Roberto. *Categories of the Impolitical*. Trans. Connal Parsley. New York: Fordham University Press. 2015.

————. *Communitas: The Origin and Destiny of Community*. Trans. Timothy Campbell. Stanford, CA: Stanford University Press. 2010.

Fabian, Johannes. "The Other Revisited: Critical Afterthoughts". *Anthropological Theory*, Vol. 6, No. 2 (2006), pp. 139–152, London: Sage Publications.

————. *Time and the Other: How Anthropology Makes Its Subject*. New York: Columbia University Press. 1983. Print.

Fahim, H.M., and K. Helmer et al. "Indigenous Anthropology in Non-Western Countries: A Further Elaboration". *Current Anthropology*, Vol. 21, No. 5 (1980), pp. 644–663.

Fanon, Frantz. *The Wretched of the Earth*. London: Penguin. 1990.

Favretto, Ilaria, and Xabier Itcaina, eds. *Protest, Popular Culture and Tradition in Modern and Contemporary Western Europe*. London: Palgrave Macmillan. 2017.

Featherstone, M. "Postmodernism and the Aestheticization of Everyday Life". In S. Lash and J. Freedman (eds.), *Modernity and Identity*. Oxford: Blackwell Publishers. 1992.

Februari, Maxim. *The Making of a Man*. Trans. Andy Brown. London: Reaktion Books. 2013.

Felski, Rita. "Fin de siècle, Fin de sexe: Transsexuality, Postmodernism, and the Death of History". *New Literary History*, Vol. 27, No. 2 (Spring 1996), pp. 337–349.

Fielding, Dan Michael. "Queernormativity: Norms, Values, and Practices in Social Justice Fandom". *Sexualities*, pp. 1–20. DOI: 10.1177/1363460719884021. Published online: January 14, 2020.

Filmer, Kath, ed. *Twentieth-Century Fantasists: Essays on Culture, Society and Belief in Twentieth-Century Mythopoeic Literature*. New York: St. Martin's. 1992.

Fine, G.A. "The Manson Family: The Folklore Traditions of a Small Group". *Journal of the Folklore Institute*, Vol. 19, No. 1 (1982), pp. 47–60.

———. "Community and Boundary: Personal Experience Stories of Mushroom Collectors". *Journal of Folklore Research*, Vol. 24, No. 3 (1987).

Finley, Chris. "Decolonizing the Queer Native Body (and Recovering the Native Bull-Dyke): Bringing 'Sexy Back' and Out of Native Studies' Closet". In Qwo-Li Driskill, Chris Finley, Brian Joseph Gilley, and Lauria Morgensen (eds.), *Queer Indigenous Studies: Critical Interventions in Theory, Politics and Literature.* Tucson: The University of Arizona Press. 2011.

Foerst, Anne. *God in the Machine: What Robots Teach Us About Humanity and God.* New York: Dutton. 2004.

Foning, A.R. *Lepcha: My Vanishing Tribe.* New Delhi: Sterling. 1987.

Foucault, Michel. *Security, Territory, Population: Lectures at the Collège de France 1977–1978.* Trans. Graham Burchell. New York: Palgrave Macmillan. 2007.

———. *Psychiatric Power: Lectures at the Collège de France 1973–1974.* Trans. Graham Burchell. New York: Palgrave Macmillan. 2006.

———. *Abnormal: Lectures at the Collège de France 1974–1975.* Trans. Graham Burchell. New York: Picador. 2003.

———. "Sex, Power and the Politics of Identity". *The Advocate* 400. 1984. Reprinted in P. Rabinow (ed.), *Ethics: Subjectivity and Truth*, Vol. 1, of *The Essential Works of Foucault, 1954–1984.* New York: The New Press. 1997.

———. "Discipline". In James D. Faubion (ed.), *Rethinking the Subject: An Anthology of Contemporary European Thought.* Boulder: Westview Press. 1995.

———. *Volume 2 of The History of Sexuality: The Use of Pleasure.* Trans. Robert Hurley. Reissue ed. New York: Vintage. 1990.

———. *Politics, Philosophy, Culture: Interviews and Other Writings 1977–1984.* Ed. L. Kritzman. New York: Routledge. 1988.

———. *The History of Sexuality Volume 1: An Introduction.* Trans. Robert Hurley. Harmondsworth: Penguin. 1981.

———. *Power/Knowledge: Selected Writings 1972–1977.* Ed. C. Gordon, trans. C. Gordon, L. Marshall, J. Meplam, and K. Soper. Brighton: Harvester Press. 1980a.

———. "Power, Moral Values, and the Intellectual". Interview with Michael Bess (November 3, 1980b), IMEC (InstitutMémoirs de l'ÉditionContemporaine) Archive folder number FCL2. A02–06.

———. *Language, Counter-Memory, Practice: Selected Essays and Interviews.* Ed. Donald F. Bouchard, trans. Donald F. Bouchard and Sherry Simon. Ithaca, NY: Cornell University Press. 1977.

Fox, Robin. *The Tribal Imagination: Civilization and the Savage Mind.* Cambridge, MA and London: Harvard University Press. 2011.

Frank, Arthur W. "For a Sociology of the Body: An Analytical Review". In Mike Featherstone, Mike Hepworth, and Bryan S. Turner (eds.), *The Body: Social Process and the Cultural Theory.* London: Sage Publications. 1991. pp. 36–102.

Frazer, J.G. *Totemism and Exogamy.* London: Palgrave Macmillan, Vol. 4. 1910.

Frei, Hans W. *The Eclipse of Biblical Narrative. A Study in Eighteenth and Nineteenth Century Hermeneutics.* New Haven: Yale University Press. 1974.

Freire, P. *Pedagogy of the Oppressed.* Middlesex: Penguin Books Ltd. 1972.

Freud, Sigmund. *The Uncanny*. Trans. David McLintock. New York: Penguin Books. 2003.

———. *The Interpretation of Dreams*. Standard Edition 4 and 5. New York: Avon. 1965.

———. *Civilization and Its Discontents*. Trans. James Strachey. New York: W.W. Norton. 1961.

———. *A General Introduction to Psychoanalysis* (1920). Trans. Joan Riviere. New York: Pocket Books. 1953.

———. *Totem and Taboo*. Trans. James Strachey. New York: W.W. Norton. 1950.

———. *Introductory Lectures on Psycho-Analysis*, Vols. 15 and 16 of *The Complete Psychological Works of Sigmund Freud: Standard Edition*. London: Hogarth Press. 1916.

Freud, S., and D.E. Oppenheim. *Dreams in Folklore*. New York: International Universities Press Inc. 1958.

Friedman, Marilyn. *What Are Friends For? Feminist Perspectives on Personal Relationships and Moral Theory*. Ithaca, NY: Cornell University Press. 1993.

Frisch, Michael. *A Shared Authority: Essays on the Craft and Meaning of Oral and Public History*. Albany: State University of New York Press. 1990.

Fruhstuck, Sabine. "Sexuality and the Nation-State". In Robert M. Buffington, Eithne Luibheid, and Donna J. Guy (eds.), *A Global History of Sexuality: The Modern Era*. West Sussex: Wiley-Blackwell. 2014.

Fuss, Diana. *Essentially Speaking*. New York: Routledge. 1989.

Gadamer, Hans-Georg. *Truth and Method*. 2nd rev. ed. Trans. and ed. Joel Weinsheimer and Donald G. Marshall. New York: Crossroad Publishing. 1989.

Gallop, J. *Intersections: A Reading of Sade with Bataille, Blanchot and Klossowski*. Lincoln, NE and London: University of Nebraska Press. 1981.

Gaylin, Willard. *The Male Ego*. New York: Viking. 1992.

Geertz, Clifford. *Local Knowledge*. New York: Basic Books. 2000.

———. *Nagara: The Theater State in Nineteenth Century Bali*. Princeton, NJ: Princeton University Press. 1980.

Gergen, Kenneth, and Mary Gergen. "Narrative and the Self as Relationship". In Leonard Berkowitz (ed.), *Advances in Experimental Social Psychology*. San Diego: Academic Press. 1988.

Ghurye, G.S. *Scheduled Tribes*. Bombay: Popular Book Depot. 1959.

Giddens, Anthony. *The Transformation of Intimacy: Sexuality, Love and Eroticism in Modern Societies*. Cambridge: Polity Press. 1992.

———. *Modernity and Self-Identity: Self and Society in Late Modern Age*. Cambridge: Polity Press. 1991.

Gilbert, Felix. "Historiography: What Ranke Meant". *The American Scholar*, Vol. 56, No. 3 (Summer 1987), pp. 393–397.

Gilroy, Paul. *The Black Atlantic: Modernity and Double-Consciousness*. Cambridge: Harvard University Press. 1993.

Godard, B. "Theorizing Feminist Discourse/Translation". In S. Bassnett and A. Lefevere (eds.), *Translation, History and Culture*. London and New York: Routledge. 1990. pp. 87–96.

Goffman, E. *Stigma: Notes on the Management of Spoiled Identity*. London: Penguin. 1990.

Goldberg, Christine. "The Construction of Folktales". *Journal of Folklore Research*, Vol. 23, No. 2/3. Special Double Issue: The Comparative Method in Folklore (May–December 1986), pp. 163–176.

Goldberg, Herb. *The New Male*. New York: Signet. 1979.

Goldberg, Isaac. *Havelock Ellis*. London: Constable. 1926.

Goldman, Jane. "Introduction: Works on the Wild(e) Side—Performing, Transgressing, Queering". In Julian Wolfreys (ed.), *Literary Theories*. New York: New York University Press. 1999. pp. 525–536.

Gordon, C., ed. *Power/Knowledge: Selected Interviews and Other Writings, 1972–1977*. London: Vintage. 1980.

Gorer, Geoffrey. *The Lepchas of Sikkim*. New Delhi: Cultural Publishing House. 1938.

Gourgouris, Stathis. *Does Literature Think? Literature as Theory for an Antimythical Era*. Stanford, CA: Stanford University Press. 2003.

Govindrajan, Radhika. *Animal Intimacies: Interspecies Relatedness in India's Central Himalayas*. Chicago and London: The University of Chicago Press. 2018.

Graham, Laura R., and H. Glenn Penny, eds. *Performing Indigeneity: Global Histories and Contemporary Experiences*. Lincoln and London: University of Nebraska Press. 2014.

Gramsci, Antonio. *Selections from Cultural Writings*. Eds. David Forgacs and Geoffrey Nowell-Smith, trans. William Boelhower. New Delhi: Aakar Books. 2015.

Greenhill, Pauline. "Fitcher's (Queer) Bird: A Fairy-Tale Heroine and Her Avatars". *Marvels & Tales: Journal of Fairy-Tale Studies*, Vol. 22, No. I (2008), pp. 143–167.

Grigson, W.V. *The Maria Gonds of Bastar*. London: Oxford University Press. 1938.

Grosz, Elizabeth. *Architecture from the Outside: Essays on Virtual and Real Spaces*. Cambridge: MIT Press. 2001.

Guedalla, Philip. Quoted in *The Facts on File Dictionary of Proverbs* by Martin H. Manser. New York: Facts on File. 2007.

Guha, Ramachandra. "Adivasis, Naxalites and Indian Democracy". *Economic and Political Weekly*, Vol. 42, No. 32 (2007), pp. 3305–3312.

Gunn, Thom. *The Man with Night Sweats: Poems*. New York: Farrar, Straus and Giroux. 2007.

Gupta, Akhil. "Governing Population: The Integrated Child Development Services Program in India". In T. Hansen and F. Stepputat (eds.), *States of Imagination. Ethnographic Explorations of the State*. Durham: Duke University Press. 2001. pp. 65–95.

Guru, Gopal. "The Politics of Naming". *Seminar*, Vol. 491 (1998), pp. 14–18.

Gutierrez, Raquel, Alvaro Garcia Linera, and Luis Tapia. "La forma multitude de la politica de las necesidadesvitales". In Alvaro Garcia Linera, RaquelGutierrez, Raul Prada, and Luis Tapia (eds.), *El retorno de la Bolivia plebeya*. La Paz: Mueladel Diablo Editores. 2000. pp. 135–184.

Haaland, Bonnie. *Emma Goldman: Sexuality and the Impurity of the State*. Montreal, New York and London: Black Rose Books. 1993.

Halberstam, Judith. *Female Masculinity*. Durham and London: Duke University Press. 1998.

———. *Skin Shows: Gothic Horror and the Technology of Monsters*. Durham: Duke University Press. 1995.

Halbwachs, Maurice. *Les cadressociaux de la mémoire [On Collective Memory]*. Ed. and trans. Lewis A. Coser. Chicago: University of Chicago Press. 1992.

Hall, Robert G. "Historical Inference and Rhetorical Effect: Another Look at Galatians 1 and 2". In Duane F. Watson (ed.), *Persuasive Artistery. Studies in New TestamentRhetoric in Honor of George A. Kennedy* (JSNTSup, 50). Sheffield: JSOT Press. 1991. pp. 308–320.

———. "Ancient Historical Method and the Training of an Orator". In Stanley E. Porter and Thomas H. Olbricht (eds.), *The Rhetorical Analysis of Scripture. Essays from the1995 London Conference* (JSNTSup, 146). Sheffield: Sheffield Academic Press. 1997. pp. 103–118.

Hamilton, Paula, and Linda Shopes, ed. *Oral History and Public Memories*. Philadelphia: Temple University Press. 2008.

Hannerz, Ulf. *Cultural Complexity: Studies in the Social Organization of Meaning*. New York: Colombia University Press. 1992.

Hardt, Michael, and Antonio Negri. *Multitude: War and Democracy in the Age of Empire*. New York: The Penguin Press. 2004.

Hargreaves, Tracy. *Androgyny in Modern Literature*. New York: Palgrave Macmillan. 2005.

Hartley, L.P. *The Go-Between*. New York: New York Review Books. 2002.

Heckert, J. "Sexuality as a State-form". In D. Rousselle and S. Evren (eds.), *Postanarchism: A Reader*. Ann Arbor, MI and London: Pluto Press. 2011.

———. "Sexuality/Identity/Politics". In J. Purkis and J. Bowden (eds.), *Changing Anarchism: Anarchist Theory and Practice in a Global Age*. Manchester and New York: Manchester University Press. 2004.

Heckert, J., and R. Cleminson, eds. *Anarchism & Sexuality: Ethics, Relationships and Power*. New York: Routledge. 2011.

Hegarty, Paul. *Georges Bataille: Core Cultural Theorist*. London: Sage Publications. 2000.

Hegel, G.W.F. *Early Theological Writings*. Trans. T.M. Knox. Chicago: University of Chicago Press. 1948.

Heidegger, Martin. *On the Way to Language*. Trans. Peter D. Hertz. New York: Harper and Row. 1971.

Heilbrun, Carolyn G. *Towards Androgyny*. New York: Harper Colophon Books. 1974.

Helgeson, Vicki S. *The Psychology of Gender*. Boston: Pearson. 2001.

Herskovits, M.J. *Man and His Works*. New York: Knopf. 1948.

Hinchman, Lewis P., and Sandra K. Hinchman, eds. *Memory, Identity, Community: The Idea of Narrative in the Human Sciences*. New York: State University of New York Press. 1997.

Hodgson, Dorothy L., ed. *Gendered Modernities, Ethnographic Perspectives*. New York: Palgrave Macmillan. 2001.

Hoffmeyer, Jesper. *Signs of Meaning in the Universe*. Trans. Barbara J. Haveland. Bloomington: Indiana University Press. 1993.

Hofstede, Geert. et al. *Masculinity and Femininity: The Taboo Dimension of National Cultures*. Thousand Oaks, CA: Sage Publications. 1998.

Holquist, Michael. *Dialogism: Bakhtin and His World*. London and New York: Routledge as an Imprint of the Taylor & Francis Group. 2002.

Hönig, H.G. "Positions, Power and Practice: Functionalist Approaches and Translation Quality Assessment". *Current Issues in Language and Society*, Vol. 4, No. 1 (1997), pp. 6–34.

Hönig, H.G., and P. Kussmaul. *Strategie der Übersetzung: Ein Lehr- und Arbeitsbuch*. Tübingen: Narr. 1982.

hooks, bell. *The Will to Change: Men, Masculinity and Love*. New York: Washington Square Press. 2004.

———. *Outlaw Culture*. New York and London: Routledge. 1994.

Horkheimer, M. *Between Philosophy and Social Science*. Cambridge: The MIT Press. 1993.

Hountondji, Paulin J. "Producing Knowledge in Africa Today: The Second Bashorun M.K.O. Abiola Distinguished Lecture". *African Studies Review*, Vol. 38, No. 3 (December 1995), pp. 1–10.

Howard, Jean E. "Crossdressing, the Theater, and Gender Struggle in Early Modern England". *Shakespeare Quarterly*, Vol. 39 (1988), pp. 418–441.

Hutton, Patrick H. *History as an Art of Memory*. Hanover, NH and London: University Press of New England. 1993.

Huyssen, Andreas. "Resistance to Memory: The Uses and Abuses of Public Forgetting". In Max Pensky (ed.), *Globalizing Critical Theory*. London: Rowan and Littlefield. 2005. pp. 165–184.

Iggers, George G. *Historiography in the Twentieth Century. From Scientific Objectivity to the Postmodern Challenge*. Hanover, NH: Wesleyan University Press. 1997.

Ignatieff, Michael. *The Needs of Strangers*. London: Chatto & Windus, The Hogarth Press. 1984.

Irwin, Lee. "Sending a Voice, Seeking a Place: Visionary Traditions Among Native Women of the Plains". In Kelly Bulkeley (ed.), *Dreams: A Reader on Religions, Cultural, and Psychological Dimensions of Dreaming*. New York: Palgrave Macmillan. 2001.

Jackson, Michael. "Ambivalence and the Last-Born: Birth-Order Position in Convention and Myth". *Man, New Series*, Vol. 13 (1978), pp. 341–361.

Jackson, Rosemary. *Fantasy: The Literature of Subversion. New Accents*. New York: Methuen. 1981.

Jaffrelot, Christophe. "The Bahujan Samaj Party in North India: No Longer Just a Dalit Party?" *Comparative Studies of South Asia, Africa and the Middle East* (formerly *South Asia Bulletin*), Vol. XVIII, No. 1 (1998).

Jagose, Annamarie. *Queer Theory: An Introduction*. New York: New York University Press. 1996.

Jameson, Frederic. *Postmodernism, or the Cultural Logic of Late Capitalism*. London: Verso. 1991.

———. *The Political Unconscious: Narrative as a Socially Symbolic Act*. Ithaca, NY: Cornell University Press. 1981.

Jervis, J. *Transgressing the Modern: Explorations in the Western Experience of Otherness*. Oxford: Blackwell Publishers. 1999.

Jones, Angela. "Queer Heterotopias: Homonormativity and the Future of Queerness". *Interalia: A Journal of Queer Studies*, Vol. 4 (2009), pp. 1–20.

Jones, Steven Swann. *The Fairy Tale: The Magic Mirror of Imagination*. New Delhi: Prentice Hall International. 1995.

Jung, C.G. *Psychology and Alchemy*. Trans. R.F.C. Hull. Princeton, NJ: Princeton University Press. 1969.

———. "The Psychology of the Child Archetype". In C.G. Jung and C. Kereny (eds.), *Essays on a Science of Mythology*. New York: Harper Torchbook. 1963. pp. 70–100.

Kalia, S.L. "Sanskritisation and Translation". *Bulletin of the Tribal Research Institute*, Vol. 2, No. 4 (1959), pp. 33–43.

Kant, Immanuel. *Religion Within the Bounds of Bare Reason*. Trans. Werner S. Pluhar. Indianapolis: Hackett. 2009. Print.

Karlsson, B.G. *Contested Belonging: An Indigenous People's Struggle for Forest and Identity in Sub-Himalayan Bengal*. Richmond, Surrey: Curzon Press. 2000.

Keeshing-Tobias, Lenore. "Poaching: Is It Irresponsible to Appropriate Native American Stories?" *Utne Reader*, March–April 1994.

Kelber, Werner H. "Narrative as Interpretation and Interpretation of Narrative: Hermeneutical Reflections on the Gospels". *Semeia*, Vol. 39 (1987), pp. 107–133.

Kelley, Robin. "On the Density of Black Being". In Christine Kim (ed.), *Scratch*. New York: Studio Museum of Harlem. 2005.

Kennedy, Jonathan, and Lawrence King. "Adivasis, Maoists and Insurgency in the Central Indian Tribal Belt". *European Journal of Sociology*, Vol. 54, No. 1 (April 2013), pp. 1–32. DOI: 10.1017./S0003975613000015. Published online: June 3, 2013.

———. "Understanding the Conviction of Binayak Sen: Neocolonialism, Political Violence and the Political Economy of Health in the Central Indian Tribal Belt". *Social Science & Medicine*, Vol. 72 (2011), pp. 1639–1642.

Kimmel, Michael S. *The Gender of Desire: Essays on Male Sexuality*. Albany: State University of New York Press. 2005.

King, Nicola. "Autobiography as Cultural Memory: Three Case Studies". *New Formations*, No. 30 (Winter 1996), pp. 50–62.

Kinnvall, Catarina. "Populism, Ontological Insecurity and Hindutva: Modi and the Masculinization of Indian Politics". *Cambridge Review of International Affairs*, Vol. 32, No. 3 (2019), pp. 283–302. DOI: 10.1080/09557571.2019.15 88851.

Kjosavik, Darley Jose. "Standpoints and Intersections: Towards an Indigenist Epistemology". In B. Hobson (ed.), *Recognition, Struggles and Social Movements: Contested Identities, Agencies and Power*. Cambridge: Cambridge University Press. 2003. pp. 119–135.

Klein, Melanie. "Weaning". In *Love, Guilt and Reparation & Other Works. 1921–1945*. N.P.: Delacorte Press. 1975. pp. 290–305.

Kojève, A. *Introduction to the Reading of Hegel*. Ed. A. Bloom, trans. J.H. Nichols (assembled R. Queneau). New York: Basic Books. 1969.

Kotturan, George. *Folk Tales from Sikkim*. New Delhi: Sterling Publishers. 1976.

Krishnaswamy, Revathi. *Effeminism: The Economy of Colonial Desire*. Ann Arbor: The University of Michigan Press. 1998.

Kristeva, Julia. *Powers of Horror: An Essay on Abjection*. Trans. L.S. Roudiez. New York: Columbia University Press. 1982.

Kropotkin, Peter. *Mutual Aid: A Factor of Evolution*. Mineola and New York: Dover Publications. 2006.

Kübler-Ross, Elisabeth. *On Death and Dying*. New York: The Macmillan Company. 1969.

Kugle, Scott. "Sultan Mahmud's Makeover: Colonial Homophobia and the Persian-Urdu Literary Tradition". In Ruth Vanita (ed.), *Queering India: Same Sex Love and Eroticism in Indian Culture and Society*. London: Routledge. 2002. pp. 30–46.

Kumar, D.V., ed. *Modernity and Ethnic Processes in India*. New Delhi: Rawat Publications. 2014.

La Barre, Weston. *The Ghost Dance: Origins of Religion*. New York: Doubleday Press. 1970.

LaFortune, Anguksuar Richard. "A Postcolonial Colonial Perspective on Western (Mis)Conceptions of the Cosmos and the Restoration of Indigenous Taxonomies". In Sue-Ellen Jacobs, Wesley Thomas, and Sabine Lang (eds.), *Two-Spirit People: Native American Gender Identity, Sexuality, and Spirituality*. Urbana: University of Illinois Press. 1997. pp. 217–222.

Lamont, Ellen. "'We Can Write the Scripts Ourselves': Queer Challenges to Heteronormative Courtship Practices". *Gender & Society*, Vol. 31, No. 5 (October 2017), pp. 624–646.

Landauer, G. *Prophet of Community: The Romantic Socialism of Gustav Landauer*. Berkeley: University of California Press. 1973.

Landsberg, Alison. "Prosthetic Memory: *Total Recall* and *Blade Runner*". In M. Featherstone and R. Burrows (eds.), *Cyberspace/Cyberbodies/Cyberpunk: Cultures of Technological Embodiment*. London: Sage Publications. 1995.

Lasch, C. *Haven in a Heartless World*. New York: Basic Books. 1977.

Lawrence, D.H. "Introduction to *Pansies*". In *Complete Poems*. London: Wordsworth Poetry Library. 1994.

Lawson, Jenny. "Good Enough to Eat: Resisting the 'Hunger Gaze' Through Performance Practice". *The Hunger Artist: Food and the Arts*, No. 15 (Winter 2011).

Le Goff, Jacques. *History and Memory*. Trans. Steven Rendall and Elizabeth Claman. New York: Columbia University Press. 1992.

Le Guin, Ursula K. *The Left Hand of Darkness*. New York: Time Warner International. 1996.

Lee, Julian C.H. *Policing Sexuality: Sex, Society, and the State*. Kuala Lumpur: Strategic Information and Research Development Centre and London and New York: Zed Books. 2011.

Leverenz, David. "The Last Real Man in America: From Natty Bumppo to Batman". *American Literary Review*, Vol. 3 (1991).

Levinas, Emmanuel. *Difficult Freedom: Essays on Judaism*. Trans. Sean Hand. Baltimore, MD: The Johns Hopkins University Press. 1990.

———. *Totality and Infinity: An Essay on Exteriority*. Trans. Alphonso Lingis. Pittsburgh: Duquesne University Press. 1969.

Lévi-Strauss, Claude. *The Elementary Structures of Kinship*. Trans. James Harle Bell and John Richard von Strurmer, ed. Rodney Needham. Boston: Beacon Press. 1969.

———. *Tristes Tropiques*. Trans. John Weightman and Doreen Weightman. New York: Atheneum. 1968.

Lingis, Alphonso. *The Community of Those Who Have Nothing in Common*. Bloomington and Indianapolis: Indiana University Press. 1994.

Linstead, S., and A. Pullen. "Gender as Multiplicity: Desire, Displacement, Difference and Dispersion". *Human Relations*, Vol. 59, No. 9 (2006), pp. 1287–1310.

Little, Graham. "Freud, Friendship and Politics". In Roy Porter and Sylvana Tomaselli (eds.), *The Dialectics of Friendship*. London: Routledge. 1989. pp. 143–158.

Locke, John. "An Essay Concerning Human Understanding. 1690". In Michael Rossington and Anne Whitehead (eds.), *Theories of Memory: A Reader*. Baltimore, MD: Johns Hopkins University Press. 2007. pp. 75–79.

Longkumer, Atola. *Religious Conversion: Rethinking Religious Encounter in Modern India*. Oxford: Church Mission Society. 2010.

Lorber, Judith. *Paradoxes of Gender*. New Haven and London: Yale University Press. 1994.

Lotter, James, and Pieter Fourie. "Queer-on-queer Violence: Homopopulism & African LGBTQ Mobility". *South African Journal of Political Studies*. DOI: 10.1080/02589346.2020.1715160. Published online: January 20, 2020.

Luz, Ulrich. "Fiktivität und Traditionstreue im Matthäusevangelium im Lichte griechischer Literatur". *Zeitschrift für die Neutestamentliche Wissenschaft*, Vol. 84 (1993), pp. 153–177.

Macherey, Pierre. *A Theory of Literary Production*. Trans. Geoffrey Wall. London: Routledge. 1978.

MacInnes, John. *The End of Masculinity*. Buckingham: Open University Press. 1998.

MacIntyre, Alasdair. *After Virtue*. Notre Dame: University of Notre Dame Press. 1981.

Mackie, J.L. "Evil and Omnipotence". In Marilyn Adams and Robert Adams (eds.), *The Problem of Evil*. New York: Oxford University Press. 1990. pp. 25–38. Print.

Mair, Miller. *Between Psychology and Psychotherapy: A Poetics of Experience*. London: Routledge. 1988.

Majumdar, Bimalendu. *A Sociological Study of the Toto Folk Tales*. Calcutta: The Asiatic Society. 1991.

———. *Rabha—Janojiban O Lokokahini*. Lokoshanskriti O Adivasi Shanskriti Kendra: Tathya O ShanskritiBivag, Poshchimbanga Sarkar. 2008.

Mali, Joseph. *Mythistory*. Chicago and London: The University of Chicago Press. 2003.

Malina, Bruce J. *The Social World of Jesus and the Gospels*. London: Routledge. 1996.

Malinowski, Bronislaw. *Argonauts of the Western Pacific*. London: Routledge and Kegan Paul. 1922.

Marcus, G.E., and M.M.J. Fischer. *Anthropology as Cultural Critique. An Experimental Moment in the Human Sciences*. Chicago: University of Chicago Press. 1986.

Marinucci, Mimi. *Feminism is Queer: The Intimate Connection Between Queer and Feminist Theory*. London. Zed Books. 2010.

Maruyama, M. "Endogenous Research: Rationale". In P. Reason and J. Rowan (eds.), *Human Inquiry: A Sourcebook of New Paradigm Research*. Chichester, UK: John Wiley. 1981.

Marx, Karl. "A Contribution to the Critique of Hegel's *Philosophy of Right*. Introduction". In *Early Writings*. L. Colleti (Introduced). Harmondsworth: Penguin. 1975.

McCall, Leslie. "The Complexity of Intersectionality". *Signs*, Vol. 30, No. 3 (2005), pp. 1771–1800.

McGillis, Roderick. "'A Fairytale Is Just a Fairytale': George MacDonald and the Queering of Fairy". *Marvels & Tales: Journal of Fairy-Tale Studies*, Vol. 17, No. I (2003), pp. 86–89.

McHoul, Alec, and Wendy Grace, ed. *A Foucault Primer: Discourse, Power and the Subject*. Carlton South: Melbourne University Press. 1993.

McNeill, William H. "Mythistory, or Truth, Myth, History, and Historians". *The American Historical Review*, Vol. 91, No. 1 (February 1986), pp. 1–10.

Mignolo, W. "Epistemic Disobedience, Independent Thought and Decolonial Freedom". *Theory, Culture & Society*, Vol. 26, No. 7–8 (2009), pp. 159–181.

Miller, Jacques-Alain. "On Perversion". In Richard Feldstein, Bruce Fink, and Maire Jaanus (eds.), *ReadIng SemInars I and II: Lacan's Return to Freud*. Albany: SUNY Press. 1996.

Mills, Margaret A. "Domains of Folkloristic Concern: The Interpretation of Scriptures". In Susan Niditch (ed.), *Text and Tradition. The Hebrew Bible and Folklore* (SBLSS). Atlanta: Scholars Press. 1990. pp. 231–241.

Mockus, Antanas. "Anfibiosculturales y divorcio entre ley, moral y cultura". *Analisis Politico*, Vol. 21 (1994), pp. 37–48.

Monier-Williams, Sir Monier. *A Sanskrit—English Dictionary Etymologically and Philologically Arranged*. New Delhi: Motilal Banarsidass. 1997.

Moore, Henriette. *A Passion for Difference: Essays in Anthropology and Gender*. Cambridge: Polity Press. 1994.

Moore, Sally Falk, ed. *Introduction: Moralizing States and the Ethnography of the Present*. American Ethnological Society Monograph Series. No. 5. Arlington, VA: American Anthropological Association. 1995. pp. 1–6.

Moraga, Cherrie. "Speaking Tongues: A Letter to 3rd World Women Writers". In Cherrie Moraga and G. Anzaldúa (eds.), *This Bridge Called My Back, Writings by Radical Women of Colour*. New York: Kitchen Table Press. 1983.

Moreton-Robinson, Aileen. "Whiteness, Epistemology and Indigenous Representation". In Aileen Moreton-Robinson (ed.), *Whitening Race: Essays in Social and Cultural Criticism*. Canberra: Aboriginal Studies Press. 2004.

Morgensen, Scott Lauria. *Spaces Between Us: Queer Settler Colonialism and Indigenous Decolonization*. Minneapolis and London: University of Minnesota. 2011.

Morrison, T. *Playing in the Dark: Whiteness and the Literary Imagination*. New York: Vintage. 1993.

Mueller, Carol. "'Recognition Struggles' and Process Theories of Social Movements". In B. Hobson (ed.), *Recognition, Struggles and Social Movements: Contested Identities, Agencies and Power*. Cambridge: Cambridge University Press. 2003. pp. 274–291.

Muñoz, José Esteban. *Cruising Utopia: The Then and There of Queer Futurity*. New York: New York University Press. 2009.

———. *Disidentifications: Queers of Color and the Performance of Politics*. Minneapolis: University of Minnesota Press. 1999.

———. "Ephemera as Evidence: Introductory Notes to Queer Acts". *Women and Performance: A Journal of Feminist Theory*, Vol. 8, No. 2 (1996), pp. 5–16.

Nagoshi, Julie L., Craig T. Nagoshi, and Stephan/ieBrzuzy, eds. *Gender and Sexual Identity: Transcending Feminist and Queer Theory*. New York: Springer. 2014.

Nakata, N. Martin. "Indigenous Knowledge and the Cultural Interface: Underlying Issues at the Intersection of Knowledge and Information Systems". *IFLA Journal*, Vol. 28, No. 5/6 (2002), pp. 281–291.

Nakata, N. Martin, Victoria Nakata, Sarah Keech, and Reuben Bolt. "Decolonial Goals and Pedagogies for Indigenous Studies". *Decolonization: Indigeneity, Education & Society*, Vol. 1, No. 1 (2012), pp. 120–140.

Nakleh, K. "On Being a Native Anthropologist". In G. Huizer and B. Mannheim (eds.), *The Politics of Anthropology*. The Hague: Mouton. 1979. pp. 343–352.

Nancy, Jean-Luc. *The Inoperative Community*. Ed. Peter Connor, trans. Peter Connor, Lisa Garbus, Michael Holland, and Simona Sawhney. Minneapolis and Oxford: University of Minnesota Press. 1991.

Nandy, Ashis. *The Intimate Enemy: Loss and Recovery of Self Under Colonialism*. New Delhi: Oxford University Press. 1983.

Narayan, K. "How Native Is a 'Native' Anthropologist?" *American Anthropologist*, Vol. 95, No. 3 (1993), pp. 671–686.

Needham, J. *Science and Civilization in China*. Cambridge: Cambridge University Press. 1956.

Negri, A. "Value and Affect". *Boundary 2*, Vol. 26, No. 2 (1999), pp. 77–88.

Newman, S. "War on the State: Stirner's and Deleuze's Anarchism". *Anarchist Studies*, Vol. 9, No. 2 (2001), pp. 147–164.

Nietzsche, F. *The Genealogy of Morals*. Trans. W. Kauffmann and P.J. Hollingdale. New York: Vintage. 1969.

———. *On the Genealogy of Morality*. Cambridge: Cambridge University Press. 1887.

———. "Thus Spake Zarathustra". In W. Kaufmann (ed.), *The Portable Nietzsche*. New York: Viking. 1885.

Niranjana, Tejaswini. "Alternative Frames? Questioning for Comparative Research in the Third World". In Kuan-Hsing Chen and Chua Beng Huat (eds.), *The Inter-Asia Cultural Studies Reader*. London and New York: Routledge. 2007. pp. 103–114.

———. *Siting Translation: History, Post-Structuralism and the Colonial Context*. Los Angeles: University of California Press. 1992.

Nora, Pierre. *Realms of Memory: The Construction of the French Past (Volume 1)*. Co-edited with Lawrence D. Kritzman, trans. Arthur Goldhammer. New York: Columbia University Press. 1996.

———, ed. *Les Lieux de memoire*, Vols. 3. Paris: Gallimard. 1984–92.

Norris, Margot. *Beasts of the Modern Imagination: Darwin, Nietzsche, Kafka, Ernst & Lawrence*. Baltimore: The Johns Hopkins University Press. 1985.

Nye, Robert A. *Masculinity and Male Codes of Honor in France*. Berkeley: University of California Press. 1998.

O' Neill, Maggie, and Lizzie Seal. *Transgressive Imaginations: Crime, Deviance and Culture*. New York: Palgrave Macmillan. 2012.

Ober, Josiah. *Political Dissent in Democratic Athens. Intellectual Critics of Popular Rule*. Princeton, NJ: Princeton University Press. 1998.

Okely, Judith. "Anthropology and Autobiography: Participatory Experience and Embodied Knowledge". In Judith Okely and Helen Callaway (eds.), *Anthropology and Autobiography* (ASA Monograph 29). London: Routledge. 1992. pp. 1–28.

Oleksy, Elzbieta H., ed. *Intimate Citizenships: Gender, Sexualities, Politics*. New York and London: Routledge. 2009.

Olick, Jeffrey, and Joyce Robbins. "Social Memory Studies: From 'Collective Memory' to the Historical Sociology of Mnemonic Practices". *Annual Review of Sociology*, Vol. 24 (1998), pp. 105–140.

Olsen, Lance. "Nameless Things and Thingless Names". In David Sandner (ed.), *Fantastic Literature: A Critical Reader*. Westport, CT: Greenwood Press. 2004. pp. 274–292.

Ong, Walter J. *Orality and Literacy: The Technologizing of the Word*. New York: Methuen. 1982.

Opie, Iona, and Peter Opie. *The Classic Fairy Tales*. London: Oxford University Press. 1974.

Orne, Jason. *Boystown: Sex and Community in Chicago*. Chicago: University of Chicago Press. 2017.

Ortiz, Roxanne Dunbar. "The Fourth World and Indigenism: Politics of Isolation and Alternatives". *Journal of Ethnic Studies*, Vol. 21, No 1 (1984), pp. 79–105.

Outka, Gene. "Character, Vision and Narrative". *Religious Studies Review*, Vol. 6, No. 2 (1980).

Pappadis, Melanie. *Limbu Folklore*. Varanasi: Pilgrims Publishing. 2001.

Pattanaik, Devdutt. *The Pregnant King*. New Delhi: Penguin. 2008.

Patterson, Orlando. *Slavery and Social Death: A Comparative Study*. Cambridge, MA: Harvard University Press. 1982.

Paulson, Ronald. *Sin and Evil: Moral Values in Literature*. New Haven: Yale University Press. 2007. Print.

Paz, O. "Translations of Literature and Letters". Trans. Irene del Corral. In R. Schulte and J. Biguenet (eds.), *Theories of Translation from Dryden to Derrida*. Chicago: University of Chicago Press. 1992. pp. 152–163.

Peacock, Philip Vinod. ' "Now We Will Have the Dalit Perspective': Dissecting the Politics of Identity". *The Ecumenical Review*, Vol. 72, No. 1 (January 2020), pp. 116–127.

Penczak, Christopher. *Gay Witchcraft: Empowering the Tribe*. Boston: Weiser Books. 2003.

Penney, James. *After Queer Theory: The Limits of Sexual Politics*. London: Pluto Press. 2014.

Pensky, Max. "Method and Time: Benjamin's Dialectical Images". In David S. Ferris (ed.), *The Cambridge Companion to Walter Benjamin*. Cambridge: Cambridge University Press. 2004. pp. 177–198.

Perry, Cindy L. *Nepali Around the World. Emphasizing Nepali Christians of the Himalayas*. Kathmandu: Ekta. 1997.

Pfeffer, Clara. "Normative Resistance and Inventive Pragmatism: Negotiating Structure and Agency in Transgender Families". *Gender and Society*, Vol. 26, No. 4 (2012), pp. 574–602.

Pfohl, Stephen. "Venus in Microsoft: Male Mas(s)ochism and Cybernetics". In A. Kroker and M. Kroker (eds.), *The Last Sex: Feminism and Outlaw Bodies*. Basingstoke: Palgrave Macmillan. 1993.

Phillips, Kendall R., ed. *Framing Public Memory*. Tuscaloosa: University of Alabama Press. 2004.

Pillemer, David B. *Momentous Events, Vivid Memories*. Cambridge: Harvard University Press. 1998.

Pinder, D. *Visions of the City*. Edinburgh: Edinburgh University Press. 2005.

Pitkin, Hannah. "Justice: On Relating Public and Private". *Political Theory*, Vol. 9, No. 3 (August 1981), pp. 327–352.

Pittman, Kimberly. "Walk Like a Man: Inside the Booming Drag King Scene". *Manhattan Pride*, June 1996.

Plato. "Philebus". In E. Hamilton and H. Cairns (eds.), *The Collected Dialogues of Plato*. Princeton, NJ: Princeton University Press. 1963.

Polkinghorne, Donald. "Narrative and Self-Concept". *Journal of Narrative and Life History*, Vol. 1, No. 2–3 (1991).

Polybius. *The Histories*. Trans. W.R. Paton, Vols. 6 (LCL). London: William Heinemann, and Cambridge, MA: Harvard University Press. 1922–1927.

Popper, Karl. *The Poverty of Historicism*. Boston: The Beacon Press. 1957.

Portelli, Alessandro. *The Order Has Been Carried Out: History, Memory, and Meaning of a Nazi Massacre in Rome*. New York: Palgrave Macmillan. 2003.

———. "What Makes Oral History Different". In Robert Perks and Alistair Thomson (eds.), *The Oral History Reader*. London: Routledge. 1998.

Prakash, Gyan. "Science 'Gone Native' in Colonial India". *Representations*, Vol. 40 (Fall 1992): 153–178.

Pratt, M.L. *Imperial Eyes: Travel Writing and Transculturation*. London and New York: Routledge. 1992.

Price, J., and M. Shildrick, eds. *Feminist Theory and the Body: A Reader*. Edinburgh: Edinburgh University Press. 1999.

Probyn, Elspeth. "Lesbians in Space: Gender, Sex and the Structure of Missing". *Gender, Place and Culture: A Journal of Feminist Geography*, Vol. 2, No. 1 (1995), pp. 77–84.

Puar, Jasbir K. *Terrorist Assemblages: Homonationalism in Queer Times*. Durham and London: Duke University Press. 2007.

Rabinow, Paul, ed. *Ethics: Subjectivity and Truth (Essential Works of Foucault, 1954–1984, Vol. 1)*. New York: The New Press. 1998.

Radway, Janice. "What's in a Name? Presidential Address to the American Studies Association, November 20, 1998". *American Quarterly*, Vol. 51, No. 1 (1999), pp. 8–18.

Raha, Manis Kumar. *Matriliny to Patriliny: A Study of the Rabha Society*. New Delhi: Gian Publishing House. 1989.

Rahman, M. "Queer as Intersectionality: Theorizing Gay Muslim Identities". *Sociology*, Vol. 44 (2010), pp. 944–958.

Ramanujan, A.K. *Folktales from India: A Selection of Oral Tales from Twenty-Two Languages*. New York: Pantheon Books. 1991.

Ranciere, Jacques. *Disagreement: Politics and Philosophy*. Trans. J. Rose. Minneapolis, MN: Berkeley: University of Minnesota Press. 1998.

Randall, Richard S. *Freedom and Taboo: Pornography and the Politics of a Self Divided*. Berkeley: University of California Press. 1989.

Rao, Rahul. "Global Homocapitalism". *Radical Philosophy*, Vol. 194 (2015), pp. 38–49.

Razack, Sherene. *Casting Out: The Eviction of Muslims from Western Law and Politics*. Toronto: University of Toronto Press. 2007.

Ricard, Alain, and Flora Veit–Wild, ed. *Interfaces Between the Oral and the Written: Versions and Subversions in African Literatures*. Amsterdam, New York: Rodopi. 2005.

Richards, Thomas. *The Imperial Archive: Knowledge and the Fantasy of Empire*. London: Verso. 1993.

Richter, Dieter, and Johannes Merkel. *Marchen, Phantasie und sozialesLernen*. Berlin: Basis. 1974.

Rickman, H.P., ed. *W. Dilthey: Selected Writings*. Cambridge: Cambridge University Press. 1976.

Ricoeur, Paul. *The Symbolism of Evil*. London: Beacon Press. 1967.

Robbins, Vernon K. *Exploring the Texture of Texts. A Guide to Socio-Rhetorical Interpretation*. Vally Forge, PA: Trinity Press International. 1996a.

———. *The Tapestry of Early Christian Discourse. Rhetoric, Society and Ideology*. London: Routledge. 1996b.

———. "Social-Scientific Criticism and Literary Studies. Prospects for Cooperation in Biblical Interpretation". In Philip F. Esler (ed.), *Modelling Early Christianity. Social-Scientific Studies of the New Testament in Its Context*. London: Routledge. 1995. pp. 274–289.

Rose, D.B. *Dingo Makes Us Human: Life and Land in an Australian Aboriginal Culture*. Cambridge: Cambridge University Press. 2009.

Rosman, Jonathan P., and Phillip J. Resnick. "Sexual Attraction to Corpses: A Psychiatric Review of Necrophilia". *The Bulletin of the American Academy of Psychiatry and the Law*, Vol. 17, No. 2 (1989), pp. 153–163.

Ross, Bruce A. *Remembering the Personal Past: Descriptions of Autobiographical Memory*. Oxford: Oxford University Press. 1991.

Roy, Sanjay K. "Conflicting Nations in North East India". *Economic and Political Weekly*, Vol. 40, No. 21 (2005), pp. 2176–2182.

Roy Burman, B.K. "Brief Statement on the Socio-Economic Situation in Totopara and Perspective and Programme of Activities in Totopara Welfare Centre" (Unpublished). Cited in Bimalendu Majumdar. *A Sociological Study of the Toto Folk Tales*. Calcutta: The Asiatic Society. 1962.

Rubin, Gayle S. "Thinking Sex: Notes for a Radical Theory of the Politics of Sexuality". In Richard Parker and Peter Aggleton (eds.), *Culture, Society and Sexuality: A Reader*. London: UCL Press. 1999. pp. 143–178.

Rubin, Lillian B. *Just Friends: The Role of Friendship in Our Lives*. New York: HarperCollins. 1985.

Rycroft, Daniel J., and Sangeeta Dasgupta, ed. *The Politics of Belonging in India: Becoming Adivasi*. London and New York: Routledge. 2011.

Sade, A. *Oxford World's Classics: The Marquis de Sade, the Crimes of Love. A Selection Translated with an Introduction and Notes by David Coward*. New York: Oxford University Press. 2005.

Saha, Rebatimohan. *The Cultural Heritage of the Rabhas*. Kolkata: Anjali Publishers. 2015.

Said, Edward. "Opponents, Audiences, Constituencies and Community". In W.J.T. Mitchell (ed.), *The Politics of Interpretation*. Chicago: University of Chicago Press. 1983.

———. *Orientalism*. London: Routledge and Kegan Paul. 1978.

Samuel, Raphael. *Theatres of Memory*. London: Verso. 1994.

Sanjek, Roger. "Anthropology's Hidden Colonialism: Assistants and Their Ethnographers". *Anthropology Today*, Vol. 9, No. 2 (1993), pp. 13–18.

Sanjines, C. Javier. *Embers of the Past: Essays in Times of Decolonization*. Durham and London: Duke University Press. 2013.

Sarsby, J.G. "Special Problems of Fieldwork in Familiar Settings". In R.F. Ellen (ed.), *Ethnographic Research*. London: Academic Press. 1984. pp. 129–132.

Sartre, Jean-Paul. *Being and Nothingness: An Essay on Phenomenological Ontology*. Trans. Hazel E. Barnes. London: Routledge. 1989. Print.

Sarukkai, Sundar. "Dalit Experience and Theory". *Economic and Political Weekly*, Vol. 42, No. 40 (October 6–12, 2007), pp. 4043–4048.

———. "The 'Other' in Anthropology and Philosophy". *Economic and Political Weekly*, Vol. 32, No. 24 (June 14–20, 1997), pp. 1406–1409.

Satriani, Luigi Lombardi. "Folklore as Culture of Contestation". *Journal of the Folklore Institute*, Vol. XI, No. 1–2 (1974), pp. 99–121.

Satyanarayana, K. "Identification, Belonging, and the Category of Dalit". In Kaustav Chakraborty (ed.), *The Politics of Belonging in Contemporary India: Anxiety and Intimacy*. London and New York: Routledge. 2020. pp. 21–28.

Saunders, Peter. "The Meaning of 'Home' in Contemporary English Culture". *Housing Studies*, Vol. 4 (1989), pp. 177–192.

Schippers, Mini. *Beyond Monogamy: Polyamory and the Future of Polyqueer Sexualities*. New York: New York University Press. 2016.

Schneider, David M. "The Meaning of Incest". *The Journal of the Polynesian Society*, Vol. 85 (1976).

Schudson, Michael. *Watergate in American Memory: How We Remember, Forget and Reconstruct the Past*. New York: Basic Books. 1992.

Schutte, Ofelia. "A Critique of Normative Heterosexuality: Identity, Embodiment, and Sexual Difference in Beauvoir and Irigaray". *Hypatia*, Vol. 12, No. 1 (Winter 1997), pp. 40–62.

Schutz, Alfred. *The Problem of Social Reality: Collected Papers*, Vol. I. The Hague: MartinusNijhoff. 1962.

Schwenger, Peter. "Corpsing the Image". *Critical Inquiry*, Vol. 26, No. 3 (2000), pp. 395–413.

Scott, James C. *The Art of Not Being Governed: An Anarchist History of Upland Southeast Asia*. New Haven and London: Yale University Press. 2009.

Scott, Joan Wallach. *Gender and the Politics of History*. New York: Columba University Press. 1988.

Searle, John R. *The Construction of Social Reality*. New York: Simon and Schuster.1995.

Sedgwick, Eve Kosofsky. "The Beast in the Closet: James and the Writing of the Homosexual Panic". In Rachel Adams and David Savran (eds.), *The Masculinity Studies Reader*. Malden, MA: Blackwell Publishers. 2002.

———. *Tendencies*. Durham, NC: Duke University Press. 1993.

———. *Between Men: English Literature and Male Homosocial Desire*. New York: Columbia University Press.1985.

Segalen, M., and F. Zonabend. "Social Anthropology and the Ethnology of France". In A. Jackson (ed.), *Anthropology at Home* (ASA Monographs 25). London: Tavistock Publications. 1987. pp. 109–119.

Seiden, Ann M., and Pauline B. Bart. "Woman to Woman: Is Sisterhood Powerful?" In Nona Yetta Glazer (ed.), *Old Family/New Family: Interpersonal Relationships*. New York: Van Nostrand Publishers. 1975. pp. 189–228.

Seidler, V.J., ed. *Men, Sex and Relationships: Writings from Achilles Heel*. London: Routledge. 1992.

Seifert, Lewis C. *Fairy Tales, Sexuality, and Gender in France 1690–1715: Nostalgic Utopias*. Cambridge: Cambridge University Press. 1996.

Seleskovitch, D., and M. Lederer. *Interpréter pour traduire*. Paris: Didier. 1984.

Sen, Soumen, ed. *Folklore in North-East India*. New Delhi: Omsons Publications. 1985.

Severn, J. Millott. "Friendship, Its Advantages and Excesses". *Phrenological Journal of Science and Health*, Vol. 106 (September 1898).

Shahani, Nishant. *Queer Retrosexualities: The Politics of Reparative Return*. Bethlehem: Lehigh University Press. 2012.

Shami, Seteney. "Studying Your Own: The Complexities of a Shared Culture". In S. Altorki and C.F. El-Solh (eds.), *Arab Women in the Field. Studying Your Own Society*. Syracuse, NY: Syracuse University Press. 1988. pp. 115–138.

Shaw, Christopher, and Malcolm Chase. *The Imagined Past: History and Nostalgia*. Manchester and New York: Manchester University Press. 1989.

Shively, Charley. "Indiscriminate Promiscuity as an Act of Revolution". 1974. In Winston Leyland (ed.), *Gay Roots: Twenty Years of Gay Sunshine*. San Francisco: Gay Sunshine Press. 1991. pp. 257–263.

Shklovsky, Victor. "Art as Technique" (1965). In David Lodge (ed.), *Modern Criticism and Theory: A Reader*. London: Longman. 1988. pp. 16–30.

Shristava, Sanjay. "Modi-Masculinity: Media, Manhood and 'Traditions' in a Time of Consumerism". *Television & New Media*, Vol. 16, No. 4 (2015), pp. 331–338.

Sinha, Mrinalini. *Colonial Masculinity: The 'Manly Englishman' and the 'Effeminate Bengali' in the Late Nineteenth Century*. Manchester and New York: Manchester University Press. 1995.

———. " 'Chathams, Pitts and Gladstones in Petticoats': The Politics of Gender and Race in the Illbert Bill Controversy, 1883–84". In Nupur Chaudhuri and Margaret Strobel (eds.), *Western Women and Imperialism: Complicity and Resistance*. Bloomington: Indiana University Press. 1992.

Sjoo, Monica, and Barbara Moor. *The Great Cosmic Mother: Discovering the Religion of the Earth*. San Francisco: HarperCollins. 1987.

Smith, Andrea. "Queer Theory and Native Studies: The Heteronormativity of Settler Colonialism". In Daniel Heath Justice, Mark Rifkin, and Bethany Schneider (eds.), *Sexuality, Nationality, Indigeneity*. Special Issue of *GLQ: A Journal of Lesbian and Gay Studies*, Vol. 16, No. 1–2 (2010), pp. 41–68.

Snell-Hornby, M. "Linguistic Transcoding or Cultural Transfer? A Critique of Translation Theory in Germany". In S. Bassnett and A. Lefevere (eds.), *Translation, History and Culture*. London and New York: Pinter. 1990. pp. 79–86.

Sone, Enongene Mirabeau. "The Folktale and Social Values in Traditional Africa". *Eastern African Literary and Cultural Studies*, Vol. 4, No. 2 (2018), pp. 142–159.

Spicer, Edward H. "Persistent Cultural Systems: A Comparative Study of Identity Systems That Can Adopt to Contrasting Environments". *Science*, Vol. 174, No. 4011 (1971), pp. 795–800.

Spivak, Gayatri C. "Questions of Multiculturalism". In S. Harasayam (ed.), *The Post-Colonial Critic: Interviews, Strategies, Dialogues*. New York: Routledge. 1990. pp. 59–60.

Srinivas, M.N. "Indian Anthropologists and the Study of Indian Culture". *Economic and Political Weekly*, Vol. XXXI, No. 11 (March 1996).

Stallybrass, P., and A. White. *The Politics and Poetics of Transgression*. London: Methuen. 1986.

Steiner, Deborah Tarn. *The Tyrant's Writ: Myths and Images of Writing in Ancient Greece*. Princeton, NJ: Princeton University Press. 1994.

Stewart, Garrett. *Death Sentences: Styles of Dying in British Fiction*. Cambridge: Harvard University Press. 1984.

Stewart, Susan. *Nonsense: Aspects of Intertextuality in Folklore and Literature*. Baltimore, MD: The Johns Hopkins University Press. 1978.

Stock, Brian. *The Implications of Literacy: Written Language and Models of Interpretation in the Eleventh and Twelfth Centuries*. Princeton, NJ: Princeton University Press. 1987.

Stoltenberg, John. *Refusing to be a Man: Essays on Sex and Justice*. London: Routledge. 1990.

Stone, S. "The 'Empire' Strikes Back: A Posttranssexual Manifesto". In K. Straub and J. Epstein (eds.), *Body Guards: The Cultural Politics of Gender Ambiguity*. New York: Routledge. 1991.

Strong, T.B. and F.A. Sposito. "Habermas's Significant Other". In Stephen White (ed.), *Cambridge Companion to Habermas*. Cambridge: Cambridge University Press. 1995.

Subba, J.R. *Yumanism, the Limboo Way of Life: A Philosophical Analysis*. Gangtok: Yakthung Mundhum Saplappa. 2012a.

———. *Ethno-Religious Views of the Limboo Mundhums [Myths]: An Analysis of Traditional Theories*. Gangtok: Yakthung Mundhum Saplappa. 2012b.

Suleiman, S. *Subversive Intent: Gender, Politics and the Avante-Garde*. Cambridge, MA: Harvard University Press. 1990.

Syme, Ronald. *Tacitus*, Vols. 2. Oxford: Clarendon Press. 1958.

Tamsang, Lyangsang. *Lepcha Folklore and Folk Songs*. New Delhi: SahityaAkademi. 2008.

Tatar, Maria. *Secrets Beyond the Door: The Story of Bluebeard and His Wives*. Princeton, NJ: Princeton University Press. 2004.

Tedlock, Dennis. "Toward a Poetics of Polyphony and Translatability". In Jerome Rothenberg and Stephen Clay (eds.), *A Book of the Book: Some Works & Projections About the Book & Writing*. New York: Granary. 2000.

Thiong'o, Ngũgĩwa. *Globalectics: Theory and the Politics of Knowing*. New York: Columbia University Press. 2012.

Thompson, Paul. *The Voice of the Past. Oral History. Opus Books*. Oxford: Oxford University Press. 1988.

Tiffin, Jessica. *Marvellous Geometry: Narrative and Metafiction in Modern Fairy Tale*. Detroit: Wayne State University Press. 2009.

Tolkien, J.R.R. *The Monsters and the Critics and Other Essays*. London: HarperCollins. 1990.

Tonkin, Elisabeth. *Narrating Our Pasts. The Social Construction of Oral History* (CSOLC, 22). Cambridge: Cambridge University Press. 1992.

Trilling, Lionel. "Freud and Literature". In *The Liberal Imagination*. London: Martin Secker. 1951. pp. 34–57. Print.

Trites, Roberta Seelinger. *Disturbing the Universe: Power and Repression in Adolescent Literature*. Iowa: University of Iowa Press. 2000.

Tuplin, Christopher. *The Failings of the Empire. A Reading of Xenophon* (Hellenica 2.7./7–7.5.27. Historia, 76). Stuttgart: Franz Steiner Verlag. 1993.

Turner, V. *Dreams, Fields and Metaphors*. New York: Cornell University Press. 1974.

Tylor, Edward B. "On a Method of Investigating the Development of Institutions; Applied to Laws of Marriage and Descent". *Journal of the Royal Anthropological Institute of Great Britain and Ireland*, Vol. 18 (1889).

Ueding, Gert, ed. *Asthetik des Vor-Scheins 1*. Frankfurt am Main: Suhrkamp. 1976.

Uexküll, Jakob von. *Umwelt und Innenwelt der Tiere*. Berlin: J. Springer. 1909 ("Environment and Inner World of Animals". Translated Excerpts by Chauncey J. Mellor and Doris Gove. *Foundations of Comparative Ethology*. Ed. Gordon M. Burghardt. New York: Van Nostrand Reinhold. 1985).

Vanita, Ruth, and Saleem Kidwai. *Same Sex Love in India: Readings from Literature and History*. New Delhi: Palgrave Macmillan. 2000.

Vansina, Jan. *Oral Tradition as History*. London: James Currey and Nairobi: Heinemann Kenya. 1985.

Venkateswar, Sita, and Emma Hughes, eds. *The Politics of Indigeneity: Dialogues and Reflections on Indigenous Activism*. London and New York: Zed Books. 2011.

Vico, Giambattista. *The New Science*. Ithaca, NY: Cornell University Press. 1984.

Vidal, Hernan. "An Aesthetic Approach to Issues of Human Rights". *Hispanic Issues On Line*, Vol. 4 (2009), pp. 14–43.

Viollet, Catharine. "Discourse Strategies—Power and Resistance: A Socio-Enunciative Approach". In Gill Seidel (ed.), *The Nature of the Right: A Feminist Analysis of Order Patterns*. Amsterdam: Benjamins. 1988. pp. 61–79.

Ward, E. *Father-Daughter Rape*. London: Women's Press. 1984.

Warner, Marina. *Joan of Arc: The Image of Female Heroism*. New York: Vintage. 1982.

Watson, Francis. *Text and Truth. Redefining Biblical Theology*. Edinburgh: Clark. 1997.

Weaver, Jace. "More Light Than Heat: The Current State of Native American Studies". *American Indian Quarterly*, Vol. 31, No. 2 (2007).

Weber, Max. *Economy and Society*, Vol. I. New York: Bedminster Press. 1968.

Weeks, Jeffrey. "The Idea of a Sexual Community". *Soundings*, Vol. 2 (Spring 1996), pp. 72–84.

———. *Sexuality and Its Discontents*. London: Routledge. 1985.

———. *Making Sexual History*. Cambridge: Polity Press. 1945.

Weiss, Margot D. "Gay Shame and BDSM Pride: Neoliberalism, Policy, and Sexual Politics". *Radical History Review: Queer Futures*, Vol. 100 (2008), pp. 87–102.

Weston, K. *Families We Choose: Lesbians, Gays, Kinship*. New York: Columbia University Press. 1991.

187

White, Hayden. *Figural Realism: Studies in the Mimesis Effect*. Baltimore, MD and London: The Johns Hopkins University Press. 1999.

———. "The Value of Narrativity in the Representation of Reality". *Critical Inquiry*, Vol. 7 (1980), pp. 5–27.

———. "Rhetoric and History". In Hayden White and Frank E. Manuel (eds.), *Theories of History*. Los Angeles: William Andrews Clark Memorial Library. 1978a. pp. 1–25.

———. *Tropics of Discourse. Essays in Cultural Criticism*. London: Johns Hopkins University Press. 1978b.

———. "The Fictions of Factual Representation". In Angus Fletcher (ed.), *The Literature of Fact: Selected Papers from the English Institute*. New York: Columbia University Press. 1976. pp. 21–44.

———. *Metahistory: The Historical Imagination in Nineteenth-Century Europe*. Baltimore, MD: Johns Hopkins University Press. 1973.

———. "The Burden of History". *History and Theory*, Vol. 5 (1966), pp. 111–134.

White, Leslie. "The Definition and Prohibition of Incest". *American Anthropologist*, Vol. 50, part I (1948).

Whitehead, Stephen M. *Men and Masculinities*. Cambridge: Polity Press. 2002.

Whitehead, Stephen M., and Frank J. Barrett, eds. *The Masculinities Reader*. Cambridge: Polity Press and Malden, MA: Blackwell Publishers. 2001.

Williams, Raymond. *Resources of Hope*. London and New York: Verso. 1989.

———. *Marxism and Literature*. Oxford: Oxford University Press. 1977.

Wilson, A.N. *C.S. Lewis: A Biography*. London: HarperCollins. 1990.

Winnicott, D. "Transitional Objects and Transitional Phenomena". *International Journal of Psychoanalysis*, Vol. 34 (1953), pp. 89–97.

Wiredu, K. *Conceptual Decolonization in African Philosophy: Four Essays*. Ibadan, Nigeria: Hope Publications. 1995.

Wolf, Arthur P., and William H. Durham, eds. *Inbreeding, Incest and the Incest Taboo: The State of Knowledge at the Turn of the Century*. Stanford, CA: Stanford University Press. 2005.

Wolfensberger, Wolf. "Social Role Valorization and, or Versus, 'Empowerment'". *MentalRetardation*, Vol. 40, No. 3 (2002), pp. 252–258.

Woodman, A.J. *Rhetoric in Classical Historiography*. London: CroomHelm and Portland, OR: Areopagitica Press. 1988.

Wylie, Macleod. *Bengal as a Field of Missions*. W.H. Dalton, Thacker, Spink. 1854.

Xaxa, Virginius. "Transformation of Tribes in India: Terms of Discourse". *Economic and Political Weekly*, Vol. 34, No. 24 (June 12–18, 1999), pp. 1519–1524.

Young, Iris Marion. *Throwing Like a Girl and Other Essays in Feminist Philosophy and Social Theory*. Bloomington and Indianapolis: Indiana University Press. 1990.

Zavarzadeh, Masud. *The Mythopoeic Reality: The Postwar American Nonfiction Novel*. Urbana: University of Illinois Press. 1976.

Zimbardo, Philip. *The Lucifer Effect: Understanding How Good People Turn Evil*. New York: Random. 2007. Print.

Zimmerman, Bonnie. "Perverse Reading: The Lesbian Appropriate of Literature". In Susan J. Wolfe and Julia Penelope (eds.), *Sexual Practice, Textual Theory: Lesbian Cultural Criticism*. Cambridge: Blackwell Publishers. 1993. pp. 135–149.

Zipes, Jack. *Breaking the Magic Spell: Radical Theories of Folk and Fairy Tales*. Austin: University of Texas Press. 1979.

Zizek, Slavoj. *Living in the End Times*. London and New York: Verso. 2010.

Zukauskaite, Audrone. "From Biopolitics to Biophilosophy, or the Vanishing Subject of Biopolitics". In S.E. Wilmer and Audrone Zukauskaite (eds.), *Resisting Biopolitics: Philosophical, Political and Performative Strategies*. New York and London: Routledge. 2016.

Zupancie, Alenka. "Sexual Difference and Ontology". *e-flux*, Vol. 32 (2012).

INDEX

For Product Safety Concerns and Information please contact our EU
representative GPSR@taylorandfrancis.com
Taylor & Francis Verlag GmbH, Kaufingerstraße 24, 80331 München, Germany

www.ingramcontent.com/pod-product-compliance
Lightning Source LLC
Chambersburg PA
CBHW071110100726
47908CB00008B/2329

* 9 7 8 0 3 6 7 5 5 4 2 4 8 *